Praise for *Dune*

"A portrayal of an alien society more complete and
deeply detailed than any other author in the field
has managed . . . a story absorbing equally for
its action and philosophical vistas . . .
An astonishing science fiction phenomenon."

—*The Washington Post*

"Powerful, convincing, and most ingenious."

—Robert A. Heinlein

"Herbert's creation of this universe, with its intricate
development and analysis of ecology, religion,
politics, and philosophy, remains one of the supreme
and seminal achievements in science fiction."

—*The Louisville Times*

OTHER BOOKS
•

BY FRANK HERBERT

Dune
Dune Messiah
Children of Dune
God Emperor of Dune
Heretics of Dune
Chapterhouse: Dune

BY FRANK HERBERT, BRIAN HERBERT, AND KEVIN J. ANDERSON

The Road to Dune
(includes the original short novel *Spice Planet*)

BY BRIAN HERBERT AND KEVIN J. ANDERSON

Dune: House Atreides
Dune: House Harkonnen
Dune: House Corrino

Dune: The Butlerian Jihad
Dune: The Machine Crusade
Dune: The Battle of Corrin

Hunters of Dune
Sandworms of Dune

Paul of Dune
The Winds of Dune

Sisterhood of Dune
Mentats of Dune
Navigators of Dune

Hellhole
Hellhole Awakening
Hellhole Inferno

BY BRIAN HERBERT

Dreamer of Dune
(biography of Frank Herbert)

FRANK HERBERT

THE DOSADI EXPERIMENT

[AND]

THE EYES OF HEISENBERG

A TOM DOHERTY ASSOCIATES BOOK | NEW YORK

NOTE: If you purchased this book without a cover, you should be aware that this book is stolen property. It was reported as "unsold and destroyed" to the publisher, and neither the author nor the publisher has received any payment for this "stripped book."

This is a work of fiction. All of the characters, organizations, and events portrayed in these novels are either products of the author's imagination or are used fictitiously.

THE DOSADI EXPERIMENT AND THE EYES OF HEISENBERG

The Dosadi Experiment copyright © 1977 by Herbert Properties LLC

The Eyes of Heisenberg copyright © 1966, 1994 by Herbert Properties LLC

All rights reserved.

A Tor Book
Published by Tom Doherty Associates
175 Fifth Avenue
New York, NY 10010

www.tor-forge.com

Tor® is a registered trademark of Macmillan Publishing Group, LLC.

ISBN 978-1-250-16454-4

Our books may be purchased in bulk for promotional, educational, or business use. Please contact your local bookseller or the Macmillan Corporate and Premium Sales Department at 1-800-221-7945, extension 5442, or by e-mail at MacmillanSpecialMarkets@macmillan.com.

First Edition: December 2017

Printed in the United States of America

0 9 8 7 6 5 4 3 2 1

THE DOSADI
EXPERIMENT

In memory of Babe
because she knew how to enjoy life.

When the Calebans first sent us one of their giant metal "beachballs," communicating through this device to offer the use of jumpdoors for interstellar travel, many in the ConSentiency covertly began to exploit this gift of the stars for their own questionable purposes. Both the "Shadow Government" and some among the Gowachin people saw what is obvious today: that instantaneous travel across unlimited space involved powers which might isolate subject populations in gross numbers.

This observation at the beginning of the Dosadi Experiment came long before Saboteur Extraordinary Jorj X. McKie discovered that visible stars of our universe were either Calebans or the manifestations of Calebans in ConSentient space. (See *Whipping Star,* an account of McKie's discovery thinly disguised as fiction.)

What remains pertinent here is that McKie, acting for his Bureau of Sabotage, identified the Caleban called "Fannie Mae" as the visible star Thyone. This discovery of the Thyone-Fannie Mae identity ignited new interest in the Caleban Question and thus contributed to the exposure of the Dosadi Experiment—which many still believe was the most disgusting use of Sentients by Sentients in ConSentient history. Certainly, it remains the most gross psychological test of Sentient Beings ever performed, and the issue of informed consent has never been settled to everyone's satisfaction.

—from the first public account, The Trial of Trials

Justice belongs to those who claim it, but let the claimant beware lest he create new injustice by his claim and thus set the bloody pendulum of revenge into its inexorable motion.

—Gowachin aphorism

"Why are you so cold and mechanical in your Human relationships?"

Jorj X. McKie was to reflect on that Caleban question later. Had she been trying to alert him to the Dosadi Experiment and to what his investigation of that experiment might do to him? He hadn't even known about Dosadi at the time and the pressures of the Caleban communications trance, the accusatory tone she took, had precluded other considerations.

Still, it rankled. He didn't like the feeling that he might be a subject of her research into Humans. He'd always thought of that particular Caleban as his friend—if one could consider being friendly with a creature whose visible manifestation in this universe was a fourth-magnitude yellow sun visible from Central Central where the Bureau of Sabotage maintained its headquarters. And there was inevitable discomfort in Caleban communication. You sank into a trembling, jerking trance while they made their words appear in your consciousness.

But his uncertainty remained: had she tried to tell him something beyond the plain content of her words?

When the weather makers kept the evening rain period short, McKie liked to go outdoors immediately afterward and stroll in the park enclosure which BuSab provided for its employees on Central Central. As a Saboteur Extraordinary, McKie had free run of the enclosure and he liked the fresh smells of the place after a rain.

The park covered about thirty hectares, deep in a well of Bureau buildings. It was a scrambling hodgepodge of plantings cut by wide paths which circled and twisted through specimens from every inhabited planet of the known universe. No care had been taken to provide a particular area for any sentient species. If there was any plan to the park it was a maintenance plan with plants requiring similar conditions and care held in their own sectors. Giant Spear Pines from Sasak occupied a knoll near one corner surrounded by mounds of Flame Briar from Rudiria. There were bold stretches of lawn and hidden scraps of lawn, and some flat stretches of greenery which were not lawns at all but mobile sheets of predatory leaf imprisoned behind thin moats of caustic water.

Rain-jeweled flowers often held McKie's attention to the exclusion of all else. There was a single planting of Lilium Grossa, its red blossoms twice his height casting long shadows over a wriggling carpet of blue Syringa, each miniature bloom opening and closing at random like tiny mouths gasping for air.

Sometimes, floral perfumes stopped his progress and held him in a momentary olfactory thralldom while his eyes searched out the source. As often as not, the plant would be a dangerous one—a flesh eater or poison-sweat variety. Warning signs in flashing Galach guarded such plantings. Sonabarriers, moats, and force fields edged the winding paths in many areas.

McKie had a favorite spot in the park, a bench with its back to a fountain where he could sit and watch the shadows collect across fat yellow bushes from the floating islands of Tandaloor. The yellow bushes thrived because their roots were washed in running water hidden beneath the soil and renewed by the fountain. Beneath the yellow bushes there were faint gleams of phosphorescent silver enclosed by a force field and identified by a low sign:

"Sangeet Mobilus, a blood-sucking perennial from Bisaj.

Extreme danger to all sentient species. Do not intrude any portion of your body beyond the force field."

As he sat on the bench, McKie thought about that sign. The universe often mixed the beautiful and the dangerous. This was a deliberate mixture in the park. The yellow bushes, the fragrant and benign Golden Iridens, had been mingled with Sangeet Mobilus. The two supported each other and both thrived. The ConSentient government which McKie served often made such mixtures . . . sometimes by accident.

Sometimes by design.

He listened to the splashing of the fountain while the shadows thickened and the tiny border lights came on along the paths. The tops of the buildings beyond the park became a palette where the sunset laid out its final display of the day.

In that instant, the Caleban contact caught him and he felt his body slip into the helpless communications trance. The mental tendrils were immediately identified—Fannie Mae. And he thought, as he often had, what an improbable name that was for a star entity. He heard no sounds, but his hearing centers responded as to spoken words, and the inward glow was unmistakable. It was Fannie Mae, her syntax far more sophisticated than during their earliest encounters.

"You admire one of us," she said, indicating his attention on the sun which had just set beyond the buildings.

"I try not to think of any star as a Caleban," he responded. "It interferes with my awareness of the natural beauty."

"Natural? McKie, you don't understand your own awareness, nor even how you employ it!"

That was her beginning—accusatory, attacking, unlike any previous contact with this Caleban he'd thought of as friend. And she employed her verb forms with new deftness, almost as though showing off, parading her understanding of his language.

"What do you want, Fannie Mae?"

"I consider your relationships with females of your species. You have entered marriage relationships which number more than fifty. Not so?"

"That's right. Yes. Why do you . . ."

"I am your friend, McKie. What is your feeling toward me?"

He thought about that. There was a demanding intensity in her question. He owed his life to this Caleban with an improbable name. For that matter, she owed her life to him. Together, they'd resolved the Whipping Star threat. Now, many Calebans provided the jumpdoors by which other beings moved in a single step from planet to planet, but once Fannie Mae had held all of those jumpdoor threads, her life threatened through the odd honor code by which Calebans maintained their contractual obligations. And McKie had saved her life. He had but to think about their past interdependence and a warm sense of camaraderie suffused him.

Fannie Mae sensed this.

"Yes, McKie, that is friendship, is love. Do you possess this feeling toward Human female companions?"

Her question angered him. Why was she prying? His private sexual relationships were no concern of hers!

"Your love turns easily to anger," she chided.

"There are limits to how deeply a Saboteur Extraordinary can allow himself to be involved with anyone."

"Which came first, McKie—the Saboteur Extraordinary or these limits?"

Her response carried obvious derision. Had he chosen the Bureau because he was incapable of warm relationships? But he really cared for Fannie Mae! He admired her . . . and she could hurt him because he admired her and felt . . . felt *this way*.

He spoke out of his anger and hurt.

"Without the Bureau there'd be no ConSentiency and no need for Calebans."

"Yes, indeed. People have but to look at a dread agent from BuSab and know fear."

It was intolerable, but he couldn't escape the underlying warmth he felt toward this strange Caleban entity, this being who could creep unguarded into his mind and talk to him as no other being dared. If only he had found a woman to share that kind of intimacy . . .

And this was the part of their conversation which came back to haunt him. After months with no contact between them, why had she chosen that moment—just three days before the Dosadi crisis burst upon the Bureau? She'd pulled out his ego, his deepest sense of identity. She'd shaken that ego and then she'd skewered him with her barbed question:

"Why are you so cold and mechanical in your Human relationships?"

Her irony could not be evaded. She'd made him appear ridiculous in his own eyes. He could feel warmth, yes . . . even love, for a Caleban but not for a Human female. This unguarded feeling he held for Fannie Mae had never been directed at any of his marital companions. Fannie Mae had aroused his anger, then reduced his anger to verbal breast-beating, and finally to silent hurt. Still, the love remained.

Why?

Human females were bed partners. They were bodies which used him and which he used. That was out of the question with this Caleban. She was a star burning with atomic fires, her seat of consciousness unimaginable to other sentients. Yet, she could extract love from him. He gave this love freely and she knew it. There was no hiding an emotion from a Caleban when she sent her mental tendrils into your awareness.

She'd certainly known he would see the irony. That had to be part of her motive in such an attack. But Calebans seldom acted from a single motive—which was part of their charm and the essence of their most irritant exchanges with other sentient beings.

"McKie?" Softly in his mind.

"Yes." Angry.

"I show you now a fractional bit of my feeling toward your node."

Like a balloon being inflated by a swift surge of gas, he felt himself suffused by a projected sense of concern, of caring. He was drowning in it . . . wanted to drown in it. His entire body radiated this white-hot sense of protective attention. For a whole minute after it was withdrawn, he still glowed with it.

A fractional bit?

"McKie?" Concerned.

"Yes." Awed.

"Have I hurt you?"

He felt alone, emptied.

"No."

"The full extent of my nodal involvement would destroy you. Some Humans have suspected this about love."

Nodal involvement?

She was confusing him as she'd done in their first encounters. How could the Calebans describe love as . . . nodal involvement?

"Labels depend on viewpoint," she said. "You look at the universe through too narrow an opening. We despair of you sometimes."

There she was again, attacking.

He fell back on a childhood platitude.

"I am what I am and that's all I am."

"You may soon learn, friend McKie, that you're more than you thought."

With that, she'd broken the contact. He'd awakened in damp, chilly darkness, the sound of the fountain loud in his ears. Nothing he did would bring her back into communication, not even when he'd spent some of his own credits on a Taprisiot in a vain attempt to call her.

His Caleban friend had shut him out.

We have created a monster—enormously valuable and even useful yet extremely dangerous. Our monster is both beautiful and terrifying. We do not dare use this monster to its full potential, but we cannot release our grasp upon it.

—Gowachin assessment of the Dosadi Experiment

A bullet went *spang!* against the window behind Keila Jedrik's desk, ricocheted and screamed off into the canyon street far below her office. Jedrik prided herself that she had not even flinched. The Elector's patrols would take care of the sniper. The patrols which swept the streets of Chu every morning would home on the sound of the shot. She held the casual hope that the sniper would escape back to the Rim Rabble, but she recognized this hope as a weakness and dismissed it. There were concerns this morning far more important than an infiltrator from the Rim.

Jedrik reached one hand into the corner of early sunlight which illuminated the contact plates of her terminal in the Master Accountancy computer. Those flying fingers—she could almost disassociate herself from them. They darted like insects at the waiting keys. The terminal was a functional instrument, symbol of her status as a Senior Liaitor. It sat all alone in its desk slot—grey, green, gold, black, white and deadly. Its grey screen was almost precisely the tone of her desk top.

With careful precision, her fingers played their rhythms on the keys. The screen produced yellow numbers, all weighted and averaged at her command—a thin strip of destiny with violence hidden in its golden shapes.

Every angel carries a sword, she thought.

But she did not really consider herself an angel or her weapon a sword. Her real weapon was an intellect hardened

and sharpened by the terrible decisions her planet required. Emotions were a force to be diverted within the self or to be used against anyone who had failed to learn what Dosadi taught. She knew her own weakness and hid it carefully: she'd been taught by loving parents (who'd concealed their love behind exquisite cruelty) that Dosadi's decisions were indeed terrible.

Jedrik studied the numbers on her computer display, cleared the screen and made a new entry. As she did this, she knew she took sustenance from fifty of her planet's Human inhabitants. Many of those fifty would not long survive this callous jape. In truth, her fingers were weapons of death for those who failed this test. She felt no guilt about those she slew. The imminent arrival of one Jorj X. McKie dictated her actions, precipitated them.

When she thought about McKie, her basic feeling was one of satisfaction. She'd waited for McKie like a predator beside a burrow in the earth. His name and identifying keys had been given to her by her chauffeur, Havvy, hoping to increase his value to her. She'd taken the information and made her usual investigation. Jedrik doubted that any other person on Dosadi could have come up with the result her sources produced: Jorj X. McKie was an adult Human who could not possibly exist. No record of him could be found on all of Dosadi—not on the poisonous Rim, not in Chu's Warrens, not in any niche of the existing power structure. McKie did not exist, but he was due to arrive in Chu momentarily, smuggled into the city by a Gowachin temporarily under her control.

McKie was the precision element for which she had waited. He wasn't merely a possible key to the God Wall (not a bent and damaged key like Havvy) but clean and certain. She'd never thought to attack this lock with poor instruments. There'd be one chance and only one; it required the best.

Thus fifty Dosadi Humans took their faceless places behind the numbers in her computer. Bait, expendable. Those

who died by this act wouldn't die immediately. Forty-nine might never know they'd been deliberately submitted to early death by her deliberate choice. Some would be pushed back to the Rim's desperate and short existence. Some would die in the violent battles she was precipitating. Others would waste away in the Warrens. For most, the deadly process would extend across sufficient time to conceal her hand in it. But they'd been slain in her computer and she knew it. She cursed her parents (and the others before them) for this unwanted sensitivity to the blood and sinew behind these computer numbers. Those loving parents had taught her well. She might never see the slain bodies, need give not another thought to all but one of the fifty; still she sensed them behind her computer display . . . warm and pulsing.

Jedrik sighed. The fifty were bleating animals staked out to lure a special beast onto Dosadi's poisonous soil. Her fifty would create a fractional surplus which would vanish, swallowed before anyone realized their purpose.

Dosadi is sick, she thought. And not for the first time, she wondered: *Is this really Hell?*

Many believed it.

We're being punished.

But no one knew what they'd done to deserve punishment.

Jedrik leaned back, looked across her doorless office to the sound barrier and milky light of the hall. A strange Gowachin shambled past her doorway. He was a frog figure on some official errand, a packet of brown paper clutched in his knobby hands. His green skin shimmered as though he'd recently come from water.

The Gowachin reminded her of Bahrank, he who was bringing McKie into her net, Bahrank who did her bidding because she controlled the substance to which he was addicted. More fool he to let himself become an addict to anything, even to living. One day soon Bahrank would sell what he knew about her to the Elector's spies; by then it would be too late and the Elector would learn only what she

wanted him to learn when she wanted him to learn it. She'd chosen Bahrank with the same care she'd used at her computer terminal, the same care which had made her wait for someone precisely like McKie. And Bahrank was Gowachin. Once committed to a project, the frog people were notorious for carrying out their orders in a precise way. They possessed an inbred sense of order but understood the limits of law.

As her gaze traversed the office, the sparse and functional efficiency of the space filled her with quiet amusement. This office presented an image of her which she had constructed with meticulous care. It pleased her that she would be leaving here soon never to return, like an insect shedding its skin. The office was four paces wide, eight long. Twelve black metal rotofiles lined the wall on her left, dark sentinels of her methodical ways. She had reset their locking codes and armed them to destroy their contents when the Elector's toads pried into them. The Elector's people would attribute this to outrage, a last angry sabotage. It would be some time before accumulating doubts would lead them to reassessment and to frustrated questions. Even then they might not suspect her hand in the elimination of fifty Humans. She, after all, was one of the fifty.

This thought inflicted her with a momentary sense of unfocused loss. How pervasive were the seductions of Dosadi's power structure! How subtle! What she'd just done here introduced a flaw into the computer system which ruled the distribution of non-poisonous food in Dosadi's only city. Food—here was the real base of Dosadi's social pyramid, solid and ugly. The flaw removed her from a puissant niche in that pyramid. She had worn the persona of Keila Jedrik-Liaitor for many years, long enough to learn enjoyment of the power system. Losing one valuable counter in Dosadi's endless survival game, she must now live and act only with the persona of Keila Jedrik-Warlord. This was an all-or-nothing move, a gambler's plunge. She felt the nakedness of

it. But this gamble had begun long ago, far back in Dosadi's contrived history, when her ancestors had recognized the nature of this planet and had begun breeding and training for the individual who would take this plunge.

I am that individual, she told herself. *This is our moment.*

But had they truly assessed the problem correctly?

Jedrik's glance fell on the single window which looked out into the canyon street. Her own reflection stared back: a face too narrow, thin nose, eyes and mouth too large. Her hair could be an interesting black velvet helmet if she let it grow, but she kept it cropped short as a reminder that she was not a magnetic sex partner, that she must rely on her wits. That was the way she'd been bred and trained. Dosadi had taught her its cruelest lessons early. She'd grown tall while still in her teens, carrying more height in her body than in her legs so that she appeared even taller when seated. She looked down on most Gowachin and Human males in more ways than one. That was another gift (and lesson) from her *loving* parents and from their ancestors. There was no escaping this Dosadi lesson.

What you love or value will be used against you.

She leaned forward to hide her disquieting reflection, peered far down into the street. There, that was better. Her fellow Dosadis no longer were warm and pulsing people. They were reduced to distant movements, as impersonal as the dancing figures in her computer.

Traffic was light, she noted. Very few armored vehicles moved, no pedestrians. There'd been only that one shot at her window. She still entertained a faint hope that the sniper had escaped. More likely a patrol had caught the fool. The Rim Rabble persisted in testing Chu's defenses despite the boringly repetitive results. It was desperation. Snipers seldom waited until the day was deep and still and the patrols were scattered, those hours when even some among the most powerful ventured out.

Symptoms, all symptoms.

Rim sorties represented only one among many Dosadi symptoms which she'd taught herself to read in that precarious climb whose early stage came to climax in this room. It was not just a thought, but more a sense of familiar awareness to which she returned at oddly reflexive moments in her life.

We have a disturbed relationship with our past which religion cannot explain. We are primitive in unexplainable ways, our lives woven of the familiar and the strange, the reasonable and the insane.

It made some insane choices magnificently attractive.

Have I made an insane choice?

No!

The data lay clearly in her mind, facts which she could not obliterate by turning away from them. Dosadi had been designed from a cosmic grab bag: "Give them one of these and one of these and one of these . . ."

It made for incompatible pairings.

The DemoPol with which Dosadi juggled its computer-monitored society didn't fit a world which used energy transmitted from a satellite in geosynchronous orbit. The DemoPol reeked of primitive ignorance, something from a society which had wandered too far down the path of legalisms—a law for everything and everything managed by law. The dogma that a God-inspired few had chosen Chu's river canyon in which to build a city insulated from this poisonous planet, and that only some twenty or so generations earlier, remained indigestible. And that energy satellite which hovered beneath the God Wall's barrier—that stank of a long and sophisticated evolution during which something as obviously flawed as the DemoPol would have been discarded.

It was a cosmic grab bag designed for a specific purpose which her ancestors had recognized.

We did not evolve on this planet.

The place was out of phase with both Gowachin and Hu-

man. Dosadi employed computer memories and physical files side by side for identical purposes. And the number of addictive substances to be found on Dosadi was outrageous. Yet this was played off against a religion so contrived, so gross in its demands for "simple faith" that the two conditions remained at constant war. The mystics died for their "new insights" while the holders of "simple faith" used control of the addictive substances to gain more and more power. The only real faith on Dosadi was that you survived by power and that you gained power by controlling what others required for survival. Their society understood the medicine of bacteria, virus and brain control, but these could not stamp out the Rim and Warren Underground where *jabua* faith healers cured their patients with the smoke of burning weeds.

And they could not stamp out (not yet) Keila Jedrik because she had seen what she had seen. Two by two the incompatible things ebbed and flowed around her, in the city of Chu and the surrounding Rim. It was the same in every case: a society which made use of one of these things could not naturally be a society which used the other.

Not naturally.

All around her, Jedrik sensed Chu with its indigestible polarities. They had only two species: Human and Gowachin. Why two? Were there no other species in this universe? Subtle hints in some of Dosadi's artifacts suggested an evolution for appendages other than the flexible fingers of Gowachin and Human.

Why only one city on all of Dosadi?

Dogma failed to answer.

The Rim hordes huddled close, always seeking a way into Chu's insulated purity. But they had a whole planet behind them. Granted it was a poisonous planet, but it had other rivers, other places of potential sanctuary. The survival of both species argued for the building of more sanctuaries, many more than that pitiful hole which Gar and Tria thought they

masterminded. No . . . Chu stood alone—almost twenty kilometers wide and forty long, built on hills and silted islands where the river slowed in its deep canyon. At last count, some eighty-nine million people lived here and three times that number eked a short life on the Rim—pressing, always pressing for a place in the poison-free city.

Give us your precious bodies, you stupid Rimmers!

They heard the message, knew its import and defied it. What had the people of Dosadi done to be imprisoned here? What had their ancestors done? It was right to build a religion upon hate for such ancestors . . . provided such ancestors were guilty.

Jedrik leaned toward the window, peered upward at the God Wall, that milky translucence which imprisoned Dosadi, yet through which those such as this Jorj X. McKie could come at will. She hungered to see McKie in person, to confirm that he had not been contaminated as Havvy had been contaminated.

It was a McKie she required now. The transparently contrived nature of Dosadi told her that there must be a McKie. She saw herself as the huntress, McKie her natural prey. The false identity she'd built in this room was part of her bait. Now, in the season of McKie, the underlying religious cant by which Dosadi's powerful maintained their private illusions would crumble. She could already see the beginnings of that dissolution; soon, everyone would see it.

She took a deep breath. There was a purity in what was about to happen, a simplification. She was about to divest herself of one of her two lives, taking all of her awareness into the persona of that other Keila Jedrik which all of Dosadi would soon know. Her people had kept her secret well, hiding a fat and sleazy blonde person from their fellow Dosadis, exposing just enough of that one to "X" that the powers beyond the God Wall might react in the proper design. She felt cleansed by the fact that the disguise of that other life had begun to lose its importance. The whole of her could begin to surface in that other place. And McKie

had precipitated this metamorphosis. Jedrik's thoughts were clear and direct now:

Come into my trap, McKie. You will take me higher than the palace apartments of the Council Hills.

Or into a deeper hell than any nightmare has imagined.

How to start a war? Nurture your own latent hungers for power. Forget that only madmen pursue power for its own sake. Let such madmen gain power—even you. Let such madmen act behind their conventional masks of sanity. Whether their masks be fashioned from the delusions of defense or the theological aura of law, war will come.

—Gowachin aphorism

The odalarm awoke Jorj X. McKie with a whiff of lemon. For just an instant his mind played tricks on him. He thought he was on Tutalsee's gentle planetary ocean floating softly on his garlanded island. There were lemons on his floating island, banks of Hibiscus and carpets of spicy Alyssum. His bowered cottage lay in the path of perfumed breezes and the lemon . . .

Awareness came. He was not on Tutalsee with a loving companion; he was on a trained bedog in the armored efficiency of his Central Central apartment; he was back in the heart of the Bureau of Sabotage; he was back at work.

McKie shuddered.

A planet full of people could die today . . . or tomorrow.

It would happen unless someone solved this Dosadi mystery. Knowing the Gowachin as he did, McKie was convinced of it. The Gowachin were capable of cruel decisions, especially where their species pride was at stake, or for reasons which other species might not understand. Bildoon, his Bureau chief, assessed this crisis the same way. Not since the Caleban problem had such enormity crossed the Con-Sentient horizon.

But where was this endangered planet, this Dosadi?

After a night of sleep suppression, the briefings about Dosadi came back vividly as though part of his mind had remained at work sharpening the images. Two operatives,

one Wreave and one Laclac, had made the report. The two were reliable and resourceful. Their sources were excellent, although the information was sparse. The two also were bucking for promotion at a time when Wreaves and Laclacs were hinting at discrimination against their species. The report required special scrutiny. No BuSab agent, regardless of species, was above some internal testing, a deception designed to weaken the Bureau and gain coup merits upon which to ride into the director's office.

However, BuSab was still directed by Bildoon, a PanSpechi in Human form, the fourth member of his creche to carry that name. It had been obvious from Bildoon's first words that he believed the report.

"McKie, this thing could set Human and Gowachin at each others' throats."

It was an understandable idiom, although in point of fact you would go for the Gowachin abdomen to carry out the same threat. McKie already had acquainted himself with the report and, from internal evidence to which his long association with the Gowachin made him sensitive, he shared Bildoon's assessment. Seating himself in a grey chairdog across the desk from the director in the rather small, windowless office Bildoon had lately preferred, McKie shifted the report from one hand to the other. Presently, recognizing his own nervous mannerism, he put the report on the desk. It was on coded memowire which played to trained senses when passed through the fingers or across other sensitive appendages.

"Why couldn't they pinpoint this Dosadi's location?" McKie asked.

"It's known only to a Caleban."

"Well, they'll . . ."

"The Calebans refuse to respond."

McKie stared across the desk at Bildoon. The polished surface reflected a second image of the BuSab director, an inverted image to match the upright one. McKie studied the reflection. Until you focused on Bildoon's faceted eyes (how

like an insect's eyes they were), this PanSpechi appeared much like a Human male with dark hair and pleasant round face. Perhaps he'd put on more than the form when his flesh had been molded to Human shape. Bildoon's face displayed emotions which McKie read in Human terms. The director appeared angry.

McKie was troubled.

"Refused?"

"The Calebans don't deny that Dosadi exists or that it's threatened. They refuse to discuss it."

"Then we're dealing with a Caleban contract and they're obeying the terms of that contract."

Recalling that conversation with Bildoon as he awakened in his apartment, McKie lay quietly thinking. Was Dosadi some new extension of the Caleban Question?

It's right to fear what we don't understand.

The Caleban mystery had eluded ConSentient investigators for too long. He thought of his recent conversation with Fannie Mae. When you thought you had something pinned down, it slipped out of your grasp. Before the Calebans' gift of jumpdoors, the ConSentiency had been a relatively slow and understandable federation of the known sentient species. The universe had contained itself in a shared space of recognizable dimensions. The ConSentiency of those days had grown in a way likened to expanding bubbles. It had been linear.

Caleban jumpdoors had changed that with an explosive acceleration of every aspect of life. Jumpdoors had been an immediately disruptive tool of power. They implied infinite usable dimensions. They implied many other things only faintly understood. Through a jumpdoor you stepped from a room on Tutalsee into a hallway here on Central Central. You walked through a jumpdoor here and found yourself in a garden on Paginui. The intervening "normal space" might be measured in light years or parsecs, but the passage from one place to the other ignored such old concepts. And to this day, ConSentient investigators did not understand

how the jumpdoors worked. Concepts such as "relative space" didn't explain the phenomenon; they only added to the mystery.

McKie ground his teeth in frustration. Calebans inevitably did that to him. What good did it do to think of the Calebans as visible stars in the space his body occupied? He could look up from any planet where a jumpdoor deposited him and examine the night sky. Visible stars: ah, yes. Those are Calebans. What did that tell him?

There was a strongly defended theory that Calebans were but a more sophisticated aspect of the equally mysterious Taprisiots. The ConSentiency had accepted and employed Taprisiots for thousands of standard years. A Taprisiot presented sentient form and size. They appeared to be short lengths of tree trunk cut off at top and bottom and with oddly protruding stub limbs. When you touched them they were warm and resilient. They were fellow beings of the ConSentiency. But just as the Calebans took your flesh across the parsecs, Taprisiots took your awareness across those same parsecs to merge you with another mind.

Taprisiots were a communications device.

But current theory said Taprisiots had been introduced to prepare the ConSentiency for Calebans.

It was dangerous to think of Taprisiots as merely a convenient means of communication. Equally dangerous to think of Calebans as "transportation facilitators." Look at the socially disruptive effect of jumpdoors! And when you employed a Taprisiot, you had a constant reminder of danger: the communications trance which reduced you to a twitching zombie while you made your call. No . . . neither Calebans nor Taprisiots should be accepted without question.

With the possible exception of the PanSpechi, no other species knew the first thing about Caleban and Taprisiot phenomena beyond their economic and personal value. They were, indeed, valuable, a fact reflected in the prices often paid for jumpdoor and long-call services. The PanSpechi

denied that they could explain these things, but the Pan-Spechi were notoriously secretive. They were a species where each *individual* consisted of five bodies and only one dominant ego. The four reserves lay somewhere in a hidden creche. Bildoon had come from such a creche, accepting the communal ego from a creche-mate whose subsequent fate could only be imagined. PanSpechi refused to discuss internal creche matters except to admit what was obvious on the surface: that they could grow a simulacrum body to mimic most of the known species in the ConSentiency.

McKie felt himself overcome by a momentary pang of xenophobia.

We accept too damned many things on the explanations of people who could have good reasons for lying.

Keeping his eyes closed, McKie sat up. His bedog rippled gently against his buttocks.

Blast and damn the Calebans! Damn Fannie Mae!

He'd already called Fannie Mae, asking about Dosadi. The result had left him wondering if he really knew what Calebans meant by friendship.

"Information not permitted."

What kind of an answer was that? Especially when it was the only response he could get.

Not permitted?

The basic irritant was an old one: BuSab had no real way of applying its "gentle ministrations" to the Calebans.

But Calebans had never been known to lie. They appeared painfully, explicitly honest . . . as far as they could be understood. But they obviously withheld information. Not permitted! Was it possible they'd let themselves be accessories to the destruction of a planet and that planet's entire population?

McKie had to admit it was possible.

They might do it out of ignorance or from some stricture of Caleban morality which the rest of the ConSentiency did not share or understand. Or for some other reason which defied translation. They said they looked upon all life as

"precious nodes of existence." But hints at peculiar exceptions remained. What was it Fannie Mae had once said?

"Dissolved well this node."

How could you look at an individual life as a "node"?

If association with Calebans had taught him anything, it was that understanding between species was tenuous at best and trying to understand a Caleban could drive you insane. In what medium did a node dissolve?

McKie sighed.

For now, this Dosadi report from the Wreave and Laclac agents had to be accepted on its own limited terms. Powerful people in the Gowachin Confederacy had sequestered Humans and Gowachin on an unlisted planet. Dosadi—location unknown, but the scene of unspecified experiments and tests on an imprisoned population. This much the agents insisted was true. If confirmed, it was a shameful act. The frog people would know that, surely. Rather than let their shame be exposed, they could carry out the threat which the two agents reported: blast the captive planet out of existence, the population and all of the incriminating evidence with it.

McKie shuddered.

Dosadi, a planet of thinking creatures—*sentients*. If the Gowachin carried out their violent threat, a living world would be reduced to blazing gases and the hot plasma of atomic particles. Somewhere, perhaps beyond the reach of other eyes, something would strike fire against the void. The tragedy would require less than a standard second. The most concise thought about such a catastrophe would require a longer time than the actual event.

But if it happened and the other ConSentient species received absolute proof that it had happened . . . ahhh, then the ConSentiency might well be shattered. Who would use a jumpdoor, suspecting that he might be shunted into some hideous experiment? Who would trust a neighbor, if that neighbor's habits, language, and body were different from his own? Yes . . . there would be more than Humans and

Gowachin *at each other's throats*. These were things all the species feared. Bildoon realized this. The threat to this mysterious Dosadi was a threat to all.

McKie could not shake the terrible image from his mind: an explosion, a bright blink stretching toward its own darkness. And if the ConSentiency learned of it . . . in that instant before their universe crumbled like a cliff dislodged in a lightning bolt, what excuses would be offered for the failure of reason to prevent such a thing?

Reason?

McKie shook his head, opened his eyes. It was useless to dwell on the worst prospects. He allowed the apartment's sleep gloom to invade his senses, absorbed the familiar presence of his surroundings.

I'm a Saboteur Extraordinary and I've a job to do.

It helped to think of Dosadi that way. Solutions to problems often depended upon the will to succeed, upon sharpened skills and multiple resources. BuSab owned those resources and those skills.

McKie stretched his arms high over his head, twisted his blocky torso. The bedog rippled with pleasure at his movements. He whistled softly and suffered the kindling of morning light as the apartment's window controls responded. A yawn stretched his mouth. He slid from the bedog and padded across to the window. The view stretched away beneath a sky like stained blue paper. He stared out across the spires and rooftops of Central Central. Here lay the heart of the domine planet from which the Bureau of Sabotage spread its multifarious tentacles.

He blinked at the brightness, took a deep breath.

The Bureau. The omnipresent, omniscient, omnivorous Bureau. The one source of unmonitored governmental violence remaining in the ConSentiency. Here lay the norm against which sanity measured itself. Each choice made here demanded utmost delicacy. Their common enemy was that never-ending sentient yearning for absolutes. And each

hour of every waking workday, BuSab in all of its parts asked itself:

"What are we if we succumb to unbridled violence?"

The answer was there in deepest awareness:

"Then we are useless."

ConSentient government worked because, no matter how they defined it, the participants believed in a common justice personally achievable. The *Government* worked because BuSab sat at its core like a terrible watchdog able to attack itself or any seat of power with a delicately balanced immunity. Government worked because there were places where it could not act without being chopped off. An appeal to BuSab made the individual as powerful as the ConSentiency. It all came down to the cynical, self-effacing behavior of the carefully chosen BuSab tentacles.

I don't feel much like a BuSab tentacle this morning, McKie thought.

In his advancing years, he'd often experienced such mornings. He had a personal way of dealing with this mood: he buried himself in work.

McKie turned, crossed to the baffle into his bath where he turned his body over to the programmed ministrations of his morning toilet. The psyche-mirror on the bath's far wall reflected his body while it examined and adjusted to his internal conditions. His eyes told him he was still a squat, dark-skinned gnome of a Human with red hair, features so large they suggested an impossible kinship with the frog people of the Gowachin. The mirror did not reflect his mind, considered by many to be the sharpest legal device in the ConSentiency.

The Daily Schedule began playing to McKie as he emerged from the bath. The DS suited its tone to his movements and the combined analysis of his psychophysical condition.

"Good morning, ser," it fluted.

McKie, who could interpret the analysis of his mood from the DS tone, put down a flash of resentment. Of course

he felt angry and concerned. Who wouldn't under these circumstances?

"Good morning, you dumb inanimate object," he growled. He slipped into a supple armored pullover, dull green and with the outward appearance of cloth.

The DS waited for his head to emerge.

"You wanted to be reminded, ser, that there is a full conference of the Bureau Directorate at nine local this morning, but the . . ."

"Of all the stupid . . ." McKie's interruption stopped the DS. He'd been meaning for some time to reprogram the damned thing. No matter how carefully you set them, they always got out of phase. He didn't bother to bridle his mood, merely spoke the key words in full emotional spate: "Now you hear me, machine: don't you ever again choose that buddy-buddy conversational pattern when I'm in this mood! I want nothing *less* than a reminder of that conference. When you list such a reminder, don't even suggest remotely that it's my wish. Understood?"

"Your admonition recorded and new program instituted, ser." The DS adopted a brisk, matter of fact tone as it continued: "There is a new reason for alluding to the conference."

"Well, get on with it."

McKie pulled on a pair of green shorts and matching kilt of armored material identical to that of the pullover.

The DS continued:

"The conference was alluded to, ser, as introduction to a new datum: you have been asked not to attend."

McKie, bending to fit his feet into self-powered racing boots, hesitated, then:

"But they're still going to have a showdown meeting with all the Gowachin in the Bureau?"

"No mention of that, ser. The message was that you are to depart immediately this morning on the field assignment which was discussed with you. Code Geevee was invoked. An unspecified Gowachin Phylum has asked that you pro-

ceed at once to their home planet. That would be Tandaloor. You are to consult there on a problem of a legal nature."

McKie finished fitting the boots, straightened. He could feel all of his accumulated years as though there'd been no geriatric intervention. Geevee invoked a billion kinds of hell. It put him on his own with but one shopside backup facility: a Taprisiot monitor. He'd have his own Taprisiot link sitting safely here on CC while he went out and risked his vulnerable flesh. The Taprisiot served only one function: to note his death and record every aspect of his final moments—every thought, every memory. This would be part of the next agent's briefing. And the next agent would get his own Taprisiot monitor etcetera, etcetera, etcetera . . . BuSab was notorious for gnawing away at its problems. The Bureau never gave up. But the astronomical cost of such a Taprisiot monitor left the operative so gifted with only one conclusion: odds were not in his favor. There'd be no accolades, no cemetery rites for a dead hero . . . probably not even the physical substance of a hero for private grieving.

McKie felt less and less heroic by the minute.

Heroism was for fools and BuSab agents were not employed for their foolishness. He saw the reasoning, though. He was the best qualified non-Gowachin for dealing with the Gowachin. He looked at the nearest DS voder.

"Was it suggested that someone doesn't want me at that conference?"

"There was no such speculation."

"Who gave you this message?"

"Bildoon. Verified voiceprint. He asked that your sleep not be interrupted, that the message be given to you on awakening."

"Did he say he'd call back or ask me to call him?"

"No."

"Did Bildoon mention Dosadi?"

"He said the Dosadi problem is unchanged. Dosadi is not in my banks, ser. Did you wish me to seek more info . . ."

"No! I'm to leave immediately?"

"Bildoon said your orders have been cut. In relationship to Dosadi, he said, and these are his exact words: 'The worst is probable. They have all the motivation required.'"

McKie ruminated aloud: "All the motivation . . . selfish interest or fear . . ."

"Ser, are you inquiring of . . ."

"No, you stupid machine! I'm thinking out loud. People do that. We have to sort things out in our heads, put a proper evaluation on available data."

"You do it with extreme inefficiency."

This startled McKie into a flash of anger. "But this job takes a sentient, a *person,* not a machine! Only a person can make the responsible decision. And I'm the only agent who understands them sufficiently."

"Why not set a Gowachin agent to ferret out their . . ."

"So you've worked it out?"

"It was not difficult, even for a machine. Sufficient clues were provided. And since you'll get a Taprisiot monitor, the project involves danger to your person. While I do not have specifics about Dosadi, the clear inference is that the Gowachin have engaged in questionable activity. Let me remind McKie that the Gowachin do not admit guilt easily. Very few non-Gowachin are considered by them to be worthy of their company and confidence. They do not like to feel dependent upon non-Gowachin. In fact, no Gowachin enjoys any dependent condition, not even when dependent upon another Gowachin. This is at the root of their law."

This was a more emotionally loaded conversation than McKie had ever before heard from his DS. Perhaps his constant refusal to accept the thing on a personal anthropomorphic basis had forced it into this adaptation. He suddenly felt almost shy with the DS. What it had said was pertinent, and more than that, vitally important in a particular way: chosen to help him to the extent the DS was capable. In McKie's thoughts, the DS was suddenly transformed into a valued confidante.

As though it knew his thoughts, the DS said:

"I'm still a machine. You are inefficient, but as you have correctly stated you have ways of arriving at accuracy which machines do not understand. We can only . . . guess, and we are not really programmed to guess unless specifically ordered to do so on a given occasion. Trust yourself."

"But you'd rather I were not killed?"

"That is my program."

"Do you have any more helpful suggestions?"

"You would be advised to waste as little time as possible here. There was a tone of urgency in Bildoon's voice."

McKie stared at the nearest voder. Urgency in Bildoon's voice? Even under the most urgent necessity, Bildoon had never sounded urgent to McKie. Certainly, Dosadi could be an urgent matter, but . . . Why should that sound a sour note?

"Are you sure he sounded urgent?"

"He spoke rapidly and with obvious tensions."

"Truthful?"

"The tone-spikes lead to that conclusion."

McKie shook his head. Something about Bildoon's behavior in this matter didn't ring true, but whatever it was it escaped the sophisticated reading circuits of the DS.

And my circuits, too.

Still troubled, McKie ordered the DS to assemble a full travel kit and to read out the rest of the schedule. He moved to the tool cupboard beside his bath baffle as the DS began reeling off the schedule.

His day was to start with the Taprisiot appointment. He listened with only part of his attention, taking care to check the toolkit as the DS assembled it. There were plastipiks. He handled them gently as they deserved. A selection of stims followed. He rejected these, counting on the implanted sense/muscle amplifiers which increased the capabilities of senior BuSab agents. Explosives in various denominations went into the kit—raygens, pentrates. Very careful with these dangerous items. He accepted multilenses, a wad of uniflesh with matching mediskin, solvos, miniputer. The DS extruded a life-monitor bead for the

Taprisiot linkage. He swallowed it to give the bead time to anchor in his stomach before the Taprisiot appointment. A holoscan and matching blanks were accepted, as were ruptors and comparators. He rejected the adapter for simulation of target identities. It was doubtful he'd have time or facilities for such sophisticated refinements. Better to trust his own instincts.

Presently, he sealed the kit in its wallet, concealed the wallet in a pocket. The DS had gone rambling on:

". . . and you'll arrive on Tandaloor at a place called Holy Running. The time there will be early afternoon."

Holy Running!

McKie riveted his attention to this datum. A Gowachin saying skittered through his mind: *The Law is a blind guide, a pot of bitter water. The Law is a deadly contest which can change as waves change.*

No doubt of what had led his thoughts into that path. Holy Running was the place of Gowachin myth. Here, so their stories said, lived Mrreg, the monster who had set the immutable pattern of Gowachin character.

And now, McKie suspected he knew which Gowachin Phylum had summoned him. It could be any one of five Phyla at Holy Running, but he felt certain it'd be the worst of those five—the most unpredictable, the most powerful, the most feared. Where else could a thing such as Dosadi originate?

McKie addressed his DS:

"Send in my breakfast. Please record that the condemned person ate a hearty breakfast."

The DS, programmed to recognize rhetoric for which there was no competent response, remained silent while complying.

All sentient beings are created unequal. The best society provides each with equal opportunity to float at his own level.

—The Gowachin Primary

B y mid-afternoon, Jedrik saw that her gambit had been accepted. A surplus of fifty Humans was just the right size to be taken by a greedy underling. Whoever it was would see the possibilities of continuing—ten here, thirty there—and because of the way she'd introduced this *flaw*, the next people discarded would be mostly Humans, but with just enough Gowachin to smack of retaliation.

It'd been difficult carrying out her daily routine knowing what she'd set in motion. It was all very well to accept the fact that you were *going* into danger. When the actual moment arrived, it always had a different character. As the subtle and not so subtle evidence of success accumulated, she felt the crazy force of it rolling over her. Now was the time to think about her true power base, the troops who would obey her slightest hint, the tight communications linkage with the Rim, the carefully selected and trained lieutenants. Now was the time to think about McKie slipping so smoothly into her trap. She concealed elation behind a facade of anger. They'd expect her to be angry.

The evidence began with a slowed response at her computer terminal. Someone was monitoring. Whoever had taken her bait wanted to be certain she was expendable. Wouldn't want to eliminate someone and then discover that the eliminated someone was essential to the power structure. She'd made damned sure to cut a wide swath into a region which could be made non-essential.

The microsecond delay from the monitoring triggered a disconnect on her telltale circuit, removing the evidence of

her preparations before anyone could find it. She didn't think there'd be that much caution in anyone who'd accept this gambit, but unnecessary chances weren't part of her plan. She removed the telltale timer and locked it away in one of the filing cabinets, there to be destroyed with the other evidence when the Elector's toads came prying. The lonely blue flash would be confined by metal walls which would heat to a nice blood red before lapsing into slag and ashes.

In the next stage, people averted their faces as they walked past her office doorway.

Ahhh, the accuracy of the rumor-trail.

The avoidance came so naturally: a glance at a companion on the other side, concentration on material in one's hands, a brisk stride with gaze fixed on the corridor's ends. Important business up there. No time to stop and chat with Keila Jedrik today.

By the Veil of Heaven! They were so transparent!

A Gowachin walked by examining the corridor's blank opposite wall. She knew that Gowachin: one of the Elector's spies. What would he tell Elector Broey today? Jedrik glared at the Gowachin in secret glee. By nightfall, Broey would know who'd picked up her gambit, but it was too small a bite to arouse his avarice. He'd merely log the information for possible future use. It was too early for him to suspect a sacrifice move.

A Human male followed the Gowachin. He was intent on the adjustment of his neckline and that, of course, precluded a glance at a Senior Liaitor in her office. His name was Drayjo. Only yesterday, Drayjo had made courting gestures, bending toward her over this very desk to reveal the muscles under his light grey coveralls. What did it matter that Drayjo no longer saw her as a useful conquest. His face was a wooden door, closed, locked, hiding nothing.

Avert your face, you clog!

When the red light glowed on her terminal screen, it came as anticlimax. Confirmation that her gambit had been ac-

cepted by someone who would shortly regret it. Communication flowed across the screen:

"Opp SD22240268523ZX."

Good old ZX!

Bad news always developed its own coded idiom. She read what followed, anticipating every nuance:

"The Mandate of God having been consulted, the following supernumerary functions are hereby reduced. If your position screen carries your job title with an underline, you are included in the reduction.

"Senior Liaitor."

Jedrik clenched her fists in simulated anger while she glared at the underlined words. It was done. Opp-Out, the good old Double-O. Through its pliable arm, the DemoPol, the Sacred Congregation of the Heavenly Veil had struck again.

None of her elation showed through her Dosadi controls. Someone able to see beyond immediate gain would note presently that only Humans had received this particular good old Double-O. Not one Gowachin there. Whoever made that observation would come sniffing down the trail she'd deliberately left. Evidence would accumulate. She thought she knew who would read that accumulated evidence for Broey. It would be Tria. It was not yet time for Tria to entertain doubts. Broey would hear what Jedrik wanted him to hear. The Dosadi power game would be played by Jedrik's rules then, and by the time others learned the rules it'd be too late.

She counted on the factor which Broey labeled "instability of the masses." Religious twaddle! Dosadi's masses were unstable only in particular ways. Fit a conscious justification to their innermost unconscious demands and they became a predictable system which would leap into predictable actions—especially with a psychotic populace whose innermost demands could never be faced consciously by the individuals. Such a populace remained highly useful to the

initiates. That was why they maintained the DemoPol with its mandate-of-God sample. The tools of government were not difficult to understand. All you needed was a pathway into the system, a place where what you did touched a new reality.

Broey would think himself the target of her action. More fool he.

Jedrik pushed back her chair, stood and strode to the window hardly daring to think about where her actions would truly be felt. She saw that the sniper's bullet hadn't even left a mark on the glass. These new windows were far superior to the old ones which had taken on dull streaks and scratches after only a few years.

She stared down at the light on the river, carefully preserving this moment, prolonging it.

I won't look up yet, not yet.

Whoever had accepted her gambit would be watching her now. Too late! Too late!

A streak of orange-yellow meandered in the river current: contaminants from the Warren factories . . . poisons. Presently, not looking too high yet, she lifted her gaze to the silvered layers of the Council Hills, to the fluting inverted-stalagmites of the high apartments to which the denizens of Chu aspired in their futile dreams. Sunlight gleamed from the power bulbs which adorned the apartments on the hills. The great crushing wheel of government had its hub on those hills, but the impetus for that wheel had originated elsewhere.

Now, having prolonged the moment while anticipation enriched it, Jedrik lifted her gaze to that region above the Council Hills, to the sparkling streamers and grey glowing of the barrier veil, to the God Wall which englobed her planet in its impenetrable shell. The Veil of Heaven looked the way it always looked in this light. There was no apparent change. But she *knew* what she had done.

Jedrik was aware of subtle instruments which revealed other suns and galaxies beyond the God Wall, places where

other planets must exist, but her people had only this one planet. That barrier up there and whoever had created it insured this isolation. Her eyes blurred with quick tears which she wiped away with real anger at herself. Let Broey and his toads believe themselves the only objects of her anger. She would carve a way beyond them through that deadly veil. No one on Dosadi would ever again cower beneath the hidden powers who lived in the sky!

She lowered her gaze to the carpet of factories and Warrens. Some of the defensive walls were faintly visible in the layers of smoke which blanketed the teeming scramble of life upon which the city fed. The smoke erased fine details to separate the apartment hills from the earth. Above the smoke, the fluted buildings became more a part of sky than of ground. Even the ledged, set-back walls of the canyon within which Chu created its sanctuary were no longer attached to the ground, but floated separate from this place where people could survive to a riper maturity on Dosadi. The smoke dulled the greens of ledges and Rim where the Rabble waged a losing battle for survival. Twenty years was old out there. In that pressure, they fought for a chance to enter Chu's protective confines by any means available, even welcoming the opportunity to eat garbage from which the poisons of this planet had been removed. The worst of Chu was better than their best, which only proved that the conditions of hell were relative.

I seek escape through the God Wall for the same reasons the Rabble seeks entrance to Chu.

In Jedrik's mind lay a graph with an undulant line. It combined many influences: Chu's precious food cycle and economics, Rim incursions, spots which flowed across their veiled sun, subtle planetary movements, atmospheric electricity, gravitational flows, magnetronic fluctuations, the dance of numbers in the Liaitor banks, the seemingly random play of cosmic rays, the shifting colors in the God Wall . . . and mysterious jolts to the entire system which commanded her most concentrated attention. There could

be only one source for such jolts: a manipulative intelligence outside the planetary influence of Dosadi. She called that force "X," but she had broken "X" into components. One component was a simulation model of Elector Broey which she carried firmly in her head, not needing any of the mechanical devices for reading such things. "X" and all of its components were as real as anything else on the chart in her mind. By their interplay she read them.

Jedrik addressed herself silently to "X":

By your actions I know you and you are vulnerable.

Despite all of the Sacred Congregation's prattle, Jedrik and her people knew the God Wall had been put there for a specific purpose. It was the purpose which pressed living flesh into Chu from the Rim. It was the purpose which jammed too many people into too little space while it frustrated all attempts to spread into any other potential sanctuary. It was the purpose which created people who possessed that terrifying mental template which could trade flesh for flesh . . . Gowachin or Human. Many clues revealed themselves around her and came through that radiance in the sky, but she refused as yet to make a coherent whole out of that purpose. Not yet.

I need this McKie!

With a Jedrik-maintained tenacity, her people knew that the regions beyond the barrier veil were not heaven or hell. Dosadi was hell, but it was a *created* hell. *We will know soon . . . soon.*

This moment had been almost nine Dosadi generations in preparation: the careful breeding of a specific individual who carried in one body the talents required for this assault on "X," the exquisitely detailed education of that weapon-in-fleshly-form . . . and there'd been all the rest of it—whispers, unremarked observations in clandestine leaflets, help for people who held particular ideas and elimination of others whose concepts obstructed, the building of a Rim-Warren communications network, the slow and secret assembly of a military force to match the others which balanced them-

selves at the peaks of Dosadi power . . . All of these things and much more had prepared the way for those numbers introduced into her computer terminal. The ones who appeared to rule Dosadi like puppets—those ones could be read in many ways and this time the rulers, both visible and hidden, had made one calculation while Jedrik had made another calculation.

Again, she looked up at the God Wall.

You out there! Keila Jedrik knows you're there. And you can be baited, you can be trapped. You are slow and stupid. And you think I don't know how to use your McKie. Ahhh, sky demons, McKie will open your veil for me. My life's a wrath and you're the objects of my wrath. I dare what you would not.

Nothing of this revealed itself on her face nor in any movement of her body.

Arm yourself when the Frog God smiles.

—Gowachin admonition

Mckie began speaking as he entered the Phylum sanctus: "I'm Jorj X. McKie of the Bureau of Sabotage."

Name and primary allegiance, that was the drill. If he'd been a Gowachin, he'd have named his Phylum or would've favored the room with a long blink to reveal the identifying Phylum tattoo on his eyelids. As a non-Gowachin, he didn't need a tattoo.

He held his right hand extended in the Gowachin peace sign, palm down and fingers wide to show that he held no weapon there and had not extended his claws. Even as he entered, he smiled, knowing the effect this would have on any Gowachin here. In a rare mood of candor, one of his old Gowachin teachers had once explained the effect of a smiling McKie.

"We feel our bones age. It is a very uncomfortable experience."

McKie understood the reason for this. He possessed a thick, muscular body—a swimmer's body with light mahogany skin. He walked with a swimmer's rolling gait. There were Polynesians in his Old Terran ancestry, this much was known in the Family Annals. Wide lips and a flat nose dominated his face; the eyes were large and placidly brown. There was a final genetic ornamentation to confound the Gowachin: red hair. He was the Human equivalent of the greenstone sculpture found in every Phylum house here on Tandaloor. McKie possessed the face and body of the Frog God, the Giver of Law.

As his old teacher had explained, no Gowachin ever fully escaped feelings of awe in McKie's presence, especially when McKie smiled. They were forced to hide a response

which went back to the admonition which every Gowachin learned while still clinging to his mother's back.

Arm yourselves! McKie thought.

Still smiling, he stopped after the prescribed eight paces, glanced once around the room, then narrowed his attention. Green crystal walls confined the sanctus. It was not a large space, a gentle oval of perhaps twenty meters in its longest dimension. A single oval window admitted warm afternoon light from Tandaloor's golden sun. The glowing yellow created a contrived *spiritual ring* directly ahead of McKie. The light focused on an aged Gowachin seated in a brown chairdog which had spread itself wide to support his elbows and webbed fingers. At the Gowachin's right hand stood an exquisitely wrought wooden swingdesk on a scrollwork stand. The desk held one object: a metal box of dull blue about fifteen centimeters long, ten wide, and six deep. Standing behind the blue box in the servant-guard position was a red-robed Wreave, her fighting mandibles tucked neatly into the lower folds of her facial slit.

This Phylum was initiating a Wreave!

The realization filled McKie with disquiet. Bildoon had not warned him about Wreaves on Tandaloor. The Wreave indicated a sad shift among the Gowachin toward a particular kind of violence. Wreaves never danced for joy, only for death. And this was the most dangerous of Wreaves, a *female*, recognizable as such by the jaw pouches behind her mandibles. There'd be two males somewhere nearby to form the breeding triad. Wreaves never ventured from their home soil otherwise.

McKie realized he no longer was smiling. These damnable Gowachin! They'd known the effect a Wreave female would have on him. Except in the Bureau, where a special dispensation prevailed, dealing with Wreaves required the most delicate care to avoid giving offence. And because they periodically exchanged triad members, they developed extended families of gigantic proportions wherein offending one member was to offend them all.

These reflections did not sit well with the chill he'd experienced at sight of the blue box on the swingdesk. He still did not know the identity of this Phylum, but he knew what that blue box had to be. He could smell the peculiar scent of antiquity about it. His choices had been narrowed.

"I know you, McKie," the ancient Gowachin said.

He spoke the ritual in standard Galach with a pronounced burr, a fact which revealed he'd seldom been off this planet. His left hand moved to indicate a white chairdog positioned at an angle to his right beyond the swingdesk, yet well within striking range of the silent Wreave.

"Please seat yourself, McKie."

The Gowachin glanced at the Wreave, at the blue box, returned his attention to McKie. It was a deliberate movement of the pale yellow eyes which were moist with age beneath bleached green brows. He wore only a green apron with white shoulder straps which outlined crusted white chest ventricles. The face was flat and sloping with pale, puckered nostrils below a faint nose crest. He blinked and revealed the tattoos on his eyelids. McKie saw there the dark, swimming circle of the Running Phylum, that which legend said had been the first to accept Gowachin Law from the Frog God.

His worst fears confirmed, McKie seated himself and felt the white chairdog adjust to his body. He cast an uneasy glance at the Wreave, who towered behind the swingdesk like a red-robed executioner. The flexing bifurcation which served as Wreave legs moved in the folds of the robe, but without tension. This Wreave was not yet ready to dance. McKie reminded himself that Wreaves were careful in all matters. This had prompted the ConSentient expression, "a Wreave bet." Wreaves were noted for waiting for the sure thing.

"You see the blue box," the old Gowachin said.

It was a statement of mutual understanding, no answer required, but McKie took advantage of the opening.

"However, I do not know your companion."

"This is Ceylang, Servant of the Box"

Ceylang nodded acknowledgment.

A fellow BuSab agent had once told McKie how to count the number of triad exchanges in which a Wreave female had participated.

"A tiny bit of skin is nipped from one of her jaw pouches by the departing companion. It looks like a little pockmark."

Both of Ceylang's pouches were peppered with exchange pocks. McKie nodded to her, formal and correct, no offense intended, none given. He glanced at the box which she served.

McKie had been a Servant of the Box once. This was where you began to learn the limits of legal ritual. The Gowachin words for this novitiate translated as "The Heart of Disrespect." It was the first stage on the road to Legum. The old Gowachin here was not mistaken: McKie as one of the few non-Gowachin ever admitted to Legum status, to the practice of law in this planetary federation, would *see* that blue box and know what it contained. There would be a small brown book printed on pages of ageless metal, a knife with the blood of many sentient beings dried on its black surface, and lastly a grey rock, chipped and scratched over the millennia in which it'd been used to pound on wood and call Gowachin courts into session. The box and its contents symbolized all that was mysterious and yet practical about Gowachin Law. The book was ageless, yet not to be read and reread; it was sealed in a box where it could be thought upon as a thing which marked a beginning. The knife carried the bloody residue of many endings. And the rock—that came from the natural earth where things only changed, never beginning or ending. The entire assemblage, box and contents, represented a window into the soul of the Frog God's minions. And now they were educating a Wreave as Servant of the Box.

McKie wondered why the Gowachin had chosen a deadly Wreave, but dared not enquire. The blue box, however, was another matter. It said with certainty that a planet called

Dosadi would be named openly here. The thing which BuSab had uncovered was about to become an issue in Gowachin Law. That the Gowachin had anticipated Bureau action spoke well of their information sources. A sense of careful choosing radiated from this room. McKie assumed a mask of relaxation and remained silent.

The old Gowachin did not appear pleased by this. He said:

"You once afforded me much amusement, McKie."

That might be a compliment, probably not. Hard to tell. Even if it were a compliment, coming from a Gowachin it would contain signal reservations, especially in legal matters. McKie held his silence. This Gowachin was big power and no mistake. Whoever misjudged him would hear the Courtarena's final trumpet.

"I watched you argue your first case in our courts," the Gowachin said. "Betting was nine-point-three to three-point-eight that we'd see your blood. But when you concluded by demonstrating that eternal sloppiness was the price of liberty . . . ahhh, that was a master stroke. It filled many a Legum with envy. Your words clawed through the skin of Gowachin Law to get at the meat. And at the same time you amused us. That was the supreme touch."

Until this moment, McKie had not even suspected that there'd been amusement for anyone in that first case. Present circumstances argued for truthfulness from the old Gowachin, however. Recalling that first case, McKie tried to reassess it in the light of this revelation. He remembered the case well. The Gowachin had charged a Low Magister named Klodik with breaking his most sacred vows in an issue of justice. Klodik's crime was the release of thirty-one fellow Gowachin from their primary allegiance to Gowachin Law and the purpose of that was to qualify the thirty-one for service in BuSab. The hapless prosecutor, a much-admired Legum named Pirgutud, had aspired to Klodik's position and had made the mistake of trying for a direct conviction. McKie had thought at the time that the wiser

choice would've been to attempt discrediting the legal structure under which Klodik had been arraigned. This would have thrown judgment into the area of popular choice, and there'd been no doubt that Klodik's early demise would've been popular. Seeing this opening, McKie had attacked the prosecutor as a legalist, a stickler, one who preferred Old Law. Victory had been relatively easy.

When it had come to the knife, however, McKie had found himself profoundly reluctant. There'd been no question of selling Pirgutud back to his own Phylum. BuSab had needed a non-Gowachin Legum . . . the whole non-Gowachin universe had needed this. The few other non-Gowachin who'd attained Legum status were all dead, every last one of them in the Courtarena. A current of animosity toward the Gowachin worlds had been growing. Suspicion fed on suspicion.

Pirgutud had to die in the traditional, the formal, way. He'd known it perhaps better than McKie. Pirgutud, as required, had bared the heart area beside his stomach and clasped his hands behind his head. This extruded the stomach circle, providing a point of reference.

The purely academic anatomy lessons and the practice sessions on lifelike dummies had come to deadly focus.

"Just to the left of the stomach circle imagine a small triangle with an apex at the center of the stomach circle extended horizontally and the base even with the bottom of the stomach circle. Strike into the lower outside corner of this triangle and slightly upward toward the midline."

About the only satisfaction McKie had found in the event was that Pirgutud had died cleanly and quickly with one stroke. McKie had not entered Gowachin Law as a "hacker."

What had there been in that case and its bloody ending to amuse the Gowachin? The answer filled McKie with a profound sense of peril.

The Gowachin were amused at themselves because they had so misjudged me! But I'd planned all along for them to misjudge me. That was what amused them!

Having provided McKie with a polite period for reflection, the old Gowachin continued:

"I'd bet against you, McKie. The odds, you understand? You delighted me nonetheless. You instructed us while winning your case in a classic manner which would've done credit to the best of us. That is one of the Law's purposes, of course: to test the qualities of those who choose to employ it. Now what did you expect to find when you answered our latest summons to Tandaloor?"

The question's abrupt shift almost caught McKie by surprise.

I've been too long away from the Gowachin, he thought. I can't relax even for an instant.

It was almost a palpable thing: if he missed a single beat of the rhythms in this room, he and an entire planet could fall before Gowachin judgment. For a civilization which based its law on the Courtarena where any participant could be sacrificed, anything was possible. McKie chose his next words with life-and-death care.

"You summoned me, that is true, but I came on official business of my Bureau. It's the Bureau's expectations which concern me."

"Then you are in a difficult position because you're also a Legum of the Gowachin Bar subject to our demands. Do you know me?"

This was a Magister, a *Foremost-Speaker* from the "Phylum of Phylums," no doubt of it. He was a survivor in one of the most cruel traditions known to the sentient universe. His abilities and resources were formidable and he was on his home ground. McKie chose the cautious response.

"On my arrival I was told to come to this place at this time. That is what I know."

The least thing that is known shall govern your acts. This was the course of evidence for the Gowachin. McKie's response put a legal burden on his questioner.

The old Gowachin's hands clutched with pleasure at the level of artistry to which this contest had risen. There was

a momentary silence during which Ceylang gathered her robe tightly and moved even closer to the swingdesk. Now, there was tension in her movements. The Magister stirred, said:

"I have the disgusting honor to be High Magister of the Running Phylum, Aritch by name."

As he spoke, his right hand thrust out, took the blue box, and dropped it into McKie's lap. "I place the binding oath upon you in the name of the book!"

As McKie had expected, it was done swiftly. He had the box in his hands while the final words of the ancient legal challenge were ringing in his ears. No matter the ConSentient modifications of Gowachin Law which might apply in this situation, he was caught in a convoluted legal maneuvering. The metal of the box felt cold against his fingers. They'd confronted him with *the* High Magister. The Gowachin were dispensing with many preliminaries. This spoke of time pressures and a particular assessment of their own predicament. McKie reminded himself that he was dealing with people who found pleasure in their own failures, could be amused by death in the Courtarena, whose most consummate pleasure came when the currents of their own Law were changed artistically.

McKie spoke with the careful formality which ritual required if he were to emerge alive from this room.

"Two wrongs may cancel each other. Therefore, let those who do wrong do it together. That is the true purpose of Law."

Gently, McKie released the simple swing catch on the box, lifted the lid to verify the contents. This must be done with precise attention to formal details. A bitter, musty odor touched his nostrils as the lid lifted. The box held what he'd expected: the book, the knife, the rock. It occurred to McKie then that he was holding the original of all such boxes. It was a thing of enormous antiquity—thousands upon thousands of standard years. Gowachin professed the belief that the Frog God had created this box, this very box, and its contents as a model, the symbol of "the only workable Law."

Careful to do it with his right hand, McKie touched each item of the box in its turn, closed the lid and latched it. As he did this, he felt that he stepped into a ghostly parade of Legums, names imbedded in the minstrel chronology of Gowachin history.

Bishkar who concealed her eggs . . .

Kondush the Diver . . .

Dritaik who sprang from the marsh and laughed at Mrreg . . .

Tonkeel of the hidden knife . . .

McKie wondered then how they would sing about him. Would it be *McKie the blunderer?* His thoughts raced through review of the necessities. The primary necessity was Aritch. Little was known about this High Magister outside the Gowachin Federation, but it was said that he'd once won a case by finding a popular bias which allowed him to kill a judge. The commentary on this coup said Aritch "embraced the Law in the same way that salt dissolves in water." To the initiates, this meant Aritch personified the basic Gowachin attitude toward their Law: "respectful disrespect" It was a peculiar form of sanctity. Every movement of your body was as important as your words. The Gowachin made it an aphorism.

"You hold your life in your mouth when you enter the Courtarena."

They provided legal ways to kill any participant—judges, Legums, clients . . . But it must be done with exquisite legal finesse, with its justifications apparent to all observers, and with the most delicate timing. Above all, one could kill in the arena only when no other choice offered the same worshipful disrespect for Gowachin Law. Even while changing the Law, you were required to revere its sanctity.

When you entered the Courtarena, you had to feel that peculiar sanctity in every fiber. The forms . . . the forms . . . the forms . . . With that blue box in his hands, the deadly forms of Gowachin Law dominated every movement, every word. Knowing McKie was not Gowachin-born, Aritch

was putting time pressures on him, hoping for an immediate flaw. They didn't want this Dosadi matter in the arena. That was the immediate contest. And if it did get to the arena . . . well, the crucial matter would be selection of the judges. Judges were chosen with great care. Both sides maneuvered in this, being cautious not to intrude a professional legalist onto the bench. Judges could represent those whom the Law had offended. They could be private citizens in any number satisfactory to the opposing forces. Judges could be (and often were) chosen for their special knowledge of a case at hand. But here you were forced to weigh the subtleties of prejudgment. Gowachin Law made a special distinction between prejudgment and bias.

McKie considered this.

The interpretation of bias was: "If I can rule for a particular side I will do so."

For prejudgment: "No matter what happens in the arena I will rule for a particular side."

Bias was permitted, but not prejudgment.

Aritch was the first problem, his possible prejudgments, his bias, his inborn and most deeply conditioned attitudes. In his deepest feelings, he would look down on all non-Gowachin legal systems as "devices to weaken personal character through appeals to illogic, irrationality, and to ego-centered selfishness in the name of high purpose."

If Dosadi came to the arena, it would be tried under modified Gowachin Law. The modifications were a thorn in the Gowachin skin. They represented concessions made for entrance into the ConSentiency. Periodically, the Gowachin tried to make their Law the basis for all ConSentient Law.

McKie recalled that a Gowachin had once said of ConSentient Law:

"It fosters greed, discontent, and competitiveness not based on excellence but on appeals to prejudice and materialism."

Abruptly, McKie remembered that this was a quotation attributed to Aritch, High Magister of the Running Phylum.

Were there even more deeply hidden motives in what the Gowachin did here?

Showing signs of impatience, Aritch inhaled deeply through his chest ventricles, said:

"You are now my Legum. To be convicted is to go free because this marks you as enemy of all government. I know you to be such an enemy, McKie."

"You know me," McKie agreed.

It was more than ritual response and obedience to forms, it was truth. But it required great effort for McKie to speak it calmly. In the almost fifty years since he'd been admitted to the Gowachin Bar, he'd served that ancient legal structure four times in the Courtarena, a minor record among the ordinary Legums. Each time, his personal survival had been in the balance. In all of its stages, this contest was a deadly battle. The loser's life belonged to the winner and could be taken at the winner's discretion. On rare occasions, the loser might be sold back to his own Phylum as a menial. Even the losers disliked this choice.

Better clean death than dirty life.

The blood-encrusted knife in the blue box testified to the more popular outcome. It was a practice which made for rare litigation and memorable court performances.

Aritch, speaking with eyes closed and the Running Phylum tattoos formally displayed, brought their encounter to its testing point.

"Now McKie, you will tell me what official matters of the Bureau of Sabotage bring you to the Gowachin Federation."

Law must retain useful ways to break with traditional forms because nothing is more certain than that the forms of Law remain when all justice is gone.

—Gowachin aphorism

He was tall for a Dosadi Gowachin, but fat and ungroomed. His feet shuffled when he walked and there was a permanent stoop to his shoulders. A flexing wheezing overcame his chest ventricles when he became excited. He knew this and was aware that those around him knew it. He often used this characteristic as a warning, reminding people that no Dosadi held more power than he, and that power was deadly. All Dosadi knew his name: Broey. And very few misinterpreted the fact that he'd come up through the Sacred Congregation of the Heavenly Veil to his post as chief steward of Control: The Elector. His private army was Dosadi's largest, most efficient, and best armed. Broey's intelligence corps was a thing to invoke fear and admiration. He maintained a fortified suite atop his headquarters building, a structure of stone and plasteel which fronted the main arm of the river in the heart of Chu. Around this core, the twisting walled fortifications of the city stepped outward in concentric rings. The only entrance to Broey's citadel was through a guarded Tube Gate in a subbasement, designated TG One. TG One admitted the select of the select and no others.

In the forenoon, the ledges outside Broey's windows were a roosting place for carrion birds, who occupied a special niche on Dosadi. Since the Lords of the Veil forbade the eating of sentient flesh by sentient, this task devolved upon the birds. Flesh from the people of Chu and even from the Rim carried fewer of the planet's heavy metals. The carrion birds prospered. A flock of them strutted along Broey's ledge,

coughing, squawking, defecating, brushing against each other with avian insolence while they watched the outlying streets for signs of food. They also watched the Rim, but it had been temporarily denied to them by a sonabarrier. Bird sounds came through a voder into one of the suite's eight rooms. This was a yellow-green space about ten meters long and six wide occupied by Broey and two Humans.

Broey uttered a mild expletive at the bird noise. The confounded creatures interfered with clear thinking. He shuffled to the window and silenced the voder. In the sudden quiet he looked out at the city's perimeter and the lower ledges of the enclosing cliffs. Another Rim foray had been repulsed out there in the night. Broey had made a personal inspection in a convoy of armored vehicles earlier. The troops liked it that he occasionally shared their dangers. The carrion birds already had cleaned up most of the mess by the time the armored column swept through. The flat back structure of Gowachin, who had no front rib cage, had been easily distinguishable from the white framework which had housed Human organs. Only a few rags of red and green flesh had marked where the birds had abandoned their feast when the sonabarriers herded them away.

When he considered the sonabarriers, Broey's thoughts grew hard and clear. The sonabarriers were one of Gar's damned affectations! *Let the birds finish it.*

But Gar insisted a few bodies be left around to make the point for the Rim survivors that their attacks were hopeless.

The bones by themselves would be just as effective.

Gar was bloody minded.

Broey turned and glanced across the room past his two Human companions. Two of the walls were taken up by charts bearing undulant squiggles in many colors. On a table at the room's center lay another chart with a single red line. The line curved and dipped, ending almost in the middle of the chart. Near this terminus lay a white card and beside it stood a Human male statuette with an enormous erection which was labeled "Rabble." It was a subversive,

forbidden artifact of Rim origin. The people of the Rim knew where their main strength lay: breed, breed, breed . . .

The Humans sat facing each other across the chart. They fitted into the space around them through a special absorption. It was as though they'd been initiated into the secrets of Broey's citadel through an esoteric ritual both forbidding and dangerous.

Broey returned to his chair at the head of the table, sat down, and quietly continued to study his companions. He experienced amusement to feel his fighting claws twitch beneath their finger shields as he looked at the two. Yes— trust them no more than they trusted him. They had their own troops, their own spies—they posed real threat to Broey but often their help was useful. Just as often they were a nuisance.

Quilliam Gar, the Human male who sat with his back to the windows, looked up as Broey resumed his seat. Gar snorted, somehow conveying that he'd been about to silence the voder himself.

Damned carrion birds! But they were useful . . . useful.

The Rim-born were always ambivalent about the birds.

Gar rode his chair as though talking down to ranks of the uninformed. He'd come up through the educational services in the Convocation before joining Broey. Gar was thin with an inner emaciation so common that few on Dosadi gave it any special notice. He had the hunter's face and eyes, carried his eighty-eight years as though they were twice that. Hairline wrinkles crawled down his cheeks. The bas-relief of veins along the backs of his hands and the grey hair betrayed his Rim origins, as did a tendency to short temper. The Labor Pool green of his clothing fooled very few, his face was that well known.

Across from Gar sat his eldest daughter and chief lieutenant, Tria. She'd placed herself there to watch the windows and the cliffs. She'd also been observing the carrion birds, rather enjoying their sounds. It was well to be reminded here of what lay beyond the city's outer gates.

Tria's face held too much brittle sharpness to be considered beautiful by any except an occasional Gowachin looking for an exotic experience or a Warren laborer hoping to use her as a step out of peonage. She often disconcerted her companions by a wide-eyed, cynical stare. She did this with an aristocratic sureness which commanded attention. Tria had developed the gesture for just this purpose. Today, she wore the orange with black trim of Special Services, but without a brassard to indicate the branch. She knew that this led many to believe her Broey's personal toy, which was true but not in the way the cynical supposed. Tria understood her special value: she possessed a remarkable ability to interpret the vagaries of the DemoPol.

Indicating the red line on the chart in front of her, Tria said, "She has to be the one. How can you doubt it?" And she wondered why Broey continued to worry at the obvious.

"Keila Jedrik," Broey said. And again: "Keila Jedrik."

Gar squinted at his daughter.

"Why would she include herself among the fifty who . . ."

"She sends us a message," Broey said. "I hear it clearly now." He seemed pleased by his own thoughts.

Gar read something else in the Gowachin's manner.

"I hope you're not having her killed."

"I'm not as quick to anger as are you Humans," Broey said.

"The usual surveillance?" Gar asked.

"I haven't decided. You know, don't you, that she lives a rather celibate life? Is it that she doesn't enjoy the males of your species?"

"More likely they don't enjoy her," Tria said.

"Interesting. Your breeding habits are so peculiar."

Tria shot a measuring stare at Broey. She wondered why the Gowachin had chosen to wear black today. It was a robe-like garment cut at a sharp angle from shoulders to waist, clearing his ventricles. The ventricles revolted her and Broey knew this. The very thought of them pressing against her . . . She cleared her throat. Broey seldom wore black; it was the

happy color of priestly celebrants. He wore it, though, with a remoteness which suggested that thoughts passed through his mind which no other person could experience.

The exchange between Broey and Tria worried Gar. He could not help but feel the oddity that each of them tried to present a threatening view of events by withholding some data and coloring other data.

"What if she runs out to the Rim?" Gar asked.

Broey shook his head.

"Let her go. She's not one to stay on the Rim."

"Perhaps we should have her picked up," Gar said.

Broey stared at him, then:

"I've gained the distinct impression that you've some private plan in mind. Are you prepared to share it?"

"I've no idea what you . . ."

"Enough!" Broey shouted. His ventricles wheezed as he inhaled.

Gar held himself very quiet.

Broey leaned toward him, noting that this exchange amused Tria.

"It's too soon to make decisions we cannot change! This is a time for ambiguity."

Irritated by his own display of anger, Broey arose and hurried into his adjoining office, where he locked the door. It was obvious that those two had no more idea than he where Jedrik had gone to ground. But it was still his game. She couldn't hide forever. Seated once more in his office, he called Security.

"Has Bahrank returned?"

A senior Gowachin officer hurried into the screen's view, looked up.

"Not yet."

"What precautions to learn where he delivers his cargo?"

"We know his entry gate. It'll be simple to track him."

"I don't want Gar's people to know what you're doing."

"Understood."

"That other matter?"

"Pcharky may have been the last one. He could be dead, too. The killers were thorough."

"Keep searching."

Broey put down a sense of disquiet. Some very un-Dosadi things were happening in Chu . . . and on the Rim. He felt that things occurred which his spies could not uncover. Presently, he returned to the more pressing matter.

"Bahrank is not to be interfered with until afterward."

"Understood."

"Pick him up well clear of his delivery point and bring him to your section. I will interview him personally."

"Sir, his addiction to . . ."

"I know the hold she has on him. I'm counting on it."

"We've not yet secured any of that substance, sir, although we're still trying."

"I want success, not excuses. Who's in charge of that?"

"Kidge, sir. He's very efficient in this . . ."

"Is Kidge available?"

"One moment, sir. I'll put him on."

Kidge had a phlegmatic Gowachin face and rumbling voice.

"Do you want a status report, sir?"

"Yes."

"My Rim contacts believe the addictive substance is de-rived from a plant called 'tibac.' We have no prior record of such a plant, but the outer Rabble has been cultivating it lately. According to my contacts, it's extremely addictive to Humans, even more so to us."

"No record? What's its origin? Do they say?"

"I talked personally to a Human who'd recently returned from upriver where the outer Rabble reportedly has exten-sive plantations of this 'tibac.' I promised my informant a place in the Warrens if he provides me with a complete re-port on the stuff and a kilo packet of it. This informant says the cultivators believe tibac has religious significance. I didn't see any point in exploring that."

"When do you expect him to deliver?"

"By nightfall at the latest."

Broey held his silence for a moment. *Religious significance.* More than likely the plant came from beyond the God Wall then, as Kidge implied. But why? What were *they* doing?

"Do you have new instructions?" Kidge asked.

"Get that substance up to me as soon as you can."

Kidge fidgeted. He obviously had another question, but was unwilling to ask it. Broey glared at him.

"Yes? What is it?"

"Don't you want the substance tested first?"

It was a baffling question. Had Kidge withheld vital information about the dangers of this tibac? One never knew from what quarter an attack might come. But Kidge was held in his own special bondage. He knew what could happen to him if he failed Broey. And Jedrik had handled this stuff. But why had Kidge asked this question? Faced with such unknowns, Broey tended to withdraw into himself, eyes veiled by the nictating membrane while he weighed the possibilities. Presently, he stirred, looked at Kidge in the screen.

"If there's enough of it, feed some to volunteers—both Human and Gowachin. Get the rest of it up to me immediately, even while you're testing, but in a sealed container."

"Sir, there are rumors about this stuff. It'll be difficult getting real volunteers."

"You'll think of something."

Broey broke the connection, returned to the outer room to make his political peace with Gar and Tria. He was not ready to blunt that pair . . . not yet.

They were sitting just as he'd left them. Tria was speaking:

". . . the highest probability and I have to go on that."

Gar merely nodded.

Broey seated himself, nodded to Tria, who continued as though there'd been no hiatus.

"Clearly, Jedrik's a genius. And her Loyalty Index! That has to be false, contrived. And look at her decisions: one questionable decision in four years. One!"

Gar moved a finger along the red line on the chart. It was a curiously sensuous gesture, as though he were stroking flesh.

Broey gave him a verbal prod.

"Yes, Gar, what is it?"

"I was just wondering if Jedrik could be another . . ."

His glance darted ceilingward, back to the chart. They all understood his allusion to intruders from beyond the God Wall.

Broey looked at Gar as though awakening from an interrupted thought. What'd that fool Gar mean by raising such a question at this juncture? The required responses were so obvious.

"I agree with Tria's analysis," Broey said. "As to your question . . ." He gave a Human shrug. "Jedrik reveals some of the classic requirements, but . . ." Again, that shrug. "This is still the world God gave us."

Colored as they were by his years in the Sacred Congregation, Broey's words took on an unctuous overtone, but in this room the message was strictly secular.

"The others have been such disappointments," Gar said. "Especially Havvy." He moved the statuette to a more central position on the chart.

"We failed because we were too eager," Tria said, her voice snappish. "Poor timing."

Gar scratched his chin with his thumb. Tria sometimes disturbed him by that accusatory tone she took toward their failures. He said:

"But . . . if she turns out to be one of *them* and we haven't allowed for it . . ."

"We'll look through that gate when we come to it," Broey said. "*If* we come to it. Even another failure could have its uses. The food factories will give us a substantial increase at the next harvest. That means we can postpone the

more troublesome political decisions which have been bothering us."

Broey let this thought hang between them while he set himself to identifying the lines of activity revealed by what had happened in this room today. Yes, the Humans betrayed unmistakable signs that they behaved according to a secret plan. Things were going well, then: they'd attempt to supersede him soon . . . and fail.

A door behind Tria opened. A fat Human female entered. Her body bulbed in green coveralls and her round face appeared to float in a halo of yellow hair.

Her cheeks betrayed the telltale lividity of *dacon* addiction. She spoke subserviently to Gar.

"You told me to interrupt if . . ."

"Yes, yes."

Gar waved to indicate she could speak freely. The gesture's significance did not escape Broey. Another part of their set piece.

"We've located Havvy but Jedrik's not with him."

Gar nodded, addressed Broey:

"Whether Jedrik's an agent or another puppet, this whole thing smells of something *they* have set in motion."

Once more, his gaze darted ceilingward.

"I will act on that assumption," Tria said. She pushed her chair back, arose. "I'm going into the Warrens."

Broey looked up at her. Again, he felt his talons twitch beneath their sheaths. He said:

"Don't interfere with them."

Gar forced his gaze away from the Gowachin while his mind raced. Often, the Gowachin were difficult to read, but Broey had been obvious just then: he was confident that he could locate Jedrik and he didn't care who knew it. That could be very dangerous.

Tria had seen it, too, of course, but she made no comment, merely turned and followed the fat woman out of the room.

Gar arose like a folding ruler being opened to its limit.

"I'd best be getting along. There are many matters requiring my personal attention."

"We depend on you for a great deal," Broey said.

He was not yet ready to release Gar, however. Let Tria get well on her way. Best to keep those two apart for a spell. He said:

"Before you go, Gar. Several things still bother me. Why was Jedrik so precipitate? And why destroy her records? What was it that we were not supposed to see?"

"Perhaps it was an attempt to confuse us," Gar said, quoting Tria. "One thing's sure: it wasn't just an angry gesture."

"There must be a clue somewhere," Broey said.

"Would you have us risk an interrogation of Havvy?"

"Of course not!"

Gar showed no sign that he recognized Broey's anger. He said:

"Despite what you and Tria say, I don't think we can afford another mistake at this time. Havvy was . . . well . . ."

"If you recall," Broey said, "Havvy was not one of Tria's mistakes. She went along with us under protest. I wish now we'd listened to her." He waved a hand idly in dismissal. "Go see to your important affairs." He watched Gar leave.

Yes, on the basis of the Human's behavior it was reasonable to assume he knew nothing as yet about this *infiltrator* Bahrank was bringing through the gates. Gar would've concealed such valuable information, would not have dared raise the issue of a God Wall intrusion . . . Or would he? Broey nodded to himself. This must be handled with great delicacy.

We will now explore the particular imprint which various governments make upon the individual. First, be sure you recognize the primary governing force. For example, take a careful look at Human history. Humans have been known to submit to many constraints: to rule by Autarchs, by Plutarchs, by the power seekers of the many Republics, by Oligarchs, by tyrant Majorities and Minorities, by the hidden suasions of Polls, by profound instincts and shallow juvenilities. And always, the governing force as we wish you now to understand this concept was whatever the individual believed had control over his immediate survival. Survival sets the pattern of imprint. During much of Human history (and the pattern is similar with most sentient species), Corporation presidents held more survival in their casual remarks than did the figurehead officials. We of the ConSentiency cannot forget this as we keep watch on the Multiworld Corporations. We dare not even forget it of ourselves. Where you work for your own survival, this dominates your imprint, this dominates what you believe.

—Instruction Manual
Bureau of Sabotage

N*ever do what your enemy wants you to do,* McKie reminded himself.

In this moment, Aritch was the enemy, having placed the binding oath of Legum upon an agent of BuSab, having demanded information to which he had no right. The old Gowachin's behavior was consistent with the demands of his own legal system, but it immediately magnified the area of conflict by an enormous factor. McKie chose a minimal response.

"I'm here because Tandaloor is the heart of the Gowachin Federation."

Aritch, who'd been sitting with his eyes closed to emphasize the formal client-Legum relationship, opened his eyes to glare at McKie.

"I remind you *once* that I am your client"

Signs indicating a dangerous new tension in the Wreave servant were increasing, but McKie was forced to concentrate his attention on Aritch.

"You name your *self* client. Very well. The client must answer truthfully such questions as the Legum asks when the legal issues demand it."

Aritch continued to glare at McKie, latent fire in the yellow eyes. Now, the battle was truly joined.

McKie sensed how fragile was the relationship upon which his survival depended. The Gowachin, signatories to the great ConSentiency Pact binding the species of the known universe, were legally subject to certain BuSab intrusions. But Aritch had placed them on another footing. If the Gowachin Federation disagreed with McKie/Agent, they could take him into the Courtarena as a Legum who had wronged a client. With the entire Gowachin Bar arrayed against him, McKie did not doubt which Legum would *taste the knife*. His one hope lay in avoiding immediate litigation. That was, after all, the real basis of Gowachin Law.

Moving a step closer to specifics, McKie said:

"My Bureau has uncovered a matter of embarrassment to the Gowachin Federation."

Aritch blinked twice.

"As we suspected."

McKie shook his head. They didn't *suspect*, they knew. He counted on this: that the Gowachin understood why he'd answered their summons. If any Sentiency under the Pact could understand his position, it had to be the Gowachin. BuSab reflected Gowachin philosophy. Centuries had passed since the great convulsion out of which BuSab had origi-

nated, but the ConSentiency had never been allowed to forget that birth. It was taught to the young of every species.

"Once, long ago, a tyrannical majority captured the government. They said they would make all individuals equal. They meant they would not let any individual be better than another at doing anything. Excellence was to be suppressed or concealed. The tyrants made their government act with great speed 'in the name of the people.' They removed delays and red tape wherever found. There was little deliberation. Unaware that they acted out of an unconscious compulsion to prevent all change, the tyrants tried to enforce a grey sameness upon every population.

"Thus the powerful governmental machine blundered along at increasingly reckless speed. It took commerce and all the important elements of society with it. Laws were thought of and passed within hours. Every society came to be twisted into a suicidal pattern. People became unprepared for those changes which the universe demands. They were unable to change.

"It was the time of *brittle money*, 'appropriated in the morning and gone by nightfall,' as you learned earlier. In their passion for sameness, the tyrants made themselves more and more powerful. All others grew correspondingly weaker and weaker. New bureaus and directorates, odd ministries, leaped into existence for the most improbable purposes. These became the citadels of a new aristocracy, rulers who kept the giant wheel of government careening along, spreading destruction, violence, and chaos wherever they touched.

"In those desperate times, a handful of people (the Five Ears, their makeup and species never revealed) created the Sabotage Corps to slow that runaway wheel of government. The original corps was bloody, violent, and cruel. Gradually, the original efforts were replaced by more subtle methods. The governmental wheel slowed, became more manageable. Deliberation returned.

"Over the generations, that original Corps became a Bureau, the Bureau of Sabotage, with its present Ministerial powers, preferring diversion to violence, but ready for violence when the need arises."

They were words from McKie's own teens, generators of a concept modified by his experiences in the Bureau. Now, he was aware that this directorate composed of all the known sentient species was headed into its own entropic corridors. Someday, the Bureau would dissolve or be dissolved, but the universe still needed them. The old imprints remained, the old futile seeking after absolutes of sameness. It was the ancient conflict between what the individual saw as personal needs for immediate survival and what the totality required if *any* were to survive. And now it was the Gowachin versus the ConSentiency, and Aritch was the champion of his people.

McKie studied the High Magister carefully, sensitive to the unrelieved tensions in the Wreave attendant. Would there be violence in this room? It was a question which remained unanswered as McKie spoke.

"You have observed that I am in a difficult position. I do not enjoy the embarrassment of revered teachers and friends, nor of their compatriots. Yet, evidence has been seen . . ."

He let his voice trail off. Gowachin disliked dangling implications.

Aritch's claws slid from the sheaths of his webbed fingers.

"Your client wishes to hear of this evidence."

Before speaking, McKie rested his hand on the latch of the box in his lap.

"Many people from two species have disappeared. Two species: Gowachin and Human. Singly, these were small matters, but these disappearances have been going on for a long time—perhaps twelve or fifteen generations by the old Human reckoning. Taken together, these disappearances are massive. We've learned that there's a planet called Dosadi where these people were taken. Such evidence as we have

has been examined carefully. It all leads to the Gowachin Federation."

Aritch's fingers splayed, a sign of acute embarrassment. Whether assumed or real, McKie could not tell.

"Does your Bureau accuse the Gowachin?"

"You know the function of my Bureau. We do not yet know the location of Dosadi, but we'll find it."

Aritch remained silent. He knew BuSab had never given up on a problem.

McKie raised the blue box.

"Having thrust this upon me, you've made me guardian of your fate, client. You've no rights to inquire as to my methods. I will not follow *old* law."

Aritch nodded.

"It was my argument that you'd react thus."

He raised his right hand.

The rhythmic "death flexion" swept over the Wreave and her fighting mandibles darted from her facial slit.

At the first movement from her, McKie whipped open the blue box, snatched out book and knife. He spoke with a firmness his body did not feel:

"If she makes the slightest move toward me, my blood will defile this book." He placed the knife against his own wrist. "Does your Servant of the Box know the consequences? The history of the Running Phylum would end. Another Phylum would be presumed to've accepted the Law from its Giver. The name of this Phylum's *last* High Magister would be erased from living thought. Gowachin would eat their own eggs at the merest hint that they had Running Phylum blood in their veins."

Aritch remained frozen, right hand raised. Then:

"McKie, you are revealed as a sneak. Only by spying on our most sacred rituals could you know this."

"Did you think me some fearful, pliable dolt, client? I am a true Legum. A Legum does not have to sneak to learn the Law. When you admitted me to your Bar you opened every door."

Slowly, muscles quivering, Aritch turned and spoke to the Wreave:

"Ceylang?"

She had difficulty speaking while her poison-tipped fighting mandibles remained extruded.

"Your command?"

"Observe this Human well. Study him. You will meet again."

"I obey."

"You may go, but remember my words."

"I remember."

McKie, knowing the death dance could not remain uncompleted, stopped her.

"Ceylang!"

Slowly, reluctantly, she looked at him.

"*Do* observe me well, Ceylang. I am what you hope to be. And I warn you: unless you shed your Wreave skin you will never be a Legum." He nodded in dismissal. "Now, you may go."

In a fluid swish of robes she obeyed, but her fighting mandibles remained out, their poison tips glittering. Somewhere in her triad's quarters, McKie knew, there'd be a small feathered pet which would die presently with poison from its mistress burning through its veins. Then the death dance would be ended and she could retract her mandibles. But the hate would remain.

When the door had closed behind the red robe, McKie restored book and knife to the box, returned his attention to Aritch. Now, when McKie spoke, it was really Legum to client without any sophistry, and they both knew it.

"What would tempt the High Magister of the renowned Running Phylum to bring down the Arch of Civilization?"

McKie's tone was conversational, between equals.

Aritch had trouble adjusting to the new status. His thoughts were obvious. If McKie had witnessed a Cleansing Ritual, McKie had to be accepted as a Gowachin. But McKie was

not Gowachin. Yet he'd been accepted before the Gowachin Bar . . . and if he'd seen that most sacred ritual . . .

Presently, Aritch spoke.

"Where did you see the ritual?"

"It was performed by the Phylum which sheltered me on Tandaloor."

"The Dry Heads?"

"Yes."

"Did they know you witnessed?"

"They invited me."

"How did you shed your skin?"

"They scraped me raw and preserved the scrapings."

Aritch took some time digesting this. The Dry Heads had played their own secret game of Gowachin politics and now the secret was out. He had to consider the implications. What had they hoped to gain? He said:

"You wear no tattoo."

"I've never made formal application for Dry Heads membership."

"Why?"

"My primary allegiance is to BuSab."

"The Dry Heads know this?"

"They encourage it."

"But what motivated them to . . ."

McKie smiled.

Aritch glanced at a veiled alcove at the far end of the sanctum, back to McKie. A likeness to the Frog God?

"It'd take more than that."

McKie shrugged.

Aritch mused aloud:

"The Dry Heads supported Klodik in his crime when you . . ."

"Not crime."

"I stand corrected. You won Klodik's freedom. And after your victory the Dry Heads invited you to the Cleansing Ritual."

"A Gowachin in BuSab cannot have divided allegiance."

"But a Legum serves only the Law!"

"BuSab and Gowachin Law are not in conflict."

"So the Dry Heads would have us believe."

"Many Gowachin believe it."

"But Klodik's case was not a true test."

Realization swept through McKie: Aritch regretted more than a lost bet. He'd put his money with his hopes. It was time then to redirect this conversation.

"I am your Legum."

Aritch spoke with resignation.

"You are."

"Your Legum wishes to hear of the Dosadi problem."

"A thing is not a problem until it arouses sufficient concern." Aritch glanced at the box in McKie's lap. "We're dealing with differences in values, changes in values."

McKie did not believe for an instant this was the tenor of Gowachin defense, but Aritch's words gave him pause. The Gowachin combined such an odd mixture of respect and disrespect for their Law and all government. At the root lay their unchanging rituals, but above that everything remained as fluid as the seas in which they'd evolved. Constant fluidity was the purpose behind their rituals. You never entered any exchange with Gowachin on a sure-footed basis. They did something different every time . . . religiously. It was their nature. *All ground is temporary. Law is made to be changed.* That was their catechism. *To be a Legum is to learn where to place your feet.*

"The Dry Heads did something different," McKie said.

This plunged Aritch into gloom. His chest ventricles wheezed, indicating he'd speak *from the stomach.*

"The people of the ConSentiency come in so many different forms: Wreaves (a flickering glance doorward), Sobarips, Laclacs, Calebans, PanSpechi, Palenki, Chithers, Taprisiots, Humans, we of the Gowachin . . . so many. The unknowns between us defy counting."

"As well count the drops of water in a sea."

Aritch grunted, then:

"Some diseases cross the barriers between species."

McKie stared at him. Was Dosadi a medical experiment station? Impossible! There would be no reason for secrecy then. Secrecy defeated the efforts to study a common problem and the Gowachin knew it.

"You are not studying Gowachin-Human diseases."

"Some diseases attack the psyche and cannot be traced to any physical agent."

McKie absorbed this. Although Gowachin definitions were difficult to understand, they permitted no aberrant behavior. Different behavior, yes; aberrant behavior, no. You could challenge the Law, not the ritual. They were compulsive in this regard. They slew the ritual deviant out of hand. It required enormous restraint on their part to deal with another species.

Aritch continued:

"Terrifying psychological abrasions occur when divergent species confront each other and are forced to adapt to new ways. We seek new knowledge in this arena of behavior."

McKie nodded.

One of his Dry Head teachers had said it: "No matter how painful, life must adapt or die."

It was a profound revelation about how Gowachin applied their insight to themselves. Law changed, but it changed on a foundation which could not be permitted the slightest change. "Else, how do we know where we are or where we have been?" But encounters with other species changed the foundation. Life adapted . . . willingly or by force.

McKie spoke with care.

"Psychological experiments with people who've not given their informed consent are still illegal . . . even among the Gowachin."

Aritch would not accept this argument.

"The ConSentiency in all of its parts has accumulated a long history of scientific studies into behavioral and biomedical questions where people are the final test site."

McKie said:

"And the first issue when you propose such an experiment is 'How great is the known risk to the subjects?' "

"But, my dear Legum, *informed consent* implies that the experimenter knows all the risks and can describe them to his test subjects. I ask you: how can that be when the experiment goes beyond what you already know? How can you describe risks which you cannot anticipate?"

"You submit a proposal to many recognized experts in the field," McKie said. "They weigh the proposed experiment against whatever value the new knowledge is expected to uncover."

"Ahh, yes. We submit our proposal to fellow researchers, to people whose *mission*, whose very view of their own personal identity is controlled by the belief that they can improve the lot of all sentient beings. Tell me, Legum: do review boards composed of such people reject many experimental proposals?"

McKie saw the direction of the argument. He spoke with care.

"They don't reject many proposals, that's true. Still, you didn't submit your Dosadi protocol to any outside review. Was that to keep it secret from your own people or from others?"

"We feared the fate of our proposal should it run the gauntlet of other species."

"Did a Gowachin majority approve your project?"

"No. But we both know that having a majority set the experimental guidelines gives no guarantee against dangerous projects."

"Dosadi has proved dangerous?"

Aritch remained silent for several deep breaths, then:

"It has proved dangerous."

"To whom?"

"Everyone."

It was an unexpected answer, adding a new dimension to Aritch's behavior. McKie decided to back up and test the revelation. "This Dosadi project was approved by a minor-

ity among the Gowachin, a minority willing to accept a dangerous risk-benefit ratio."

"You have a way of putting these matters, McKie, which presupposes a particular kind of guilt."

"But a majority in the ConSentiency might agree with my description?"

"Should they ever learn of it."

"I see. Then, in accepting a dangerous risk, what were the future benefits you expected?"

Aritch emitted a deep grunt.

"Legum, I assure you that we worked only with volunteers and they were limited to Humans and Gowachin."

"You evade my question."

"I merely defer an answer."

"Then tell me, did you explain to your volunteers that they had a choice, that they could say 'no'? Did you tell them they might be in danger?"

"We did not try to frighten them . . . no."

"Was any one of you concerned about the free destiny of your *volunteers*?"

"Be careful how you judge us, McKie. There is a fundamental tension between science and freedom—no matter how science is viewed by its practitioners nor how freedom is sensed by those who believe they have it."

McKie was reminded of a cynical Gowachin aphorism: *To believe that you are free is more important than being free.* He said:

"Your volunteers were lured into this project."

"Some would see it that way."

McKie reflected on this. He still did not know precisely what the Gowachin had done on Dosadi, but he was beginning to suspect it'd be something repulsive. He could not keep this fear from his voice.

"We return to the question of expected benefits."

"Legum, we have long admired your species. You gave us one of our most trusted maxims: *No species is to be trusted farther than it is bound by its own interests.*"

"That's no longer sufficient justification for . . ."

"We derive another rule from your maxim: *It is wise to guide your actions in such a way that the interests of other species coincide with the interests of your species.*"

McKie stared at the High Magister. Did this crafty old Gowachin seek a Human-Gowachin conspiracy to suppress evidence of what had been done on Dosadi? Would he dare such a gambit? Just how bad was this Dosadi fiasco?

To test the issue, McKie asked:

"What benefits did you expect? I insist."

Aritch slumped. His chairdog accommodated to the new position. The High Magister favored McKie with a heavy-lidded stare for a long interval, then:

"You play this game better than we'd ever hoped."

"With you, Law and Government are always a game. I come from another arena."

"Your Bureau."

"And I was trained as a Legum."

"Are you *my* Legum?"

"The binding oath is binding on me. Have you no faith in . . ."

McKie broke off, overwhelmed by a sudden insight. Of course! The Gowachin had known for a long time that Dosadi would become a legal issue.

"Faith in what?" Aritch asked.

"Enough of these evasions!" McKie said. "You had your Dosadi problem in mind when you trained me. Now, you act as though you distrust your own plan."

Aritch's lips rippled.

"How strange. You're more Gowachin than a Gowachin."

"What benefits did you expect when you took this risk?"

Aritch's fingers splayed, stretching the webs.

"We hoped for a quick conclusion and benefits to offset the natural animosities we knew would arise. But it's now more than twenty of your generations, not twelve or fifteen, that we've grasped the firebrand. Benefits? Yes, there are some, but we dare not use them or free Dosadi from bond-

age lest we raise questions which we cannot answer without revealing our . . . source."

"The benefits!" McKie said. "Your *Legum* insists."

Aritch exhaled a shuddering breath through his ventricles.

"Only the Caleban who guards Dosadi knows its location and she is charged to give access without revealing that place. Dosadi is peopled by Humans and Gowachin. They live in a single city they call Chu. Some ninety million people live there, almost equally divided between the two species. Perhaps three times that number live outside Chu, on the Rim, but they're outside the experiment. Chu is approximately eight hundred square kilometers."

The population density shocked McKie. Millions per kilometer. He had difficulty visualizing it. Even allowing for a city's vertical dimension . . . and burrowing . . . There'd be some, of course, whose power bought them space, but the others . . . Gods! Such a city would be crawling with people, no escaping the pressure of your fellows anywhere except on that unexplained Rim. McKie said as much to Aritch.

The High Magister confirmed this.

"The population density is very great in some areas. The people of Dosadi call these areas 'Warrens' for good reason."

"But why? With an entire planet to live on . . ."

"Dosadi is poisonous to our forms of life. All of their food comes from carefully managed hydroponics factories in the heart of Chu. Food factories and the distribution are managed by warlords. Everything is under a quasi-military form of management. But life expectancy in the city is four times that outside."

"You said the population outside the city was much larger than . . ."

"They breed like mad animals."

"What possible benefits could you have expected from . . ."

"Under pressure, life reveals its basic elements."

McKie considered what the High Magister had revealed. The picture of Dosadi was that of a seething mass. Warlords . . . He visualized walls, some people living and working in comparative richness of space while others . . . Gods! It was madness in a universe where some highly habitable planets held no more than a few thousand people. His voice brittle, McKie addressed himself to the High Magister.

"These basic elements, the *benefits* you sought . . . I wish to hear about them."

Aritch hitched himself forward.

"We have discovered new ways of association, new devices of motivation, unsuspected drives which can impose themselves upon an entire population."

"I require specific and explicit enumeration of these discoveries."

"Presently, Legum . . . presently."

Why did Aritch delay? Were the so-called benefits insignificant beside the repulsive horror of such an experiment? McKie ventured another tack.

"You say this planet is poisonous. Why not remove the inhabitants a few at a time, subject them to memory erasure if you must, and feed them out into the ConSentiency as new . . ."

"We dare not! First, the inhabitants have developed an immunity to erasure, a by-product of those poisons which do get into their diet. Second, given what they have become on Dosadi . . . How can I explain this to you?"

"Why don't the people just leave Dosadi? I presume you deny them jumpdoors, but rockets and other mechanical . . ."

"We will not permit them to leave. Our Caleban encloses Dosadi in what she calls a 'tempokinetic barrier' which our test subjects cannot penetrate."

"Why?"

"We will destroy the entire planet and everything on it rather than loose this population upon the ConSentiency."

"What are the people of Dosadi that you'd even contemplate such a thing?"

Aritch shuddered.

"We have created a monster."

Every government is run by liars and nothing they say should be believed.

—Attributed to an ancient Human journalist

As she hurried across the roof of the adjoining parking spire at midafternoon of her final day as a Liaitor, Jedrik couldn't clear her mind of the awareness that she was about to shed another mark of rank. Stacked in the building beneath her, each one suspended by its roof grapples on the conveyor track, were the vehicles of the power merchants and their minions. The machines varied from the giant *jaigers* heavy with armor and weapons and redundant engine systems, of the ruling few, down to the tiny black skitters assigned to such as herself. Ex-minion Jedrik knew she was about to take a final ride in the machine which had released her from the morning and evening crush on the underground walkways.

She had timed her departure with care. The ones who rode in the *jaigers* would not have reassigned her *skitter* and its driver. That driver, Havvy, required her special attentions in this last ride, this narrow time slot which she had set aside for dealing with him.

Jedrik sensed events rushing at their own terrible pace now. Just that morning she had loosed death, against fifty Humans. Now, the avalanche gathered power.

The parking spire's roof pavement had been poorly repaired after the recent explosive destruction of three Rim guerrillas. Her feet adjusted to the rough paving as she hurried across the open area to the drop chute. At the chute, she paused and glanced westward through Chu's enclosing cliffs. The sun, already nearing its late afternoon line on the cliffs, was a golden glow beyond the God Wall's milky bar-

CONTENTS

rier. To her newly sensitized fears, that was not a sun but a malignant eye which peered down at her.

By now, the rotofiles in her office would've been ignited by the clumsy intrusion of the LP toads. There'd be a delay while they reported this, while it was bucked up through the hierarchy to a level where somebody dared make an important decision.

Jedrik fought against letting her thoughts fall into trembling shadows. After the rotofiles, other data would accumulate. The Elector's people would grow increasingly suspicious. But that was part of her plan, a layer with many layers.

Abruptly, she stepped into the chute, dropped to her parking level, stared across the catwalks at her *skitter* dangling among the others. Havvy sat on the sloping hood, his shoulders in their characteristic slouch. Good. He behaved as expected. A certain finesse was called for now, but she expected no real trouble from anyone as shallow and transparent as Havvy. Still, she kept her right hand in the pocket where she'd secreted a small but adequate weapon. Nothing could be allowed to stop her now. She had selected and trained lieutenants, but none of them quite matched her capabilities. The military force which had been prepared for this moment needed Jedrik for that extra edge which could pluck victory from the days ahead of them.

For now, I must float like a leaf above the hurricane.

Havvy was reading a book, one of those pseudodeep things he regularly affected, a book which she knew he would not understand. As he read, he pulled at his lower lip with thumb and forefinger, the very picture of a deep intellectual involvement with important ideas. But it was only a picture. He gave no sign that he heard Jedrik hurrying toward him. A light breeze flicked the pages and he held them with one finger. She could not yet see the title, but assumed this book would be on the contraband list as was much of his reading. That was about the peak of Havvy's risk taking, not great but imbued with a certain false glamor. Another picture.

She could see him quite distinctly now in readable detail. He should have looked up by now but still sat absorbed in his book. Havvy possessed large brown eyes which he obviously believed he employed with deceptive innocence. The real innocence went far beyond his shallow attempts at deception. Jedrik's imagination easily played the scene should one of Broey's people confront Havvy in this pose.

"*A contraband book?*" Havvy would ask, playing his brown eyes for all their worthless innocence. "*I didn't think there were any more of those around. Thought you'd burned them all. Fellow handed it to me on the street when I asked what he was reading.*"

And the Elector's spy would conceal a sneer while asking, "*Didn't you question such a gift?*"

Should it come to that, things would grow progressively stickier for Havvy along the paths he could not anticipate. His innocent brown eyes would deceive one of the Elector's people no more than they deceived her. In a view of this, she read other messages in the fact that Havvy had produced her key to the God Wall—this Jorj X. McKie. Havvy had come to her with his heavy-handed conspiratorial manner:

"The Rim wants to send in a new agent. We thought you might . . ."

And every datum he'd divulged about this oddity, every question he'd answered with his transparent candor, had increased her tension, surprise, and elation.

Jedrik thought upon these matters as she approached Havvy.

He sensed her presence, looked up. Recognition and something unexpected—a watchfulness half-shielded—came over him. He closed his book.

"You're early."

"As I said I'd be."

This new manner in Havvy set her nerves on edge, raised old doubts. No course remained for her except attack.

"Only toads don't break routine," she said.

Havvy's gaze darted left, right, returned to her face. He hadn't expected this. It was a bit more open risk than Havvy relished. The Elector had spy devices everywhere. Havvy's reaction told her what she wanted to know, however. She gestured to the *skitter*.

"Let's go."

He pocketed his book, slid down, and opened her door. His actions were a bit too brisk. The button tab on one of his green-striped sleeves caught a door handle. He freed himself with an embarrassed flurry.

Jedrik slipped into the passenger harness. Havvy slammed the door a touch too hard. Nervous. Good. He took his place at the power bar to her left, kept his profile to her when he spoke.

"Where?"

"Head for the apartment."

A slight hesitation, then he activated the grapple tracks. The skitter jerked into motion, danced sideways, and slid smoothly down the diveway to the street.

As they emerged from the parking spire's enclosing shadows, even before the grapple released and Havvy activated the skitter's own power, Jedrik firmed her decision not to look back. The Liaitor building had become part of her past, a pile of grey-green stones hemmed by other tall structures with, here and there, gaps to the cliffs and the river's arms. That part of her life she now excised. Best it were done cleanly. Her mind must be clear for what came next. What came next was war.

It wasn't often that a warrior force lifted itself out of Dosadi's masses to seek its place in the power structure. And the force she had groomed would strike fear into millions. It was the fears of only a few people that concerned her now, though, and the first of these was Havvy.

He drove with his usual competence, not overly proficient

but adequate. His knuckles were white on the steering arms, however. It was still the Havvy she knew moving those muscles, not one of the evil identities who could play their tricks in Dosadi flesh. That was Havvy's usefulness to her and his failure. He was Dosadi-flawed, corrupted. That could not be permitted with McKie.

Havvy appeared to have enough good sense to fear her. Jedrik allowed this emotion to ferment in him while she studied the passing scene. There was little traffic and all of that was armored. The occasional tube access with its sense of weapons in the shadows and eyes behind the guard slits—all seemed normal. It was too soon for the hue and cry after an errant Senior Liaitor.

They went through the first walled checkpoint without delay. The guards were efficiently casual, a glance at the skitter and the identification brassards of the occupants. It was all routine.

The danger with routines, she told herself, was that they very soon became boring. Boredom dulled the senses. That was a boredom which she and her aides constantly guarded against among their warriors. This new force on Dosadi would create many shocks.

As Havvy took them up the normal ring route through the walls, the streets became wide, more open. There were garden plantings in the open here, poisonous but beautiful. Leaves were purple in the shadows. Barren dirt beneath the bushes glittered with corrosive droplets, one of Dosadi's little ways of protecting territory. Dosadi taught many things to those willing to learn.

Jedrik turned, studied Havvy, the way he appeared to concentrate on his driving with an air of stored-up energy. That was about as far as Havvy's learning went. He seemed to know some of his own deficiencies, must realize that many wondered how he held a driver's job, even for the middle echelons, when the Warrens were jammed with people violently avaricious for any step upward. Obviously, Havvy carried valuable secrets which he sold on a hidden market.

She had to nudge that hidden market now. Her act must appear faintly clumsy, as though events of this day had confused her.

"Can we be overheard?" she asked.

That made no difference to her plans, but it was the kind of clumsiness which Havvy would misinterpret in precisely the way she now required.

"I've disarmed the transceiver the way I did before," he said. "It'll look like a simple-breakdown if anyone checks."

To no one but you, she thought.

But it was the level of infantile response she'd come to expect from Havvy. She picked up his gambit, probing with real curiosity.

"You expected that we'd require privacy today?"

He almost shot a startled look at her, caught himself, then:

"Oh, no! It was a precaution. I have more information to sell you."

"But you *gave* me the information about McKie."

"That was to demonstrate my value."

Oh, Havvy! Why do you try?

"You have unexpected qualities," she said, and marked that he did not even detect the first level of her irony. "What's this information you wish to sell?"

"It concerns this McKie."

"Indeed?"

"What's it worth to you?"

"Am I your only market, Havvy?"

His shoulder muscles bunched as his grip grew even tighter on the steering arms. The tensions in his voice were remarkably easy to read.

"Sold in the right place my information could guarantee maybe five years of easy living—no worries about food or good housing or anything."

"Why aren't you selling it in such a place?"

"I didn't say I *could* sell it. There are buyers and then there are buyers."

"And then there are the ones who just take?"

There was no need for him to answer and it was just as well. A barrier dropped in front of the skitter, forcing Havvy to a quick stop. For just an instant, fear gripped her and she felt her reflexes prevent any bodily betrayal of the emotion. Then she saw that it was a routine stop while repair supplies were trundled across the roadway ahead of them.

Jedrik peered out the window on her right. The interminable repair and strengthening of the city's fortifications was going on at the next lower level. Memory told her this was the eighth layer of city protection on the southwest. The noise of pounding rock hammers filled the street. Grey dust lay everywhere, clouds of it drifting. She smelled burnt flint and that bitter metallic undertone which you never quite escaped anywhere in Chu, the smell of the poison death which Dosadi ladled out to its inhabitants. She closed her mouth and took shallow breaths, noted absently that the labor crew was all Warren, all Human, and about a third of them women. None of the women appeared older than fifteen. They already had that hard alertness about the eyes which the Warren-born never lost.

A young male strawboss went by trailing a male assistant, an older man with bent shoulders and straggly grey hair. The older man walked with slow deliberation and the young strawboss seemed impatient with him, waving the assistant to keep up. The important subtleties of the relationship thus revealed were entirely lost on Havvy, she noted. The strawboss, as he passed one of the female laborers, looked her up and down with interest. The worker noted his attention and exerted herself with the hammer. The strawboss said something to his assistant, who went over and spoke to the young female. She smiled and glanced at the strawboss, nodded. The strawboss and assistant walked on without looking back. The obvious arrangement for later assignation would have gone without Jedrik's conscious notice except that the young female strongly resembled a woman she'd once known . . . dead now as were so many of her early companions.

A bell began to ring and the barrier lifted.

Havvy drove on, glancing once at the strawboss as they passed him. The glance was not returned, telling Jedrik that the strawboss had assessed the skitter's occupants much earlier.

Jedrick picked up the conversation with Havvy where they'd left it.

"What makes you think you could get more from me than from someone else?"

"Not more . . . It's just that there's less risk with you."

The truth was in his voice, that innocent instrument which told so much about Havvy. She shook her head.

"You want me to take the risk of selling higher up?"

After a long pause, Havvy said:

"You know a safer way for me to operate?"

"I'd have to use you somewhere along the line for verification."

"But I'd be under your protection then."

"Why should I protect you when you're no longer of value?"

"What makes you think this is all the information I can get?"

Jedrik allowed herself a sigh, wondered why she continued this empty game.

"We might both run into a taker, Havvy."

Havvy didn't respond. Surely, he'd considered this in his foolish game plan.

They passed a squat brown building on the left. Their street curved upward around the building and passed through a teeming square at the next higher level. Between two taller buildings on the right, she glimpsed a stretch of a river channel, then it was more buildings which enclosed them like the cliffs of Chu, growing taller as the skitter climbed.

As she'd known, Havvy couldn't endure her silence.

"What're you going to do?" he asked.

"I'll pay one year of such protection as I can offer."

"But this is . . ."

"Take it or leave it."

He heard the finality but, being Havvy, couldn't give up. It was his one redeeming feature.

"Couldn't we even discuss a . . ."

"We won't discuss anything! If you won't sell at my price, then perhaps I should become a taker."

"That's not like you!"

"How little you know. I can buy informants of your caliber far cheaper."

"You're a hard person."

Out of compassion, she ventured a tiny lesson. "That's how to survive. But I think we should forget this now. Your information is probably something I already know, or something useless."

"It's worth a lot more than you offered."

"So you say, but I know you, Havvy. You're not one to take big risks. Little risks sometimes, big risks never. Your information couldn't be of any great value to me."

"If you only knew."

"I'm no longer interested, Havvy."

"Oh, that's great! You bargain with me and then pull out after I've . . ."

"I was *not* bargaining!" Wasn't the fool capable of anything?

"But you . . ."

"Havvy! Hear me with care. You're a little tad who's stumbled onto something you believe is important. It's actually nothing of great importance, but it's big enough to frighten you. You can't think of a way to sell this information without putting your neck in peril. That's why you came to me. You presume to have me act as your agent. You presume too much."

Anger closed his mind to any value in her words.

"I take risks!"

She didn't even try to keep amusement from her voice. "Yes, Havvy, but never where you think. So here's a risk for you right out in the open. Tell me your valuable information. No strings. Let me judge. If I think it's worth more than I've already offered I'll pay more. If I already have this information or it's otherwise useless, you get nothing."

"The advantage is all on your side!"

"Where it belongs."

Jedrik studied Havvy's shoulders, the set of his head, the rippling of muscles under stretched fabric as he drove. He was supposed to be pure Labor Pool and didn't even know that silence was the guardian of the LP: *Learning silence, you learn what to hear.* The LP seldom volunteered anything. And here was Havvy, so far from that and other LP traditions that he might never have experienced the Warren. *Had* never experienced it until he was too old to learn. Yet he talked of friends on the Rim, acted as though he had his own conspiratorial cell. He held a job for which he was barely competent. And everything he did revealed his belief that all of these things would not tell someone of Jedrik's caliber the essential facts about him.

Unless his were a marvelously practiced act.

She did not believe such a marvel, but there was a cautionary element in recognizing the remote possibility. This and the obvious flaws in Havvy had kept her from using him as a key to the God Wall.

They were passing the Elector's headquarters now. She turned and glanced at the stone escarpment. Her thoughts were a thorn thicket. Every assumption she made about Havvy required a peculiar protective reflex. A non-Dosadi reflex. She noted workers streaming down the steps toward the tube entrance of the Elector's building. Her problem with Havvy carried an odd similarity to the problem she knew Broey would encounter when it came to deciding about an ex-Liaitor named Keila Jedrik. She had studied Broey's decisions with a concentrated precision which had tested the limits of her abilities. Doing this, she had changed basic things about herself, had become oddly non-Dosadi.

They would no longer find Keila Jedrik in the DemoPol. No more than they'd find Havvy or this McKie there. But if she could do this . . .

Pedestrian traffic in this region of extreme caution had slowed Havvy to a crawl. More of the Elector's workers were coming up from the Tube Gate One exit, a throng of them as though released on urgent business. She wondered if any of her fifty flowed in that throng.

I must not allow my thoughts to wander.

To float like an aware leaf was one thing, but she dared not let herself enter the hurricane . . . not yet. She focused once more on the silent, angry Havvy.

"Tell me, Havvy, did you ever kill a person?"

His shoulders stiffened.

"Why do you ask such a question?"

She stared at his profile for an adequate time, obviously reflecting on this same question.

"I presumed you'd answer. I understand now that you will not answer. This is not the first time I've made that mistake."

Again, Havvy missed the lesson.

"Do you ask many people that question?"

"That doesn't concern you now."

She concealed a profound sadness.

Havvy hadn't the wit to read even the most blatant of the surface indicators. He compounded the useless.

"You can't justify such an intrusion into my . . ."

"Be still, little man! Have you learned nothing? Death is often the only means of evoking an appropriate answer."

Havvy saw this only as an utterly unscrupulous response as she'd known he would. When he shot a probing stare at her, she lifted an eyebrow in a cynical shrug. Havvy continued to divide his attention between the street and her face, apprehensive, fearful. His driving degenerated, became actively dangerous.

"Watch what you're doing, you fool!"

He turned more of his attention to the street, presuming this the greater danger.

The next time he glanced at her, she smiled, knowing Havvy would be unable to detect any lethal change in this gesture. He already wondered if she would attack, but guessed she wouldn't do it while he was driving. He doubted, though, and his doubts made him even more transparent. Havvy was no marvel. One thing certain about him: he came from beyond the God Wall, from the lands of "X," from the place of McKie. Whether he worked for the Elector was immaterial. In fact, it grew increasingly doubtful that Broey would employ such a dangerous, a *flawed* tool. No pretense at foolhardy ignorance of Dosadi's basic survival lessons could be this perfect. The pretender would not survive. Only the truly ignorant could have survived to Havvy's age, allowed to go on living as a curiosity, a possible source of interesting data . . . *interesting* data, not necessarily useful.

Having left resolution of the Havvy Problem to the ultimate moment, wringing every last bit of usefulness from him, she knew her course clearly. Whoever protected Havvy, her questions placed the precisely modulated pressure upon them and left her options open.

"What is your valued information?" she asked.

Sensing now that he bought life with every response, Havvy pulled the skitter to the curb at a windowless building wall, stopped, and stared at her.

She waited.

"McKie . . ." He swallowed. "McKie comes from beyond the God Wall."

She allowed laughter to convulse her and it went deeper than she'd anticipated. For an instant, she was helpless with it and this sobered her. Not even Havvy could be permitted such an advantage.

Havvy was angry.

"What's funny?"

"You are. Did you imagine for even a second that I wouldn't recognize someone alien to Dosadi? Little man, how *have* you survived?"

This time, he read her correctly. It threw him back on his only remaining resource and it even answered her question.

"Don't underestimate my value."

Yes, of course: the unknown value of "X." And there was a latent threat in his tone which she'd never heard there before. Could Havvy call on protectors from beyond the God Wall? That didn't seem possible, given his circumstances, but it had to be considered. It wouldn't do to approach her larger problem from a narrow viewpoint. People who could enclose an entire planet in an impenetrable barrier would have other capabilities she had not even imagined. Some of these creatures came and went at will, as though Dosadi were merely a casual stopping point. And the travelers from "X" could change their bodies; that was the single terrible fact which must never be forgotten; that was what had led her ancestors to breed for a Keila Jedrik.

Such considerations always left her feeling almost helpless, shaken by the ultimate unknowns which lay in her path. Was Havvy still Havvy? Her trusted senses answered: yes. Havvy was a spy, a diversion, an amusement. And he was something else which she could not fathom. It was maddening. She could read every nuance of his reactions, yet questions remained. How could you ever understand these creatures from beyond the Veil of Heaven? They were transparent to Dosadi eyes, but that transparency itself confused one.

On the other hand, how could the people of "X" hope to understand (and thus anticipate) a Keila Jedrik? Every evidence of her senses told her that Havvy saw only a surface Jedrik which she wanted him to see. His spying eyes reported what she wanted them to report. But the enormous interests at stake here dictated a brand of caution beyond anything she'd ever before attempted. The fact that she saw this arena of explosive repercussions, however, armed her with grim satisfaction. The idea that a Dosadi *puppet* might rebel against "X" and fully understand the nature of such rebellion, surely that idea lay beyond their capabilities. They were overconfident while she was filled with wariness. She saw no way of hiding her movements from the people beyond the God Wall as she hid from her fellow Dosadis. "X" had ways of spying that no one completely evaded. They would know about the two Keila Jedriks. She counted on only one thing: that they could not see her deepest thoughts, that they'd read only that surface which she revealed to them.

Jedrik maintained a steady gaze at Havvy while these considerations flowed through her mind. Not by the slightest act did she betray what went on in her mind. That, after all, was Dosadi's greatest gift to its survivors.

"Your information is valueless," she said.

He was accusatory. "You already knew!"

What did he hope to catch with such a gambit? Not for the first time, she asked herself whether Havvy might represent the best that "X" could produce? Would they knowingly send their dolts here? It hardly seemed possible. But how could Havvy's childish incompetence command such tools of power as the God Wall implied? Were the people of "X" the decadent descendants of greater beings?

Even though his own survival demanded it, Havvy would not remain silent.

"If you didn't already know about McKie . . . then you . . . you don't believe me!"

This was too much. Even for Havvy it was too much and she told herself: *Despite the unknown powers of "X," he will have to die. He muddies the water. Such incompetence cannot be permitted to breed.*

It would have to be done without passion, not like a Gowachin male weeding his own tads, but with a kind of clinical decisiveness which "X" could not misunderstand.

For now, she had arranged that Havvy take her to a particular place. He still had a role to perform. Later, with discreet attention to the necessary misdirections, she would do what had to be done. Then the next part of her plan could be assayed.

All persons act from beliefs they are conditioned not to question, from a set of deeply seated prejudices. Therefore, whoever presumes to judge must be asked: "How are you affronted?" And this judge must begin there to question inwardly as well as outwardly.

—"The Question" from Ritual of the Courtarena Guide
to Servants of the Box

O ne might suspect you of trying to speak under water," McKie, accused.

He still sat opposite Aritch in the High Magister's sanctus, and this near-insult was only one indicator marking the changed atmosphere between them. The sun had dropped closer to the horizon and its *spiritual ring* no longer outlined Aritch's head. The two of them were being more direct now, if not more candid, having explored individual capacities and found where profitable discourse might be directed.

The High Magister flexed his thigh tendons.

Knowing these people from long and close observation, McKie realized the old Gowachin was in pain from prolonged inactivity. That was an advantage to be exploited. McKie held up his left hand, enumerated on his fingers:

"You say the original volunteers on Dosadi submitted to memory erasure, but many of their descendants are immune to such erasure. The present population knows nothing about our ConSentient Universe."

"As far as the present Dosadi population comprehends, they are the only people on the only inhabited planet in existence."

McKie found this hard to believe. He held up a third finger.

Aritch stared with distaste at the displayed hand. *There were no webs between the alien fingers!*

McKie said, "And you tell me that a DemoPol backed up by certain religious injunctions is the primary tool of government there?"

"An original condition of our experiment," Aritch said.

It was not a comprehensive answer, McKie observed. Original conditions invariably changed. McKie decided to come back to this after the High Magister had submitted to more muscle pain.

"Do the Dosadi know the nature of the Caleban barrier which encloses them?"

"They've tried rocket probes, primitive electromagnetic projections. They understand that those energies they can produce will not penetrate their 'God Wall.'"

"Is that what they call the barrier?"

"That or 'The Heavenly Veil.' To some degree, these labels measure their attitude toward the barrier."

"The DemoPol can serve many governmental forms," McKie said. "What's the basic form of their government?"

Aritch considered this, then:

"The form varies. They've employed some eighty different governmental forms."

Another nonresponsive answer. Aritch did not like to face the fact that their experiment had assumed warlord trappings. McKie thought about the DemoPol. In the hands of adepts and with a population responsive to the software probes by which the computer data was assembled, the DemoPol represented an ultimate tool for manipulation of a populace. The ConSentiency outlawed its use as an assault on individual rights and freedoms. The Gowachin had broken this prohibition, yes, but a more interesting datum was surfacing: Dosadi had employed some eighty different governmental forms without rejecting the DemoPol. That implied frequent changes.

"How often have they changed their form of government?"

"You can divide the numbers as easily as I," Aritch said. His tone was petulant.

McKie nodded. One thing had become quite clear.

"Dosadi's masses know about the DemoPol, but you won't let them remove it!"

Aritch had not expected this insight. He responded with revealing sharpness which was amplified by his muscle pains.

"How did you learn that?"

"You told me."

"I?"

"Quite plainly. Such frequent change is responsive to an irritant—the DemoPol. They change the forms of government, but leave the irritant. Obviously, they cannot remove the irritant. That was clearly part of your experiment—to raise a population resistant to the DemoPol."

"A resistant population, yes," Aritch said. He shuddered.

"You've fractured ConSentient Law in many places," McKie said.

"Does my Legum presume to judge me?"

"No. But if I speak with a certain bitterness, please recall that I am a Human. I embrace a profound sympathy for the Gowachin, but I remain Human."

"Ahhhh, yes. We must not forget the long Human association with DemoPols."

"We survive by selecting the best decision makers," McKie said.

"And a DemoPol elevates mediocrity."

"Has that happened on Dosadi?"

"No."

"But you wanted them to try many different governmental forms?"

The High Magister shrugged, remained silent.

"We Humans found that the DemoPol does profound damage to social relationships. It destroys preselected portions of a society."

"And what could we hope to learn by *damaging* our Dosadi society?"

"Have we arrived back at the question of expected benefits?"

Aritch stretched his aching muscles.

"You are persistent, McKie. I will say that."

McKie shook his head sadly.

"The DemoPol was always held up to us as the ultimate equalizer, a source of decision-making miracles. It was supposed to produce a growing body of knowledge about what a society really needed. It was thought to produce justice in all cases despite any odds."

Aritch was irritated. He leaned forward, wincing at the pain of his old muscles.

"One might make the same accusations about the *Law* as practiced everywhere except on Gowachin worlds!"

McKie suppressed a sharp response. Gowachin training had forced him to question assumptions about the uses of law in the ConSentiency, about the inherent rightness of any aristocracy, any power bloc whether majority or minority. It was a BuSab axiom that all power blocs tended toward aristocratic forms, that the descendants of decision makers dominated the power niches. BuSab never employed offspring of their agents.

Aritch repeated himself, a thing Gowachin seldom did.

"Law is delusion and fakery, McKie, everywhere except on the Gowachin worlds! You give your law a theological aura. You ignore the ways it injures your societies. Just as with the DemoPol, you hold up your law as the unvarying source of justice. When you . . ."

"BuSab has . . ."

"No! If something's wrong in your societies, what do you do? You create new law. You never think to remove law or disarm the law. You make more law! You create more legal professionals. We Gowachin sneer at you! We always strive to reduce the number of laws, the number of Legums. A Legum's first duty is to avoid litigation. When we create new Legums, we always have specific problems in mind. We anticipate the ways that laws damage our society."

It was the opening McKie wanted.

"Why are you training a Wreave?"

Belatedly, Aritch realized he had been goaded into re-vealing more than he had wanted.

"You are good, McKie. Very good."

"Why?" McKie persisted. "Why a Wreave?"

"You will learn why in time."

McKie saw that Aritch would not expand on this answer, but there were other matters to consider now. It was clear that the Gowachin had trained him for a specific problem; Dosadi. To train a Wreave as Legum, they'd have an equally important problem in mind . . . perhaps the same problem. A basic difference in the approach to law, species differenti-ated, had surfaced, however, and this could not be ignored. McKie well understood the Gowachin disdain for all legal systems, including their own. They were educated from in-fancy to distrust any community of professionals, especially legal professionals. A Legum could only tread their reli-gious path when he completely shared that distrust.

Do I share that distrust?

He thought he did. It came naturally to a BuSab agent. But most of the ConSentiency still held its professional com-munities in high esteem, ignoring the nature of the intense competition for new achievements which invariably over-came such communities: *new* achievements, *new* recogni-tion. But the *new* could be illusion in such communities because they always maintained a peer review system nicely balanced with peer pressures for ego rewards.

"Professional always means power," the Gowachin said.

The Gowachin distrusted power in all of its forms. They gave with one hand and took with the other. Legums faced death whenever they used the Law. To make *new* law in the Gowachin Courtarena was to bring about the elegant dissolution of old law with a concomitant application of justice.

Not for the first time, McKie wondered about the un-known problems a High Magister must face. It would have to be a delicate existence indeed. McKie almost formed a question about this, thought better of it. He shifted instead to the unknowns about Dosadi. *God Wall? Heavenly Veil?*

"Does Dosadi often accept a religious oligarchy?"

"As an outward form, yes. They currently are presided over by a supreme Elector, a Gowachin by the name of Broey."

"Have Humans ever held power equal to Broey's?"

"Frequently."

It was one of the most responsive exchanges that McKie had achieved with Aritch. Although he knew he was following the High Magister's purpose, McKie decided to explore this.

"Tell me about Dosadi's *social* forms."

"They are the forms of a military organization under constant attack or threat of attack. They form certain cabals, certain power enclaves whose influences shift."

"Is there much violence?"

"It is a world of constant violence."

McKie absorbed this. Warlords. Military society. He knew he had just lifted a corner of the real issue which had brought the Gowachin to the point of obliterating Dosadi. It was an area to be approached with extreme caution. McKie chose a flanking approach.

"Aside from the military forms, what are the dominant occupations? How do they perceive guilt and innocence? What are their forms of punishment, of absolution? How do they . . ."

"You do not confuse me, McKie. Consider, Legum: there are better ways to answer such questions."

Brought up short by the Magister's chiding tone, McKie fell into silence. He glanced out the oval window, realizing he'd been thrown onto the defensive with exquisite ease. McKie felt the nerves tingling along his spine. Danger! Tandaloor's golden sun had moved perceptibly closer to the horizon. That horizon was a blue-green line made hazy by kilometer after kilometer of hair trees whose slender female fronds waved and hunted in the air. Presently, McKie turned back to Aritch.

Better ways to answer such questions.

It was obvious where the High Magister's thoughts trended. The experimenters would, of course, have ways of watching their experiment. They could also influence their experiment, but it was obvious there were limits to this influence. A population resistant to outside influences? The implied complications of this Dosadi problem daunted McKie. Oh, the circular dance the Gowachin always performed!

Better ways.

Aritch cleared his ventricle passages with a harsh exhalation, then:

"Anticipating the possibility that others would censure us, we gave our test subjects the Primary."

Devils incarnate! The Gowachin set such store on their damned Primary! Of course all people were created unequal and had to find their own level!

McKie knew he had no choice but to plunge into the maelstrom.

"Did you also anticipate that you'd be charged with violating sentient rights on a massive scale?"

Aritch shocked him by a brief puffing of jowls, the Gowachin shrug.

McKie allowed himself a warning smile.

"I remind the High Magister that *he* raised the issue of the Primary."

"Truth is truth."

McKie shook his head sharply, not caring what this revealed. The High Magister couldn't possibly have that low an estimation of his Legum's reasoning abilities. *Truth indeed*!

"I'll give you truth: the ConSentiency has laws on this subject to which the Gowachin are signatories!"

Even as the words fell from his lips, McKie realized this was precisely where Aritch had wanted him to go. *They've learned something from Dosadi! Something crucial!*

Aritch massaged the painful muscles of his thighs, said, "I remind *you*, Legum, that we peopled Dosadi with volunteers."

"Their descendants volunteered for nothing!"

"Ancestors always volunteer their descendants—for better or for worse. Sentient rights? Informed consent? The ConSentiency has been so busy building law upon law, creating its great illusion of rights, that you've almost lost sight of the Primary's guiding principle: to develop our capacities. People who are never challenged never develop *survival* strengths!"

Despite the perils, McKie knew he had to press for the answer to his original question: *benefits*.

"What've you learned from your monster?"

"You'll soon have a complete answer to that question."

Again, the implication that he could actually watch Dosadi. But first it'd be well to disabuse Aritch of any suspicion that McKie was unaware of the root implications. The issue had to be met head on.

"You're not going to implicate me."

"Implicate you?" There was no mistaking Aritch's surprise.

"No matter how you use what you've learned from Dosadi, you'll be suspected of evil intent. Whatever anyone learns from . . ."

"Oh, that. New data gives one power."

"And *you* do not confuse *me,* Aritch. In the history of every species there are many examples of places where new data has been gravely abused."

Aritch accepted this without question. They both knew the background. The Gowachin distrusted power in all of its forms, yet they used power with consummate skill. The trend of McKie's thoughts lay heavily in this room now. To destroy Dosadi would be to hide whatever the Gowachin had learned there. McKie, a non-Gowachin, therefore, would learn these things, would share the mantle of suspicion should it be cast. The historical abuses of new data occurred between the time that a few people learned the important thing and the time when that important thing became general knowledge. To the Gowachin and to BuSab it was the "Data Gap," a source of constant danger.

"We would not try to hide *what* we've learned," Aritch said, "only how we learned it."

"And it's just an academic question whether you destroy an entire planet and every person on it!"

"Ahh, yes: academic. What you don't know, McKie, is that one of our test subjects on Dosadi has initiated, all on her own, a course of events which will destroy Dosadi very quickly whether we act or not. You'll learn all about this very soon when, like the good Legum we know you to be, you go there to experience this monster with your own flesh."

*In the name of all that we together hold holy I promise
three things to the sacred congregation of people who are
subject to my rule. In the first place, that the holy religion
which we mutually espouse shall always preserve their
freedom under my auspices; secondly, that I will temper
every form of rapacity and inequity which may inflict itself upon us all; and thirdly, that I will command swift
mercy in all judgments, that to me and to you the gracious
Lord may extend His Recognition.*

—The Oath of Power,
Dosadi Sacred Congregation papers

B roey arose from prayer, groped behind him for the
chair, and sank into it. Enclosed darkness surrounded
him. The room was a shielded bubble attached to the bottom of his Graluz. Around the room's thick walls was the
warm water which protected his females and their eggs.
Access to the bubble was through a floor hatch and a twisting flooded passage from the Graluz. Pressure in the bubble
excluded the water, but the space around Broey smelled
reassuringly of the Graluz. This helped reinforce the mood
he now required.

Presently, the God spoke to him. Elation filled Broey.
God spoke to him, only to him. Words hissed within his
head. Scenes impinged themselves upon his vision centers.
Yes! Yes! I keep the DemoPol!

God was reassured and reflected that reassurance.

Today, God showed him a ritual Broey had never seen
before. The ritual was only for Gowachin. The ritual was
called Laupuk. Broey saw the ritual in all of its gory details,
felt the *rightness* of it as though his very cells accepted it.

Responsibility, expiation—these were the lessons of Laupuk. God approved when Broey expressed understanding.

They communicated by words which Broey expressed silently in his thoughts, but there were other thoughts which God could not perceive. Just as God no doubt held thoughts which were not communicated to Broey. God used people, people used God. Divine intervention with cynical overtones. Broey had learned the Elector's role through a long and painful apprenticeship.

I am your servant, God.

As God admonished, Broey kept the secret of his private communion. It suited his purpose to obey, as it obviously suited God's purpose. There were times, though, when Broey wanted to shout it:

"You fools! I speak with the voice of God!"

Other Electors had made that mistake. They'd soon fallen from the seat of power. Broey, drawing on several lifetimes of assembled experiences, knew he must keep this power if he ever were to escape from Dosadi.

Anyway, the fools did his bidding (and therefore God's) without divine admonition. All was well. One presented a selection of thoughts to God . . . being careful always where and when one reviewed private thoughts. There were times when Broey felt God within him when there'd been no prayer, no preparations here in the blackness of this bubble room. God might peer out of Broey's eyes at any time— softly, quietly—examining His world and its works through mortal senses.

"I guard My servant well."

The warmth of reassurance which flowed through Broey then was like the warmth of the Graluz when he'd still been a tad clinging to his mother's back. It was a warmth and sense of safety which Broey tempered with a deep awareness of that other Graluz time: a giant grey-green adult male Gowachin ravening through the water, devouring those tads not swift enough, alert enough to escape.

I was one of the swift.

Memory of that plunging, frantic flight in the Graluz had taught Broey how to behave with God.

In his bubble room's darkness, Broey shuddered. Yes, the ways of God were cruel. Thus armed, a servant of God could be equally cruel, could surmount the fact that he knew what it was to be both Human and Gowachin. He need only be the pure servant of God. This thought he shared.

Beware, McKie. God has told me whence you come. I know your intentions. Hold fast to the narrow path, McKie. You risk my displeasure.

Behavioral engineering in all of its manifestations always degenerates into merciless manipulation. It reduces all (manipulators and manipulated alike) to a deadly "mass effect." The central assumption, that manipulation of individual personalities can achieve uniform behavioral responses, has been exposed as a lie by many species but never with more telling effect than by the Gowachin on Dosadi. Here, they showed us the "Walden Fallacy" in ultimate foolishness, explaining: "Given any species which reproduces by genetic mingling such that every individual is a unique specimen, all attempts to impose a decision matrix based on assumed uniform behavior will prove lethal."

—The Dosadi Papers,
BuSab reference

McKie walked through the jumpdoor and, as Aritch's aides had said, found himself on sand at just past Dosadi's midmorning. He looked up, seeking his first real-time view of the God Wall, wanting to share the Dosadi feeling of that enclosure. All he saw was a thin haze, faintly silver, disappointing. The sun circle was more defined than he'd expected and he knew from the holographic reproductions he'd seen that a few of the third-magnitude stars would be filtered out at night. What else he'd expected, McKie could not say, but somehow this milky veil was not it. Too thin, perhaps. It appeared insubstantial, too weak for the power it represented.

The visible sun disk reminded him of another urgent necessity, but he postponed that necessity while he examined his surroundings.

A tall white rock? Yes, there it was on his left.

They'd warned him to wait beside that rock, that he'd be

relatively safe there. Under no circumstances was he to wander from this contact point.

"We can tell you about the dangers of Dosadi, but words are not enough. Besides, the place is always developing new threats."

Things he'd learned in the briefing sessions over the past weeks reinforced the warning. The rock, twice as tall as a Human, stood only a few paces away, massive and forbidding. He went over and leaned against it. Sand grated beneath his feet. He smelled unfamiliar perfumes and acridities. The sun-warmed surface of the rock gave its energy to his flesh through the thin green coveralls they'd insisted he wear.

McKie longed for his armored clothing and its devices to amplify muscles, but such things were not permitted. Only a reduced version of his toolkit had been allowed and that reluctantly, a compromise. McKie had explained that the contents would be destroyed if anyone other than himself tried to pry into the kit's secrets. Still, they'd warned him never to open the kit in the presence of a Dosadi native.

"The most dangerous thing you can do is to underestimate any of the Dosadi."

McKie, staring around him, saw no Dosadi.

Far off across a dusty landscape dotted with yellow bushes and brown rocks, he identified the hazy spires of Chu rising out of its river canyon. Heat waves dizzied the air above the low scrub, giving the city a magical appearance.

McKie found it difficult to think about Chu in the context of what he'd learned during the crash course the Gowachin had given him. Those magical fluting spires reached heavenward from a muck where "you can buy anything . . . anything at all."

Aritch's aides had sewn a large sum in Dosadi currency into the seams of his clothing but, at the same time, had forced him to digest hair-raising admonitions about "any show of unprotected wealth."

The jumpdoor attendants had recapitulated many of the most urgent warnings, adding:

"You may have a wait of several hours. We're not sure. Just stay close to that rock where you'll be relatively safe. We've made protective arrangements which should work. Don't eat or drink anything until you get into the city. You'll be faintly sick with the diet change for a few days, but your body should adjust."

"*Should* adjust?"

"Give it time."

He'd asked about specific dangers to which he should be most alert.

"Stay clear of any Dosadi natives except your contacts. Above all, don't even appear to threaten anyone."

"What if I get drowsy and take a nap?"

They'd considered this, then:

"You know, that might be the safest thing to do. Anyone who'd dare to nap out there would have to be damned well protected. There'd be some risk, of course, but there always is on Dosadi. But they'd be awfully leery of anyone casual enough to nap out there."

Again, McKie glanced around.

Sharp whistlings and a low rasp like sand across wood came from behind the tall rock. Quietly, McKie worked his way around to where he could see the sources of these noises. The whistling was a yellow lizard almost the color of the bushes beneath which it crouched. The rasp came from a direction which commanded the lizard's attention. Its source appeared to be a small hole beneath another bush. McKie thought he detected in the lizard only a faint curiosity about himself. Something about that hole and the noise issuing from it demanded a great deal of concentrated attention.

Something stirred in the hole's blackness.

The lizard crouched, continued to whistle.

An ebony creature about the size of McKie's fist emerged from the hole, darted forward, saw the lizard. Wings shot from the newcomer's sides and it leaped upward, but it was too late. With a swiftness which astonished McKie, the lizard shot forward, balled itself around its prey. A slit opened in the lizard's stomach, surrounded the ebony creature. With a final rasping, the black thing vanished into the lizard.

All this time, the lizard continued to whistle. Still whistling it crawled into the hole from which its prey had come.

"Things are seldom what they seem to be on Dosadi," McKie's teachers had said.

He wondered now what he had just seen.

The whistling had stopped.

The lizard and its prey reminded McKie that, as he'd been warned, there had not been time to prepare him for every new detail on Dosadi. He crouched now and, once more, studied his immediate surroundings.

Tiny jumping things like insects inhabited the narrow line of shade at the base of the white rock. Green (blossoms?) opened and closed on the stems of the yellow bushes. The ground all around appeared to be a basic sand and clay, but when he peered at it closely he saw veins of blue and red discoloration. He turned his back on the distant city, saw far away mountains: a purple graph line against silver sky. Rain had cut an arroyo in that direction. He saw touches of darker green reaching from the depths. The air tasted bitter.

Once again, McKie made a sweeping study of his surroundings, seeking any sign of threat. Nothing he could identify. He palmed an instrument from his toolkit, stood casually and stretched while he turned toward Chu. When he stole a glance at the instrument, it revealed a sonabarrier at the city. Absently scratching himself to conceal the motion, he returned the instrument to his kit. Birds floated in the silver sky above the sonabarrier.

Why a sonabarrier? he wondered.

It would stop wild creatures, but not people. His teachers had said the sonabarrier excluded pests, vermin. The explanation did not satisfy McKie.

Things are seldom what they seem.

Despite the God Wall, that sun was hot. McKie sought the shady side of the rock. Seated there, he glanced at the small white disk affixed to the green lapel at his left breast: OP40331-D404. It was standard Galach script, the lingua franca of the ConSentiency.

"They speak only Galach on Dosadi. They may detect an accent in your speech, but they won't question it."

Aritch's people had explained that this badge identified McKie as an open-contract worker, one with slightly above average skills in a particular field, but still part of the Labor Pool and subject to assignment outside his skill.

"This puts you three hierarchical steps from the Rim," they'd said.

It'd been his own choice. The bottom of the social system always had its own communications channels flowing with information based on accurate data, instinct, dream stuff, and what was fed from the top with deliberate intent. Whatever happened here on Dosadi, its nature would be revealed in the unconscious processes of the Labor Pool. In the Labor Pool, he could tap that revealing flow.

"I'll be a weaver," he'd said, explaining that it was a hobby he'd enjoyed for many years.

The choice had amused his teachers. McKie had been unable to penetrate the reason for their amusement.

"It is of no importance right now. One choice is as good as another."

They'd insisted he concentrate on what he'd been doing at the time, learning the signal mannerisms of Dosadi. Indeed, it'd been a hectic period on Tandaloor after Aritch's insistence (with the most reasonable of arguments) that the best way for his Legum to proceed was to go personally to Dosadi. In retrospect, the arguments remained persuasive, but McKie had been surprised. For some reason which he could not now identify, he had expected a less involved *overview* of the experiment, watching through instruments and the spying abilities of the Caleban who guarded the place.

McKie was still not certain how they expected him to pull this hot palip from the cooker, but it was clear they expected it. Aritch had been mysteriously explicit:

"You are Dosadi's best chance for survival and our own best chance for . . . understanding."

They expected their Legum to save Dosadi while exonerating the Gowachin. It was a Legum's task to win for his client, but these had to be the strangest circumstances, with the client retaining the absolute power of destruction over the threatened planet.

On Tandaloor, McKie had been allowed just time for short naps. Even then, his sleep had been restless, part of his mind infernally aware of where he lay: the bedog strange and not quite attuned to his needs, the odd noises beyond the walls—water gurgling somewhere, always water.

When he'd trained there as a Legum, that had been one of his first adjustments: the uncertain rhythms of disturbed water. Gowachin never strayed far from water. The Graluz—that central pool and sanctuary for females, the place where Gowachin raised those tads which survived the ravenous *weeding* by the male parent—the Graluz always remained a central fixation for the Gowachin. As the saying put it:

"If you do not understand the Graluz, you do not understand the Gowachin."

As such sayings went, it was accurate only up to a point.

But there was always the water, contained water, the nervous slapping of wavelets against walls. The sound conveyed no fixed rhythms, but it was a profound clue to the Gowachin: contained, yet always different.

For all short distances, swimming tubes connected Gowachin facilities. They traversed long distances by jumpdoor or in hissing jetcars which moved on magnetic cushions. The comings and goings of such cars had disturbed

McKie's sleep during the period of the crash course on Dosadi. Sometimes, desperately tired, his body demanding rest, he would find himself awakened by voices. And the subtle interference of the other sounds—the cars, the waves—made eavesdropping difficult. Awake in the night, McKie would strain for meaning. He felt like a spy listening for vital clues, seeking every nuance in the casual conversations of people beyond his walls. Frustrated, always frustrated, he had retreated into sleep. And when, as happened occasionally, all sound ceased, this brought him to full alert, heart pounding, wondering what had gone wrong.

And the odors! What memories they brought back to him. Graluz musk, the bitter pressing of exotic seeds, permeated every breath. Fern tree pollen intruded with its undertones of citrus. And the caraeli, tiny, froglike pets, invaded your sleep at every dawning with their exquisite belling arias.

During those earlier days of training on Tandaloor, McKie had felt more than a little lost, hemmed in by threatening strangers, constantly aware of the important matters which rode on his success. But things were different after the interview with Aritch. McKie was now a trained, tested, and proven Legum, not to mention a renowned agent of BuSab. Yet there were times when the mood of those earlier days intruded. Such intrusions annoyed him with their implication that he was being maneuvered into peril against his will, that the Gowachin secretly laughed as they prepared him for some ultimate humiliation. They were not above such a jest. Common assessment of Gowachin by non-Gowachin said the Frog God's people were so ultimately civilized they had come full circle into a form of primitive savagery. Look at the way Gowachin males slaughtered their own newborn tads!

Once, during one of the rare naps Aritch's people permitted him, McKie had awakened to sit up and try to shake off that depressing mood of doom. He told himself true things: that the Gowachin flattered him now, deferred to him, treated him with that quasireligious respect which they paid to all Legums. But there was no evading another truth: the Gowachin had groomed him for their Dosadi problem over a long period of time, and they were being less than candid with him about that long process and its intentions.

There were always unfathomed mysteries when dealing with Gowachin.

When he'd tried returning to sleep that time, it was to encounter disturbing dreams of massed sentient flesh (both pink and green) all naked and quite defenseless before the onslaughts of gigantic Gowachin males.

The dream's message was clear. The Gowachin might very well destroy Dosadi in the way (and for similar reasons) that they winnowed their own tads—searching, endlessly searching, for the strongest and most resilient survivors.

The problem they'd dumped in his lap daunted McKie. If the slightest inkling of Dosadi leaked into common awareness without a concurrent justification, the Gowachin Federation would be hounded unmercifully. The Gowachin had clear and sufficient reason to destroy the evidence—or to let the evidence destroy itself.

Justification.

Where was that to be found? In the elusive benefits which had moved the Gowachin to mount this experiment?

Even if he found that justification, Dosadi would be an upheaval in the ConSentiency. It'd be the subject of high drama. More than twenty generations of Humans and Gowachin surfacing without warning! Their lonely history would titillate countless beings. The limits of language would be explored to wring the last drop of emotive essence from this revelation.

No matter how explained, Gowachin motives would come in for uncounted explorations and suspicions.

Why did they *really* do it? What happened to their original volunteers?

People would look backward into their own ancestry—Human and Gowachin alike. "Is that what happened to

Uncle Elfred?" Gowachin phylum records would be explored. "Yes! Here are two—gone without record!"

Aritch's people admitted that "a very small minority" had mounted this project and kept the lid on it. Were they completely sane, this Gowachin cabal?

McKie's short naps were always disturbed by an obsequious Gowachin bowing over his bedog, begging him to return at once to the briefing sessions which prepared him for survival on Dosadi.

Those briefing sessions! The implied prejudices hidden in every one raised more questions than were answered. McKie tried to retain a reasoned attitude, but irritants constantly assailed him.

Why had the Gowachin of Dosadi taken on Human emotional characteristics? Why were Dosadi's Humans aping Gowachin social compacts? Were the Dosadi truly aware of why they changed governmental forms so often?

The bland answer to these frequent questions enraged McKie.

"All will be made clear when you experience Dosadi for yourself."

He'd finally fallen into a counterirritant patter:

"You don't really know the answer, do you? You're hoping I'll find out for you!"

Some of the data recitals bored McKie. While listening to a Gowachin explain what was known about Rim relationships, he would find himself distracted by people passing in the multisentient access way outside the briefing area.

Once, Ceylang entered and sat at the side of the room, watching him with a hungry silence which rubbed McKie's sensibilities to angry rawness. He'd longed for the blue metal box then, but once the solemn investment had pulled the mantle of Legumic protection around him, the box had been removed to its sacred niche. He'd not see it again unless this issue entered the Courtarena. Ceylang remained an unanswered question among many. Why did that dangerous Wreave female haunt this room without contributing one thing? He suspected they allowed Ceylang to watch him through remote spy devices. Why did she choose that once to come in person? To let him know he was being observed? It had something to do with whatever had prompted the Gowachin to train a Wreave. They had some future problem which only a Wreave could solve. They were grooming this Wreave as they'd groomed him. Why? What Wreave capabilities attracted the Gowachin? How did this Wreave female differ from other Wreaves? Where were her loyalties? What was the 'Wreave Bet'?

This led McKie into another avenue never sufficiently explored: what Human capabilities had led the Gowachin to him? Dogged persistence? A background in Human law? The essential individualism of the Human?

There were no sure answers to these questions, no more than there were about the Wreave. Her presence continued to fascinate him, however. McKie knew many things about Wreave society not in common awareness outside the Wreave worlds. They were, after all, integral and valued partners in BuSab. In shared tasks, a camaraderie developed which often prompted intimate exchanges of information. Beyond the fact that Wreaves required a breeding triad for reproduction, he knew that Wreaves had never discovered a way to determine in advance which of the Triad would be capable of nursing the offspring. This formed an essential building stone in Wreave society. Periodically, this person from the triad would be exchanged for a like person from another triad. This insured their form of genetic dispersion and, of equal importance, built countless linkages throughout their civilization. With each such linkage went requirements for unquestioning support in times of trouble.

A Wreave in the Bureau had tried to explain this:

"Take, for example, the situation where a Wreave is murdered or, even worse, deprived of essential vanity. The guilty party would be answerable *personally* to millions upon millions of us. Wherever the triad exchange has linked us, we are required to respond intimately to the insult. The closest thing you have to this, as I understand it, is familial responsibility. We have this familial responsibility for vendetta where such affronts occur. You have no idea how difficult it was to release those of us in BuSab from this . . . this bondage, this network of responsibility."

The Gowachin would know this about the Wreaves, McKie thought. Had this characteristic attracted the Gowachin or had they chosen in spite of it, making their decision because of some other Wreave aspect? Would a Wreave Legum continue to share that network of familial responsibility? How could that be? Wreave society could only offend a basic sensibility of the Gowachin. The Frog God's people were even more . . . more *exclusive* and individual than Humans. To the Gowachin, family remained a private thing, walled off from strangers in an isolation which was abandoned only when you entered your chosen phylum.

As he waited beside the white rock on Dosadi, McKie reflected on these matters, biding his time, listening. The alien heat, the smells and unfamiliar noises, disturbed him. He'd been told to listen for the sound of an internal combustion engine. Internal combustion! But the Dosadi used such devices outside the city because they were more powerful (although much larger) than the beamed impulse drivers which they used within Chu's walls.

"The fuel is alcohol. Most of the raw materials come from the Rim. It doesn't matter how much poison there is in such fuel. They ferment bushes, trees, ferns . . . anything the Rim supplies."

A sleepy quiet surrounded McKie now. For a long time he'd been girding himself to risk the thing he knew he would have to do once he were alone on Dosadi. He might never again be this alone here, probably not once he was into Chu's Warrens. He knew the futility of trying to contact his Taprisiot monitor. Aritch, telling him the Gowachin knew BuSab had bought "Taprisiot insurance," had said:

"Not even a Taprisiot call can penetrate the God Wall."

In the event of Dosadi's destruction, the Caleban contract

ended. McKie's Taprisiot might even have an instant to complete the death record of McKie's memories. Might. That was academic to McKie in his present circumstances. The Calebans owed him a debt. The Whipping Star threat had been as deadly to Calebans as to any other species which had ever used jumpdoors. The threat had been real and specific. Users of jumpdoors and the Caleban who controlled those jumpdoors had been doomed. "Fannie Mae" had expressed the debt to McKie in her own peculiar way:

"The owing of me to thee connects to no ending."

Aritch could have alerted his Dosadi guardian against any attempt by McKie to contact another Caleban. McKie doubted this. Aritch had specified a ban against Taprisiot calls. But all Calebans shared an awareness at some level. If Aritch and company had been lulled into a mistaken assumption about the security of their barrier around Dosadi . . .

Carefully, McKie cleared his mind of any thoughts about Taprisiots. This wasn't easy. It required a Sufi concentration upon a particular *void*. There could be no accidental thrust of his mind at the Taprisiot waiting in the safety of Central Central with its endless patience. Everything must be blanked from awareness except a clear projection toward Fannie Mae.

McKie visualized her: the star Thyone. He recalled their long hours of mental give and take. He projected the warmth of emotional attachment, recalling her recent demonstration of "nodal involvement."

Presently, he closed his eyes, amplified that internal image which now suffused his mind. He felt his muscles relax. The warm rock against his back, the sand beneath him, faded from awareness. Only the glowing presence of a Caleban remained in his mind.

"Who calls?"

The words touched his auditory centers, but not his ears.

"It's McKie, friend of Fannie Mae. Are you the Caleban of the God Wall?"

"I am the God Wall. Have you come to worship?"

McKie felt his thoughts stumble. Worship? The projection from this Caleban was echoing and portentous, not at all like the probing curiosity he always sensed in Fannie Mae. He fought to regain that first clear image. The inner glow of a Caleban contact returned. He supposed there might be something worshipful in this experience. You were never absolutely certain of a Caleban's meaning.

"It's McKie, friend of Fannie Mae," he repeated.

The glow within McKie dimmed, then: "But you occupy a point upon Dosadi's wave."

That was a familiar kind of communication, one to which McKie could apply previous experience in the hope of a small understanding, an approximation.

"Does the God Wall permit me to contact Fannie Mae?"

Words echoed in his head:

"One Caleban, all Caleban."

"I wish converse with Fannie Mae."

"You are not satisfied with your present body?"

McKie felt his body then, the trembling flesh, the zombielike trance state which went with Caleban or Taprisiot contact. The question had no meaning to him, but the body contact was real and it threatened to break off communication. Slowly, McKie fought back to that tenuous mind-presence.

"I am Jorj X. McKie. Calebans are in my debt."

"All Calebans know this debt."

"Then honor your debt."

He waited, trying not to grow tense.

The glow within his head was replaced by a new presence. It insinuated itself into McKie's awareness with penetrating familiarity—not full mental contact, but rather a playing upon those regions of his brain where sight and sound were interpreted. McKie recognized this new presence.

"Fannie Mae!"

"What does McKie require?"

For a Caleban, it was quite a direct communication. McKie, noting this, responded more directly:

"I require your help."

"Explain."

"I may be killed here . . . ahh, have an end to my node here on Dosadi."

"Dosadi's wave," she corrected him.

"Yes. And if that happens, if I die here, I have friends on Central Central . . . on Central Central's wave . . . friends there who must learn everything that's in my mind when I die."

"Only Taprisiot can do this. Dosadi contract forbids Taprisiots."

"But if Dosadi is destroyed . . ."

"Contract promise passes no ending, McKie."

"You cannot help me?"

"You wish advice from Fannie Mae?"

"Yes."

"Fannie Mae able to maintain contact with McKie while he occupies Dosadi's wave."

Constant trance? McKie was shocked.

She caught this.

"No trance. McKie's nexus known to Fannie Mae."

"I think not. I can't have any distractions here."

"Bad choice."

She was petulant.

"Could you provide me with a personal jumpdoor to . . ."

"Not with node ending close to ending for Dosadi wave."

"Fannie Mae, do you know what the Gowachin are doing here on Dosadi? This . . ."

"Caleban contract, McKie."

Her displeasure was clear. You didn't question the honor of a Caleban's word-writ. The Dosadi contract undoubtedly contained specific prohibitions against any revelations of what went on here. McKie was dismayed. He was tempted to leave Dosadi immediately.

Fannie Mae got this message, too.

"McKie can leave now. Soon, McKie cannot leave in his own body/node."

"Body/node?"

"Answer not permitted."

Not permitted!

"I thought you were my friend, Fannie Mae!"

Warmth suffused him.

"Fannie Mae possesses friendship for McKie."

"Then why won't you help me?"

"You wish to leave Dosadi's wave in this instant?"

"No!"

"Then Fannie Mae cannot help."

Angry, McKie began to break the contact.

Fannie Mae projected sensations of frustration and hurt. "Why does McKie refuse advice? Fannie Mae wishes . . ."

"I must go. You know I'm in a trance while we're in contact. That's dangerous here. We'll speak another time. I appreciate your wish to help and your new clarity, but . . ."

"Not clarity! Very small hole in understanding but Human keeps no more dimension!"

Obvious unhappiness accompanied this response, but she broke the contact. McKie felt himself awakening, his fingers and toes trembling with cold. Caleban contact had slowed his metabolism to a dangerous low. He opened his eyes.

A strange Gowachin clad in the yellow of an armored vehicle driver stood over him. A tracked machine rumbled and puffed in the background. Blue smoke enveloped it. McKie stared upward in shock.

The Gowachin nodded companionably.

"You are ill?"

*We of the Sabotage Bureau remain legalists of a special
category. We know that too much law injures a society; it
is the same with too little law. One seeks a balance. We
are like the balancing force among the Gowachin: without hope of achieving heaven in the society of mortals, we
seek the unattainable. Each agent knows his own conscience and why he serves such a master. That is the key
to us. We serve a mortal conscience for immortal reasons.
We do it without hope of praise or the sureness of success.*

—The early writings of Bildoon,
PanSpechi Chief of BuSab

They moved out onto the streets as soon as the afternoon shadows gloomed the depths of the city, Tria
and six carefully chosen companions, all of them young
Human males. She'd musked herself to key them up and
she led them down dim byways where Broey's spies had been
eliminated. All of her troop was armored and armed in the
fashion of an ordinary sortie team.

There'd been rioting nearby an hour earlier, not sufficiently disruptive to attract large military attention, but a
small Gowachin salient had been eliminated from a Human
enclave. A sortie team was the kind of thing this Warren
could expect after such a specific species adjustment. Tria
and her six companions were not likely to suffer attack.
None of the rioters wanted a large-scale mopping up in the
area.

A kind of hushed, suspenseful waiting pervaded the
streets.

They crossed a wet intersection, green and red ichor in
the gutters. The smell of the dampness told her that a Graluz
had been broached and its waters freed to wash through the
streets.

That would attract retaliation. Some Human children were certain to be killed in the days ahead. An old pattern.

The troop crossed the riot area presently, noting the places where bodies had fallen, estimating casualties. All bodies had been removed. Not a scrap remained for the birds.

They emerged from the Warrens soon afterward, passing through a Gowachin-guarded gate, Broey's people. A few blocks along they went through another gate, Human guards, all in Gar's pay. Broey would learn of her presence here soon, Tria knew, but she'd said she was going into the Warrens. She came presently to an alleyway across from a Second Rank building. The windowless grey of the building's lower floors presented a blank face broken only by the lattice armor of the entrance gate. Behind the gate lay a dimly lighted passage. Its deceptively plain walls concealed spy devices and automatic weapons.

Holding back her companions with a hand motion, Tria waited in the dark while she studied the building entrance across from her. The gate was on a simple latch. There was one doorguard in an alcove on the left near the door which was dimly visible beyond the armorwork of the gate. A building defense force stood ready to come at the doorguard's summons or at the summons of those who watched through the spy devices.

Tria's informants said this was Jedrik's bolt hole. Not in the deep Warrens at all. Clever. But Tria had maintained an agent in this building for years, as she kept agents in many buildings. A conventional precaution. Everything depended on timing now. Her agent in the building was poised to eliminate the inner guards at the spy device station. Only the doorguard would remain. Tria waited for the agreed upon moment.

The street around her smelled of sewage: an open reclamation line. Accident? Riot damage? Tria didn't like the feeling of this place. What was Jedrik's game? Were there unknown surprises built into this guarded building? Jedrik must know by now that she was suspected of inciting the riot—and of other matters. But would she feel safe there in her own enclave? People tended to feel safe among their own people. She couldn't have a very large force around her, though. Still, some private plot worked itself through the devious pathways of Jedrik's mind, and Tria had not yet fathomed all of that plot. There were surface indicators enough to risk a confrontation, a parley. It was possible that Jedrik flaunted herself here to attract Tria. The potential in that possibility filled Tria with excitement.

Together, we'd be unbeatable!

Yes, Jedrik fitted the image of a superb agent. With the proper organization around her . . .

Once more, Tria glanced left and right. The streets were appropriately empty. She checked the time. Her moment had come. With hand motions, she sent flankers out left and right and another young male probing straight across the street to the gate. When they were in place, she slipped across with her three remaining companions in a triangular shield ahead.

The doorguard was a Human with grey hair and a pale face which glistened yellow in the dim light of the passage. His lids were heavy with a recent dose of his personal drug, which Tria's agent had supplied.

Tria opened the gate, saw that the guard carried a round dead-man switch in his right hand as expected. His grin was gap toothed as he held the switch toward her. She knew he'd recognized her. Much depended now on her agent's accuracy.

"Do you want to die for the frogs?" Tria asked.

He knew about the rioting, the trouble in the streets. And he was Human, with Human loyalties, but he knew she worked for Broey, a Gowachin. The question was precisely calculated to fill him with indecision. Was she a turncoat? He had his Human loyalties and a fanatic's dependence upon this guard post which kept him out of the depths. And there was his personal addiction. All doorguards were addicted to something, but this one took a drug which dulled his senses and made it difficult for him to correlate several lines of thought. He wasn't supposed to use his drug on duty and this troubled him now. There were so many matters to be judged, and Tria had asked the right question. He didn't want to die for the frogs.

She pointed to the dead-man switch, a question.

"It's only a signal relay," he said. "No bomb in this one."

She remained silent, forcing him to focus on his doubts.

The guard swallowed. "What do you . . ."

"Join us or die."

He peered past her at the others. Things such as this happened frequently in the Warrens, not very often here on the slopes which led up to the heights. The guard was not a one trusted with full knowledge of whom he guarded. He had explicit instructions and a dead-man relay to warn of intruders. Others were charged with making the more subtle distinctions, the real decisions. That was this building's weak point.

"Join who?" he asked.

There was false belligerency in his voice, and she knew she had him then.

"Your own kind."

This locked his drug-dulled mind onto its primary fears. He knew what he was supposed to do: open his hand. That released the alarm device in the dead-man switch. He could do this of his own volition and it was supposed to deter attackers from killing him. A dead man's hand opened anyway. But he'd been fed with suspicions to increase his doubts. The device in his hand might not be a simple signal transmitter. What if it actually were a bomb? He'd had many long hours to wonder about that.

"We'll treat you well," Tria said.

She put a companionable arm around his shoulder, letting him get the full effect of her musk while she held out her other hand to show that it carried no weapon. "Demonstrate to my companion here how you pass that to your relief."

One of the young males stepped forward.

The guard showed how it was done, explaining slowly as he passed the device. "It's easy once you get the trick of it."

When her companion had the thing firmly in hand, she raised her arm from the guard's shoulder, touched his carotid artery with a poisoned needle concealed in a fingernail. The guard had only time to draw one gasping breath, his eyes gaping, before he sank from her embrace.

"I treated him well," she said.

Her companions grinned. It was the kind of thing you learned to expect from Tria. They dragged the body out of sight into the guard alcove, and the young male with the signal device took his place at the door. The others protected Tria with their bodies as they swept into the building. The whole operation had taken less than two minutes. Everything was working smoothly, as Tria's operations were expected to work.

The lobby and its radiating hallways were empty.

Good.

Her agent in this building deserved a promotion.

They took a stairway rather than trust an elevator. It was only three short flights. The upper hallway also was empty. Tria led the way to the designated door, used the key her agent had supplied. The door opened without a sound and they surged into the room.

Inside, the shades had been pulled, and there was no artificial illumination. Her companions took up their places at the closed door and along both flanking walls. This was the most dangerous moment, something only Tria could handle.

Light came from thin strips where shades did not quite seal a south window. Tria discerned dim shapes of furniture, a bed with an indeterminate blob of darkness on it.

"Jedrik?" A whisper.

Tria's feet touched soft fabric, a sandal.

"Jedrik?"

Her shin touched the bed. She held a weapon ready while

she felt for the dark blob. It was only a mound of bedding. She turned.

The bathroom door was closed, but she could make out a thin slot of light at the bottom of the door. She skirted the clothing and sandal on the floor, stood at one side, and motioned a companion to the other side. Thus far they had operated with a minimum of sound.

Gently, she turned the knob, thrust open the door. There was water in a tub and a body face down, one arm hanging flaccidly over the edge, fingers dangling. A dark purple welt was visible behind and beneath the left ear. Tria lifted the head by the hair, stared at the face, lowered it gently to avoid splashing. It was her agent, the one she'd trusted for the intelligence to set up this operation. And the death was characteristic of a Gowachin ritual slaying: that welt under the ear. A Gowachin talon driven in there to silence the victim before drowning? Or had it just been made to appear like a Gowachin slaying?

Tria felt the whole operation falling apart around her, sensed the uneasiness of her companions. She considered calling Gar from where she stood, but a feeling of fear and revulsion came over her. She stepped out into the bedroom before opening her communicator and thumbing the emergency signal.

"Central." The voice was tense in her ear.

She kept her own voice flat. "Our agent's dead."

Silence. She could imagine them centering the locator on her transmission, then: "There?"

"Yes. She's been murdered."

Gar's voice came on: "That can't be. I talked to her less than an hour ago. She . . ."

"Drowned in a tub of water," Tria said. "She was knocked out first—something sharp driven in under an ear."

There was silence again while Gar absorbed this data. He would have the same uncertainties as Tria.

She glanced at her companions. They had taken up guard

positions facing the doorway to the hall. Yes, if attack came, it would come from there.

The channel to Gar remained open, and now Tria heard a babble of terse orders with only a few words intelligible: ". . . team . . . don't let . . . time . . ." Then, quite clearly: "They'll pay for this!"

Who will pay? Tria wondered.

She was beginning to make a new assessment of Jedrik.

Gar came back on: "Are you in immediate danger?"

"I don't know." It was a reluctant admission.

"Stay right where you are. We'll send help. I've notified Broey."

So that was the way Gar saw it. Yes. That was most likely the proper way to handle this new development. Jedrik had eluded them. There was no sense in proceeding alone. It would have to be done Broey's way now.

Tria shuddered as she issued the necessary orders to her companions. They prepared to sell themselves dearly if an attack came, but Tria was beginning to doubt there'd be an immediate attack. This was another message from Jedrik. The trouble came when you tried to interpret the message.

The military mentality is a bandit and raider mentality.
Thus, all military represents a form of organized banditry
where the conventional mores do not prevail. The military is
a way of rationalizing murder, rape, looting, and other
forms of theft which are always accepted as part of war-
fare. When denied an outside target, the military mental-
ity always turns against its own civilian population, using
identical rationalizations for bandit behavior.

—BuSab Manual, Chapter Five:
"The Warlord Syndrome"

Mckie, awakening from the communications trance;
realized how he must've appeared to this strange
Gowachin towering over him. Of course a Dosadi
Gowachin would think him ill. He'd been shivering and
mumbling in the trance, perspiration rolling from him.
McKie took a deep breath.

"No, I'm not ill."

"Then it's an addiction?"

Recalling the many substances to which the Dosadi could
be addicted, McKie almost used this excuse but thought better of it. This Gowachin might demand some of the addictive substance.

"Not an addiction," McKie said. He lifted himself to his
feet, glanced around. The sun had moved perceptibly toward the horizon behind its streaming veil.

And something new had been added to the landscape—
that gigantic tracked vehicle, which stood throbbing and
puffing smoke from a vertical stack behind the Gowachin
intruder. The Gowachin maintained a steady, intense concentration on McKie, disconcerting in its unwavering directness. McKie had to ask himself: was this some threat, or

his Dosadi contact? Aritch's people had said a vehicle would be sent to the contact point, but . . .

"Not ill, not an addiction," the Gowachin said. "Is it some strange condition which only Humans have?"

"I *was* ill," McKie said. "But I'm recovered. The condition has passed."

"Do you often have such attacks?"

"I can go years without a recurrence."

"Years? What causes this . . . condition?"

"I don't know."

"I . . . ahhhh." The Gowachin nodded, gestured upward with his chin. "An affliction of the Gods, perhaps."

"Perhaps."

"You were completely vulnerable."

McKie shrugged. Let the Gowachin make of that what he could.

"You were not vulnerable?" Somehow, this amused the Gowachin, who added: "I am Bahrank. Perhaps that's the luckiest thing which has ever happened to you."

Bahrank was the name Aritch's aides had given as McKie's first contact.

"I am McKie."

"You fit the description, McKie, except for your, ahhh, condition. Do you wish to say more?"

McKie wondered what Bahrank expected. This was supposed to be a simple contact handing him on to more important people. Aritch was certain to have knowledgeable observers on Dosadi, but Bahrank was not supposed to be one of them. The warning about this Gowachin had been specific.

"Bahrank doesn't know about us. Be extremely careful what you reveal to him. It'd be very dangerous to you if he were to learn that you came from beyond the God Veil."

The jumpdoor aides had reinforced the warning.

"If the Dosadi penetrate your cover, you'll have to return to your pickup point on your own. We very much doubt that you could make it. Understand that we can give you little help once we've put you on Dosadi."

Bahrank visibly came to a decision, nodding to himself.

"Jedrik expects you."

That was the other name Aritch's people had provided. "Your cell leader. She's been told that you're a new infiltrator from the Rim. Jedrik doesn't know your true origin."

"Who does know?"

"We cannot tell you. If you don't know, then that information cannot be wrested from you. We assure you, though, that Jedrik isn't one of our people."

McKie didn't like the sound of that warning. ". . . wrested from you." As usual, BuSab sent you into the tiger's mouth without a full briefing on the length of the tiger's fangs.

Bahrank gestured toward his tracked vehicle. "Shall we go?"

McKie glanced at the machine. It was an obvious war device, heavily armored with slits in its metal cab, projectile weapons protruding at odd angles. It looked squat and deadly. Aritch's people had mentioned such things.

"We saw to it that they got only primitive armored vehicles, projectile weapons and relatively unimportant explosives, that sort of thing. They've been quite resourceful in their adaptations of such weaponry, however."

Once more, Bahrank gestured toward his vehicle, obviously anxious to leave.

McKie was forced to suppress an abrupt feeling of profound anxiety. What had he gotten himself into? He felt that he had awakened to find himself on a terrifying slide into peril, unable to control the least threat. The sensation passed, but it left him shaken. He delayed while he continued to stare at the vehicle. It was about six meters long with heavy tracks, plus other wheels faintly visible within the shadows behind the tracks. It sported a conventional antenna at the rear for tapping the power transmitter in orbit beneath the barrier veil, but there was a secondary system which burned a stinking fuel. The smoke of that fuel filled the air around them with acridity.

"For what do we wait?" Bahrank demanded. He glared at McKie with obvious fear and suspicion.

"We can go now," McKie said.

Bahrank turned and led the way swiftly, clambering up over the tracks and into a shadowed cab. McKie followed, found the interior a tightly cluttered place full of a bitter, oily smell. There were two hard metal seats with curved backs higher than the head of a seated Human or Gowachin. Bahrank already occupied the seat on the left, working switches and dials. McKie dropped into the other seat. Folding arms locked across his chest and waist to hold him in place; a brace fitted itself to the back of his head. Bahrank threw a switch. The door through which they'd entered closed with a grinding of servomotors and the solid clank of locks.

An ambivalent mood swept over McKie. He had always felt faint agoraphobia in open places such as the area around the rock. But the dim interior of this war machine, with its savage reminders of primitive times, touched an atavistic chord in his psyche and he fought an urge to claw his way outside. This was a trap!

An odd observation helped him overcome the sensation. There was glass over the slits which gave them their view of the outside. Glass. He felt it. Yes, glass. It was common stuff in the ConSentiency—strong yet fragile. He could see that this glass wasn't very thick. The fierce appearance of this machine had to be more show than actuality, then.

Bahrank gave one swift, sweeping glance to their surroundings, moved levers which set the vehicle into lurching motion. It emitted a grinding rumble with an overriding whine.

A track of sorts led from the white rock toward the distant city. It showed the marks of this machine's recent passage, a roadway to follow. Glittering reflections danced from bright rocks along the track. Bahrank appeared very busy with whatever he was doing to guide them toward Chu.

McKie found his own thoughts returning to the briefings he'd received on Tandaloor.

"Once you enter Jedrik's cell you're on your own."

Yes . . . he felt very much alone, his mind a clutter of data which had little relationship to any previous experience. And this planet could die unless he made sense out of that data plus whatever else he might learn here.

Alone, alone . . . If Dosadi died there'd be few sentient watchers. The Caleban's tempokinetic barrier would contain most of that final destructive flare. The Caleban would, in fact, feed upon the released energy. That was one of the things he'd learned from Fannie Mae. One consuming blast, a *meal* for a Caleban, and BuSab would be forced to start anew and without the most important piece of physical evidence—Dosadi.

The machine beneath McKie thundered, rocked, and skidded, but always returned to the track which led toward Chu's distant spires.

McKie studied the driver covertly. Bahrank showed uncharacteristic behavior for a Gowachin: more direct, more Human. That was it! His Gowachin instincts had been contaminated by contact with Humans. Aritch was sure to despise that, fear it. Bahrank drove with a casual expertise, using a complex control system. McKie counted eight different levers and arms which the Gowachin employed. Some were actuated by knees, others by his head. His hands reached out while an elbow deflected a lever. The war machine responded.

Bahrank spoke presently without taking his attention from driving.

"We may come under fire on the second ledge. There was quite a police action down there earlier."

McKie stared at him.

"I thought we had safe passage through."

"You Rimmers are always pressing."

McKie peered out the slits: bushes, barren ground, that lonely track they followed.

Bahrank spoke.

"You're older than any Rimmer I ever saw before."

Aritch's people had warned McKie about this as a basic flaw in his cover, the need to conceal the subtle signs of age.

They'd provided him with some geriatric assistance and an answer to give when challenged. He used that answer now.

"It ages you in a hurry out here."

"It must."

McKie felt that something in Bahrank's response eluded him, but dared not pursue this. It was an unproductive exchange. And there was that reference to a "police action." McKie knew that the Rim Rabble, excluded from Chu, tried periodic raids, most often fruitless. Barbaric!

"What excuse did you use to come out here?" McKie asked.

Bahrank shot a probing glance at him, raised one webbed hand from the controls to indicate a handle in the roof over his head. The handle's purpose was unknown to McKie, and he feared he had already betrayed too much ignorance. But Bahrank was speaking.

"Officially, I'm scouting this area for any hidden surprises the Rimmers may have stored out here. I often do that. Unofficially, everyone thinks I've a secret pond out here full of fertile females."

A pond . . . not a Graluz. Again, it was a relatively fruitless exchange with hidden undertones.

McKie stared silently ahead through a slit. Their dusty track made a slow and wide sweep left, abruptly angled down onto a narrow ledge cut from red rock walls. Bahrank put them through a series of swift changes in speed: slow, fast, slow, fast. The red rock walls raced past. McKie peered out and downward on his side. Far below lay jungle verdure and, in the distance, the smoke and spires of Chu—fluted buildings ranked high over dim background cliffs.

The speed changes appeared purposeless to McKie. And the dizzy drop off the cliff on his side filled him with awe. Their narrow ledge hugged the cliff, turning as the cliff turned—now into shadows and now into light. The machine roared and groaned around him. The smell of oil made his stomach heave. And the faraway city seemed little closer than it had from the cliff top, except that it was taller, more mysterious in its smoky obscurity.

"Don't expect any real trouble until we reach the first ledge," Bahrank said.

McKie glanced at him. First ledge? Yes, that'd be the first elevation outside the city's walls. The gorge within which Chu had been raised came down to river level in broad steps, each one numbered. Chu had been anchored to island hills and flats where the river slowed and split into many arms. And the hills which had resisted the river were almost solid iron ore, as were many of the flanking ledges.

"Glad to get off there," Bahrank said.

Their narrow ledge had turned at right angles away from the cliff onto a broad ramp which descended into grey-green jungle. The growth enclosed them in abrupt green shadows. McKie, looking out to the side, identified hair fronds and broad leaf ficus, giant spikes of barbed red which he had never before seen. Their track, like the jungle floor, was grey mud. McKie looked from side to side; the growth appeared an almost equal mixture of Terran and Tandaloor, interspersed with many strange plants.

Sunlight made him blink as they raced out of the overhanging plants onto a plain of tall grass which had been trampled, blasted, and burned by recent violence. He saw a pile of wrecked vehicles off to the left, twisted shards of metal with, here and there, a section of track or a wheel aimed at the sky. Some of the wrecks looked similar to the machine in which he now rode.

Bahrank skirted a blast hole at an angle which gave McKie a view into the hole's depths. Torn bodies lay there. Bahrank made no comment, seemed hardly to notice.

Abruptly, McKie saw signs of movement in the jungle, the flitting presence of both Humans and Gowachin. Some carried what appeared to be small weapons—the glint of a metal tube, bandoliers of bulbous white objects around their necks. McKie had not tried to memorize all of Dosadi's weaponry; it was, after all, primitive, but he reminded himself now that primitive weapons had created these scenes of destruction.

Their track plunged again into overhanging growth, leaving the battlefield behind. Deep green shadows enclosed the lurching, rumbling machine. McKie, shaken from side to side against the restraints, carried an odor memory with him: deep, bloody musks and the beginnings of rot. Their shaded avenue made a sharp right turn, emerged onto another ledge slashed by a plunging cut into which Bahrank took them, turning onto another cliff-hugging ledge.

McKie stared across Bahrank through the slits. The city was nearer now. Their rocking descent swept his gaze up and down Chu's towers, which lifted like silvery organ pipes out of the Council Hills. The far cliff was a series of misted steps fading into purple grey. Chu's Warrens lay smokey and hazed all around the fluted towers. And he could make out part of the city's enclosing outer wall. Squat forts dotted the wall's top, offset for enfilading fire. The city within the wall seemed so tall. McKie had not expected it to appear so tall—but that spoke of the population pressures in a way that could not be misunderstood.

Their ledge ended at another battlefield plain strewn with bodies of metal and flesh, the death stink an inescapable vapor. Bahrank spun his vehicle left, right, dodged piles of torn equipment, avoided craters where mounds of flesh lay beneath insect blankets. Ferns and other low growth were beginning to spring upright after the monstrous trampling. Grey and yellow flying creatures sported in the ferntops, uncaring of all that death. Aritch's aides had warned McKie that Dosadi's life existed amidst brutal excesses, but the actuality sickened him. He identified both Gowachin and

Human forms among the sprawled corpses. The sleek green skin of a young Gowachin female, orange fertility marks prominent along her arms, especially revolted him. McKie turned sharply away, found Bahrank studying him with tawny mockery in the shining Gowachin eyes. Bahrank spoke as he drove.

"There're informers everywhere, of course, and after this . . ." His head nodded left and right. ". . . you'll have to move with more caution than you might've anticipated."

A brittle explosion punctuated his words. Something struck the vehicle's armor on McKie's side. Again they were a target. And again. The clanging of metal against metal came thickly, striking all around them, even on the glass over the view slits.

McKie suppressed his shock. That thin glass did not shatter. He knew about thick shields of tempered glass, but this put a new dimension on what he'd been told about the Dosadi. Quite resourceful, indeed!

Bahrank drove with apparent unconcern.

More explosive attacks came from directly in front of them, flashes of orange in the jungle beyond the plain.

"They're testing," Bahrank said. He pointed to one of the slits. "See? They don't even leave a mark on that new glass."

McKie spoke from the depths of his bitterness.

"Sometimes you wonder what all this proves except that our world runs on distrust."

"Who trusts?"

Bahrank's words had the sound of a catechism.

McKie said:

"I hope our friends know when to stop testing."

"They were told we couldn't take more'n eighty millimeter."

"Didn't they agree to pass us through?"

"Even so, they're expected to try a few shots if just to keep me in good graces with my superiors."

Once more, Bahrank put them through a series of dazzling speed changes and turns for no apparent reason.

McKie lurched against the restraints, felt bruising pain as an elbow hit the side of the cab. An explosion directly behind rocked them up onto the left track. As they bounced, Bahrank spun them left, avoided another blast which would've landed directly on them along their previous path. McKie, his ears ringing from the explosions, felt the machine bounce to a stop, reverse as more explosions erupted ahead. Bahrank spun them to the right, then left, once more charged full speed ahead right into an unbroken wall of jungle. With explosions all around, they crashed through greenery, turned to the right along another shadowed muddy track. McKie had lost all sense of direction, but the attack had ceased.

Bahrank slowed them, took a deep breath through his ventricles.

"I knew they'd try that."

He sounded both relieved and amused.

McKie, shaken by the brush with death, couldn't find his voice.

Their shadowy track snaked through the jungle for a space, giving McKie time to recover. By then, he didn't know what to say. He couldn't understand Bahrank's amusement, the lack of enduring concern over such violent threat.

Presently, they emerged onto an untouched, sloping plain as smooth and green as a park lawn. It dipped gently downward into a thin screen of growth through which McKie could see a silver-green tracery of river. What caught and held McKie's attention, however, was a windowless, pock-walled grey fortress which lifted from the plain in the middle distance. It towered over the growth screening the river. Buttressed arms reached toward them to enclose a black metal barrier.

"That's our gate," Bahrank said.

Bahrank turned them left, lined up with the center of the buttressed arms. "Gate Nine and we're home through the tube," he said.

McKie nodded. Walls, tubes, and gates: those were the

keys to Chu's defenses. They had "barrier and fortress minds" on Dosadi. This tube would run beneath the river. He tried to place it on the map which Aritch's people had planted in his mind. He was supposed to know the geography of this place, its geology, religions, social patterns, the intimate layout of each island's walled defenses, but he found it hard to locate himself now on that mental map. He leaned forward to the slit, peered upward as the machine began to gather speed, saw the great central spire with its horizontal clock. All the hours of map briefing snicked into place.

"Yes, Gate Nine."

Bahrank, too busy driving, did not reply.

McKie dropped his gaze to the fortress, stifled a gasp.

The rumbling machine was plunging downslope at a frightening pace, aimed directly toward that black metal barrier. At the last instant, when it seemed they would crash into it, the barrier leaped upward. They shot through into a dimly illuminated tube. The gate thundered closed behind them. Their machine made a racketing sound on metal grating beneath the tracks.

Bahrank slowed them, shifted a lever beside him. The machine lifted onto wheels with an abrupt reduction in noise which made McKie feel that he'd been deafened. The feeling was heightened by the realization that Bahrank had said the same thing to him several times.

"Jedrik says you come from beyond the far mountains. Is that true?"

"Jedrik says it." He tried to make it sound wry, but it came out almost questioning.

Bahrank was concentrating on a line of thought, however, as he drove them straight down the grating floor of the dim tube.

"There's a rumor that you Rimmers have started a secret settlement back there, that you're trying to build your own city."

"An interesting rumor."

"Isn't it, though?"

The single line of overhead lights in the tube left the cab's interior darker than it'd been outside, illuminated by only the faint reflections from instruments and dials. But McKie had the odd sensation that Bahrank saw him clearly, was studying every expression. Despite the impossibility of this, the thought persisted. What was behind Bahrank's probing?

Why do I feel that he sees right through me?

These disquieting conjectures ended as they emerged from the tube onto a Warren street. Bahrank spun them to the right along a narrow alleyway in deep grey shadows.

Although he'd seen many representations of these streets the actuality deepened McKie's feelings of misgiving. So dirty . . . oppressive . . . so many people. They were everywhere!

Bahrank drove slowly now on the silent wheels, the tracks raised off the paving. The big machine eased its way through narrow little streets, some paved with stone, some with great slabs of gleaming black. All the streets were shaded by overhanging upper stories whose height McKie could not judge through the slits. He saw shops barred and guarded. An occasional stairway, also guarded, led up or down into repellent darkness. Only Humans occupied these streets, and no casual, pedestrian expressions on any of them. Jaws were set on grim mouths. Hard, questioning eyes peered at the passing vehicle. Both men and women wore the universal dark, one-piece clothing of the Labor Pool.

Noting McKie's interest, Bahrank spoke.

"This is a Human enclave and you have a Gowachin driver."

"Can they see us in here?"

"They know. And there's trouble coming."

"Trouble?"

"Gowachin against Human."

This appalled McKie, and he wondered if this were the source of those forebodings which Aritch and aides would not explain: destruction of Dosadi from within. But Bahrank continued:

"There's a growing separation between Humans and Gowachin, worse than it's ever been. You may be the last Human to ride with me."

Aritch and company had prepared McKie for Dosadi's violence, hunger, and distrust, but they'd said nothing about species against species . . . only that someone they refused to name could destroy the place from within. What was Bahrank trying to say? McKie dared not expose his ignorance by probing, and this inability dismayed him.

Bahrank, meanwhile, nosed their machine out of a narrow passage onto a wider street which was crowded by carts, each piled with greenery. The carts moved aside slowly as the armored vehicle approached, hatred plain in the eyes of the Humans who moved with the carts. The press of people astonished McKie: for every cart (and he lost count of them within a block) there were at least a hundred people crowding around, lifting arms high, shouting at the ring of people who stood shoulder to shoulder around each cart, their backs to the piled contents and obviously guarding those contents.

McKie, staring at the carts, realized with a shocked sense of recognition that he was staring at carts piled with garbage. The crowds of people were buying garbage.

Again, Bahrank acted the part of tour guide.

"This is called the Street of the Hungry. That's very select garbage, the best."

McKie recalled one of Aritch's aides saying there were restaurants in Chu which specialized in garbage from particular areas of the city, that no poison-free food was wasted.

The passing scene compelled McKie's attention: hard faces, furtive movements, the hate and thinly suppressed violence, all of this immersed in a *normal* commercial operation based on garbage. And the numbers of these people! They were everywhere around: in doorways, guarding and pushing the carts, skipping out of Bahrank's path. New smells assaulted McKie's nostrils, a fetid acridity, a stink such as he had never before experienced. Another thing surprised him: the appearance of antiquity in this Warren. He wondered if all city populations crowded by threats from outside took on this ancient appearance. By ConSentient standards, the population of Chu had lived here only a few generations, but the city looked older than any he'd ever seen.

With an abrupt rocking motion, Bahrank turned their machine down a narrow street, brought them to a stop. McKie, looking out the slit on his right, saw an arched entry in a grimy building, a stairway leading downward into gloom.

"Down there's where you meet Jedrik," Bahrank said. "Down those stairs, second door on your left. It's a restaurant."

"How'll I know her?"

"Didn't they tell you?"

"I . . ." McKie broke off. He'd seen pictures of Jedrik during the Tandaloor briefings, realized now that he was trying to delay leaving Bahrank's armored cocoon.

Bahrank appeared to sense this.

"Have no fear, McKie. Jedrik will know you. And McKie . . ."

McKie turned to face the Gowachin.

". . . go directly to the restaurant, take a seat, wait for Jedrik. You'll not survive long here without her protection. Your skin's dark and some Humans prefer even the green to the dark in this quarter. They remember Pylash Gate here. Fifteen years isn't long enough to erase that from their minds."

Nothing about a Pylash Gate had been included in McKie's briefings and now he dared not ask.

Bahrank moved the switch which opened McKie's door. Immediately, the stink of the street was amplified to almost overpowering proportions. Bahrank, seeing him hesitate, spoke sharply.

"Go quickly!"

McKie descended in a kind of olfactory daze, found himself standing on the side of the street, the object of suspicious stares from all around. The sight of Bahrank driving away was the cutting of his last link to the ConSentiency and all the familiar things which might protect him. Never in his long life had McKie felt this much alone.

No legal system can maintain justice unless every participant—magisters, prosecutors, Legums, defendants, witnesses, all—risks life itself in whatever dispute comes before the bar. Everything must be risked in the Court-arena. If any element remains outside the contest and without personal risk, justice inevitably fails.

—Gowachin Law

Near sunset there was a fine rain which lasted well into darkness, then departed on the gorge wind which cleared Dosadi's skies. It left the air crystalline, cornices dripping puddles in the streets. Even the omnipresent Warren stink was diluted and Chu's inhabitants showed a predatory lightness as they moved along the streets.

Returning to headquarters in an armored troop carrier which carried only his most trusted Gowachin, Broey noted the clear air even while he wondered at the reports which had brought him racing from the Council Hills. When he entered the conference room, Broey saw that Gar already was there standing with his back to the dark window which looked out on the eastern cliffs. Broey wondered how long Gar had been there. No sign of recognition passed between Gowachin and Human, but this only emphasized the growing separation of the species. They'd both seen the reports which contained that most disturbing datum: the killing of a Human double agent under circumstances which pointed at Broey himself.

Broey crossed to the head of the conference table, flipped the toggle which activated his communicator, addressed the screen which only he could see.

"Assemble the Council and link for conference."

The response came as a distorted buzz filtered through scramblers and suppressed by a privacy cone. Gar, standing across the room, could make no sense out of the noises coming from the communicator.

While he waited for the Council members to come on the conference link, Broey seated himself at the communicator, summoned a Gowachin aide to the screen, and spoke in a low voice masked by the privacy cone.

"Start a security check on all Humans in positions where they might threaten us. Use Plan D."

Broey glanced up at Gar. The Human's mouth worked silently. He was annoyed by the privacy cone and his inability to tell exactly what Broey was doing. Broey continued speaking to his aide.

"I'll want the special force deployed as I told you earlier . . . Yes . . ."

Gar pointedly turned his back on this conversation, stared out at the night.

Broey continued to address his aide in the screen.

"No! We must include even the Humans in this conference. Yes, that's the report Gar made to me. Yes, I also received that information. Other Humans can be expected to riot and drive out their Gowachin neighbors, and there'll be retaliations. Yes, that was my thought when I saw the report."

Broey turned off the privacy cone and scrambler. Tria had just come onto his screen with an override, interrupting the conversation with his security aide She spoke in a low, hurried voice with only a few words intelligible to Gar across the room. But Broey's suspicions were becoming obvious. He heard Tria out, then:

"Yes . . . it would be logical to suppose that such a killing was made to look like Gowachin work for . . . I see. But the scattered incidents which . . . Indeed? Well, under the circumstances . . ."

He left the thought incomplete, but his words drew a line between Human and Gowachin, even at the highest levels of his Advisory Council.

"Tria, I must make my own decisions on this."

While Broey was speaking, Gar brought up a chair and

placed it near the communicator, then sat down. Broey had finished his conversation with Tria and restored the privacy circuits, however, and even though he sat nearby Gar could not penetrate their protective screen. He was close enough now, though, to hear the buzzing of the privacy system and the sound annoyed Gar. He did not try to conceal his annoyance.

Broey saw Gar, but gave no indication that he approved or disapproved Gar's nearness.

"So I understand," Broey said. "Yes . . . I'll issue those orders as soon as I've finished here. No . . . Agreed. That would be best." He closed the circuit. The annoying buzz stopped.

"Jedrik means to set Gowachin against Human, Human against Gowachin," Gar said.

"If so, it's been a long time in secret preparation," Broey said.

His words implied many things: that there was conspiracy in high places, that the situation had achieved dangerous momentum without being detected, that all of the inertial forces could not now be anticipated.

"You expect it to get worse," Gar said.

"Hopefully."

Gar stared at him for a long period, then:

"Yes."

It was clear that Broey wanted a well-defined condition to develop, one which would provide clear predictions of the major consequences. He was prepared for this. When Broey understood the situation to his own satisfaction, he'd use his own undeniable powers to gain as much as possible during a period of upset.

Gar broke the silence.

"But if we've misunderstood Jedrik's intent—"

"It helps us when the innocent suffer," Broey said, paraphrasing part of an old axiom which every Dosadi knew.

Gar completed the thought for him.

"But who's innocent?"

Before Broey could respond, his screen came alight with the assembled faces of his Council, each face in its own little square. Broey conducted the conference quickly, allowing few interruptions. There were no house arrests, no direct accusations, but his words and manner divided them by species. When he was through, Gar imagined the scrambling which must be going on right then in Chu while the powerful assembled their defenses.

Without knowing how he sensed this, Gar felt that this was exactly what Jedrik had wanted, and that it'd been a mistake for Broey to increase the tensions.

After turning off the communicator, Broey sat back and addressed himself to Gar with great care.

"Tria tells me that Jedrik cannot be found."

"Didn't we expect that?"

"Perhaps." Broey puffed his jowls. "What I don't understand is how a simple Liaitor could elude my people *and* Tria."

"I think we've underestimated this Jedrik. What if she comes from . . ." His chin jerked ceilingward.

Broey considered this. He'd been supervising the interrogation of Bahrank at a secure post deep in the Council Hills when the summons to headquarters had interrupted. The accumulating reports indicated a kind of trouble Chu had known at various times, but never at this magnitude. And Bahrank's information had been disappointing. He'd delivered this Rim infiltrator named McKie to such and such an address. (Security had been unable to check this in time because of the riots.) Bahrank's beliefs were obvious. And perhaps the Rimmers *were* trying to build their own city beyond the mountains. Broey thought this unlikely. His sources in the Rim had proved generally trustworthy and his special source was always trustworthy. Besides, such a venture would require gigantic stocks of food, all of it subject to exposure in the regular accounting. That, after all, was the Liaitor function, why he had . . . No, that was not probable. The Rim subsisted on the lowest of Chu's leavings and what-

ever could be wrested from Dosadi's poisonous soil. No . . .
Bahrank was wrong. This McKie was peculiar, but in quite
another way. And Jedrik must've known this before anyone
else—except himself. The paramount question remained:
who'd helped her?

Broey sighed.

"We have a long association, Gar. A person of your powers who has worked his way from the Rim through the
Warrens . . ."

Gar understood. He was being told that Broey looked
upon him with active suspicion. There'd never been any real
trust between them, but this was something else: nothing
openly spoken, nothing direct or specific, but the meaning
clear. It was not even sly; it was merely Dosadi.

For a moment, Gar didn't know which way to turn.
There'd always been this possibility in his relationship with
Broey, but long acceptance had lulled Gar into a dangerous
dependency. Tria had been his most valuable counter. He
needed her now, but she had other, much more demanding,
duties at this juncture.

Gar realized now that he would have to precipitate his
own plans, calling in all of the debts and dependencies
which were his due. He was distracted by the sound of many
people hurrying past in the outer hall. Presumably, things
were coming to a head faster than expected.

Gar stood up, stared vaguely out the windows at those dark
shadows in the night which were the Rim cliffs. While waiting for Broey, Gar had watched darkness settle there, watched
the spots of orange appear which were the Rim's cookfires.
Gar knew those cookfires, knew the taste of the food which
came from them, knew the flesh-dragging dullness which
dominated existence out there. Did Broey expect him to
flee back to that? Broey would be astonished at the alternatives open to Gar.

"I will leave you now," Broey said. He arose and wad-
dled from the room. What he meant was: "Don't be here
when I return."

Gar continued to stare out the windows. He seemed lost in angry reverie. Why hadn't Tria reported yet? One of Broey's Gowachin aides came in, fussed over papers on a corner table.

It was actually no more than five minutes that Gar remained standing thus. He shook himself presently, turned, and let himself out of the room.

Scarcely had he set foot in the outer passage than a troop of Broey's Gowachin shouldered their way past him into the conference room. They'd been waiting for him to leave.

Angry with himself for what he knew he must do, Gar turned left, strode down the hall to the room where he knew he'd find Broey. Three Gowachin wearing Security brassards followed him, but did not interfere. Two more Gowachin guarded Broey's door, but they hesitated to stop him. Gar's power had been felt here too long. And Broey, not expecting Gar to follow, had failed to issue specific orders. Gar counted on this.

Broey, instructing a group of Gowachin aides, stood over a table cluttered with charts. Yellow light from fixtures directly overhead played shifting shadows on the charts as the aides bent over the table and made notes. Broey broke off at the intrusion, his surprise obvious.

Gar spoke before Broey could order him removed.

"You still need me to keep you from making the worst mistake of your life."

Broey straightened, did not speak, but the invitation for Gar to continue was there.

"Jedrik's playing you like a fine instrument. You're doing precisely what she wants you to do."

Broey's cheeks puffed. The shrug angered Gar.

"When I first came here, Broey, I took certain precautions to insure my continued health should you ever consider violence against me."

Again, Broey gave that maddening Gowachin shrug. This was all so mundane. Why else did this fool Human continue alive and at liberty?

"You've never been able to discover what I did to insure myself against you," Gar said. "I have no addictions. I'm a prudent person and, naturally, have means of dying before your experts on pain could overcome my reason. I've done all of the things you might expect of me . . . and something more, something you now need *desperately* to know."

"I have my own precautions, Gar."

"Of course, and I admit I don't know what they are."

"So what do you propose?"

Gar gave a little laugh, not quite gloating.

"You know my terms."

Broey shook his head from side to side, an exquisitely Human gesture.

"Share the rule? I'm astonished at you, Gar."

"Your astonishment hasn't reached its limits. You don't know what I've really done."

"Which is?"

"Shall we retire to a more private place and discuss it?"

Broey looked around at his aides, waved for them to leave.

"We will talk here."

Gar waited until he heard the door close behind him on the last of the departing aides.

"You probably know about the death fanatics we've groomed in the Human enclaves."

"We are prepared to deal with them."

"Properly motivated, fanatics can keep great secrets, Broey."

"No doubt. Are you now going to reveal such a secret?"

"For years now, my fanatics have lived on reduced rations, preserving and exporting their surplus rations to the Rim. We have enough, megatons of food out there. With a whole planet in which to hide it, you'll never find it. City food, every bit of it and we will . . ."

"Another city!"

"More than that. Every weapon the city of Chu has, we have."

Broey's ventricle lips went almost green with anger.

"So you never really left the Rim?"

"The Rim-born cannot forget."

"After all that Chu has done for you . . ."

"I'm glad you didn't mention blasphemy."

"But the Gods of the Veil gave us a mandate!"

"Divide and rule, subdivide and rule even more powerfully, fragment and rule absolutely."

"That's not what I meant." Broey breathed deeply several times to restore his calm. "One city and only one city. That is our mandate."

"But the other city will be built"

"Will it?"

"We've dug in the factories to provide our own weapons and food. If you move against our people inside Chu, we'll come at you from the outside, shatter your walls and . . ."

"What do you propose?"

"Open cooperation for a separation of the species, one city for Gowachin, one for Human. What you do in Chu will be your own business then, but I'll tell you that we of the new city will rid ourselves of the DemoPol and its aristocracy."

"You'd create another aristocracy?"

"Perhaps. But my people will die for the vision of freedom we share. We no longer provide our bodies for Chu!"

"So that's why your fanatics are all Rim-born."

"I see that you don't yet understand, Broey. My people are not merely Rim-born; they are willing, even *eager*, to die for their vision."

Broey considered this. It was a difficult concept for a Gowachin, whose Graluz guilt was always transformed into a profound respect for the survival drive. But he saw where Gar's words must lead, and he built an image in his mind of fleshly Human waves throwing themselves onto all opposition without inhibitions about pain, death, or survival in any respect. They might very well capture Chu. The idea that countless Rim immigrants lived within Chu's walls in readiness for such sacrifice filled him with deep disquiet. It required strong self-control to conceal this reaction. He did not for an instant doubt Gar's story. It was just the kind of thing this dry-fleshed Rimmer would do. But why was Gar revealing this now?

"Did Jedrik order you to prepare me for . . ."

"Jedrik isn't part of our plan. She complicates matters for us, but the kind of upset she's igniting is just the sort of thing we can exploit better than you."

Broey weighed this with what he knew about Gar, found it valid as far as it went, but it still did not answer the basic question.

"Why?"

"I'm not ready to sacrifice my people," Gar said.

That had the ring of partial truth. Gar had shown many times that he could make hard decisions. But numbered among his fanatic hordes there doubtless were certain skills he'd prefer not losing—not yet. Yes, that was the way Gar's mind worked. And Gar would know the profound respect for life which matured in a Gowachin breast after the weeding frenzy. Gowachin, too, could make bloody decisions, but the guilt . . . oh, the guilt . . . Gar counted on the guilt. Perhaps he counted too much.

"Surely, you don't expect me to take an open and active part in your Rim city project?"

"If not open, then passive."

"And you insist on sharing the rule of Chu?"

"For the interim."

"Impossible!"

"In substance if not in name."

"You have been my advisor."

"Will you precipitate violence between us with Jedrik standing there to pick up whatever she can gain from us?"

"Ahhhhhh . . ." Broey nodded.

So that was it! Gar was not part of this Jedrik thing. Gar was afraid of Jedrik, more afraid of her than he was of Broey. This gave Broey cause for caution. Gar was not easily made fearful. What did he know of this Jedrik that Broey did not know? But now there was a sufficient reason for compromise. The unanswered questions could be answered later.

"You will continue as my chief advisor," Broey said.

It was acceptable. Gar signified his consent by a curt nod.

The compromise left an empty feeling in Broey's digestive nodes, though. Gar knew he'd been manipulated to reveal his fear of Jedrik. Gar could be certain that Broey would try to neutralize the Rim city project. But the magnitude of Gar's plotting went far beyond expectations, leaving too many unknowns. One could not make accurate decisions with insufficient data. Gar had given away information without receiving an equal exchange. That was not like Gar. Or was that a correct interpretation of what'd happened here? Broey knew he had to explore this, risking one piece of accurate information as bait.

"There's been a recent increase of mystical experiences by Gowachin in the Warrens."

"You know better than to try that religious nonsense on me!"

Gar was actually angry.

Broey concealed his amusement. Gar did not know then (or did not accept) that the God of the Veil sometimes created illusions in his flock, that God spoke truly to his anointed and would even answer some questions.

Much had been revealed here, more than Gar suspected. Bahrank had been right. And Jedrik would know about Gar's Rim city. It was possible that Jedrik wanted Broey to know and had maneuvered Gar into revealing the plot. If Gar saw this, that would be enough to make him fearful.

Why didn't the God reveal this to me? Broey wondered. *Am I being tested?*

Yes, that had to be the answer, because there was one thing certain now:

This time, I'll do what the God advises.

People always devise their own justifications. Fixed and immovable Law merely provides a convenient structure within which to hang your justifications and the prejudices behind them. The only universally acceptable law for mortals would be one which fitted every justification. What obvious nonsense. Law must expose prejudice and question justification. Thus, Law must be flexible, must change to fit new demands. Otherwise, it becomes merely the justification of the powerful.

—Gowachin Law
(The BuSab Translation)

It required a moment after Bahrank drove away for McKie to recover his sense of purpose. The buildings rose tall and massive over him, but through a quirk of this Warren's growth, an opening to the west allowed a spike of the silvery afternoon sunlight to slant into the narrow street. The light threw hard shadows on every object, accented the pressure of Human movement. McKie did not like the way people looked at him: as though everyone measured him for some private gain.

Slowly, McKie pressed through the passing throng to the arched entry, observing all he could without seeming to do so. After all those years in BuSab, all of the training and experience which had qualified him for such a delicately powerful agency, he possessed superb knowledge of the ConSentiency's species. He drew on that knowledge now, sensing the powerful secrecy which governed these people. Unfortunately, his experience also was replete with knowledge of what species could do to species, not to mention what a species could do to itself. The Humans around him reminded him of nothing more than a mob about to explode.

Moving with a constant readiness to defend himself, he went down a short flight of stairs into cool shadows where the foot traffic was lighter but the smells of rot and mold were more pronounced.

Second door on the left.

He went to the doorway to which Bahrank had directed him, peered into the opening: another stairway down. Somehow, this dismayed him. The picture of Chu growing in his mind was not at all what Aritch's people had drawn. Had they deliberately misled him? If so, why? Was it possible they really didn't understand their monster? The array of answers to his questions chilled him. What if a few of the observers sent here by Aritch's people had chosen to capitalize on whatever power Dosadi provided?

In all of his career, McKie had never before come across a world so completely cut off from the rest of the universe. This planet was *alone*, without many of the amenities which graced the other ConSentient worlds: no common access to jumpdoors, no concourse of the known species, none of the refined pleasures nor the sophisticated traps which occupied the denizens of other worlds. Dosadi had developed its own ways. And the instructors on Tandaloor had returned time and again to that constant note of warning—that these lonely *primitives* would take over the ConSentiency if released upon the universe.

"Nothing restrains them. Nothing."

That was, perhaps, an overstatement. Some things did restrain the Dosadi physically. But they were not held back by the conventions or mores of the ConSentiency. Anything could be purchased here, any forbidden depravity which the imagination might conceive. This idea haunted McKie. He thought of this and of the countless substances to which many Dosadi were addicted. The power leverage such things gave to the unprincipled few was terrifying.

He dared not pause here wrestling with his indecisions, though. McKie stepped into the stairwell with a boldness which he did not feel, following Bahrank's directions because he had no choice. The bottom landing was a wider space in deep shadows, one dim light on a black door. Two Humans dozed in chairs beside the door while a third squatted beside them with what appeared to be a crude projectile weapon in his hands.

"Jedrik summoned me," McKie said.

The guard with the weapon nodded for him to proceed.

McKie made his way past them, glanced at the weapon: a length of pipe with a metal box at the back and a flat trigger atop the box held by the guard's thumb. McKie almost missed a step. The weapon was a dead-man bomb! Had to be. If that guard's thumb relaxed for any reason, the thing no doubt would explode and kill everyone in the stairwell. McKie glanced at the two sleepers. How could they sleep in such circumstances?

The black door with its one dim light commanded his attention now. A strong smell of highly seasoned cooking dominated the other stinks here. McKie saw that it was a heavy door with a glittering spyeye at face level. The door opened at his approach. He stepped through into a large low room crowded—*jammed*!—with people seated on benches at trestle tables. There was barely room for passage between the benches. And everywhere that McKie looked he saw people spooning food into their mouths from small bowls. Waiters and waitresses hurried through the narrow spaces slapping down bowls and removing empties.

The whole scene was presided over by a fat woman seated at a small desk on a platform at his left. She was positioned in such a way that she commanded the entry door, the entire room, and swinging doors at the side through which the serving people flowed back and forth. She was a monstrous woman and she sat her perch as though she had never been anywhere else. Indeed, it was easy for McKie to imagine that she could not move from her position. Her arms were bloated where they squeezed from the confines of short-sleeved green coveralls. Her ankles hung over her shoe tops in folds.

Take a seat and wait.

Bahrank had been explicit and the warning clear.

McKie looked for an opening on the benches. Before he could move, the fat woman spoke in a squeaky voice.

"Your name?"

McKie's gaze darted toward those beady eyes in their folds of fat.

"McKie."

"Thought so."

She raised a dimpled finger. From somewhere in the crush a young boy came hurrying. He could not have been over nine years old but his eyes were cold with adult wisdom. He looked up to the fat woman for instructions.

"This is the one. Guide him."

The boy turned and, without looking to see if McKie followed, hurried down the narrow pathway where the doors swung back and forth to permit the passage of the servitors. Twice, McKie was almost run down by waiters. His guide was able to anticipate the opening of every door and skipped aside.

At the end of this passage, there was another solid black door with spyeye. The door opened onto a short passage with closed doors on both sides, a blank wall at the end. The blank wall slid aside for them and they descended into a narrow, rock-lined way lighted by widely spaced bulbs overhead. The walls were damp and evil smelling. Occasionally, there were wide places with guards. They passed through several guarded doors, climbed up and went down. McKie lost track of the turns, the doors, and guard posts. After a time, they climbed to another short hallway with doors along its sides. The boy opened the second door on the right, waited for McKie to enter, closed the door. It was all done without words. McKie heard the boy's footsteps recede.

The room was small and dimly lighted by windows high in the wall opposite the door. A trestle table about two meters long with benches down both sides and a chair at each end almost filled the space. The walls were grey stone and unadorned. McKie worked his way around to the chair at the far end, sat down. He remained seated there silently for several minutes, absorbing this place. It was cold in the room: Gowachin temperature. One of the high windows behind him was open a crack and he could hear street noises: a heavy vehicle passing, voices arguing, many feet. The sense of the Warren pressing in upon this room was very strong. Nearer at hand from beyond the single door, he heard crockery banging and an occasional hiss as of steam.

Presently, the door opened and a tall, slender woman entered, slipping through the door at minimal opening. For a moment as she turned, the light from the windows concentrated on her face, then she sat down at the end of the right-hand bench, dropping into shadows.

McKie had never before seen such hard features on a woman. She was brittle rock with ice crystal eyes of palest blue. Her black hair was closely cropped into a stiff bristle. He repressed a shudder. The rigidity of her body amplified the hard expression on her face. It was not the hardness of suffering, not that alone, but something far more determined, something anchored in a kind of agony which might explode at the slightest touch. On a ConSentient world where the geriatric arts were available, she could have been any age between thirty-five and one hundred and thirty-five. The dim light into which she had seated herself complicated his scrutiny, but he suspected she was younger than thirty-five.

"So *you* are McKie."

He nodded.

"You're fortunate Adril's people got my message. Broey's already searching for you. I wasn't warned that you were so dark."

He shrugged.

"Bahrank sent word that you could get us all killed if we're not careful with you. He says you don't have even rudimentary survival training."

This surprised McKie, but he held his silence.

She sighed. "At least you have the good sense not to protest. Well . . . welcome to Dosadi, McKie. Perhaps I'll be able to keep you alive long enough for you to be of some use to us."

Welcome to Dosadi!

"I'm Jedrik as you doubtless already know."

"I recognize you."

This was only partly true. None of the representations he'd seen had conveyed the ruthless brutality which radiated from her.

A hard smile flickered on her lips, was gone.

"You don't respond when I welcome you to our planet."

McKie shook his head. Aritch's people had been specific in their injunction:

"She doesn't know your origin. Under no circumstances may you reveal to her that you come from beyond the God Wall. It could be immediately fatal."

McKie continued to stare silently at her.

A colder look came over Jedrik's features, something in the muscles at the corners of the mouth and eyes.

"We shall see. Now: Bahrank says you carry a wallet of some kind and that you have currency sewn into your clothing. First, hand me the wallet."

My toolkit?

She reached an open hand toward him.

"I'll warn you once, McKie. If I get up and walk out of here you'll not live more than two minutes."

Every muscle quivering protest, he slipped the toolkit from its pocket, extended it.

"And I'll warn you, Jedrik: I'm the only person who can open this without being killed and the contents destroyed."

She accepted the toolkit, turned its flat substance over in her hands.

"Really?"

McKie had begun to interest her in a new way. He was less than she'd expected, yet more. Naive, of course, incredibly naive. But she'd already known that of the people from beyond the God Wall. It was the most suitable explanation. Something was profoundly wrong in the Dosadi situation. The people beyond the Veil would have to send their best here. This McKie was their best? Astonishing.

She arose, went to the door, rapped once.

McKie watched her pass the toolkit to someone outside, heard a low-voiced conversation, neither half of it intelligible. In a flashing moment of indecision, he'd considered trying for some of the toolkit's protective contents. Something in Jedrik's manner and the accumulation of unknowns all around had stopped him.

Jedrik returned to her seat empty-handed. She stared at him a moment, head cocked to one side, then:

"I'll say several things to you. In a way, this is a test. If you fail, I guarantee you'll not survive long on Dosadi. Understood?"

When McKie failed to respond, she pounded a fist on the table.

"Understood?"

"Say what you have to say."

"Very well. It's obvious to me that those who instructed you about Dosadi warned you not to reveal your true origin. Yet, most of those who've talked to you for more than a few seconds suspect you're not one of us—not from Chu, not from the Rim, not from anywhere on Dosadi." Her voice took on a new harshness. "But I know it. Let me tell you, McKie, that there's not even a child among us who's failed to realize that the people imprisoned on Dosadi did not originate here!"

McKie stared at her, shocked.

Imprisoned.

As she spoke, he knew she was telling him the truth. Why hadn't Aritch or the others warned him? Why hadn't he seen this for himself? Since Dosadi was poison to both Human and Gowachin, rejected them, of course they'd know they hadn't originated here.

She gave him time to absorb this before continuing.

"There are others among us from your realm, perhaps some we've not identified, better trained. But I was taught to act only on certainty. Of you I'm certain. You do not originate on Dosadi. I've put it to the question and I've the present confirmation of my own senses. You come from beyond the God Wall. Your actions with Bahrank, with Adril, with me . . ." She shook her head sadly.

Aritch set me up for this!

This thought brought back a recurrent question which continued to nag McKie; BuSab's discovery of the Dosadi Experiment. Were the Gowachin that clumsy? Would they make such slips? The original plan to conceal this project must have been extensive. Yet, key facts had leaked to BuSab agents. McKie felt overwrought from asking himself the same questions over and over without satisfaction. And now, Jedrik's pressures compounded the burden. The only suitable answer was that Aritch's people had done everything with the intent of putting him in this position. They'd deliberately leaked information about Dosadi. And McKie was their target.

To what purpose?

"Can we be overheard?" he asked.

"Not by my enemies on Dosadi."

He considered this. She'd left open the question of whether anyone from beyond the God Wall might eavesdrop. McKie pursed his lips with indecision. She'd taken his toolkit with such ridiculous ease . . . yet, what choice had he? They wouldn't get anything from the kit and someone out there, one of Jedrik's underlings, would die. That could have a useful effect on Jedrik. He decided to play for time.

"There're many things I could tell you. So many things. I hardly know where to begin."

"Begin by telling me how you came through the God Wall."

Yes, he might be able to confuse her with a loose description of Calebans and jumpdoors. Nothing in her Dosadi experience could've prepared Jedrik for such phenomena. McKie took a deep breath. Before he could speak there was a rap on the door.

Jedrik raised a hand for silence, leaned over, and opened the door. A skinny young man with large eyes beneath a high forehead and thin blond hair slipped through, placed McKie's toolkit on the table in front of Jedrik.

"It wasn't very difficult," he said.

McKie stared at the kit in shock. It lay open with all of its contents displayed in perfect order.

Jedrik gestured the youth to the seat opposite her. She reached for a raygen.

McKie could no longer contain himself.

"Careful! That's dangerous!"

"Be still, McKie. You know nothing of danger."

She removed the raygen, examined it, replaced it neatly, looked at the young man.

"All right, Stiggy. Tell me."

The youth began removing the items from the toolkit one by one, handling each with a knowledgeable correctness, speaking rapidly.

McKie tried hard to follow the conversation, but it was in a code he could not understand. The expressions on their faces were eloquent enough, however. They were elated. Whatever Stiggy was saying about the dangerous toys in McKie's toolkit, his revelations profited both of them.

The uncertainties which had begun during McKie's ride with Bahrank reached a new intensity. The feeling had built up in him like a sickness: disquiet stomach, pains in his chest, and, lastly, an ache across his forehead. He'd wondered for a time if he might be the victim of some new disease native to Dosadi. It could not be the planet's food because he'd eaten nothing yet. The realization came over him as he watched Jedrik and Stiggy that his reactions were his own reasoning system trying to reject something, some assumption or set of assumptions which he'd accepted without question. He tried to empty his mind, not asking any questions in particular. Let come into his awareness what may. It would all have a fresh appraisal.

Dosadi requires you to be coldly brutal in all of your decisions. No exceptions.

Well . . . he'd let go of the toolkit in the belief that someone would die trying to open it. But he'd issued a warning. That warning could've helped them. Probably did.

I must become exactly like them or I cannot survive—let alone succeed.

At last, McKie felt Aritch's fear of Dosadi, understood the Gowachin desperation. What a terrible training ground for the recognition and use of power!

Jedrik and Stiggy finished their conversation over the toolkit. Stiggy closed the kit, arose with it in one hand, speaking at last in words McKie understood.

"Yes, we must lose no time."

Stiggy left with the kit.

Jedrik faced McKie. The toolkit and its contents had helped answer the most obvious question about McKie and his kind. The people beyond the God Wall were the degenerate descendants of those who'd invented such devices. It was the only workable explanation. She felt almost sorry for this poor fool. But that was not a permissible emotion. He must be made to understand that he had no choice but to obey her.

"Now, McKie, you will answer all of my questions."

"Yes."

It was utter submission and she knew it.

"When you've satisfied me in all matters," she said, "then we'll eat and I'll take you to a place where you'll be reasonably safe."

*The Family/Clan/Factions of the Rim are still responding
to their defeat in the mass attempt on our defenses of last
Decamo. They appear severely chastened. Small police actions are all that we need anticipate over the next planning
period. Further, our operatives in the Rim find no current
difficulties in steering the F/C/F toward a natural and acceptable cultural rejection of economic developments which
might lead them to improved food production.*

—from a Dosadi Bureau of Control document

An angry Broey, full out and uninhibited anger, was
something to see and quite a number of his Gowachin
aides had seen this emotional display during the night. It
was now barely dawn. Broey had not slept in two days; but
the fourth group of his aides stood before him in the sanctum to receive the full spate of his displeasure. The word
had already gone out through their ranks and they, like the
others, did not try to hide their fear or their anxious eagerness to restore themselves in Broey's good graces.

Broey stood near the end of the long table where, earlier,
he had met with Gar and Tria. The only visible sign of his
long sleepless hours was a slight pitting of the fatty nodes
between his ventricles. His eyes were as sharp as ever and
his voice had lost none if its bite.

"What I'd like explained is how this could happen without a word of warning. And it's not just that we failed to
detect this, but that we continued to grind out complacent
reports, reports which went exactly contrary to what actually was happening."

The aides massed at the other end of the table, all standing, all fidgeting, were not assuaged by Broey's use of
"we." They heard him clearly. He was saying: "You! You!
You!"

"I will be satisfied by nothing less than an informant," Broey said. "I want a Human informant, either from Chu or from the Rim. I don't care how you get this informant. We must find that store of city food. We must find where they have started their blasphemous Rim city."

One of his aides, a slender young Gowachin in the front rank, ventured a cautious question which had been repeated several times by other chastened aides during the night.

"If we move too strongly against Humans in the Warrens, won't that feed the unrest that . . ."

"We'll have more riots, more turning of Gowachin against Human and Human against Gowachin," Broey agreed. "That's a consequence we are prepared to accept."

This time they understood that Broey used the royal "we." Broey would accept the consequences. Some of his aides, however, were not ready to accept a war between the species within the city's walls. One of the aides farther back in the ranks raised an arm.

"Perhaps we should use only Human troops in the Warrens. If we . . ."

"Who would that fool?" Broey demanded. "We have taken the proper steps to maintain our hold on Chu. You have one task and one task only: find that store of food and those hidden factories. Unless we find them we're finished. Now, get out of here. I don't want to see any of you until you can report success!"

They filed out silently.

Broey stood looking down at the blank screen of his communicator. Alone at last, he allowed his shoulders to slump, breathed heavily through both mouth and ventricles.

What a mess! What a terrible mess.

He knew in his node of nodes that he was behaving precisely as Jedrik wanted him to behave. She had left him no alternatives. He could only admire her handling of the situation while he waited for the opening which he knew must come. But what a magnificent intellect operated in that Human head. And a female at that! Gowachin females never developed such qualities. Only on the Rim were Gowachin females used as other than breeders. Human females, on the other hand, never ceased to amaze him. This Jedrik possessed real leadership qualities. Whether she was the one to take over the Electorship remained to be seen.

Broey found himself recalling those first moments of terrible awareness in the Graluz. Yes, this was the way of the world. If one chose the survivors by other than a terrible testing process, all would die. It would be the end of both species. At least, it would be the end of them on Dosadi and only Dosadi mattered.

He felt bereft, though. He felt betrayed by his God. Why had God failed to warn him? And when questioned, how could God respond that only evil could penetrate the mind of a fanatic? Wasn't God omnipotent? Could any awareness be closed to God? How could God be *God* then?

I am your God!

He could never forget that voiceless voice reverberating in his head.

Was that a lie?

The idea that they were puppets of a false god was not a new one. But if this were the case, then the other uses of those like Pcharky eluded him. What was the purpose of being a Gowachin in Human form or vice versa if not to elude the God of the Veil? Quite obviously, Jedrik operated on such a premise. What other motive could she have than to prolong her own life? As the City was to the Rim, so was the power to elude the God (false God or true) to those of the City. No other assumption fitted a Dosadi justification.

We are plagued by a corrupt polity which promotes un-
lawful and/or immoral behavior. Public interest has no
practical significance in everyday behavior among the
ruling factions. The real problems of our world are not be-
ing confronted by those in power. In the guise of public ser-
vice, they use whatever comes to hand for personal gain.
They are insane with and for power.

—from a clandestine document circulated on Dosadi

It was dark when a disguised Jedrik and undisguised McKie emerged onto the streets. She led them down narrow passages, her mind full of things McKie had revealed. Jedrik wore a blonde wig and puff-out disguise which made her appear heavy and hunched.

As they passed an open courtyard, McKie heard music. He almost stumbled. The music came from a small orchestra—delicate tympany, soft strings, and a rich chorus of wind instruments. He did not recognize the melody, but it moved him more deeply than any other music of his experience. It was as though the music were played only for him. Aritch and company had said nothing about such magnificent music here.

People still thronged the streets in numbers which astonished him. But now they appeared to pay him little notice.

Jedrik kept part of her attention on McKie, noting the fools with their musical dalliance, noting how few people there were on the streets—little more than her own patrols in this quarter. She'd expected that, but the actuality held an eerie mood in the dim and scattered illumination from lighted corners.

She had debated providing McKie with a crude disguise, but he obviously didn't have the cunning to carry off the double deception she required. She'd begun to sense a real intelligence in him, though. McKie was an enigma. Why had he never encountered the opportunities to sharpen that intelligence? Sensing the sharpness in him, she could not put off the thought that she had missed something vital in his accounts of that social entity which he called the Con-Sentiency. Whether this failure came from actual conceal-ment by McKie or through his inadequacies, she was not yet willing to judge. The enigma set her on edge. And the mood in the streets did nothing to ease her emotions. She was glad when they crossed the line into the area completely controlled by her own personal cell.

The bait having been trailed through the streets by one who would appear a tame underling, Jedrik allowed herself a slight relaxation. Broey would have learned by this time about the killing of Tria's double agent. He would react to that and to the new bait. It was almost time for phase two of her design for Broey.

McKie followed her without question, acutely aware of every strange glance cast their way. He was emptied of all resistance, knowing he could not survive if he failed to fol-low Jedrik through the smelly, repellent darkness of her streets.

The food from the restaurant sat heavily in his stomach. It had been tasty: a stew of odd shapes full of shredded greenery, and steaming hot. But he could not shake the re-alization that his stew had been compounded of someone's garbage.

Jedrik had left him very little. She hadn't learned of the Taprisiot, or the bead in his stomach which probably would not link him to the powers of the ConSentiency if he died. She had not learned of the standard BuSab implantation de-vices which amplified his senses. And, oddly, she had not explored many of his revelations about BuSab. She'd seemed much more interested in the money hidden about his per-son and had taken possession of all of it. She'd examined the currency carefully.

"This is real."

He wasn't sure, but he thought she'd been surprised.

"This was given to you *before* you were sent to Dosadi?"

"Yes."

She was a while absorbing the implications, but appeared satisfied. She'd given him a few small currency tokens from her own pockets.

"Nobody'll bother you for these. If you need anything, ask. We may be able to gratify some of your needs."

It was still dark, lighted only by illumination at corners, when they came to the address Jedrik sought. Grey light suffused the street. A young Human male of about ten squatted with his back against the stone wall at the building's corner. As Jedrik and McKie approached, he sprang up, alert. He nodded once to Jedrik.

She did not acknowledge, but by some hidden signal the boy knew she had received his message. He relaxed once more against the wall.

When McKie looked back a few paces beyond where the boy had signaled, he was gone. No sound, no sign—just gone.

Jedrik stopped at a shadowed entryway. It was barred by an openwork metal gate flanked by two armed guards. The guards opened the gate without words. Beyond the gate there was a large, covered courtyard illuminated by glowing tubes on right and left. Three of its sides were piled to the courtyard cover with boxes of various sizes—some taller than a Human and narrow, others short and fat. Set into the stacks as though part of the courtyard's walls was one narrow passage leading to a metal door opposite the gateway.

McKie touched Jedrik's arm.

"What's in the boxes?"

"Weapons." She spoke as though to a cretin.

The metal door was opened from within. Jedrik led McKie into a large room at least two stories tall. The door clanged shut behind them. McKie sensed several Humans along the courtyard wall on both sides of him, but his attention had been captured by something else.

Dominating the room was a gigantic cage suspended from the ceiling. Its bars sparkled and shimmered with hidden energies. A single Gowachin male sat cross-legged in a hammock at the cage's center. McKie had seldom seen a ConSentient Gowachin that aged. His nose crest was fringed by flaking yellow crusts. Heavy wrinkles wormed their way beneath watery eyes beginning to glaze with the degeneration which often blinded Gowachin who lived too long away from water. His body had a slack appearance, with loose muscles and pitted indentations along the nodes between his ventricles. The hammock suspended him off the cage floor and that floor shimmered with volatile energies.

Jedrik paused, divided her attention between McKie and the old Gowachin. She seemed to expect a particular reaction from McKie, but he wasn't certain she found what she sought.

McKie stood a moment in silent examination of the Gowachin. Prisoner? What was the significance of that cage and its shimmering energies? Presently, he glanced around the room, recording the space. Six armed Human males flanked the door through which he and Jedrik had entered. A remarkable assortment of objects crammed the room's walls, some with purpose unknown to him but many recognizable as weapons: spears and swords, flame-throwers, garish armor, bombs, pellet projectors . . .

Jedrik moved a pace closer to the cage. The occupant stared back at her with faint interest. She cleared her throat.

"Greetings, Pcharky. I have found my key to the God Wall."

The old Gowachin remained silent, but McKie thought he saw a sparkle of interest in the glazed eyes.

Jedrik shook her head slowly from side to side, then: "I have a new datum, Pcharky. The Veil of Heaven was created by creatures called Calebans. They appear to us as suns."

Pcharky's glance flickered to McKie, back to Jedrik. The Gowachin knew the source of her new datum.

McKie renewed his speculations about the old Gowachin. That cage must be a prison, its walls enforced by dangerous energies. Bahrank had spoken of conflict between the species. Humans controlled this room. Why did they imprison a Gowachin? Or . . . was this caged Gowachin, this Pcharky, another agent from Tandaloor? With a tightening of his throat, McKie wondered if his own fate might be to live out his days in such a cage.

Pcharky grunted, then:

"The God Wall is like this cage but more powerful."

His voice was a husky croaking, the words clear Galach with an obvious Tandaloor accent. McKie, his fears reinforced, glanced at Jedrik, found her studying him. She spoke.

"Pcharky has been with us for a long time, very long. There's no telling how many people he has helped to escape from Dosadi. Soon, I may persuade him to be of service to me."

McKie found himself shocked to silence by the possibilities glimpsed through her words. Was Dosadi in fact an investigation of the Caleban mystery? Was that the secret Aritch's people concealed here? McKie stared at the shimmering bars of Pcharky's cage. Like the God Wall? But the God Wall was enforced by a Caleban.

Once more, Jedrik looked at the caged Gowachin.

"A sun confines enormous energies, Pcharky. Are your energies inadequate?"

But Pcharky's attention was on McKie. The old voice croaked.

"Human, tell me: Did you come here willingly?"

"Don't answer him," Jedrik snapped.

Pcharky closed his eyes. Interview ended.

Jedrik, accepting this, whirled and strode to the left around the cage.

"Come along, McKie." She didn't look back, but continued speaking. "Does it interest you that Pcharky designed his own cage?"

"He designed it? Is it a prison?"

"Yes."

"If he designed it . . . how does it hold him?"

"He knew he'd have to serve my purposes if he were to remain alive."

She had come to another door which opened onto a narrow stairway. It climbed to the left around the cage room. They emerged into a long hallway lined with narrow doors dimly lighted by tiny overhead bulbs. Jedrik opened one of these doors and led the way into a carpeted room about four meters wide and six long. Dark wood panels reached from floor to waist level, shelves loaded with books above. McKie peered closely: books . . . actual paper books. He tried to recall where he'd ever before seen such a collection of primitive . . . But, of course, these were not primitive. These were one of Dosadi's strange recapitulations.

Jedrik had removed her wig, stopped midway in the room to turn and face McKie.

"This is my room. Toilet there." She pointed to an opening between shelves. "That window . . ." Again, she pointed, this time to an opening opposite the toilet door. ". . . is one-way to admit light, and it's our best. As Dosadi measures such things, this is a relatively secure place."

He swept his gaze around the room.

Her room?

McKie was struck by the amount of living space, a mark of power on Dosadi; the absence of people in the hall. By the standards of this planet, Jedrik's room, this building, represented a citadel of power.

Jedrik spoke, an odd note of nervousness in voice and manner.

"Until recently, I also had other quarters: a prestigious apartment on the slopes of the Council Hills. I was considered a climber with excellent prospects, my own skitter and driver. I had access to all but the highest codes in the master banks, and that's a powerful tool for those who can use it. Now . . ." She gestured. ". . . this is what I have chosen. I must eat swill with the lowest. No males of rank will pay the slightest attention to me. Broey thinks I'm cowering somewhere, a pallet in the Warrens. But I have this . . ." Again, that sweeping gesture. ". . . and this." One finger tapped her head. "I need nothing more to bring those Council Hills crashing down."

She stared into McKie's eyes.

He found himself believing her.

She was not through speaking.

"You're definitely male Human, McKie."

He didn't know what to make of that, but her air of braggadocio fascinated him.

"How did you lose that other . . ."

"I didn't lose it. I threw it away. I no longer needed it. I've made things move faster than our precious Elector, or even your people, can anticipate. Broey thinks to wait for an opening against me?" She shook her head.

Captivated, McKie watched her cross to the window, open a ventilator above it. She kicked a wooden knob below the adjoining bookshelves, pulled out a section of paneling which trailed a double bed. Standing across the bed from McKie, she began to undress. She dropped the wig to the floor, slipped off the coveralls, peeled the bulging inner disguise from her flesh. Her skin was pale cream.

"McKie, I am your teacher."

He remained silent. She was long waisted, slim, and graceful. The creamy skin was marked by two faint scars to the left of the pubic wedge.

"Take off your clothes," she said.

He swallowed.

She shook her head.

"McKie, McKie, to survive here you must become Dosadi. You don't have much time. Get your clothes off."

Not knowing what to expect, McKie obeyed.

She watched him carefully.

"Your skin is lighter than I expected where the sun has not darkened you. We will bleach the skin of your face and hands tomorrow."

McKie looked at his hands, at the sharp line where his cuffs had protected his arms. Dark skin. He recalled Bahrank talking of dark skin and a place called Pylash Gate. To mask the unusual shyness he felt, he looked at Jedrik, asked about Pylash Gate.

"So Bahrank mentioned that? Well, it was a stupid mistake. The Rim sent in shock troops and foolish orders were given for the gate's defenses. Only one troop survived there, all dark-skinned like you. The suspicion of treachery was natural."

"Oh."

He found his attention compelled toward the bed. A dark maroon spread covered it.

Jedrik approached him around the foot of the bed. She stopped less than a hand's width away from him . . . creamy flesh, full breasts. He looked up into her eyes. She stood half a head over him, an expression of cold amusement on her face.

McKie found the musky smell of her erotically stimulating. She looked down, saw this, laughed, and abruptly hurled him onto the bed. She landed with him and her body was all over him, hot and hard and demanding.

It was the strangest sexual experience of McKie's life. Not lovemaking, but violent attack. She groaned, bit at him, clawed. And when he tried to caress her, she became even more violent, frenzied. Through it all, she was oddly careful of his pleasure, watching his reactions, reading him. When it was over, he lay back, spent. Jedrik sat up on the edge of the bed. The blankets were a twisted mess. She grabbed a blanket, threw it across the room, stood up, whirled back to look down at him.

"You are very sly and tricky, McKie."

He drew in a trembling breath, remained silent.

"You tried to catch me with softness," she accused. "Better than you have tried that with me. It will not work."

McKie marshalled the energy to sit up and restore some order to the bed. His shoulder pained him where she'd scratched. He felt the ache of a bite on his neck. He crawled into the bed, pulled the blankets up to his chin. She was a madwoman, absolutely mad. Insane.

Presently, Jedrik stopped looking at him. She recovered the blanket from across the room, spread it on the bed, joined him. He was acutely conscious of her staring at him with an openly puzzled frown.

"Tell me about the relationships between men and women on your worlds."

He recounted a few of the love stories he knew, fighting all the while to stay awake. It was difficult to stifle the gaping yawns. She kept punching his shoulder.

"I don't believe it. You're making this up."

"No . . . no. It's true."

"You have women of your own there?"

"Women of my . . . Well, it's not like that, not ownership . . . ahhh, not possession."

"What about children?"

"What about them?"

"How're they treated, educated?"

He sighed, sketched in some details from his own childhood.

After a while she let him go to sleep. He awakened several times during the night, conscious of the strange room and bed, of Jedrik breathing softly beside him. Once, he thought he felt her shoulders shaking with repressed sobs.

Shortly before dawn, there was a scream in the next block, a terrifying sound of agony loud enough to waken all but the most hardened or the most fatigued. McKie, awake and thinking, felt Jedrik's breathing change. He lay tense and watchful, awaiting a repetition or another sound which might explain that eerie scream. A threatening silence gripped the night. McKie built an image in his mind of what could be happening in the buildings around them: some people starting from sleep not knowing (perhaps not caring) what had awakened them; lighter sleepers grumbling and sinking back into restless slumber.

Finally, McKie sat up, peered into the room's shadows. His disquiet communicated itself to Jedrik. She rolled over, looked up at him in the pale dawn light now creeping into the shadows.

"There are many noises in the Warrens that you learn to ignore," she said.

Coming from her, it was almost conciliatory, almost a gesture of apology, of friendship.

"Someone screamed," he said.

"I knew it must be something like that."

"How can you sleep through such a sound?"

"I didn't."

"But how can you ignore it?"

"The sounds you ignore are those which aren't immediately threatening to you, those which you can do nothing about."

"Someone was hurt."

"Very likely. But you must not burden your soul with things you cannot change."

"Don't you want to change . . . that?"

"I am changing it."

Her tone, her attitude were those of a lecturer in a schoolroom, and now there was no doubt that she was being deliberately helpful. Well, she'd said she was his teacher. And he must become completely Dosadi to survive.

"How're you changing things?"

"You're not capable of understanding yet. I want you to take it one step at a time, one lesson at a time."

He couldn't help asking himself then:

What does she want from me now?

He hoped it was not more sex.

"Today," she said, "I want you to meet the parents of three children who work in our cell."

If you think of yourselves as helpless and ineffectual, it is certain that you will create a despotic government to be your master. The wise despot, therefore, maintains among his subjects a popular sense that they are helpless and ineffectual

—The Dosadi Lesson: A Gowachin Assessment

Aritch studied Ceylang carefully in the soft light of his green-walled relaxation room. She had come down immediately after the evening meal, responsive to his summons. They both knew the reason for that summons: to discuss the most recent report concerning McKie's behavior on Dosadi.

The old Gowachin waited for Ceylang to seat herself, observing how she pulled the red robe neatly about her lower extremities. Her features appeared composed, the fighting mandibles relaxed in their folds. She seemed altogether a figure of secure competence, a Wreave of the ruling classes—not that Wreaves recognized such classes. It disturbed Aritch that Wreaves tested for survival only through a complex understanding of sentient behavior, rigid performance standards based on ancient ritual, whose actual origins could only be guessed; there was no written record.

But that's why we chose her.

Aritch grunted, then:

"What can you say about the report?"

"McKie learns rapidly."

Her spoken Galach had a faint sibilance.

Aritch nodded.

"I would say rather that he *adapts* rapidly. It's why we chose him."

"I've heard you say he's more Gowachin than the Gowachin."

"I expect him soon to be more Dosadi than the Dosadi."

"If he survives."

"There's that, yes. Do you still hate him?"

"I have never hated him. You do not understand the spectrum of Wreave emotions."

"Enlighten me."

"He has violated my essential pride of self. This requires a specific reaction in kind. Hate would only dull my abilities."

"But *I* was the one who gave you the orders which had to be countermanded."

"My oath of service to the Gowachin contains a specific injunction, that I cannot hold any one of my teachers responsible for either understanding or obeying the Wreave protocols of courtesy. It is the same injunction which frees us to serve McKie's Bureau."

"You do not consider McKie one of your teachers?"

She studied him for a moment, then:

"Not only do I exclude him, but I know him to be one who has learned much about our protocols."

"What if I were to say he is one of your teachers?"

Again, she stared at him.

"I would revise my estimations of him—and of you."

Aritch took a deep breath.

"Yet, you must learn McKie as though you lived in his skin. Otherwise, you will fail us."

"I will not fail you. I know the reasons you chose me. Even McKie will know in time. He dares not spill my blood in the Courtarena, or even subject me to public shame. Were he to do either of these things, half the Wreave universe would go hunting him with death in their mandibles."

Aritch shook his head slowly from side to side.

"Ceylang! Didn't you hear him warn you that you must shed your Wreave skin?"

She was a long time responding and he noted the subtle characteristics which he'd been told were the Wreave adjustments to anger: a twitching of the jowls, tension in the pedal bifurcations . . .

Presently, she said:

"Tell me what that means, Teacher."

"You will be charged with performing under *Gowachin* Law, performing as though you were another McKie. He adapts! Haven't you observed this? He is capable of defeating you—and us—in such a way, *in such a way* that your Wreave universe would shower him with adulation for his victory. That cannot be permitted. Too much is at stake."

Ceylang trembled and showed other signs of distress.

"But I am Wreave!"

"If it comes to the Courtarena, you no longer can be Wreave."

She inhaled several shallow breaths, composed herself.

"If I become too much McKie, aren't you afraid I might hesitate to slay him?"

"McKie would not hesitate."

She considered this.

"Then there's only one reason you chose me for this task." He waited for her to say it.

"Because we Wreaves are the best in the universe at learning the behavior of others—both overt and covert."

"And you dare not rely on any supposed inhibitions he may or may not have!"

After a long pause, she said:

"You are a better teacher than I'd suspected. Perhaps you're even better than *you* suspected."

"Their law! It is a dangerous foundation for nonauthentic traditions. It is no more than a device to justify false ethics!"

—Gowachin comment on ConSentient Law

While they dressed in the dim dawn light coming through the single window, McKie began testing what Jedrik meant by being his teacher.

"Will you answer any question I ask about Dosadi?"

"No."

Then what areas would she withhold from him? He saw it at once: those areas where she gained and held personal power.

"Will anyone resent it that we . . . had sex together?"

"Resent? Why should anyone resent that?"

"I don't . . ."

"Answer my question!"

"Why do I have to answer your every question?"

"To stay alive."

"You already know everything I . . ."

She brushed this aside.

"So the people of your ConSentiency sometimes resent the sexual relationships of others. They are not sure, then, how they use sex to hold power over others."

He blinked. Her quick, slashing analysis was devastating. She peered at him.

"McKie, what can you do here without me? Don't you know yet that the ones who sent you intended you to die here?"

"Or survive in my own peculiar way."

She considered this. It was another idea about McKie which she had put aside for later evaluation. Indeed, he might well have hidden talents which her questions had not yet exposed. What annoyed her now was the sense that she didn't know enough about the ConSentiency to explore this. Could not take the time right now to explore it. His response disturbed her. It was as though everything she could possibly do had already been decided for her by powers of which she knew next to nothing. They were leading her by the nose, perhaps, just as she led Broey . . . just as those mysterious Gowachin of the ConSentiency obviously had led McKie . . . poor McKie. She cut this short as unprofitable speculation. Obviously, she had to begin at once to search out McKie's talent. Whatever she discovered would reveal a great deal about his ConSentiency.

"McKie, I hold a great deal of power among the Humans and even among some Gowachin in the Warrens—and elsewhere. To do this, I must maintain certain fighting forces, including those who fight with physical weapons."

He nodded. Her tone was that of lecturing to a child, but he accepted this, recognizing the care she took with him.

"We will go first," she said, "to a nearby training area where we maintain the necessary edge on one of my forces."

Turning, she led him out into the hall and down a stairway which avoided the room of the cage. McKie was reminded of Pcharky, though, thinking about that gigantic expenditure of space with its strange occupant.

"Why do you keep Pcharky caged?" he asked, addressing Jedrik's back.

"So I can escape."

She refused to elaborate on this odd answer.

Presently, they emerged into a courtyard nestled into the solid walls of towering buildings. Only a small square of sky was visible directly overhead and far away. Artificial lighting from tubes along the walls provided an adequate illumination. It revealed two squads facing each other in the center of the courtyard. They were Humans, both male and female; all carried weapons: a tube of some sort with a wandlike protrusion from the end near their bodies. Several other Humans stood at observation positions around the two squads. There was a guard station with a desk at the door through which McKie and Jedrik had emerged.

"That's an assault force," Jedrik said, indicating the squads in the courtyard. She turned and consulted with the two young men at the guard station.

McKie made a rough count of the squads: about two hundred. It was obvious that everything had stopped because of Jedrik's presence. He thought the force was composed of striplings barely blooded in Dosadi's cruel necessities. This forced him to a reevaluation of his own capabilities.

From Jedrik's manner with the two men, McKie guessed she knew them well. They paid close attention to everything she said. They, too, struck him as too young for responsibility.

The training area was another matter. It bore a depressing similarity to other such facilities he'd seen in the backwaters of the ConSentiency. War games were a constant lure among several species, a lure which BuSab had managed thus far to channel into such diversions as weapons fetishes.

Through the omnipresent stink, McKie smelled the faint aroma of cooking. He sniffed.

Turning to him, Jedrik spoke:

"The trainees have just been fed. That's part of their pay."

It was as though she'd read his mind, and now she watched him for some reaction.

McKie glanced around the training area. They'd just been fed here? There wasn't a scrap or crumb on the ground. He thought back to the restaurant, belatedly aware of a fastidious care with food that he'd seen and passed right over.

Again, Jedrik demonstrated the ease with which she read his reactions, his very thoughts.

"Nothing wasted," she said.

She turned away.

McKie looked where her attention went. Four women stood at the far side of the courtyard, weapons in their hands. Abruptly, McKie focused on the woman to the left, a competent-looking female of middle years. She was carrying a . . . it couldn't be, but . . .

Jedrik headed across the courtyard toward the woman. McKie followed, peered closely at the woman's weapon. It was an enlarged version of the pentrate from his kit! Jedrik spoke briefly to the woman.

"Is that the new one?"

"Yes. Stiggy brought it up this morning."

"Useful?"

"We think so. It focuses the explosion with somewhat more concentration than our equipment."

"Good. Carry on."

There were more training cadre near the wall behind the women. One, an older man with one arm, tried to catch Jedrik's attention as she led McKie toward a nearby door.

"Could you tell us when we . . ."

"Not now."

In the passage beyond the door, Jedrik turned and confronted McKie.

"Your impressions of our training? Quick!"

"Not sufficiently versatile."

She'd obviously probed for his most instinctive reaction, demanding the gut response unmonitored by reason. The answer brought a glowering expression to her face, an emotional candor which he was not to appreciate until much later. Presently, she nodded.

"They are a commando. More functions of a commando should be interchangeable. Wait here."

She returned to the training area. McKie, watching through the open door, saw her speak to the woman with the pentrate. When Jedrik returned, she nodded to McKie with an expression of approval.

"Anything else?"

"They're awfully damned young. You should have a few seasoned officers among them to put a rein on dangerous impetuosity."

"Yes, I've already set that in motion. Hereafter, McKie,

I want you to come out with me every morning for about an hour. Watch the training, but don't interfere. Report your reactions to me"

He nodded. Clearly, she considered him useful and that was a step in the right direction. But it was an idiotic assignment. These violent infants possessed weapons which could make Dosadi uninhabitable. There was an atavistic excitement in the situation, though. He couldn't deny that. Something in the Human psyche responded to mass violence—really, to violence of any sort. It was related to Human sexuality, an ancient stirring from the most primitive times.

Jedrik was moving on, however.

"Stay close."

They were climbing an inside stairway now and McKie, hurrying to keep up, found his thoughts locked on that pentrate in the hands of one of Jedrik's people. The speed with which they'd copied and enlarged it dazzled him. It was another demonstration of why Aritch feared Dosadi.

At the top of the stairs, Jedrik rapped briefly at a door. A male voice said, "Come in."

The door swung open, and McKie found himself presently in a small, unoccupied room with an open portal at the far wall into what appeared to be a larger, well-lighted area. Voices speaking so softly as to be unintelligible came from there. A low table and five cramped chairs occupied the small room. There were no windows, but a frosted overhead fixture provided shadowless illumination. A large sheet of paper with colored graph lines on it covered the low table.

A swish of fabric brought McKie's attention to the open portal. A short, slender woman in a white smock, grey hair, and the dark, penetrating stare of someone accustomed to command entered, followed by a slightly taller man in the same white. He looked older than the woman, except his hair remained a lustrous black. His eyes, too, held that air of command. The woman spoke.

"Excuse the delay, Jedrik. We've been changing the summation. There's now no point where Broey can anticipate and change the transition from riots to full-scale warfare."

McKie was surprised by the abject deference in her voice. This woman considered herself to be far below Jedrik. The man took the same tone, gesturing to chairs.

"Sit down, please. This chart is our summation."

As the woman turned toward him, McKie caught a strong whiff of something pungent on her breath, a not unfamiliar smell. He'd caught traces of it several times in their passage through the Warrens. She went on speaking as Jedrik and McKie slipped into chairs.

"This is not unexpected." She indicated the design on the paper.

The man intruded.

"We've been telling you for some time now that Tria is ready to come over."

"She's trouble," Jedrik said.

"But Gar . . ."

It was the woman, arguing, but Jedrik cut her off.

"I know: Gar does whatever she tells him to do. The daughter runs the father. He thinks she's the most wonderful thing that ever happened, able to . . ."

"Her abilities are not the issue," the man said.

The woman spoke eagerly.

"Yes, it's her influence on Gar that . . ."

"Neither of them anticipated my moves," Jedrik said, "but I anticipated their moves."

The man leaned across the table, his face close to Jedrik's. He appeared suddenly to McKie like a large, dangerous animal—dangerous because his actions could never be fully predicted. His hands twitched when he spoke.

"We've told you every detail of our findings, every source, every conclusion. Now, are you saying you don't share our assessment of . . ."

"You don't understand," Jedrik said.

The woman had drawn back. Now, she nodded.

Jedrik said:

"It isn't the first time I've had to reassess your conclusions. Hear me: Tria will leave Broey when she's ready, not when he's ready. It's the same for anyone she serves, even Gar."

They spoke in unison:

"Leave Gar?"

"Leave anyone. Tria serves only Tria. Never forget that. Especially don't forget it if she comes over to us."

The man and woman were silent.

McKie thought about what Jedrik had said. Her words were another indication that someone on Dosadi might have other than personal aims. Jedrik's tone was unmistakable: she censured and distrusted Tria because Tria served *only* selfish ambition. Therefore, Jedrik (and this other pair by inference) served some unstated mutual purpose. Was it a form of patriotism they served, species-oriented? BuSab agents were always alert for this dangerous form of tribal madness, not necessarily to suppress it, but to make certain it did not explode into a violence deadly to the ConSentiency.

The white-smocked woman, after mulling her own thoughts, spoke:

"If Tria can't be enlisted for . . . what I mean is, we can use her own self-serving to hold her." She corrected herself. "Unless you believe we cannot convince her we'll overcome Broey." She chewed at her lip, a fearful expression in her eyes.

A shrewd look came over Jedrik's face.

"What is it you suspect?"

The woman pointed to the chart on the table.

"Gar still shares in the major decisions. That shouldn't be, but it is. If he . . ."

The man spoke with subservient eagerness.

"He has some hold on Broey!"

The woman shook her head.

"Or Broey plays a game other than the one we anticipated."

Jedrik looked at the woman, the man, at McKie. She spoke as though to McKie, but McKie realized she was addressing the air.

"It's a specific thing. Gar has revealed something to Broey. I know what he's revealed. Nothing else could force Broey to behave this way." She nodded at the chart. "We *have* them!"

The woman ventured a question.

"Have we done well?"

"Better than you know."

The man smiled, then:

"Perhaps this is the time to ask if we could have larger rooms. The damn' children are always moving the furniture. We bump . . ."

"Not now!"

Jedrik arose. McKie followed her example.

"Let me see the children," Jedrik said.

The man turned to the open portal.

"Get out here, you! Jedrik wants you!"

Three children came scurrying from the other room. The woman didn't even look at them. The man favored them with an angry glare. He spoke to Jedrik.

"They've brought no food into this house in almost a week."

McKie studied the children carefully as he saw Jedrik was doing. They stood in a row just inside the room and, from their expressions, it was impossible to tell their reaction to the summons. They were two girls and a boy. The one on the right, a girl, was perhaps nine; on the left, another girl, was five or six. The boy was somewhat older, perhaps twelve or thirteen. He favored McKie with a glance. It was the glance of a predator who recognizes ready prey, but who already has eaten. All three bore more resemblance to the woman than to the man, but the parentage was obvious: the eyes, the set of the ears, nose . . .

Jedrik had completed her study. She gestured to the boy. "Start sending him to the second training team."

"About time," the woman said. "We'll be glad to get him out of here."

"Come along, McKie."

In the hall, Jedrik said:

"To answer your question, they're pretty typical."

McKie, who had only wondered silently, swallowed in a dry throat. The petty goals of these people: to get a bigger room where they could live without bumping into furniture. He'd sensed no affection for each other in that couple. They were companions of convenience. There had been not the smallest hint of emotion for each other when they spoke. McKie found it difficult to imagine them making love, but apparently they did. They had produced three children.

Realization came like an explosion in his head. Of course they showed no emotion! What other protection did they have? On Dosadi, anything cared for was a club to beat you into somebody else's line. And there was another thing.

McKie spoke to Jedrik's back as they went down the stairs.

"That couple—they're addicted to something."

Surprisingly, Jedrik stopped, looked back up at him.

"How else do you think I hold such a pair? The substance is called *dis*. It's very rare. It comes from the far mountains, far beyond the . . . far beyond. The Rim sends parties of children as bearers to obtain *dis* for me. In a party of fifty, thirty can expect to die on such a trek. Do you get the measure of it, McKie?"

Once more, they headed down the stairs.

McKie, realizing she'd taken the time to teach him another lesson about Dosadi, could only follow, stunned, while she led him into a room where technicians bleached the sun-darkened areas of his skin.

When they emerged, he no longer carried the stigma of Pylash Gate.

When the means of great violence are widespread nothing is more dangerous to the powerful than that they create outrage and injustice, for outrage and injustice will certainly ignite retaliation in kind.

—BuSab Manual

I t is no longer classifiable as rioting," the aide said.

He was a short Gowachin with pinched features, and he looked across the room to where Broey sat facing a dead communicator. There was a map on the wall behind the aide, its colors made brilliant by harsh morning light coming in the east windows. Below the map, a computer terminal jutted from the wall. Occasionally it clicked.

Gar came into the room from the hall, peered around as though looking for someone, left.

Broey noted the intrusion, glanced at the map.

"Still no sign of where she's gone to ground?"

"Nothing certain."

"The one who paraded McKie through the streets . . ."

"Clearly an expendable underling."

"Where did they go?"

The aide indicated a place on the map, a group of buildings in the Warrens to the northwest.

Broey stared at the blank face of his communications screen. He'd been tricked again. He knew it. That damnable Human female! Violence in the city teetered on the edge of full-scale war: Gowachin against Human. And still nothing, not even a hint at the location of Gar's Rim stores, the blasphemous factories. It was an unstable condition which could not continue much longer.

His communications screen came alive with a report: violent fighting near Gate Twenty-One. Broey glanced at the map. That made it more than one hundred clearly defined battles between the species along an unresolved perimeter. The report spoke of new weapons and unsuccessful attempts to capture specimens.

Gate Twenty-One?

That wasn't far from the place where McKie had been paraded through . . .

Several things slipped into a new relationship in Broey's mind. He looked at his aide, who stood waiting obediently at the map.

"Where's Gar?"

Aides were summoned, sent running. Gar was not to be found.

"Tria?"

She, too, was unavailable.

Gar's fanatics remained neutral, but more of Jedrik's pattern was emerging. Everything pointed to an exquisite understanding of the weakness implicit in the behavior of Gar and Tria.

And I thought I was the only one who saw that!

Broey hesitated.

Why would the God not speak to him other than to say "I am watched."

Broey felt tricked and betrayed in his innermost being. This had a cleansing effect on his reason. He could only depend on himself. And he began to sense a larger pattern in Jedrik's behavior. Was it possible that Jedrik shared *his* goals? The possibility excited him.

He looked at the aides who'd come running with the negative information about Gar and Tria, began to snap orders.

"Get our people out of all those Warrens, except that corridor to the northeast. Reinforce that area. Everyone else fall back to the secondary walls. Let no Humans inside that perimeter. Block all gates. Get moving!"

This last was shouted as his aides hesitated.

Perhaps it already was too late. He realized now that he'd allowed Jedrik to bait and distract him. It was clear that she'd created in her mind an almost perfect simulation model of Broey. And she'd done it from a Liaitor position! Incredible. He could almost feel sorry for Gar and Tria. They were like puppets dancing to Jedrik's strings.

I was no better.

It came over him that Jedrik's simulation probably encompassed this very moment of realization. Admiration for her permeated him.

Superb!

Quietly, he issued orders for the sequestering of Gowachin females within the inner Graluz bastions which he'd had the foresight to prepare. His people would thank him for that.

Those who survived the next few hours.

The attack by those who want to die—this is the attack against which you cannot prepare a perfect defense.

—Human aphorism

By the third morning, McKie felt that he might have lived all of his life on Dosadi. The place demanded every element of attention he could muster.

He stood alone in Jedrik's room, staring absently at the unmade bed. She expected him to put the place in order before her return. He knew that. She'd told him to wait here and had gone away on urgent business. He could only obey.

Concerns other than an unmade bed distracted him, though. He felt now that he understood the roots of Aritch's fears. The Gowachin of Tandaloor might very well destroy this place, even if they knew that by doing so they blasted open that bloody region where every sentient hid his most secret fears. He could see this clearly now. How the Running Phylum expected him to avoid that monstrous decision was a more elusive matter.

There were secrets here.

McKie sensed Dosadi like a malignant organism beneath his feet, jealously keeping those secrets from him. This place was the enemy of the ConSentiency, but he found himself emotionally siding with Dosadi. It was betrayal of BuSab, of his Legum oath, everything. But he could not prevent that feeling or recognition of it. In the course of only a few generations, Dosadi had become a particular thing. Monstrous? Only if you held to your own precious myths. Dosadi might be the greatest cleansing force the ConSentiency had ever experienced.

The whole prospect of the ConSentiency had begun to sicken him. And Aritch's Gowachin. Gowachin Law? Stuff Gowachin Law!

It was quiet in Jedrik's room. Painfully quiet.

He knew that out on the streets of Chu there was violent warfare between Gowachin and Human. Wounded had been rushed through the training courtyard while he was there with Jedrik. Afterward, she'd taken him to her command post, a room across the hall and above Pcharky's cage. He'd stood nearby, watched her performance as though she were a star on an entertainment circuit and he a member of the audience. It was fascinating. *Broey will do this. Broey will give that order.* And each time, the reports revealed how precisely she had anticipated her opponent

Occasionally, she mentioned Gar or Tria. He was able to detect the subtle difference in her treatment of that pair.

On their second night together, Jedrik had aroused his sexual appetites softly, deftly. She had treated him to a murmurous compliance, and afterward had leaned over him on an elbow to smile coldly.

"You see, McKie: I can play your game."

Shockingly, this had opened an area of awareness within him which he'd not even suspected. It was as though she'd held up his entire previous life to devastating observation.

And *he* was the observer!

Other beings formed lasting relationships and operated from a secure emotional base. But he was a product of BuSab, the Gowachin . . . and much that had gone before. It had become increasingly obvious to him why the Gowachin had chosen him to groom for this particular role.

I was damaged and they could rebuild me the way they wanted!

Well, the Gowachin could still be surprised by what they produced. Dosadi was evidence of that. They might not even suspect what they'd actually produced in McKie.

He was bitter with a bitterness he knew must've been fermenting in him for years. The loneliness of his own life with its central dedication to BuSab had been brought to a head by the loneliness of this imprisoned planet. An incredible jumble of emotions had sorted themselves out, and he felt new purpose burning within him.

Power!

Ahhhh . . . that was how it felt to be Dosadi!

He'd turned away from Jedrik's cold smile, pulled the blankets around his shoulder.

Thank you, loving teacher.

Such thoughts roamed through his mind as he stood alone in the room the following day and began to make the bed. After her revelation, Jedrik had resumed her interest in his memories, napping only to awaken him with more questions.

In spite of his sour outlook, he still felt it his duty to examine her behavior in every possible light his imagination could produce. Nothing about Dosadi was too absurd. He had to build a better picture of this society and its driving forces.

Before returning to Jedrik's room, he'd made another tour of the training courtyard with her. There'd been more new weapons adapted from his kit, and he'd realized the courtyard was merely Jedrik's testing ground, that there must be many more training areas for her followers.

McKie had not yet revealed to her that Aritch's people might terminate Dosadi's people with violence. She'd been centering on this at dawn. Even while they shared the tiny toilet cubicle off her room she'd pressed for answers.

For a time, McKie had diverted her with questions about Pcharky. What were the powers in that cage? At one point, he'd startled her.

"Pcharky knows something valuable he hopes to trade for his freedom."

"How'd you know?"

"It's obvious. I'll tell you something else: he came here of his own free will . . . for whatever purpose."

"You learn quickly, McKie."

She was laughing at him and he glared at her.

"All right! I don't know that purpose, but it may be that you only think you know it."

For the briefest flicker, something dangerous glared from her eyes, then:

"Your *jumpdoors* have brought us many fools, but Pcharky is one of the biggest fools. I know why he came. There've been many like him. Now . . . there is only one. Broey, for all of his power, cannot search out his own Pcharky. And Keila Jedrik is the one who frustrates him."

Too late, she realized that McKie had goaded her into this performance. How had he done that? He'd almost found out too much too soon. It was dangerous to underestimate this naive intruder from beyond the God Wall.

Once more, she'd begun probing for things he had not yet revealed. Time had protected him. Aides had come urging an early inspection of the new weapons. They were needed.

Afterward, they'd gone to the command post and then to breakfast in a Warren dining room. All through breakfast, he'd plied her with questions about the fighting. How extensive was it? Could he see some of the prisoners? Were they using the weapons built from the patterns in his kit? Were they winning?

Sometimes she merely ignored his questions. Most of her answers were short, distracted. Yes. No. No. Yes. McKie realized she was answering in monosyllables to fend him off. He was a distraction. Something important had been communicated to her and he'd missed it. Although this angered him, he tried to mask the emotion, striving to penetrate her wall of concern. Oddly, she responded when he changed his line of questioning to the parents of the three children and the conversation there.

"You started to designate a particular place: 'Beyond the . . .' Beyond what?"

"It's something Gar thinks I don't know. He thinks only his death fanatics have that kind of rapport with the Rim."

He stared at her, caught by a sudden thought. By now, he knew much about Gar and Tria. She answered his questions about them with candor, often using him openly to clarify her own thoughts. But—death fanatics?

"Are these fanatics homosexual?"

She pounced.

"How'd you know?"

"A guess."

"What difference would it make?"

"Are they?"

"Yes."

McKie shuddered.

She was peremptory.

"Explain!"

"When Humans for any reason go terminal where survival of their species is concerned, it's relatively easy to push them the short step further into *wanting* to die."

"You speak from historical evidence?"

"Yes."

"Example."

"With rare exceptions, primitive Humans of the tribal eras reserved their homosexuals as the ultimate shock troops of desperation. They were the troops of last resort, sent into battle as berserkers who expected, who *wanted*, to die."

She had to have the term *berserkers* explained, then showed by her manner that she believed him. She considered this, then:

"What does your ConSentiency do about this susceptibility?"

"We take sophisticated care to guide all natural sexual variants into constructive survival activities. We protect them from the kinds of pressures which might tip them over into behavior destructive of the species."

Only later had McKie realized she had not answered his question: *beyond what?* She'd rushed him off to a conference room where more than twenty Humans were assembled, including the two parents who'd made the chart about Tria and Gar. McKie realized he didn't even know their names.

It put him at a disadvantage not knowing as many of these people by sight and name as he should. They, of course, had ready memories of everyone important around them and, when they used a name, often did it with such blurred movement into new subjects that he was seldom sure who had been named. He saw the key to it, though. Their memories were anchored in explicit references to relative abilities of those around them, relative dangers. And it wasn't so much that they concealed their emotions as that they *managed* their emotions. Nowhere in their memories could there be any emotive clouding such as thoughts of love or friendship. Such things weakened you. Everything operated on the strict basis of *quid pro quo*, and you'd better have the cash ready—whatever that cash might be. McKie, pressed all around by questions from the people in the conference room, knew he had only one real asset: he was a key they might use to open the God Wall. Very important asset, but unfortunately owned by an idiot.

Now, they wanted his information about death fanatics. They milked him dry, then sent him away like a child who has performed for his elders but is sent to his room when important matters are brought up for discussion.

The more control, the more that requires control. This is the road to chaos.

By the fourth morning of the battle for Chu, Tria was in a vile humor. Her forces had established lines holding about one-eighth of the total Warren territory, mostly low buildings, except along Broey's corridor to the Rim. She did not like the idea that Jedrik's people held an unobstructed view down onto most of the death fanatics' territory. And most of those leaders who'd thrown in their lot with Tria were beginning to have second thoughts, especially since they'd come to realize that this enclave had insufficient food production facilities to maintain itself. The population density she'd been forced to accept was frightening: almost triple the Warren norm.

Thus far, neither Broey nor Jedrik had moved in force against her. Tria had finally been brought to the inescapable conclusion that she and Gar were precisely where Jedrik wanted them. They'd been cut out of Broey's control as neatly and cleanly as though by a knife. There was no going back. Broey would never accept Human help under present circumstances. That, too, spoke of the exquisite care with which Jedrik had executed her plan.

Tria had moved her command post during the night to a high building which faced the canyon walls to the north. Only the river, with a single gate under it, separated her from the Rim. She'd slept badly, her mind full of worries. Chief among her worries was the fact that none of the contact parties she'd sent out to the Rim had returned. There'd been no fires on the Rim ledges during the night. No word from *any* of her people out there.

Why?

Once more, she contemplated her position, seeking some advantage, any advantage. One of her lines was anchored on Broey's corridor to the Rim, one line on the river wall with its single gate, and the rest of her perimeter meandered through a series of dangerous salients from the fifth wall to the river.

She could hear sounds of battle along the far side of Broey's corridor. Jedrik's people used weapons which made a great deal of noise. Occasionally, an explosive projectile landed in Tria's enclave. These were rare, but she'd taken casualties and the effect on morale was destructive. That was a major problem with fanatics: they demanded to be used, to be wasted.

Tria stared down at the river, aware of the bodies drifting on its poison currents—both Human and Gowachin bodies, but more Gowachin than Human. Presently, she turned away from the scene, padded into the next room, and roused Gar.

"We must contact Jedrik," she said.

He rubbed sleep from his eyes.

"No! We must wait until we make contact with our people on the Rim. Then we can . . ."

"Faaaaa!"

She'd seldom showed that much disgust with him.

"We're not going to make contact with our people on the Rim. Jedrik and Broey have seen to that. It wouldn't surprise me if they were cooperating to isolate us."

"But we've . . ."

"Shut up, Father!" She held up her hands, stared at them. "I was never really good enough to be one of Broey's chief advisors. I always suspected that. I always pressed too hard. Last night, I reviewed as many of my decisions as I could. Jedrik deliberately made me look good. She did it oh so beautifully!"

"But our forces on the Rim . . ."

"May not be ours! They may be Jedrik's."

"Even the Gowachin?"

"Even the Gowachin."

Gar could hear a ringing in his ears. Contact Jedrik? Throw away all of their power?

"I'm good enough to recognize the weakness of a force such as ours," Tria said. "We can be goaded into spending ourselves uselessly. Even Broey didn't see that, but Jedrik obviously did. Look at the salients along her perimeter!"

"What have salients . . ."

"They can be pinched off and obliterated! Even *you* must see that."

"Then pull back and . . ."

"Reduce our territory?" She stared at him, aghast. "If I even intimate I'm going to do that, our auxiliaries will desert wholesale. Right now they're . . ."

"Then attack!"

"To gain what?"

Gar nodded. Jedrik would fall back across mined areas, blast the fanatics out of existence. She held enough territory that she could afford such destruction. Clearly, she'd planned on it.

"Then we must pinch off Broey's corridor."

"That's what Jedrik wants us to do. It's the only negotiable counter we have left. That's why we must contact Jedrik."

Gar shook his head in despair.

Tria was not finished, though.

"Jedrik might restore us to a share of power in the Rim city if we bargain for it now. Broey would never do that. Do you understand now the mistake you made with Broey?"

"But Broey was going to . . ."

"You failed to follow my orders, Father. You must see now why I always tried to keep you from making independent decisions."

Gar fell into abashed silence. This was his daughter, but he could sense his peril.

Tria spoke.

"I will issue orders presently to all of our commanders.

They will be told to hold at all costs. They will be told that you and I will try to contact Jedrik. They will be told why."

"But how can . . ."

"We will permit ourselves to be captured."

QUESTION: Who governs the governors?
ANSWER: Entropy.

—Gowachin riddle

Many things conspired to frustrate McKie. Few people other than Jedrik answered his questions. Most responded as though to a cretin. Jedrik treated him as though he were a child of unknown potential. At times, he knew he amused her. Other times, she punished him with an angry glance, by ignoring him, or just by going away—or worse, sending him away.

It was now late afternoon of the fifth day in the battle for Chu, and Broey's forces still held out in the heart of the city with their slim corridor to the Rim. He knew this from reports he'd overheard. He stood in a small room off Jedrik's command post, a room containing four cots where, apparently she and/or her commanders snatched occasional rest. One tall, narrow window looked out to the south Rim. McKie found it difficult to realize that he'd come across that Rim just six days previously.

Clouds had begun to gather over the Rim's terraced escarpments, a sure sign of a dramatic change in the weather. He knew that much, at least, from his Tandaloor briefings. Dosadi had no such thing as weather control. Awareness of this left him feeling oddly vulnerable. Nature could be so damnably capricious and dangerous when you had no grip on her vagaries.

McKie blinked, held his breath for a moment.

Vagaries of nature.

The vagaries of sentient nature had moved the Gowachin to set up this experiment. Did they really hope to control that vast, seething conglomerate of motives? Or had they some other reason for Dosadi, a reason which he had not yet penetrated? Was this, after all, a test of Caleban mysteries? He thought not.

He knew the way Aritch and aides *said* they'd set up this experiment. Observations here bore out their explanations. None of that data was consistent with an attempt to understand the Calebans. Only that brief encounter with Pcharky, a thing which Jedrik no longer was willing to discuss.

No matter how he tried, McKie couldn't evade the feeling that something essential lay hidden in the way this planet had been set upon its experimental course; something the Gowachin hadn't revealed, something they perhaps didn't even understand themselves. What'd they done at the beginning? They had this place, Dosadi, the subjects, the Primary . . . yes, the Primary. The inherent inequality of individuals dominated Gowachin minds. And there was that damnable DemoPol. How had they mandated it? Better yet: how did they maintain that mandate?

Aritch's people had hoped to expose the inner workings of sentient social systems. So they said. But McKie was beginning to look at that explanation with Dosadi eyes, with Dosadi scepticism. What had Fannie Mae meant about not being able to leave here in his own body/node? How could he be Jedrik's *key* to the God Wall? McKie knew he needed more information than he could hope to get from Jedrik. Did Broey have this information? McKie wondered if he might in the end have to climb the heights to the Council Hills for his answers. Was that even possible now?

When he'd asked for it, Jedrik had given him almost the run of this building, warning:

"Don't interfere."

Interfere with what?

When he'd asked, she'd just stared at him.

She had, however, taken him around to familiarize everyone with his status. He was never quite sure what that status might be, except that it was somewhere between guest and prisoner.

Jedrik had required minimal conversation with her people. Often, she'd used only hand waves to convey the necessary signals of passage. The whole traverse was a lesson for McKie, beginning with the door-guards.

"McKie." Pointing at him.

The guards nodded.

Jedrik had other concerns.

"Team Nine?"

"Back at noon."

"Send word."

Everyone subjected McKie to a hard scrutiny which he felt certain would let them identify him with minimal interruption.

There were two elevators: one an express from a heavily guarded street entrance on the side of the building, the other starting above the fourth level at the ceiling of Pcharky's cage. They took this one, went up, pausing at each floor for guards to see him.

When they returned to the cage room, McKie saw that a desk had been installed just inside the street door. The father of those three wild children sat there watching Pcharky, making occasional notations in a notebook. McKie had a name for him now, Ardir.

Jedrik paused at the desk.

"McKie can come and go with the usual precautions."

McKie, addressing himself finally to Jedrik, had said:

"Thanks for taking this time with me."

"No need to be sarcastic, McKie."

He had not intended sarcasm and reminded himself once more that the usual amenities of the ConSentiency suffered a different interpretation here.

Jedrik glanced through Ardir's notes, looked up at Pcharky, back to McKie. Her expression did not change.

"We will meet for dinner."

She left him then.

For his part, McKie had approached Pcharky's cage, noting the tension this brought to the room's guards and observers. The old Gowachin sat in his hammock with an indifferent expression on his face. The bars of the cage emitted an almost indiscernible hissing as they shimmered and glowed.

"What happens if you touch the bars?" McKie asked.

The Gowachin jowls puffed in a faint shrug.

McKie pointed.

"There's energy in those bars. What is that energy? How is it maintained?"

Pcharky responded in a hoarse croaking.

"How is the universe maintained? When you first see a thing, is that when it was created?"

"Is it a Caleban thing?"

Shrug.

McKie walked around the cage, studying it. There were glistening bulbs wherever the bars crossed each other. The rods upon which the hammock was suspended came from the ceiling. They penetrated the cage top without touching it. The hammock itself appeared to be fabric. It was faintly blue. He returned to his position facing Pcharky.

"Do they feed you?"

No answer.

Ardir spoke from behind him.

"His food is lowered from the ceiling. His excreta are hosed into the reclamation lines."

McKie spoke over his shoulder.

"I see no door into the cage. How'd he get in there?"

"It was built around him according to his own instructions."

"What are the bulbs where the bars cross?"

"They came into existence when he activated the cage."

"How'd he do that?"

"We don't know. Do you?"

McKie shook his head from side to side.

"How does Pcharky explain this?"

"He doesn't."

McKie had turned away to face Ardir, probing, moving

the focus of questions from Pcharky to the planetary society itself. Ardir's answers, especially on matters of religion and history, were banal.

Later, as he stood in the room off the command post reviewing the experience, McKie found his thoughts touching on a matter which had not even come into question.

Jedrik and her people had known for a long time that Dosadi was a Gowachin creation. They'd known it long before McKie had appeared on the scene. It was apparent in the way they focused on Pcharky, in the way they reacted to Broey. McKie had added one significant datum: that Dosadi was a Gowachin *experiment*. But Jedrik's people were not using him in the ways he might expect. She said he was the key to the God Wall, but how was he that key?

The answer was not to be found in Ardir. That one had not tried to evade McKie's questions, but the answers betrayed a severely limited scope to Ardir's knowledge and imagination.

McKie felt deeply disturbed by this insight. It was not so much what the man said as what he did not say when the reasons for speaking openly in detail were most demanding. Ardir was no dolt. This was a Human who'd risen high in Jedrik's hierarchy. Many speculations would've crossed his mind. Yet he made no mention of even the more obvious speculations. He raised no questions about the way Dosadi history ran to a single cutoff point in the past without any trace of evolutionary beginnings. He did not appear to be a religious person and even if he were, Dosadi would not permit the more blatant religious inhibitions. Yet Ardir refused to explore the most obvious discrepancies in those overt religious attitudes McKie had been told to expect. Ardir played out the right attitudes, but there was no basis for them underneath. It was all surface.

McKie suddenly despaired of ever getting a deep answer from any of these people—even from Jedrik.

An increase in the noise level out in the command post

caught McKie's attention. He opened the door, stood in the doorway to study the other room.

A new map had been posted on the far wall. There was a position board, transparent and covered with yellow, red, and blue dots, over the map. Five women and a man—all wearing earphones—worked the board, moving the colored markers. Jedrik stood with her back to McKie, talking to several commanders who'd just come in from the streets. They still carried their weapons and packs. It was their conversation which had attracted McKie. He scanned the room, noted two communications screens at the left wall, both inactive. They were new since his last view of the room and he wondered at their purpose.

An aide leaned in from the hallway, called out:

"Gate Twenty-One just reported. Everything has quieted there. They want to know if they should keep their reserves on the alert."

"Have them stand down," Jedrik said.

"The two prisoners are being brought here," the aide added.

"I see it," Jedrik said.

She nodded toward the position board.

McKie, following the direction of her gaze, saw two yellow markers being moved with eight blue companions. Without knowing how he understood this, he saw that this must be the prisoners and their escort. There were tensions in the command post which told him this was an important event. Who were those prisoners?

One of Jedrik's commanders spoke.

"I saw the monitor at . . ."

She was not listening to him and he broke off. Two people on the position board exchanged places, trading earphones. The messenger who'd called out the information about the gate and the prisoners had gone. Another messenger came in presently, conferred in a soft voice with people near the door.

In a few moments, eight young Human males entered

carrying Gar and Tria securely trussed with what appeared to be shining wire. McKie recognized the pair from Aritch's briefings. The escort carried their prisoners like so much meat, one at each leg and each arm.

"Over here," Jedrik said, indicating two chairs facing her.

McKie found himself suddenly aware, in an extremely Dosadi way, of many of the nuances here. It filled him with elation.

The escort crossed the room, not bothering to steer clear of all the furniture. The messenger from the hallway delayed his departure, reluctant to leave. He'd recognized the prisoners and knew something important was about to happen.

Gar and Tria were dumped into the two chairs.

"Release their bindings," Jedrik said.

The escort obeyed.

Jedrik waited, staring across at the position board. The two yellow and eight blue markers had been removed. She continued to stare at the board, though. Something there was more important than these two prisoners. She pointed to a cluster of red markers in an upper corner.

"See to that."

One of her commanders left the room.

McKie took a deep breath. He'd spotted the flicker of her movement toward the commander who'd obeyed. So that was how she did it! McKie moved farther into the room to put Jedrik in profile to him. She made no response to his movement, but he knew she was aware of him. He stepped closer to what he saw as the limit of her tolerance, noted a faint smile as she turned toward the prisoners.

There was an abrupt silence, one of those uncomfortable moments when people realize there are things they must do, but everyone is reluctant to start. The messenger still stood by the door to the hall, obviously wanting to see what would happen here. The escort who'd brought the prisoners remained standing in a group at one side. They were almost huddled, as though seeking protection in their own numbers.

Jedrik glanced across at the messenger.

"You may go."

She nodded to the escort.

"And you."

McKie held his cautious distance, waiting, but Jedrik took no notice of him. He saw that he not only would be allowed to stay, but that he was expected to use his wits, his off-world knowledge. Jedrik had read things in his presence: a normal distrust, caution, patience. And the fears, of course.

Jedrik took her time with the prisoners. She leaned forward, examined first Tria, then Gar. From the way she looked at them, it was clear to McKie she weighed many possibilities on how to deal with this pair. She was also building the tensions and this had its effect. Gar broke.

"Broey has a way of describing people such as you," Gar said. "He calls you 'rockets,' which is to say you are like a display which shoots up into the sky—and falls back."

Jedrik grinned.

McKie understood. Gar was not managing his emotions very well. It was a weakness.

"Many rockets in this universe must die unseen," Jedrik said.

Gar glared at her. He didn't like this response, glanced at Tria, saw from her expression that he had blundered.

Tria spoke now, smiling faintly.

"You've taken a personal interest in us, Jedrik."

To McKie, it was as though he'd suddenly crossed a threshold into the understanding of another language. Tria's was a Dosadi statement, carrying many messages. She'd said that Jedrik saw an opportunity for personal gain here and that Tria knew this. The faint smile had been the beginning of the statement. McKie felt a new awe at the special genius of the Dosadi awareness. He moved a step closer. There was something else about Tria . . . something odd.

"What is that one to you?"

Tria spoke to Jedrik, but a flicker of the eyes indicated McKie.

"He has a certain utility," Jedrik said.

"Is that the reason you keep him near you?"

"There's no single reason."

"There've been certain rumors . . ."

"One uses what's available," Jedrik said.

"Did you plan to have children by him?"

Jedrik shook with silent mirth. McKie understood that Tria probed for weaknesses, found none.

"The breeding period is so incapacitating for a female," Tria said.

The tone was deliberately goading, and McKie waited for a response.

Jedrik nodded.

"Offspring produce many repercussions down through the generations. Never a casual decision for those of us who understand."

Jedrik looked at Gar, forcing McKie to shift his attention.

Gar's face went suddenly bland, which McKie interpreted as shock and anger. The man had himself under control quickly, however. He stared at McKie, directed a question to Jedrik.

"Would his death profit us?"

Jedrik glanced at McKie.

Shocked by the directness of the question, McKie was at least as intrigued by the assumptions in Gar's question. "*Us!*" Gar assumed that he and Jedrik had common cause. Jedrik was weighing that assumption and McKie, filled with elation, understood. He also recognized something else and realized he could now repay all of Jedrik's patient teaching. *Tria!*

Something about Tria's way of holding her head, the inflections in her spoken Galach, struck a chord in McKie's memory. Tria was a Human who'd been trained by a PanSpechi—that way of moving the eyes before the head moved, the peculiar emphasis in her speech mannerisms. But there were no PanSpechi on Dosadi. Or were there?

None of this showed on McKie's face. He continued to

radiate distrust, caution, patience. But he began to ask himself if there might be another loose thread in this Dosadi mystery. He saw Jedrik looking at him and, without thinking about it, gave her a purely Dosadi eye signal to follow him, returned to the adjoining room. It was a measure of how she read him that she came without question.

"Yes?"

He told her what he suspected.

"These PanSpechi, they are the ones who can grow a body to simulate that of another species?"

"Except for the eyes. They have faceted eyes. Any PanSpechi who could act freely and simulate another species would be only the surface manifestation. The freely moving one is only one of five bodies; it's the holder of the ego, the identity. This passes periodically to another of the five. It's a PanSpechi crime to prevent that transfer by surgically fixing the ego in only one of the bodies."

Jedrik glanced out the doorway. "You're sure about her?"

"The pattern's there."

"The faceted eyes, can that be disguised?"

"There are ways: contact lenses or a rather delicate operation. I've been trained to detect such things, however, and I can tell you that the one who trained her is not Gar."

She looked at him.

"Broey?"

"A Graluz would be a great place to conceal a creche but . . ." He shook his head. ". . . I don't think so. From what you tell me about Broey . . ."

"Gowachin," she agreed. "Then who?"

"Someone who influenced her when she was quite young."

"Do you wish to interrogate the prisoners?"

"Yes, but I don't know their potential value."

She stared at him in open wonder. His had been an exquisitely penetrating Dosadi-style statement. It was as though a McKie she thought she knew had been transformed suddenly right in front of her eyes. He was not yet sufficiently Dosadi to trust completely, but she'd never expected him to come this far this quickly. He did deserve a more detailed assessment of the military situation and the relative abilities of Tria and Gar. She delivered this assessment in the Dosadi way: barebones words, swift, clipped to an essential spareness which assumed a necessary broad understanding by the listener.

Absorbing this, McKie sensed where she limited her recital, tailoring it for his abilities. In a way, it was similar to a response by his Daily Schedule back on Central Central. He could see himself in her attitudes, read her assessment of him. She was favoring him with a limited, grudging respect tempered by a certain fondness as by a parent toward a child. And he knew that once they returned to the other room, the fondness would be locked under a mask of perfect concealment. It was there, though. It was there. And he dared not betray her trust by counting on that fondness, else it would be locked away forever.

"I'm ready," he said.

They returned to the command post, McKie with a clearer picture of how to operate here. There was no such thing as mutual, unquestioning trust. You always questioned. You always managed. A sort of grudging respect was the nearest they'd reveal openly. They worked together to survive, or when it was overwhelmingly plain that there was personal advantage in mutual action. Even when they united, they remained ultimate individualists. They suspected any gift because no one gave away anything freely. The safest relationships were those in which the niches of the hierarchy were clear and solidly held—minimum threat from above and from below. The whole thing reminded McKie of stories told about behavior in Human bureaucracies of the classical period before deep space travel. And many years before he had encountered a multispecies corporation which had behaved similarly until the ministrations of BuSab had shown them the error of their ways. They'd used every dirty trick available: bribing, spying and other forms of covert and overt espionage, fomenting dissent in the opposition, assassination, blackmail, and kidnapping. Few in the ConSentiency had not heard of InterRealm Supply, now defunct.

McKie stopped three paces from the prisoners.

Tria spoke first.

"Have you decided what to do with us?"

"There's useful potential in both of you," McKie said, "but we have other questions."

The "we" did not escape Tria or Gar. They both looked at Jedrik, who stood impassively at McKie's shoulder.

McKie addressed himself to Gar.

"Is Tria really your daughter, your natural child?"

Tria appeared surprised and, with his new understanding, McKie realized she was telling him she didn't care if he saw this reaction, that it suited her for him to see this. Gar, however, had betrayed a flicker of shock. By Dosadi standards, he was dumbfounded. Then Tria was not his natural daughter, but until this moment, Tria had never questioned their relationship.

"Tell us," McKie said.

The Dosadi spareness of the words struck Gar like a blow. He looked at Jedrik. She gave every indication of willingness to wait forever for him to obey, which was to say that she made no response either to McKie's words or Gar's behavior.

Visibly defeated, Gar returned his attention to McKie.

"I went with two females, only the three of us, across the far mountains. We tried to set up our own production of pure food there. Many on the Rim tried that in those days. They seldom came back. Something always happens: the plants die for no reason, the water source runs dry, something steals what you grow. The Gods are jealous. That's what we always said."

He looked at Tria, who studied him without expression.

"One of the two women died the first year. The other was sick by the following harvest season, but survived through the next spring. It was during that harvest . . . we went to the garden . . . ha! The garden! This child was there. We had no idea of where she'd come from. She appeared to be seven or eight years old, but her reactions were those of an infant. That happens often enough on the Rim—the mind retreats from something too terrible to bear. We took her in. Sometimes you can train such a child back to usefulness. When the woman died and the crop failed, I took Tria and we headed back to the Rim. That was a very bad time. When we returned . . . I was sick. Tria helped me then. We've been together ever since."

McKie found himself deeply touched by this recital and hard put to conceal his reaction. He was not positive that he did conceal it. With his new Dosadi awareness, he read an entire saga into that sparse account of events which probably were quite ordinary by Rim standards. He found himself enraged by the other data which could be read into Gar's words.

PanSpechi trained!

That was the key. Aritch's people had wanted to maintain the purity of their experiment: only two species permitted. But it would be informative to examine PanSpechi applications. Simple. Take a Human female child. Put her exclusively under PanSpechi influence for seven or eight years. Subject that child to selective memory erasure. Hand her over to convenient surrogate parents on Dosadi.

And there was more: Aritch lied when he said he knew little about the Rim, that the Rim was outside the experiment.

As these thoughts went through his head, McKie returned to the small adjoining room. Jedrik followed. She waited while he assembled his thoughts.

Presently, McKie looked at her, laid out his deductions. When he finished, he glanced at the doorway.

"I need to learn as much as I can about the Rim."

"Those two are a good source."

"But don't you require them for your other plans, the attack on Broey's corridor?"

"Two things can go forward simultaneously. You will return to their enclave with them as my lieutenant. That'll confuse them. They won't know what to make of that. They will answer your questions. And in their confusion they'll reveal much that they might otherwise conceal from you."

McKie absorbed this. Yes . . . Jedrik did not hesitate to put him into peril. It was an ultimate message to everyone. McKie would be totally at the mercy of Gar and Tria. Jedrik was saying, "See! You cannot influence me by any threat to McKie." In a way, this protected him. In an extremely devious Dosadi way, this removed many possible threats to McKie, and it told him much about what her true feelings toward him could be. He spoke to this.

"I detest a cold bed."

Her eyes sparkled briefly, the barest touch of moisture, then, arming him:

"No matter what happens to me, McKie—free us!"

Given the proper leverage at the proper point, any sentient awareness may be exploded into astonishing self-understanding.

—from an ancient Human mystic

U nless she makes a mistake, or we find some unexpected advantage, it's only a matter of time until she overruns us," Broey said.

He sat in his aerie command post at the highest point of the dominant building on the Council Hills. The room was an armored oval with a single window about fifteen meters away directly in front of Broey looking out on sunset through the river's canyon walls. A small table with a communicator stood just to his left. Four of his commanders waited near the table. Maps, position boards, and the other appurtenances of command, with their attendants, occupied most of the room's remaining space.

Broey's intelligence service had just brought him the report that Jedrik had taken Gar and Tria captive.

One of his commanders, slender for a Gowachin and with other deprivation marks left from birth on the Rim, glanced at his three companions, cleared his throat.

"Is it time to capitulate?"

Broey shook his head in a Human gesture of negation.

It's time I told them, he thought.

He felt emptied. God refused to speak to him. Nothing in his world obeyed the old mandates.

We've been tricked.

The Powers of the God Wall had tricked him, had tricked his world and all of its inhabitants. They'd . . .

"This McKie," the commander said.

Broey swallowed, then:

"I doubt if McKie has even the faintest understanding of how she uses him."

He glanced at the reports on his communicator table, a stack of reports about McKie. Broey's intelligence service had been active.

"If we captured or killed him . . ." the commander ventured.

"Too late for that," Broey said.

"Is there a chance we won't have to capitulate?"

"There's always that chance."

None of the four commanders liked this answer. Another of them, fat and silky green, spoke up:

"If we have to capitulate, how will we know the . . ."

"We must never capitulate, and we must make certain she knows this," Broey said. "She means to exterminate us."

There! He'd told them.

They were shocked but beginning to understand where his reasoning had led him. He saw the signs of understanding come over their faces.

"The corridor . . ." one of them ventured.

Broey merely stared at him. The fool must know they couldn't get more than a fraction of their forces onto the Rim before Jedrik and Tria closed off that avenue. And even if they could escape to the Rim, what could they do? They hadn't the faintest idea of where the damned factories and food stores were buried.

"If we could rescue Tria," the slim commander said.

Broey snorted. He'd prayed for Tria to contact him, to open negotiations. There'd been not a word, even after she'd fallen back into that impossible enclave. Therefore, Tria had lost control of her people outside the city. All the other evidence supported this conclusion. There was no contact with the Rim. Jedrik's people had taken over out there. Tria would've sent word to him the minute she recognized the impossibility of her position. Any valuable piece of information, any counter in this game would've leaped into Tria's awareness, and she'd have recognized who the highest bidder must be.

Who was the highest bidder? Tria, after all, was Human. Broey sighed.

And McKie—an idiot savant from beyond the God Wall, a *weapons* expert. Jedrik must've known. But how? Did the Gods talk to her? Broey doubted this. Jedrik gave every evidence of being too clever to be sucked in by trickster Gods.

More clever, more wary, more Dosadi than I.

She deserved the victory.

Broey arose and went to the window. His commanders exchanged worried glances behind him. Could Broey *think* them out of this mess?

A corner of his slim corridor to the Rim was visible to Broey. He could not hear the battle, but explosive orange blossoms told him the fighting continued. He knew the gamble Jedrik took. Those Gowachin beyond the God Wall, the ones who'd created this hellish place, were slow—terrifyingly slow. But eventually they would be unable to misunderstand Jedrik's intentions. Would they step in, those mentally retarded Gowachin out there, and try to stop Jedrik? She obviously thought they would. Everything she did told Broey of the care with which Jedrik had prepared for the stupids from Outside. Broey almost wished her success, but he could not bear the price he and his people would have to pay.

Jedrik had the time-edge on him. She had McKie. She had played McKie like a superb instrument. And what would McKie do when he realized the final use Jedrik intended to make of him? Yes . . . McKie was a perfect tool for Jedrik. She'd obviously waited for that perfect instrument, had known when it arrived.

Gods! She was superb!

Broey scratched at the nodes between his ventricles. Well, there were still things a trapped people could do. He returned to his commanders.

"Abandon the corridor. Do it quietly, but swiftly. Fall back to the prepared inner walls."

As his commanders started to turn away, Broey stopped them.

"I also want some carefully selected volunteers. The fix we're in must be explained to them in such a way that there's no misunderstanding. They will be asked to sacrifice themselves in a way no Gowachin has ever before contemplated."

"How?"

It was the slender one.

Broey addressed himself to this one. A Gowachin born on the Rim should be the first to understand.

"We must increase the price Jedrik's paying. Hundreds of their people for every *one* of ours."

"Suicide missions," the slender one said.

Broey nodded, continued:

"One more thing. I want Havvy brought up here and I want orders issued to increase the food allotment to those Humans we've held in special reserve."

Two of his commanders spoke in unison:

"They won't sacri . . ."

"I have something else in mind for them."

Broey nodded to himself. Yes indeed. Some of those Humans could still serve his purposes. It wasn't likely they could serve him as McKie served Jedrik, but there was still a chance . . . yes, a chance. Jedrik might not be certain of what Broey could do with his Humans. Havvy, for example. Jedrik had certainly considered and discarded Havvy. In itself, that might be useful. Broey waved for his commanders to leave and execute his orders. They'd seen the new determination in him. They'd pass that along to the ones beneath them. That, too, would serve his purposes. It would delay the moment when his people might suspect that he was making a desperate gamble.

He returned to his communicator, called his search people, urged them to new efforts. They might still achieve what Jedrik obviously had achieved with Pcharky . . . if they could find a Pcharky.

*Knowledge is the province of the Legum, just as knowledge
is a source of crime.*

—Gowachin Law

Mckie told himself that he might've known an assignment from Jedrik could not be simple. There had to
be Dosadi complications.

"There can be no question in their minds that you're really my lieutenant."

"Then I must be your lieutenant."

This pleased her, and she gave him the bare outline of
her plan, warning him that the upcoming encounter could
not be an act. He must respond as one who was fully aware
of this planet's demands.

Night fell over Chu while she prepared him and, when
they returned to the command post where Gar and Tria
waited, the occasion presented itself as Jedrik had told
him it would. It was a sortie by Broey's people against
Gate Eighteen. Jedrik snapped the orders at him, sent him
running.

"Find the purpose of that!"

McKie paused only to pick up four waiting guards at the
command post door, noting the unconcealed surprise in Gar
and Tria. They'd formed a particular opinion of McKie's position and now had to seek a new assessment. Tria would
be most upset by this, confused by self-doubts. McKie knew
Jedrik would immediately amplify those doubts, telling Gar
and Tria that McKie would go with them when he returned
from Gate Eighteen.

"You must consider his orders as my orders."

Gate Eighteen turned out to be more than a minor problem. Broey had taken the gate itself and two buildings. One
of the attackers, diving from an upper window into one of

Jedrik's best units, had blown himself up with a nasty lot of casualties.

"More than a hundred dead," a breathless courier told him.

McKie didn't like the implications of a suicide attack, but couldn't pause to assess it. They had to eliminate this threat. He gave orders for two feints while a third force blasted down one of the captured buildings, smothering the gate in rubble. That left the other captive building isolated. The swiftness of this success dazzled Jedrik's forces, and the commanders snapped to obedience when McKie issued orders for them to take captives and bring those captives to him for interrogation.

At McKie's command, one of his original four guards brought a map of the area, tacked it to a wall. Less than an hour had passed since he'd left Jedrik, but McKie felt that he'd entered another world, one even more primitive than that surrounding the incredible woman who'd set all of this in motion. It was the difference between second- and third-hand reports of action and the physical feeling of that action all around him. Explosions and the hissing of flamers down on the streets jarred his awareness.

Staring at the map, McKie said, "This has all the marks of a trap. Get all but a holding force out of the area. Tell Jedrik."

People scurried to obey.

One of the guards and two sub-commanders remained. The guard spoke.

"What about this place?"

McKie glanced around him. It was a square room with brown walls. Two windows looked out on the street away from the battle for the isolated building near the gate. He'd hardly looked at the room when they'd brought him here to set up his command post. Four streets with isolated hold-outs cushioned him from the main battle. They could shoot a cable bridge to another building if things became hot here. And it'd help morale if he remained in the danger area.

He spoke to one of the sub-commanders:

"Go down to the entry. Call all the elevators down there and disable all but one. Stand by that one with a holding force and put guards in the stairway. Stand by yourself to bring up captives. Comment?"

"I'll send up two cable teams and make sure the adjoining buildings are secure."

Of course! McKie nodded.

Gods! How these people reacted in emergencies. They were as direct and cutting as knives.

"Do it," McKie said.

He had less than a ten-minute wait before two of Jedrik's special security troops brought up the first captive, a young Gowachin whose eyelids bore curious scars—scroll-like and pale against the green skin.

The two security people stopped just inside the doorway. They held the Gowachin firmly, although he did not appear to be struggling. The sub-commander who'd brought them up closed the door as he left.

One of the captors, an older man with narrow features, nodded as he caught McKie's attention.

"What'll we do with him?"

"Tie him in a chair," McKie instructed.

He studied the Gowachin as they complied.

"Where was he captured?"

"He was trying to escape from that building through a perimeter sewage line."

"Alone?"

"I don't know. He's the first of a group of prisoners. The others are waiting outside."

They had finished binding the young Gowachin, now took up position directly behind him.

McKie studied the captive. He wore black coveralls with characteristic deep vee to clear the ventricles. The garment had been cut and torn in several places. He'd obviously been searched with swift and brutal thoroughness. McKie put down a twinge of pity. The scar lines on the prisoner's eyelids precluded anything but the most direct Dosadi necessities.

"They did a poor job removing your Phylum tattoos," McKie said. He'd already recognized the scar lines: Deep Swimmers. It was a relatively unimportant Phylum, small in numbers and sensitive about their status.

The young Gowachin blinked. McKie's opening remark had been so conversational, even-toned, that the shock of his words came after. Shock was obvious now in the set of the captive's mouth.

"What is your name, please?" McKie asked, still in that even, conversational way.

"Grinik."

It was forced out of him.

McKie asked one of the guards for a notebook and stylus, wrote the Gowachin's name in it, adding the Phylum identification.

"Grinik of the Deep Swimmers," he said. "How long have you been on Dosadi?"

The Gowachin took a deep, ventricular breath, remained silent. The security men appeared puzzled. This interrogation wasn't going as they'd expected. McKie himself did not know what to expect. He still felt himself recovering from surprise at recognition of the badly erased Phylum tattoos.

"This is a very small planet," McKie said. "The universe from which we both come is very big and can be very cruel. I'm sure you didn't come here expecting to die."

If this Grinik didn't know the deadly plans of his superiors, that would emerge shortly. McKie's words could be construed as a personal threat beyond any larger threat to Dosadi as a whole. It remained to see how Grinik reacted.

Still, the young Gowachin hesitated.

When in doubt, remain silent.

"You appear to've been adequately trained for this project," McKie said. "But I doubt if you were told everything you should know. I even doubt if you were told things essential to you in your present position."

"Who are you?" Grinik demanded. "How dare you speak here of matters which . . ." He broke off, glanced at the two guards standing at his shoulders.

"They know all about us," McKie lied.

He could smell the sweet perfume of Gowachin fear now, a floral scent which he'd noted only on a few previous occasions. The two guards also sensed this and showed faint smiles to betray that they knew its import.

"Your masters sent you here to die," McKie said. "They may very well pay heavily for this. You ask who I am? I am Jorj X. McKie, Legum of the Gowachin Bar, Saboteur Extraordinary, senior lieutenant of Jedrik who will shortly rule all of Dosadi. I make formal imposition upon you. Answer my questions for the Law is at stake."

On the Gowachin worlds, that was a most powerful motivator. Grinik was shaken by it.

"What do you wish to know?"

He barely managed the words.

"Your mission on Dosadi. The precise instructions you were given and who gave them to you."

"There are twenty of us. We were sent by Mrreg."

That name! The implications in Gowachin lore stunned McKie. He waited, then:

"Continue."

"Two more of our twenty are out there."

Grinik motioned to the doorway, clearly pleading for his captive associates.

"Your instructions?"

"To get our people out of this terrible place."

"How long?"

"Just . . . sixty hours remain."

McKie exhaled slowly. So Aritch and company had given up on him. They were going to eliminate Dosadi.

"Where are the other members of your party?"

"I don't know."

"You were, of course, a reserve team trained and held in readiness for this mission. Do you realize how poorly you were trained?"

Grinik remained silent.

McKie put down a feeling of despair, glanced at the two guards. He understood that they'd brought him this particular captive because this was one of three who were not Dosadi. Jedrik had instructed them, of course. Many things became clearer to him in this new awareness. Jedrik had put sufficient pressure on the Gowachin beyond the God Wall. She still had not imagined the extremes to which those Gowachin might go in stopping her. It was time Jedrik learned what sort of fuse she'd lighted. And Broey must be told. Especially Broey—before he sent many more suicide missions.

The outer door opened and the sub-commander leaned in to speak.

"You were right about the trap. We mined the area before pulling back. Caught them nicely. The gate's secure now, and we've cleared out that last building."

McKie pursed his lips, then:

"Take the prisoners to Jedrik. Tell her we're coming in."

A flicker of surprise touched the sub-commander's eyes.

"She knows."

Still the man hesitated.

"Yes?"

"There's one Human prisoner out here you should question before leaving."

McKie waited. Jedrik knew he was coming in, knew what had gone on here, knew about the Human prisoner out there. She wanted him to question this person. Yes . . . of course. She left nothing to chance . . . by her standards. Well, her standards were about to change, but she might even know that.

"Name?"

"Havvy. Broey holds him, but he once served Jedrik. She says to tell you Havvy is a reject, that he was contaminated."

"Bring him in."

Havvy surprised him. The surface was that of a bland-faced nonentity, braggadocio clearly evident under a mask of secret knowledge. He wore a green uniform with a driver's brassard. The uniform was wrinkled, but there were no visible rips or cuts. He'd been treated with more care than the Gowachin who was being led out of the room. Havvy replaced the Gowachin in the chair. McKie waved away the bindings.

Unfocused questions created turmoil in McKie's mind. He found it difficult to delay. Sixty hours! But he felt that he could almost touch the solution to the Dosadi mystery, that in only a few minutes he would know names and real motives for the ones who'd created this monster. Havvy? He'd served Jedrik. In what way? Why rejected? Contaminated?

Unfocused questions, yes.

Havvy sat in watchful tension, casting an occasional glance around the room, at the windows. There were no more explosions out there.

As McKie studied him more carefully, certain observations emerged. Havvy was small but solid, one of those Humans of lesser stature who concealed heavy musculature which could surprise you if you suddenly bumped into them. It was difficult to guess his age, but he was not Dosadi. A member of Grinik's team? Doubtful. Clearly not Dosadi, though. He didn't examine those around him with an automatic status assessment. His reactions were slow. Too much that should remain under shutters flowed from within him directly to the surface. Yes, that was the ultimate revelation. It bothered McKie that so much went unseen beneath the surface here, so much for which Aritch and company had not prepared him. It would take a lifetime to learn all the nuances of this place, and he had less than sixty hours remaining to him.

All of this flowed through McKie's mind in an eyeblink. He reached his decision, motioned the guards and others to leave.

One of the security people started to protest, but McKie silenced him with a glance, pulled up a chair, and sat down facing the captive.

The door closed behind the last of the guards.

"You were sent here deliberately to seek me out," McKie said.

It was not the opening Havvy had expected. He stared into McKie's eyes. A door slammed outside. There was the sound of several doors opening and shutting, the shuffling of feet. An amplified voice called out:

"Move these prisoners out!"

Havvy chewed at his upper lip. He didn't protest. A deep sigh shook him, then:

"You're Jorj X. McKie of BuSab?"

McKie blew out through pursed lips. Did Havvy doubt the evidence of his own senses? Surprising. McKie shook his head, continued to study the captive.

"You can't be McKie!" Havvy said.

"Ahhhhhh . . ." It was pressed out of McKie.

Something about Havvy: the body moved, the voice spoke, but the eyes did not agree.

McKie thought about what the Caleban, Fannie Mae, had said. *A light touch.* He was overtaken by an abrupt certainty: someone other than Havvy looked out through the man's eyes. Yesssss. Aritch's people controlled the Caleban who maintained the barrier around Dosadi. The Caleban could contact selected people here. She'd have a constant updating on everything such people learned. There must be many such spies on Dosadi, all trained not to betray the Caleban contact—no twitching, no lapses into trance. No telling how many agents Aritch possessed here.

Would all the other people on Dosadi remain unaware of such a thing, though? That was a matter to question.

"But you must be McKie," Havvy said. "Jedrik's still working out of . . ." He broke off.

"You must've provided her with some amusement by your bumbling," McKie said. "I assure you, however, that BuSab is *not* amused."

A gloating look came over Havvy's face.

"No, she hasn't made the transfer yet."

"Transfer?"

"Haven't you figured out yet how Pcharky's supposed to buy his freedom?"

McKie felt off balance at this odd turn.

"Explain."

"He's supposed to transfer your identity into Jedrik's body and her identity into your body. I think she was going to try that with me once, but . . ."

Havvy shrugged.

It was like an explosion in McKie's newly sensitized awareness. Rejected! Contaminated! Body exchange! McKie was accusatory!

"Broey sent you!"

"Of course." Offensive.

McKie contained his anger. The Dosadi complexities no longer baffled him as once they had. It was like peeling back layer upon layer of concealment. With each new layer you expected to find *the* answer. But that was a trap the whole universe set for the unwary. It was the ultimate mystery and he hated mystery. There were those who said this was a necessary ingredient for BuSab agents. You eliminated that which you hated. But everything he'd uncovered about this planet showed him how little he'd known previously about any mystery. Now, he understood something new about Jedrik. There was little doubt that Broey's Human messenger told the truth.

Pcharky had penetrated the intricacies of PanSpechi ego transfer. He'd done it without a PanSpechi as his subject, unless . . . yes . . . that expanded the implications in Tria's history. Their PanSpechi experiment had assumed even more grotesque proportions.

"I will speak directly to your Caleban monitor," McKie said.

"My what?"

It was such obvious dissimulation that McKie only snorted. He leaned forward.

"I will speak directly to Aritch. See that he gets this message without any mistakes."

Havvy's eyes became glassy. He shuddered.

McKie felt the inner tendrils of an attempted Caleban contact in his own awareness, thrust them aside.

"No! I will speak openly through your agent. Pay close attention, Aritch. Those who created this Dosadi horror cannot run far enough, fast enough, or long enough to escape. If you wish to make every Gowachin in the universe a target for violence, you are proceeding correctly. Others, including BuSab, can employ mass violence if you force it upon them. Not a pleasant thought. But unless you adhere to your own Law, to the honored relationship between Legum and Client, your shame will be exposed. Innocent Gowachin as well as you others whose legal status has yet to be determined—all will pay the bloody price."

Havvy's brows drew down in puzzlement.

"Shame?"

"They plan to blast Dosadi out of existence"

Havvy pressed back into the chair, glared at McKie.

"You're lying."

"Even you, Havvy, are capable of recognizing a truth. I'm going to release you, pass you back through the lines to Broey. Tell him what you learned from me."

"It's a lie! They're not going to . . ."

"Ask Aritch for yourself."

Havvy didn't ask "Aritch who?" He lifted himself from the chair.

"I will."

"Tell Broey we've less than sixty hours. None of us who can resist mind erasure will be permitted to escape."

"Us?"

McKie nodded, thinking: *Yes, I am Dosadi now.* He said: "Get out of here."

It afforded him a measure of amusement that the door was opened by the sub-commander just as Havvy reached it.

"See to him yourself," McKie said, indicating Havvy. "I'll be ready to go in a moment."

Without any concern about whether the subcommander understood the nature of the assignment, McKie closed his eyes in thought. There remained the matter of Mrreg, who'd sent twenty Gowachin from Tandaloor to get *his people* off the planet. Mrreg. That was the name of the mythical monster who'd tested the first primitive Gowachin people almost to extinction, setting the pattern of their deepest instincts.

Mrreg?

Was it code, or did some Gowachin actually use that name? Or was it a role that some Gowachin filled?

THE DOSADI EXPERIMENT

Does a populace have informed consent when a ruling minority acts in secret to ignite a war, doing this to justify the existence of the minority's forces? History already has answered that question. Every society in the ConSentiency today reflects the historical judgment that failure to provide full information for informed consent on such an issue represents an ultimate crime.

—from The Trial of Trials

L ess than an hour after closing down at Gate Eighteen, McKie and his escort arrived back at Jedrik's headquarters building. He led them to the heavily guarded side entrance with its express elevator, not wanting to pass Pcharky at this moment. Pcharky was an unnecessary distraction. He left the escort in the hallway with instructions to get food and rest, signaled for the elevator. The elevator door was opened by a small Human female of about fifteen years who nodded him into the dim interior.

McKie, his natural distrust of even the young on this planet well masked, nevertheless kept her under observation as he accepted the invitation. She was a gamin child with dirty face and hands, a torn grey single garment cut off at the knees. Her very existence as a Dosadi survivor said she'd undoubtedly sold her body many times for scraps of food. He realized how much Dosadi had influenced him when he found that he couldn't raise even the slightest feeling of censure at this knowledge. You did what the conditions around you demanded when those conditions were overwhelming. It was an ultimate question: this or death? And certainly some of them chose death.

"Jedrik," he said.

She worked her controls and he found himself presently in an unfamiliar hallway. Two familiar guards stood at a doorway down the hall, however. They betrayed not the slightest interest in him as he opened the door between them swiftly and strode through.

It was a tiny anteroom, empty, but another door directly in front of him. He opened this with more confidence than he felt, entered a larger space full of projection-room gloom with shadowed figures seated facing a holographic focus on his left. McKie identified Jedrik by her profile, slipped into a seat beside her.

She kept her attention on the h-focus where a projection of Broey stood looking out at something over their shoulders. McKie recognized the subtle slippage of computer simulation. That was not a flesh-and-blood Broey in the focus.

Someone on the far side of the room stood up and crossed to sit beside another figure in the gloom. McKie recognized Gar as the man moved through one of the projection beams.

McKie whispered to Jedrik, "Why simulation?"

"He's beginning to do things I didn't anticipate."

The suicide missions. McKie looked at the simulation, wondered why there was no sync-sound. Ahhh, yes. They were lip-reading, and it was silent to reduce distractions, to amplify concentration. Yes, Jedrik was reworking the simulation model of Broey which she carried in her head. She would also carry another model, even more accurate than the one of Broey, which would give her a certain lead time on the reactions of one Jorj X. McKie.

"Would you really have done it?" he asked.

"Why do you distract me with such nonsense?"

He considered. Yes, it was a good question. He already knew the answer. She would have done it: traded bodies with him and escaped outside the God Wall as McKie. She might still do it, unless he could anticipate the mechanics of the transfer.

By now, she knew about the sixty-hour limit and would suspect its significance. Less than sixty hours. And the

Dosadi could make extremely complex projections from limited data. Witness this Broey simulation.

The figure in the focus was talking to a fat Human female who held a tube which McKie recognized as a communicator for field use.

Jedrik spoke across the room to Gar.

"She still with him?"

"Addicted."

A two-sentence exchange, and it condensed an entire conversation about possible uses of that woman. McKie did not ask addicted to what. There were too many such substances on Dosadi, each with peculiar characteristics, often involving odd monopolies with which everyone seemed familiar. This was a telltale gap in Aritch's briefings: the monopolies and their uses.

As McKie absorbed the action in the focus, the reasons behind this session became more apparent. Broey was refusing to believe the report from Havvy.

And there was Havvy in the focus.

Jedrik favored McKie with one flickering glance as Havvy-simulation appeared. Certainly. She factored McKie into her computations.

McKie compressed his lips. *She knew Havvy would contaminate me. They couldn't say "I love you" on this damned planet. Oh, no. They had to create a special Dosadi production number.*

"Most of the data for this originated before the breakup," McKie said. "It's useless. Rather than ask the computer to play pretty pictures for us, why don't we examine our own memories? Surely, somewhere in the combined experiences with Broey . . ."

A chuckle somewhere to the left stopped him.

Too late, McKie saw that every seat in the room had an arm keyed to the simulations. They were doing precisely what he'd suggested, but in a more sophisticated way. The figures at the focus were being adjusted to the combined memories. There was such a keyed arm at McKie's right hand. He suddenly realized how tactless and lecturing he still must appear to these people. They didn't waste energy on unnecessary words. Anyone who did must be subnormal, poorly trained or . . . or not from Dosadi.

"Does he always state the obvious?" Gar asked.

McKie wondered if he'd blown his lieutenancy, lost the opportunity to explore the mystery of the Rim, but . . . no, there wasn't time for that now. He'd have to penetrate the Rim another way.

"He's new," Jedrik said. "New is not necessarily naive, as you should know."

"He has you doing it now," Gar said.

"Guess again."

McKie put a hand to the simulation controls under his right hand, tested the keys. He had it in a moment. They were similar to such devices in the ConSentiency, an adaptation from the DemoPol inputs, no doubt. Slowly, he changed the Broey at the focus, heavier, the sagging jowls and node wattles of a breeding male Gowachin. McKie froze the image.

"Tentative?" Gar asked.

Jedrik answered for him.

"It's knowledge he brought here with him." She did something to her controls, stopped the projection, and raised the room lights.

McKie noted that Tria was nowhere in the room.

"The Gowachin have sequestered their females somewhere," McKie said. "That somewhere should not be difficult to locate. Send word to Tria that she must not mount her attack on Broey's corridor just yet."

"Why delay?" Gar demanded.

"Broey will have all but evacuated the corridor by now," McKie said.

Gar was angry and showing it.

"Not a single one of them has gone through that Rim gate."

"Not to the Rim," Jedrik said.

It was clear to her now. McKie had supplied the leverage she needed. It was time now to employ him as she'd always intended. She glanced at McKie.

"We have unfinished business. Are you ready?"

He held his silence. How could he answer such a Dosadi-weighted question? There were so many things left unspoken on this planet, only the native-born could understand them all. McKie felt once more that he was a dull outsider, a child of dubious potential among normal adults.

Jedrik arose, looked across at Gar.

"Send word to Tria to hold herself in readiness for another assignment. Tell Broey. Call him on an open line. We now have an excellent use for your fanatics. If only a few of your people fight through to that Graluz complex, it'll be enough and Broey will know it."

McKie noted that she spoke to Gar with a familiar teaching emphasis. It was the curiously weighted manner she'd once used with McKie, but no longer found necessary. His recognition of this amused her.

"Come along, McKie. We haven't much time."

Does a population have informed consent when that population is not taught the inner workings of its monetary system, and then is drawn, all unknowing, into economic adventures?

—from The Trial of Trials

For almost an hour after the morning meal, Aritch observed Ceylang as she worked with the McKie simulator. She was pushing herself hard, believing Wreave honor at stake, and had almost reached the pitch Aritch desired.

Ceylang had set up her own simulator situation: McKie interviewing five of Broey's Gowachin. She had the Gowachin come to McKie in surrender, hands extended, the webbed fingers exposed to show that the talons were withdrawn.

Simulator-McKie merely probed for military advantages.

"Why does Broey attack in this fashion?"

Or he'd turn to some places outside the h-focus of the simulator.

"Send reinforcements into that area."

Nothing about the Rim.

Earlier, Ceylang had tried the issue with a prisoner simulation where the five Gowachin tried to confuse McKie by presenting a scenario in which Broey massed his forces at the corridor. The makings of a breakout to the Rim appeared obvious.

Simulator-McKie asked the prisoners why they lied.

Ceylang cleared the simulator and sat back. She saw Aritch at the observation window, opened a channel to him.

"Something has to be wrong in the simulation. McKie cannot be led into questioning the purposes of the Rim."

"I assure you that simulation is remarkable in its accuracy. Remarkable."

"Then why . . ."

"Perhaps he already knows the answer. Why don't you try him with Jedrik? Here . . ." Aritch operated the controls at the observer station. "This might help. This is a record of McKie in recent action on Dosadi."

The simulator presented a view down a covered passage through a building. Artificial light. Darkness at the far end of the passage. McKie, two blocky guards in tow, approached the viewers.

Ceylang recognized the scene. She'd watched this action at Gate Eighteen from several angles; had seen this passage empty before the battle, acquainting herself with the available views. As she'd watched it then, the passage had filled with Human defenders. There was a minor gate behind the viewer and she knew the viewer itself to be only a bright spot, a fleck of glittering impurity in an otherwise drab brick over the gate's archway.

Now, the long passage seemed strange to Ceylang without its throng of defenders. There were only a few workmen along its length as McKie passed. The workmen repaired service pipes in the ceiling. A cleanup crew washed down patches of blood at the far end of the passage, the high-water mark of the Gowachin attack. An officer leaned against a wall near the viewer, a bored expression on his face which did not mislead Ceylang. He was there to watch McKie. Three soldiers squatted nearby rolling hexi-bones for coins which lay in piles before each man. Every now and then, one of the gamblers would pass a coin to the watching officer. A repair supervisor stood with his back to the viewer, notebook in hand, writing a list of supplies to complete the job. McKie and his guards were forced to step around these people. As they passed, the officer turned, looked directly into the viewer, smiled.

"That officer," Ceylang said. "One of your people?"

"No."

The viewpoint shifted, looking down on the gate itself, McKie in profile. The gatekeeper was a teenager with a scar down his right cheek and a broken nose. McKie showed no signs of recognition, but the youth knew McKie.

"You go through on request."

"When did she call?"

"Ten."

"Let us through."

The gate was opened. McKie and his guards went through, passed beyond the viewer's focus.

The youthful gatekeeper stood up, smashed the viewer. The h-focus went blank.

Aritch looked down from his observation booth for a moment before speaking.

"Who called?"

"Jedrik?" Ceylang spoke without thinking.

"What does that conversation tell you? Quickly!"

"That Jedrik anticipated his movements, was observing him all the time."

"What else?"

"That McKie . . . knows this, knows she can anticipate him."

"She carries a better simulation of him in her head than we have . . . there."

Aritch pointed at the h-focus area.

"But they left so much unspoken!" Ceylang said.

Aritch remained silent.

Ceylang closed her eyes. It was like mind reading. It confused her.

Aritch interrupted her musings.

"What about that officer and the gatekeeper?"

She shook her head.

"You're wise to use living observers there. They all seem to know when they're being watched. And how it's done."

"Even McKie."

"He didn't look at the viewers."

"Because he assumed from the first that we'd have him under almost constant observation. He's not concerned about the mechanical intrusions. He has built a simulation McKie of his own who acts on the surface of the real McKie."

"That's your assumption?"

"We arrived at this from observation of Jedrik in her dealings with McKie. She peels away the simulation layers one at a time, coming closer and closer to the actuality at the core."

Another observation bothered Ceylang.

"Why'd the gatekeeper shut down that viewer just then?"

"Obviously because Jedrik told him to do that."

Ceylang shuddered.

"Sometimes I think those Dosadi play us like a fine instrument."

"But of course! That's why we sent them our McKie."

The music of a civilization has far-reaching consequences on consciousness and, thus, influences the basic nature of a society. Music and its rhythms divert and compel the awareness, describing the limits within which a consciousness, thus fascinated, may operate. Control the music, then, and you own a powerful tool with which to shape the society.

—The Dosadi Analysis, BuSab Documents

It was a half-hour before Jedrik and McKie found themselves in the hallway leading to her quarters. McKie, aware of the effort she was expending to conceal a deep weariness, watched her carefully. She concentrated on presenting a show of vitality, her attention glued on the prospect ahead. There was no way of telling what went on in her mind. McKie did not attempt to break the silence. He had his own worries.

Which was the real Jedrik? How was she going to employ Pcharky? Could he resist her?

He knew he was close to a solution of the Dosadi mystery, but the prospect of the twin gambles he was about to take filled him with doubts.

On coming from the projection room, they'd found themselves in a strange delaying situation, as though it were something planned for their frustration. Everything had been prepared for their movement—guards warned, elevator waiting, doors opened. But every time they thought the way clear, they met interference. Except for the obvious importance of the matters which delayed them, it was easy to imagine a conspiracy.

A party of Gowachin at Gate Seventy wanted to surrender, but they demanded a parley first. One of Jedrik's aides didn't like the situation. Something about the assessment of the offer bothered her, and she wanted to discuss it with Jedrik. She stopped them halfway down the first hall outside the projection room.

The aide was an older woman who reminded McKie vaguely of a Wreave lab worker at BuSab, one who'd always been suspicious of computers, even antagonistic toward them. This Wreave had read every bit of history he could find about the evolution of such instruments and liked to remind his listeners of the misuses of the DemoPol. Human history had provided him with abundant ammunition, what with its periodic revolts against "enslavement by machines." Once, he'd cornered McKie.

"Look here! See this sign: 'Gigo.' That's a very old sign that was hung above one of your ancient computers. It's an acronym: Garbage In, Garbage Out.' You see! They knew."

Yes. Jedrik's female aide reminded him of that Wreave.

McKie listened to her worries. She roamed all around a central disquiet, never settling on a particular thing. Aware of Aritch's deadline and Jedrik's fatigue, McKie felt the pressures bearing down upon him. The aide's data was accurate. Others had checked it. Finally, he could hold his impatience no longer.

"Who fed this data into your computer?"

The aide was startled at the interruption, but Jedrik turned to him, waiting.

"I think it was Holjance," the aide said. "Why?"

"Get him in here."

"Her."

"Her, then! Make sure she's actually the one who fed in that data."

Holjance was a pinch-faced woman with deep wrinkles around very bright eyes. Her hair was dark and wiry, skin almost the color of McKie's. Yes, she was the one who'd fed the data into the computer because it had arrived on her shift, and she'd thought it too important to delegate.

"What is it you want?" she demanded.

He saw no rudeness in this. It was Dosadi directness. Important things were happening all around. *Don't waste time*.

"You saw this assessment of the surrender offer?" he asked.

"Yes."

"Are you satisfied with it?"

"The data went in correctly."

"That's not my question"

"Of course I'm satisfied!"

She stood ready to defend herself against any charge that she'd slighted her job.

"Tell me, Holjance," he said, "if you wanted the Gowachin computers to produce inaccurate assessments, what would you do?"

She thought about this a moment, blinked, glanced almost furtively at Jedrik who appeared lost in thought. "Well, sir, we have a regular filtering procedure for preventing . . ."

"That's it," Jedrik said. "If I were a Gowachin, I would not be doing that right now."

Jedrik turned, barked orders to the guards behind her.

"That's another trap! Take care of it."

As they emerged from the elevator on Jedrik's floor, there was another delay, one of the escort who'd been with McKie at Gate Eighteen. His name was Todu Pellas and McKie addressed him by name, noting the faint betrayal of pleasure this elicited. Pellas, too, had doubts about carrying out a particular order.

"We're supposed to back up Tria's move by attacking across the upper parkway, but there are some trees and other growth knocked down up there that haven't been moved for two days."

"Who knocked down those trees?" McKie asked.

"We did."

McKie understood. You feinted. The Gowachin were supposed to believe this would provide cover for an attack, but there'd been no attack for two days.

"They must be under pretty heavy strain," Jedrik said.

McKie nodded. That, too, made sense. The alternative Gowachin assumption was that the Humans were trying to fake them into an attack at that point. But the cover had not been removed by either side for two days.

Jedrik took a deep breath.

"We have superior firepower and when Tria . . . well, you should be able to cut right through there to . . ."

McKie interrupted.

"Call off that attack."

"But . . ."

"Call it off!"

She saw the direction of his reasoning. Broey had learned much from the force which Gar and Tria had trained. And Jedrik herself had provided the final emphasis in the lesson. She saw there was no need to change her orders to Pellas.

Pellas had taken it upon himself to obey McKie, not waiting for Jedrik's response, although she was his commander. He already had a communicator off his belt and was speaking rapidly into it.

"Yes! Dig in for a holding action."

He spoke in an aside to Jedrik.

"I can handle it from here."

In a few steps, Jedrik and McKie found themselves in her room. Jedrik leaned with her back against the door, no longer trying to conceal her fatigue.

"McKie, you're becoming very Dosadi."

He crossed to the concealing panels, pulled out the bed.

"You need rest."

"No time."

Yes, she knew all about the sixty-hour deadline—less than fifty-five hours now. Dosadi's destruction was a reaction she hadn't expected from "X," and she blamed herself.

He turned, studied her, saw that she'd passed some previously defined limit of personal endurance. She possessed no amplifiers of muscles or senses, none of the sophisticated aids McKie could call upon in emergencies. She had nothing but her own magnificent mind and body. And she'd almost run them out. Still, she pressed on. This told him a great deal about her motivation.

McKie found himself deeply touched by the fact that she'd not once berated him for hiding that ultimate threat which Aritch held over Dosadi. She'd accepted it that someone in Aritch's position could erase an entire planet, that McKie had been properly maneuvered into concealing this.

The alternative she offered filled McKie with misgivings.

Exchange bodies?

He understood now that this was Pcharky's function, the price the old Gowachin paid for survival. Jedrik had explained.

"He will perform this service one more time. In exchange, we release him from Dosadi."

"If he's one of the original . . . I mean, why doesn't he just leave?"

"We haven't provided him with a body he can use."

McKie had suppressed a feeling of horror. But the history of Dosadi which Jedrik unfolded made it clear that a deliberate loophole had been left in the Caleban contract which imprisoned this planet. Fannie Mae had even said it. He could leave in another body. That was the basic purpose behind this experiment.

New bodies for old!

Aritch had expected this to be the ultimate enticement, luring McKie into the Gowachin plot, enlisting McKie's supreme abilities and his powerful position in BuSab.

A new body for his old one.

All he'd have to do would be to cooperate in the destruction of a planet, conceal the real purpose of this project, and help set up another body-trade planet better concealed.

But Aritch had not anticipated what might be created by Jedrik plus McKie. They now shared a particular hate and motivation.

Jedrik still stood at the door waiting for him to decide.

"Tell me what to do," he said.

"You're sure that you're willing to . . ."

"Jedrik!"

He thought he saw the beginning of tears. It wasn't that she hid them, but that they reached a suppression level barely visible and she defied them. She found her voice, pointed.

"That panel beside the bed. Pressure latch."

The panel swung wide to reveal two shimmering rods about two centimeters in diameter. The rods danced with the energies of Pcharky's cage. They emerged from the floor, bent at right angles about waist height and, as the panel opened, they rotated to extend into the room—two glowing handles about a meter apart.

McKie stared at them. He felt a tightness in his breast. What if he'd misread Jedrik? Could he be sure of any Dosadi? This room felt as familiar to him now as his quarters on CC. It was here that Jedrik had taught him some of the most essential Dosadi lessons. Yet . . . he knew the old pattern of what she proposed. The discarded body with its donor ego had always been killed immediately. Why?

"You'll have your answer to that question when we've done this thing."

A Dosadi response, ambiguous, heavy with alternatives.

He glanced around the room, found it hard to believe that he'd known this place only these few days. His attention returned to the shimmering rods. Another trap?

He knew he was wasting precious time, that he'd have to go through with this. But what would it be like to find himself in Jedrik's flesh, wearing her body as he now wore his own? PanSpechi transferred an ego from body to body. But something unspeakable which they would not reveal happened to the donor.

McKie took a trembling breath.

It had to be done. He and Jedrik shared a common purpose. She'd had many opportunities to use Pcharky simply to escape or to extend her life . . . the way, he realized now, that Broey had used the Dosadi secret. The fact that she'd waited for a McKie forced him to believe her. Jedrik's followers trusted her—and they were Dosadi. And if he and Jedrik escaped, Aritch would find himself facing a far different McKie from the one who'd come so innocently across the Rim. They might yet stay Aritch's hand.

The enticement had been real, though. No doubting that. Shed an old body, get a new one. And the Rim had been the major source of *raw material:* strong, resilient bodies. Survivors.

"What do I do?" he asked.

He felt a hand on his shoulder, and she spoke from beside him.

"You are very Dosadi, McKie. Astonishing."

He glanced at her, saw what it had cost her to move here from the door. He slipped a hand around her waist, eased her to a sitting position on the bed and within reach of the rods.

"Tell me what to do."

She stared at the rods, and McKie realized it was rage driving her, rage against Aritch, the embodiment of "X," the embodiment of a contrived fate. He understood this. The solution of the Dosadi mystery had left him feeling empty, but on the edges there was such a rage as he'd never before experienced. He was still BuSab, though. He wanted no more bloodshed because of Dosadi, no more Gowachin justifications.

Jedrik's voice interrupted his thoughts and he saw that she also shared some of his misgivings.

"I come from a long line of heretics. None of us doubted that Dosadi was a crime, that somewhere there was a justice to punish the criminals."

McKie almost sighed. Not the old Messiah dream! Not that! He would not fill that role, even for Dosadi.

It was as though Jedrik read his mind. Perhaps, with that simulation model of him she carried in her head, this was exactly what she did.

"We didn't expect a hero to come and save us. We knew that whoever came would suffer from the same deficiencies as the other non-Dosadi we saw here. You were so . . . slow. Tell me, McKie, what drives a Dosadi?"

He almost said, "Power."

She saw his hesitation, waited.

"The power to change your condition," he said.

"You make me very proud, McKie."

"But how did you know I was . . ."

"McKie!"

He swallowed, then: "Yes, I guess that was the easiest part for you."

"It was much more difficult finding your abilities and shaping you into a Dosadi."

"But I might've been . . ."

"Tell me how I did it, McKie."

It was a test. He saw that. How had she known absolutely that he was the one she needed?

"I was sent here in a way that evaded Broey."

"And that's not easy." Her glance flickered ceilingward. "They tried to bait us from time to time. Havvy . . ."

"Compromised, contaminated . . ."

"Useless. Sometimes, a stranger looks out of Havvy's eyes."

"My eyes are my own."

"The first thing Bahrank reported about you."

"But even before that . . ."

"Yes?"

"They used Havvy to tell you I was coming . . . and he told you that you could use my body. He had to be truthful with you up to a point. You could read Havvy! How clever they thought they were being! I had to be vulnerable . . . really vulnerable."

"The first thing . . ."

". . . you found out about me." He nodded. "Suspicions confirmed. All of that money on my person. Bait. I was someone to be eliminated. I was a powerful enemy of your enemies."

"And you were angered by the right things."

"You saw that?"

"McKie, you people are so easy to read. So *easy!*"

"And the weapons I carried. You were supposed to use those to destroy yourselves. The implications . . ."

"I would've seen that if I'd had first-hand experience of Aritch. You *knew* what he intended for us. My mistake was to read your fears as purely personal. In time . . ."

"We're wasting time."

"You fear we'll be too late?"

Once more, he looked at the shimmering rods. What was it Pcharky did? McKie felt events rushing over him, engulfing him. What bargain had Jedrik really driven with Pcharky? She saw the question on his face.

"My people knew all along that Pcharky was just a tool of the God who held us prisoner. We forced a bargain on that God—that Caleban. Did you think we would not recognize the identity between the powers of that cage and the powers of our God Wall? No more delays, McKie. It's time to test our bargain."

Geriatric or other life extension for the powerful poses a similar threat to a sentient species as that found histori-cally in the dominance of a self-perpetuating bureaucracy. Both assume prerogatives of immortality, collecting more and more power with each passing moment. This is power which draws a theological aura about itself: the unassail-able Law, the God-given mandate of the leader, manifest destiny. Power held too long within a narrow framework moves farther and farther away from the adaptive demands of changed conditions. The leadership grows ever more paranoid, suspicious of inventive adaptations to change, fearfully protective of personal power and, in the terrified avoidance of what it sees as risk, blindly leads its people into destruction.

—BuSab Manual

Very well, I'll tell you what bothers me," Ceylang said.

"There are too many things about this problem that I fail to understand."

From her seated position, she looked across a small, round room at Aritch, who floated gently in a tiny blue pool. His head at the pool's lip was almost on a level with Ceylang's. Again, they had worked late into the night. She understood the reasons for this, the time pressures were quite appar-ent, but the peculiar Gowachin flavor of her training kept her in an almost constant state of angry questioning.

This whole thing was so un-Wreave!

Ceylang smoothed the robe over her long body. The robe was blue now, one step away from Legum black. Appropri-ately, there was blue all around her: the walls, the floor, the ceiling, Aritch's pool.

The High Magister rested his chin on the pool's edge to speak.

"I require specific questions before I can even hope to penetrate your puzzlement."

"Will McKie defend or prosecute? The simulator . . ."

"Damn the simulator! Odds are that he'll make the mistake of prosecuting. Your own reasoning powers should . . ."

"But if he doesn't?"

"Then selection of the judicial panel becomes vital."

Ceylang twisted her body to one side, feeling the chairdog adjust for her comfort. As usual, Aritch's answer only deepened her sense of uncertainty. She voiced that now.

"I continue to have this odd feeling that you intend me to play some role which I'm not supposed to discover until the very last instant."

Aritch breathed noisily through his mouth, splashed water onto his head.

"This all may be moot. By this time day after tomorrow, Dosadi *and* McKie may no longer exist."

"Then I will not advance to Legum?"

"Oh, I'm fairly certain you'll be a Legum."

She studied him, sensing irony, then:

"What a delicate line you walk, High Magister."

"Hardly. My way is wide and clear. You know the things I cannot countenance. I cannot betray the Law or my people."

"I have similar inhibitions. But this Dosadi thing—so tempting."

"So dangerous! Would a Wreave don Human flesh to learn the Human condition? Would you permit a Human to penetrate Wreave society in this . . ."

"There are some who might conspire in this! There are even Gowachin who . . ."

"The opportunities for misuse are countless."

"Yet you say that McKie already is more Gowachin than a Gowachin."

Aritch's webbed hands folded over the pool's edge, the claws extended.

"We risked much in training him for this task."

"More than you risk with me?"

Aritch withdrew his hands, stared at her, unblinking.

"So that's what bothers you."

"Precisely."

"Think, Ceylang, how near the core of Wreavedom you would permit me to come. Thus far and no farther will we permit you."

"And McKie?"

"May already have gone too far for us to permit his continued existence."

"I heed your warning, Aritch. But I remain puzzled as to why the Calebans couldn't prevent . . ."

"They profess not to understand the ego transfer. But who can understand a Caleban, let alone control one in a matter so delicate? Even this one who created the God Wall . . ."

"It's rumored that McKie understands Calebans."

"He denies it."

She rubbed her pocked left jowl with a prehensile mandible, felt the many scars of her passage through the Wreave triads. Family to family to family until it was a single gigantic family. Yet, all were Wreave. This Dosadi thing threatened a monstrous parody of Wreavedom. Still . . .

"So fascinating," she murmured.

"That's its threat."

"We should pray for the death of Dosadi."

"Perhaps."

She was startled.

"What . . ."

"This might not die with Dosadi. Our sacred bond assures that you will leave here with this knowledge. Many Gowachin know of this thing."

"And McKie."

"Infections have a way of spreading," Aritch said. "Remember *that* if this comes to the Courtarena."

There are some forms of insanity which, driven to an ultimate expression, can become the new models of sanity.

—BuSab Manual

M cKie?"

It was the familiar Caleban presence in his awareness, as though he heard and felt someone (or some-*thing*) which he knew was not there.

The preparation had been deceptively simple. He and Jedrik clasped hands, his right hand and her left, and each grasped one of the shimmering rods with the other hand.

McKie did not have a ready identity for this Caleban and wondered at the questioning in her *voice*. He agreed, however, that he was indeed McKie, shaping the thought as sub-vocalized conversation. As he spoke, McKie was acutely aware of Jedrik beside him. She was more than just another person now. He carried a tentative simulation model of her, sometimes anticipating her responses.

"You make mutual agreement?" the Caleban asked.

McKie sensed Pcharky then: a distant presence, the monitor for this experience. It was as though Pcharky had been reduced to a schematic which the Caleban followed, a set of complex rules, many of which could not be translated into words. Some part of McKie responded to this as though a monster awakened within him, a sleeping monster who sat up full of anger at being aroused thus, demanding:

"Who is it that dares awaken me?"

McKie felt his body trembling, felt Jedrik trembling beside him. The Caleban/Taprisiot-trembling, the sweaty response to trance! He saw these phenomena now in a different light. When you walked at the edge of this abyss . . .

While these thoughts passed through his mind, he felt a slight shift, no more than the blurred reflection of something which was not quite movement. Now, while he still felt his own flesh around him, he also felt himself possessed of an inner contact with Jedrik's body and knew she shared this experience.

Such a panic as he had not thought possible threatened to overwhelm him. He felt Jedrik trying to break the contact, to stop this hideous sharing, but they were powerless in the grip of a force which would not be stopped.

No time sense attached itself to this experience, but a fatalistic calm overcame them almost simultaneously. McKie felt awareness of Jedrik/flesh deepen. Curiosity dominated him now.

So this is woman!

This is man?

They shared the thoughts across an indistinct bridge.

Fascination gripped McKie. He probed deeper.

He/She could feel himself/herself breathing. And the differences! It was not the genitalia, the presence or lack of breasts. She felt bereft of breasts. He felt acutely distressed by their presence, self-consciously aware of profound implications. The sense of difference went back beyond gamete McKie/Jedrik.

McKie sensed her thoughts, her reactions.

Jedrik: "You cast your sperm upon the stream of time."

McKie: "You enclose and nurture . . ."

"I cast/I nurture."

It was as though they looked at an object from opposite sides, aware belatedly that they both examined the same thing.

"We cast/we, nurture."

Obscuring layers folded away and McKie found himself in Jedrik's mind, she in his. Their thoughts were one entity.

The separate Dosadi and ConSentient experiences melted into a single relationship.

"Aritch . . . ah, yes. You see? And your PanSpechi friend, Bildoon. Note that. You suspected, but now you know . . ."

Each set of experiences fed on the other, expanding, re-fining . . . condensing, discarding, creating . . .

So that's the training of a Legum.

Loving parents? Ahhh, yes, loving parents.

"I/we will apply pressure there . . . and there . . . They must be maneuvered into choosing that one as a judge. Yes, that will give us the required leverage. Let them break their own code."

And the awakened monster stirred within them. It had no dimension, no place, only existence. They felt its power.

"I do what I do!"

The power enveloped them. No other awareness was per-mitted. They sensed a primal current, unswerving purpose, a force which could override any other thing in their uni-verse. It was not God, not Life, not any particular species. It was something so far beyond such articulations that Jedrik/McKie could not even contemplate it without a sense that the next instant would bring obliteration. They felt a ques-tion hurled at their united, fearful awareness. The question was framed squarely in anger, astonishment, cold amuse-ment, and threat.

"For *this* you awaken *me*?"

Now, they understood why the old body and donor-ego had always been slain immediately. This terrible sharing made a . . . made a noise. It awakened a questioner.

They understood the question without words, know-ing they could never grasp the full meaning and emotive thrust, that it would burn them out even to try. Anger . . . astonishment . . . cold amusement . . . threat. The question as their own united mind(s) interpreted it represented a limit. It was all that Jedrik/McKie could accept.

The intrusive questioner receded.

They were never quite sure afterward whether they'd been expelled or whether they'd fled in terror, but the part-ing words were burned into their combined awareness.

"Let the sleeper sleep."

They walked softly in their minds then. They understood

the warning, but knew it could never be translated in its fullest threat for any other sentient being.

Concurrent: McKie/Jedrik felt a projection of terror from the God Wall Caleban, unfocused, unexplained. It was a new experience in the male-female collective memory. Caleban Fannie Mae had not even projected this upon original McKie when she'd thought herself doomed.

Concurrent: McKie/Jedrik felt a burntout fading from Pcharky. Something in that terrible contact had plunged Pcharky into his death spiral. Even as McKie/Jedrik realized this, the old Gowachin died. It was a slammed door. But this came after a blazing realization by McKie/Jedrik that Pcharky had shared the original decision to set up the Dosadi Experiment.

McKie found himself clothed in living, breathing flesh which routed its messages through his awareness. He wasn't sure which of their two bodies he possessed, but it was distinct, separate. It wrapped him in Human senses: the taste of salt, the smell of perspiration, and the omnipresent Warren stink. One hand held cold metal, the other clasped the hand of a fellow Human. Perspiration drenched this body, made the clasped hands slippery. He felt that knowing which hand held another hand was of utmost importance, but he wasn't ready to face that knowledge. Awareness of self, this new self, and a whole lifetime of new memories, demanded all of the attention he could muster.

Focus: A Rim city, never outside Jedrik's control because she had fed the signals through to Gar and Tria with exquisite care, and because those who gave the orders on the Rim had shared in the generations of selective breeding which had produced Jedrik. She was a biological weapon whose sole target was the God Wall.

Focus: Loving parents can thrust their child into deadly peril when they know everything possible has been done to prepare that child for survival.

The oddity to McKie was that he felt such things as personal memories.

"I did that."

Jedrik suffered the throes of similar experiences.

Which body?

So that was the training of a BuSab agent. Clever . . . almost adequate. Complex and full of much that she found to be new, but why did it always stop short of a full development?

She reviewed the sessions with Aritch and Ceylang. A matched pair. The choice of Ceylang and the role chosen for her appeared obvious. How innocent! Jedrik felt herself free to pity Ceylang. When allowed to run its course, this was an interesting emotion. She had never before felt pity in uncolored purity.

Focus: McKie actually loved her. She savored this emotion in its ConSentient complexity. The straight flow of selected emotions fascinated her. They did not have to be bridled!

In and out of this creative exchange there wove an intimacy, a pure sexuality without inhibitions.

McKie, savoring the amusement Jedrik had felt when Tria had suggested a McKie/Jedrik breeding, found himself caught by demanding male eroticism and knew by the sensation that he retained his old body.

Jedrik, understanding McKie's long search for a female to complete him, found her amusement converted to the desire to demonstrate that completion. As she turned toward him, releasing the dull rod which had once shimmered in contact with Pcharky, she found herself in McKie's flesh looking into her own eyes.

McKie gasped in the mirror experience.

Just as abruptly, driven by shock, they shifted back into familiar flesh: McKie male, Jedrik female. Instantly, it became a thing to explore—back—and forth. Eroticism was forgotten in this new game.

"We can be either sex/body at will!"

It was something beyond Taprisiots and Calebans, far more subtle than the crawling progression of a PanSpechi ego through the bodies from its creche.

They knew the source of this odd gift even as they sank back on the bed, content to be familiar male and female for a time.

The sleeping monster.

This was a gift with barbs in it, something *loving parents* might give their child in the knowledge that it was time for this lesson. Yet they felt revitalized, knowing they had for an instant tapped an energy source without limits.

A pounding on the door interrupted this shared reverie.

"Jedrik! Jedrik!"

"What is it?"

"It's Broey. He wishes to talk to McKie."

They were off the bed in an instant.

Jedrik glanced at McKie, knowing she had not one secret from him, that they shared a reasoning base. Out of the mutual understanding in this base, she spoke for both of them.

"Does he say why?"

"Jedrik . . ."

They both recognized the voice of a trusted aide and heard the fear in it.

". . . it's midmorning and there is no sun. God has turned off the sun!"

"Sealed us in . . ."

". . . to conceal the final blast."

Jedrik opened the door, confronted the frightened aide.

"Where is Broey?"

"Here—in your command post. He came alone without escort."

She glanced at McKie. "You will speak for us."

Broey waited near the position board in the command post. Watchful Humans stood within striking distance. He turned as McKie and Jedrik entered. McKie noted that the Gowachin's body was, indeed, heavy with breeding juices as anticipated. Unsettling for a Gowachin.

"What are your terms, McKie?"

Broey's voice was guttural, full of heavy breathing.

McKie's features remained Dosadi-bland, but he thought: *Broey thinks I'm responsible for the darkness. He's terrified.*

McKie glanced at the threatening black of the windows before speaking. He knew this Gowachin from Jedrik's painstaking study. Broey was a sophisticate, a collector of sophistication who surrounded himself with people of the same stripe. He was a professional sophisticate who read everything through that peculiar Dosadi screen. No one could come into his circle who didn't share this pose. All else remained outside and inferior. He was an ultimate Dosadi, a distillation, almost as Human as Gowachin because he'd obviously once worn a Human body. He was Gowachin at his origins, though—no doubt of it.

"You followed my scent," McKie said.

"Excellent!"

Broey brightened. He had not expected a Dosadi exchange, pared to the nonemotional essentials.

"Unfortunately," McKie said, "you have no position from which to negotiate. Certain things will be done. You will comply willingly, your compliance will be forced, or we will act without you."

It was a deliberate goading on McKie's part, a choice of non-Dosadi forms to abbreviate this confrontation. It said more than anything else that McKie came from beyond the God Wall, that the darkness which held back the daylight was the least of his resources.

Broey hesitated, then:

"So?"

The single word fell on the air with countless implications: an entire exchange discarded, hopes dashed, a hint of sadness at lost powers, and still with that sophisticated reserve which was Broey's signature. It was more subtle than a shrug, more powerful in its Dosadi overtones than an entire negotiating session.

"Questions?" McKie asked.

Broey glanced at Jedrik, obviously surprised by this. It was as though he appealed to her: they were both Dosadi, were they not? This outsider came here with his gross manners, his lack of Dosadi understanding. How could one speak to such one? He addressed Jedrik.

"Have I not already stated my submission? I came alone, I . . ."

Jedrik picked up McKie's cue.

"There are certain . . . peculiarities to our situation."

"Peculiarities?"

Broey's nictating membrane blinked once.

Jedrik allowed her manner to convey a slight embarrassment.

"Certain delicacies of the Dosadi condition must be overlooked. We are now, all of us, abject supplicants . . . and we are dealing with people who do not speak as we speak, act as we act . . ."

"Yes." He pointed upward. "The mentally retarded ones. We are in danger then."

It was not a question. Broey peered upward, as though trying to see through the ceiling and intervening floors. He drew in a deep breath.

"Yes."

Again, it was compressed communication. Anyone who could put the God Wall there could crush an entire planet. Therefore, Dosadi and all of its inhabitants had been brought to a common subjection. Only a Dosadi could have accepted it this quickly without more questions, and Broey was an ultimate Dosadi.

McKie turned to Jedrik. When he spoke, she anticipated every word, but she waited him out.

"Tell your people to stop all attacks."

He faced Broey.

"And your people."

Broey looked from Jedrik to McKie, back to Jedrik with a puzzled expression openly on his face, but he obeyed.

"Which communicator?"

Where pain predominates, agony can be a valued teacher.

—Dosadi aphorism

McKie and Jedrik had no need to discuss the decision. It was a choice which they shared and knew they shared through a memory-selection process now common to both of them. There was a loophole in the God Wall and even though that wall now blanketed Dosadi in darkness, a Caleban contract was still a Caleban contract. The vital question was whether the Caleban of the God Wall would respond.

Jedrik in McKie's body stood guard outside her own room while a Jedrik-fleshed McKie went alone into the room to make the attempt. Who should he try to contact? Fannie Mae? The absolute darkness which enclosed Dosadi hinted at an absolute withdrawal of the guardian Caleban. And there was so little time.

McKie sat cross-legged on the floor of the room and tried to clear his mind. The constant strange discoveries in the female body he now wore interfered with concentration. The moment of exchange left an aftershock which he doubted would ever diminish. They had but to share the desire for the change now and it occurred. But this different body—ahh, the multiplicity of differences created its own confusions. These went far beyond the adjustments to different height and weight. The muscles of his/her arms and hips felt wrongly attached. The bodily senses were routed through different unconscious processes. Anatomy created its own patterns, its own instinctual behavior. For one thing, he found it necessary to develop consciously monitored movements which protected his/her breasts. The movements were reminiscent of those male adjustments by which he prevented injury to testes. These were movements which a male learned early and relegated to an automatic behavior pattern. The problem in the female body was that he had to *think* about such behavior. And it went far beyond the breast-testes interlock.

As he tried to clear his mind for the Caleban contact, these webbed clusters of memory intruded. It was maddening: He needed to clear away bodily distractions, but this female body demanded his attention. In desperation, he hyperventilated and burned his awareness into a pineal focus whose dangers he knew only too well. This was the way to permanent identity loss if the experience were prolonged. It produced a sufficient clarity, however, that he could fill his awareness with memories of Fannie Mae.

Silence.

He sensed time's passage as though each heartbeat were a blow.

Fear hovered at the edges of the silence.

It came to him that something had put a terrible fear into the God Wall Caleban.

McKie felt anger.

"Caleban! You owe me!"

"McKie?"

The response was so faint that he wondered whether it might be his hopes playing tricks on him.

"Fannie Mae?"

"Are you McKie?"

That was stronger, and he recognized the familiar Caleban presence in his awareness.

"I am McKie and you owe me a debt."

"If you are truly McKie . . . why are you so . . . strange . . . changed?"

"I wear another body."

McKie was never sure, but he thought he sensed consternation. Fannie Mae responded more strongly then.

"I remove McKie from Dosadi now? Contract permits."

"I will share Dosadi's fate."

"McKie!"

"Don't argue with me, Fannie Mae. I will share Dosadi's fate unless you remove another node/person with me."

He projected Jedrik's patterns then, an easy process since he shared all of her memories.

"She wears McKie's body!"

It was accusatory.

"She wears *another* body," McKie said. He knew the Caleban saw his new relationship with Jedrik. Everything depended now on the interpretation of the Caleban contract.

"Jedrik is Dosadi," the Caleban protested.

"So am I Dosadi . . . now."

"But you are McKie!"

"And Jedrik is also McKie. Contact her if you don't believe me."

He broke the contact with an angry abruptness, found himself sprawled on the floor, still twitching. Perspiration bathed the female body which he still wore. The head ached.

Would Fannie Mae do as he'd told her? He knew Jedrik was as capable of projecting his awareness as he was of projecting hers. How would Fannie Mae interpret the Dosadi contract?

Gods! The ache in this head was a burning thing. He felt alien in Jedrik's body, misused. The pain persisted and he wondered if he'd done irreparable harm to Jedrik's brain through that intense pineal focus.

Slowly, he pushed himself upright, got to his feet. The Jedrik legs felt weak beneath him. He thought of Jedrik outside that door, trembling in the zombielike trance required for this mind-to-mind contact. What was taking so long? Had the Calebans withdrawn?

Have we lost?

He started for the door but before he'd taken the second step, light blazed around him. For a fractional heartbeat he thought it was the final fire to consume Dosadi, but the light held steady. He glanced around, found himself in the open air. It was a place he recognized immediately: the courtyard of the Dry Head compound on Tandaloor. He saw the familiar phylum designs on the surrounding walls: green Gowachin script on yellow bricks. There was the sound of water splashing in the corner pool. A group of Gowachin stood in an arched entry directly ahead of him and he recognized one of his old teachers. Yes—this was a Dry Head sanctum. These people had protected him, trained him, introduced him to their most sacred secrets.

The Gowachin in the shadowed entry were moving excitedly into the courtyard, their attention centered on a figure sprawled near them. The figure stirred, sat up.

McKie recognized his own body there.

Jedrik!

It was an intense mutual need. The body exchange required less than an eyeblink. McKie found himself in his own familiar body, seated on cool tiles. The approaching Gowachin bombarded him with questions.

"McKie, what is this?"

"You fell through a jumpdoor!"

"Are you hurt?"

He waved the questions away, crossed his legs, and fell into the long-call trance focused on that bead in his stomach. That bead Bildoon had never expected him to use!

As it was paid to do, the Taprisiot waiting on CC enfolded his awareness. McKie rejected contact with Bildoon, made six calls through the responsive Taprisiot. The calls went to key agents in BuSab, all of them ambitious and resourceful, all of them completely loyal to the agency's mandate. He transmitted his Dosadi information in full bursts, using the technique derived from his exchanges with Jedrik—mind-to-mind.

There were few questions and those easily answered.

"The Caleban who holds Dosadi imprisoned plays God. It's the letter of the contract."

"Do the Calebans approve of this?"

That question came from a particularly astute Wreave agent sensitive to the complications implicit in the fact that the Gowachin were training Ceylang, a Wreave female, as a Legum.

"The concepts of approval or disapproval are not applicable. The role was necessary for that Caleban to carry out the contract."

"It was a game?"

The Wreave agent was outraged.

"Perhaps. There's one thing certain: the Calebans don't understand harmful behavior and ethics as we understand them."

"We've always known that."

"But now we've really learned it."

When he's made the six calls, McKie sent his Taprisiot questing for Aritch, found the High Magister in the Running Phylum's conference pool.

"Greetings, Client."

McKie projected wry amusement. He sensed the Gowachin's shock.

"There are certain things which your Legum instructs you to do under the holy seal of our relationship," McKie said.

"You will take us into the Courtarena, then?"

The High Magister was perceptive and he was a beneficiary of Dosadi's peculiar gifts, but he was not a Dosadi. McKie found it relatively easy to manipulate Aritch now, enlisting the High Magister's deepest motivations. When Aritch protested against cancelling the God Wall contract, McKie revealed only the first layer of stubborn determination.

"You will not add to your Legum's difficulties."

"But what will keep them on Dosadi?"

"Nothing."

"Then you will defend rather than prosecute?"

"Ask your pet Wreave," McKie said. "Ask Ceylang."

He broke the contact then, knowing Aritch could only obey him. The High Magister had few choices, most of them bad ones. And Gowachin Law prevented him from disregarding his Legum's orders once the pattern of the contest was set.

McKie awoke from the call to find his Dry Head friends clustered around Jedrik. She was explaining their predicament. Yes . . . There were advantages to having two bodies with one purpose. McKie got to his feet. She saw him, spoke.

"My head feels better."

"It was a near thing." And he added:

"It still is. But Dosadi is free."

In the classical times of several species, it was the custom of the powerful to nudge the power-counters (money or other economic tabulators, status points, etc.) into occasional violent perturbations from which the knowledgeable few profited. Human accounts of this experience reveal edifying examples of this behavior (for which, see Appendix G). Only the PanSpechi appear to have avoided this phenomenon, possibly because of creche slavery.

—Comparative History, The BuSab Text

McKie made his next series of calls from the room the Dry Heads set aside for him. It was a relatively large room reserved for Human guests and contained well-trained chairdogs and a wide bedog which Jedrik eyed with suspicion despite her McKie memories of such things. She knew the things had only a rudimentary brain, but still they were . . . *alive.*

She stood by the single window which looked out on the courtyard pool, turning when she heard McKie awaken from his Taprisiot calls.

"Suspicions confirmed," he said.

"Will our agent friends leave Bildoon for us?" she asked

"Yes."

She turned back to the window.

"I keep thinking how the Dosadi sky must look now . . . without a God Wall. As bright as this." She nodded toward the courtyard seen through the window. "And when we get jumpdoors . . ."

She broke off. McKie, of course, shared such thoughts. This new intimacy required considerable adjustment.

"I've been thinking about your training as a Legum," she said.

McKie knew where her thoughts had gone.

The Gowachin chosen to train him had all appeared open in their relationship. He had been told that his teachers were a select group, chosen for excellence, the best available for the task: making a Gowachin Legum out of a non-Gowachin.

A silk purse from a sow's ear!

His teachers had appeared to lead conventional Gowachin lives, keeping the usual numbers of fertile females in family tanks, weeding the Graluz tads with necessary Gowachin abandon. On the surface of it, the whole thing had assumed a sense of the ordinary. They had introduced him to intimate aspects of their lives when he'd inquired, answered his questions with disarming frankness.

McKie's Jedrik-amplified awareness saw this in a different light now. The contests between Gowachin phylums stood out sharply. And McKie knew now that he had not asked the right questions, that his teachers had been selected by different rules than those revealed to him at the time, that their private instructions from their Gowachin superiors contained nuances of vital importance which had been hidden from their student.

Poor Ceylang.

These were unsettling reflections. They changed his understanding of Gowachin honor, called into question all of those inadvertent comparisons he'd made between Gowachin forms and the mandate of his own BuSab. His BuSab training came in for the same questioning examination.

Why . . . why . . . why . . . why . . .

Law? Gowachin Law?

The value in having a BuSab agent as a Legum of the Gowachin had gained a new dimension. McKie saw these matters now as Jedrik had once seen through the God Wall. There existed other forces only dimly visible behind the visible screen. An unseen power structure lay out there— people who seldom appeared in public, decision makers whose slightest whim carried terrible import for countless worlds. Many places, many worlds would be held in various degrees of bondage. Dosadi had merely been an extreme case for a special purpose.

New bodies for old. Immortality. And a training ground for people who made terrible decisions.

But none of them would be as completely Dosadi as this Jedrik-amplified McKie.

He wondered where the Dosadi decision had been made. Aritch had not shared in it; that was obvious. There were others behind Aritch—Gowachin and non-Gowachin. A shadowy power group existed. It could have its seat on any world of the ConSentiency. The power merchants would have to meet occasionally, but not necessarily face to face. And never in the public eye. Their first rule was secrecy. They would employ many people who lived at the exposed fringes of their power, people to carry out shadowy commands— people such as Aritch.

And Bildoon.

What had the PanSpechi hoped to gain? A permanent hold on his creche's ego? Of course. That . . . plus new bodies—Human bodies, undoubtedly, and unmarked by the stigmata of his PanSpechi origins.

Bildoon's behavior—and Aritch's—appeared so transparent now. And there'd be a Mrreg nearby creating the currents in which Aritch swam. Puppet leads to Puppet Master.

Mrreg.

That poor fool, Grinik, had revealed more than he thought.

And Bildoon.

"We have two points of entry," McKie said.

She agreed.

"Bildoon and Mrreg. The latter is the more dangerous."

A crease beside McKie's nose began to itch. He scratched at it absently, grew conscious that something had changed.

He stared around, found himself standing at the window and clothed in a female body.

Damn! It happened so easily.

Jedrik stared up at him with his own eyes. She spoke with his voice, but the overtones were pure Jedrik. They both found this amusing.

"The powers of your BuSab."

He understood.

"Yes, the watchdogs of justice."

"Where were the watchdogs when my ancestors were lured into this Dosadi trap?"

"Watchdogs of justice, very dangerous role," he agreed.

"You know our feelings of outrage," she said.

"And I know what it is to have loving parents."

"Remember that when you talk to Bildoon."

Once more, McKie found himself on the bed, his old familiar body around him.

Presently, he felt the mental tendrils of a Taprisiot call, sensed Bildoon's awareness in contact with him. McKie wasted no time. The shadow forces were taking the bait.

"I have located Dosadi. The issue will come to the Court-arena. No doubt of that. I want you to make the preliminary arrangements. Inform the High Magister Aritch that I make the formal imposition of the Legum. One member of the judicial panel must be a Gowachin from Dosadi. I have a particular Gowachin in mind. His name is Broey."

"Where are you?"

"On Tandaloor."

"Is that possible?"

McKie masked his sadness. *Ahhh, Bildoon, how easily you are read.*

"Dosadi is temporarily out of danger. I have taken certain retaliatory precautions."

McKie broke the contact.

Jedrik spoke in a musing voice.

"Ohh, the perturbations we spread."

McKie had no time for such reflections.

"Broey will need help, a support team, an extremely reliable troop which I want you to select for him."

"Yes, and what of Gar and Tria?"

"Let them run free. Broey will pick them up later."

Communal/managed economics have always been more destructive of their societies than those driven by greed. This is what Dosadi says: Greed sets its own limits, is self-regulating.

—The Dosadi Analysis/BuSab Text

McKie looked around the Legum office they'd assigned him. Afternoon smells from Tandaloor's fern jungles came in an open window. A low barrier separated him from the Courtarena with its ranks of seats all around. His office and adjoining quarters were small but fitted with all requisite linkages to libraries and the infrastructure to summon witnesses and experts. It was a green-walled space so deceptively ordinary that its like had beguiled more than one non-Gowachin into believing he knew how to perform here. But these quarters represented a deceptive surface riding on Gowachin currents. No matter that the ConSentient Pact modified what the Gowachin might do here, this was Tandaloor, and the forms of the frog people dominated.

Seating himself at the single table in the office space, McKie felt the chairdog adjust itself beneath him. It was good to have a chairdog again after Dosadi's unrelenting furniture. He flipped a toggle and addressed the Gowachin face which appeared on the screen inset into his table.

"I require testimony from those who made the actual decision to set up the Dosadi Experiment? Are you prepared to meet this request?"

"Do you have the names of these people?"

Did this fool think he was going to blurt out: "Mrreg"?

"If you force me to it," McKie warned, "I will bind Aritch to the Law and extract the names from him."

This had no apparent effect on the Gowachin. He addressed McKie by name and title, adding:

"I leave the formalities to you. Any witness I summon must have a name."

McKie suppressed a smile. Suspicions confirmed. This was a fact which the watchful Gowachin in the screen was late recognizing. Someone else had read the interchange correctly, however. Another, older, Gowachin face replaced the first one on the screen.

"What're you doing, McKie?"

"Determining how I will proceed with this case."

"You will proceed as a Legum of the Gowachin Bar."

"Precisely."

McKie waited.

The Gowachin peered narrowly at him from the screen. "Jedrik?"

"You are speaking to Jorj X. McKie, a Legum of the Gowachin Bar."

Belatedly, the older Gowachin saw something of the way the Dosadi experience had changed McKie.

"Do you wish me to place you in contact with Aritch?"

McKie shook his head. They were so damned obvious, these underlings.

"Aritch didn't make the Dosadi decision. Aritch was chosen to take the blow if it came to that. I will accept nothing less than the one who made that ultimate decision which launched the Dosadi Experiment."

The Gowachin stared at him coldly, then:

"One moment. I will see what I can do."

The screen went blank, but the audio remained. McKie heard the voices.

"Hello . . . Yes, I'm sorry to interrupt at this time."

"What is it?"

That was a deep and arrogant Gowachin voice, full of annoyance at the interruption. It was also an accent which a Dosadi could recognize in spite of the carefully overlaid masking tones. Here was one who'd used Dosadi.

The voice of the older Gowachin from McKie's screen continued:

"The Legum bound to Aritch has come up with a sensitive line of questioning. He wishes to speak to you."

"To me? But I am preparing for Laupuk."

McKie had no idea what Laupuk might be, but it opened a new window on the Gowachin for him. Here was a glimpse of the rarified strata which had been concealed from him all of those years. This tiny glimpse confirmed him in the course he'd chosen.

"He is listening to us at this time."

"Listening . . . why?"

The tone carried threats, but the Gowachin who'd intercepted McKie's demands went on, unwavering:

"To save explanations. It's clear that he'll accept nothing less than speaking to you. This caller is McKie, but . . ."

"Yes?"

"You will understand."

"I presume you have interpreted things correctly. Very well. Put him on."

McKie's screen flickered, revealed a wide view of a Gowachin room such as he'd never before seen. A far wall held spears and cutting weapons, streamers of colorful pennants, glistening rocks, ornate carvings in a shiny black substance. All of this was backdrop for a semireclining chairdog occupied by an aged Gowachin who sat spraddle-legged being anointed by two younger Gowachin males. The attendants poured a thick, golden substance onto the aged Gowachin from green crystal flasks. The flasks were of a spiral design. The contents were gently massaged into the Gowachin's skin. The old Gowachin glistened with the stuff and when he blinked—no Phylum tattoos.

"As you can see," he said, "I'm being prepared for . . ."

He broke off, recognizing that he spoke to a non-Gowachin. Certainly, he'd known this. It was a slow reaction for a Dosadi.

"This is a mistake," he said.

"Indeed." McKie nodded pleasantly. "Your name?"

The old Gowachin scowled at this gaucherie, then chuckled.

"I am called Mrreg."

As McKie had suspected. And why would a Tandaloor Gowachin assume the name, no, the *title* of the mythical monster who'd imbued the frog people with a drive toward savage testing? The implications went far beyond this planet, colored Dosadi.

"You made the decision for the Dosadi Experiment?"

"Someone had to make it."

That was not a substantive answer, and McKie decided to take it to issue. "You are not doing me any favors! I now know what it means to be a Legum of the Gowachin Bar and I intend to employ my powers to their limits."

It was as though McKie had worked some odd magic which froze the scene on his screen. The two attendants stopped pouring unguent, but did not look toward the pickup viewer which was recording their actions for McKie. As for Mrreg, he sat utterly still, his eyes fixed unblinking upon McKie.

McKie waited.

Presently, Mrreg turned to the attendant on his left.

"Please continue. There is little time."

McKie took this as though spoken to himself.

"You're my client. Why did you send a proxy?"

Mrreg continued to study McKie.

"I see what Ekris meant." Then, more briskly: "Well, McKie, I followed your career with interest. It now appears I did not follow you closely enough. Perhaps if we had not . . ."

He left the thought incomplete.

McKie picked up on this.

"It was inevitable that I escape from Dosadi."

"Perhaps."

The attendants finished their work, departed, taking the oddly shaped crystal flasks with them.

"Answer my question," McKie said.

"I am not required to answer your question."

"Then I withdraw from this case."

Mrreg hunched forward in sudden alarm. "You cannot! Aritch isn't . . ."

"I have no dealings with Aritch. My client is that Gowachin who made the Dosadi decision."

"You are engaging in strange behavior for a Legum. Yes, bring it." This last was addressed to someone offscreen. Another attendant appeared, carrying a white garment shaped somewhat like a long apron with sleeves. The attendant proceeded to put this onto Mrreg, who ignored him, concentrating on McKie.

"Do you have any idea what you're doing, McKie?"

"Preparing to act for my client."

"I see. Who told you about me?"

McKie shook his head.

"Did you really believe me unable to detect your presence or interpret the implications of what my own senses tell me?"

McKie saw that the Gowachin failed to see beneath the surface taunting. Mrreg turned to the attendant who was tying a green ribbon at the back of the apron. The old Gowachin had to lean forward for this. "A little tighter," he said.

The attendant retied the ribbon.

Addressing McKie, Mrreg said, "Please forgive the distraction. This must proceed at its own pace."

McKie absorbed this, assessed it Dosadi fashion. He could see the makings of an important Gowachin ritual here, but it was a new one to him. No matter. That could wait. He continued speaking, probing this Mrreg.

"When you found your own peculiar uses for Dosadi . . ."

"Peculiar? It's a universal motivation, McKie, that one tries to reduce the competition."

"Did you assess the price correctly, the price you might be asked to pay?"

"Oh, yes. I knew what I might have to pay."

There was a clear tone of resignation in the Gowachin's voice, a rare tone for his species. McKie hesitated. The attendant who'd brought the apron left the room, never once glancing in McKie's direction, although there had to be a screen to show whatever Mrreg saw of his caller.

"You wonder why I sent a proxy to hire the Legum?" Mrreg asked.

"Why Aritch?"

"Because he's a candidate for . . . greater responsibilities. You know, McKie, you astonish me. Undoubtedly you know what I could have done to you for this impertinence, yet that doesn't deter you."

This revealed more than Mrreg might have intended, but he remained unaware (or uncaring) of what McKie saw. For his part, McKie maintained a bland exterior, as blank as that of any Dosadi.

"I have a single purpose," McKie said. "Not even my client will sway me from it."

"The function of a Legum," Mrreg said.

The attendant of the white apron returned with an unsheathed blade. McKie glimpsed a jeweled handle and glittering sweep of cutting edge about twenty centimeters long. The blade curved back upon itself in a tight arc at the tip. The attendant, his back to McKie, stood facing Mrreg. The blade no longer was visible.

Mrreg, his left side partly obscured from McKie by the attendant, leaned to the right and peered up at the screen through which he watched McKie.

"You've never been appraised of the ceremony we call Laupuk. It's very important and we've been remiss in leaving this out of your education. Laupuk was essential before such a . . . project as Dosadi could be set in motion. Try to understand this ritual. It will help you prepare your case."

"What was your Phylum?" McKie asked.

"That's no longer important but . . . very well. It was Great Awakening. I was High Magister for two decades before we made the Dosadi decision."

"How many Rim bodies have you used up?"

"My final one. That, too, is no longer important. Tell me, McKie, when did you suspect Aritch was only a proxy?"

"When I realized that not all Gowachin were born Gowachin."

"But Aritch . . ."

"Ahh, yes: Aritch aspires to greater responsibilities."

"Yes . . . of course. I see. The Dosadi decision had to go far beyond a few phylums or a single species. There had to be a . . . I believe you Humans call it a 'High Command.' Yes, that would've become obvious to one as alert as you now appear. Your many marriages deceived us, I think. Was that deliberate?"

Secure behind his Dosadi mask, McKie decided to lie.

"Yes."

"Ahhhhhhhhh."

Mrreg seemed to shrivel into himself, but rallied.

"I see. We were made to believe you some kind of dilettante with perverted emotions. It'd be judged a flaw which we could exploit. Then there's another High Command and we never suspected."

It all came out swiftly, revealing the wheels within wheels which ruled Mrreg's view of the ConSentient universe. McKie marveled at how much more was said than the bare words. This one had been a long time away from Dosadi and had not been born there, but there were pressures on Mrreg now forcing him to the limits of what he'd learned on Dosadi.

McKie did not interrupt:

"We didn't expect you to penetrate Aritch's role, but that was not our intent, as you know. I presume . . ."

Whatever Mrreg presumed, he decided not to say it, musing aloud instead.

"One might almost believe you were born on Dosadi."

McKie remained silent, allowing the fear in that conjecture to fill Mrreg's consciousness.

Presently, Mrreg asked, "Do you blame all Gowachin?"

Still, McKie remained silent.

Mrreg became agitated.

"We are a government of sorts, my High Command. People can be induced not to question a government."

McKie decided to press this nerve.

"Governments always commit their entire populations when the demands grow heavy enough. By their passive acceptance, these populations become accessories to whatever is done in their name."

"You've provided free use of jumpdoors for the Dosadi?"

McKie nodded. "The Calebans are aware of their obligation. Jedrik has been busy instructing her compatriots."

"You think to loose the Dosadi upon the ConSentiency and hunt down my High Command? Have a care, McKie. I warn you not to abandon your duties as a Legum, or to turn your back on Aritch."

McKie continued silent.

"Don't make that error, McKie. Aritch is your client. Through him you represent all Gowachin."

"A Legum requires a responsible client," McKie said. "Not a proxy, but a client whose acts are brought into question by the case being tried."

Mrreg revealed Gowachin signs of deep concern.

"Hear me, McKie. I haven't much time."

In a sudden rush of apprehension, McKie focused on the attendant with the blade who stood there partly obscuring the seated Gowachin. Mrreg spoke in a swift spill of words.

"By our standards, McKie, you are not yet very well educated in Gowachin necessities. That was our error. And now your . . . impetuosity has put you into a position which is about to become untenable."

The attendant shifted slightly, arms moving up. McKie glimpsed the blade tip at the attendant's right shoulder.

"Gowachin don't have families as do Humans or even Wreaves," Mrreg said. "We have graduated advancement into groups which hold more and more responsibility for those beneath them. This was the pattern adopted by our

High Command. What you see as a Gowachin family is only a breeding group with its own limited rules. With each step up in responsibility goes a requirement that we pay an increasing price for failure. You ask if I know the price? Ahhh, McKie. The breeding male Gowachin makes sure that only the swiftest, most alert of his tads survive. A Magister upholds the forms of the Law. The High Command answers to a . . . Mrreg. You see? And a Mrreg must make only the best decisions. No failures. Thus . . . Laupuk."

As he spoke the final word, the blade in the attendant's hands flashed out and around in a shimmering arc. It caught the seated Gowachin at the neck. Mrreg's head, neatly severed, was caught in the loop at the blade's tip, lifted high, then lowered onto the white apron which now was splashed with green gore.

The scene blanked out, was replaced by the Gowachin who had connected McKie with Mrreg.

"Aritch wishes to consult his Legum," the Gowachin said.

In a changing universe, only a changing species can hope to be immortal and then only if its eggs are nurtured in widely scattered environments. This predicts a wealth of unique individuals.

—Insights (a glimpse of early Human philosophy),
BuSab Text

Jedrik made contact with McKie while he waited for the arrival of Aritch and Ceylang. He had been staring absently at the ceiling, evaluating in a profoundly Dosadi way how to gain personal advantage from the upcoming encounter, when he felt the touch of her mind on his.

McKie locked himself in his body.

"No transfer."

"Of course not."

It was a tiny thing, a subtle shading in the contact which could have been overlooked by anyone with a less accurate simulation model of Jedrik.

"You're angry with me," McKie said.

He projected irony, knew she'd read this correctly.

When she responded, her anger had been reduced to irritation. The point was not the shading of emotion, it was that she allowed such emotion to reveal itself.

"You remind me of one of my early lovers," she said.

McKie thought of where Jedrik was at this moment: safely rocked in the flower-perfumed air of his floating island on the planetary sea of Tutalsee. How strange such an environment must be for a Dosadi—no threats, fruit which could be picked and eaten without a thought of poisons. The memories she'd taken from him would coat the island with familiarity, but her flesh would continue to find that a strange experience. His memories—yes. The island would remind her of all those wives he'd taken to the honeymoon bowers of that place.

McKie spoke from this awareness.

"No doubt that early lover failed to show sufficient appreciation of your abilities, outside the bedroom, that is. Which one was it . . ."

And he named several accurate possibilities, lifting them from the memories he'd taken from Jedrik.

Now, she laughed. He sensed the untainted response, real humor and unchecked.

McKie was reminded in his turn of one of his early wives, and this made him think of the breeding situation from which Jedrik had come—no confusions between a choice for breeding mate and a lover taken for the available enjoyment of sex. One might even actively dislike the breeding mate.

Lovers . . . wives . . . What was the difference, except for the socially imprinted conventions out of which the roles arose? But Jedrik did remind him of that one particular woman, and he explored this memory, wondering if it might help him now in his relationship with Jedrik. He'd been in his midthirties and assigned to one of his first personal BuSab cases, sent out with no oldtimer to monitor and instruct him. The youngest Human agent in the Bureau's history ever to be released on his own, so it was rumored. The planet had been one of the Ylir group, very much unlike anything in McKie's previous experience: an ingrown place with deep entryways in all of the houses and an oppressive silence all around. No animals, no birds, no insects—just that awesome silence within which a fanatic religion was reported forming. All conversations were low voiced and full of subtle intonations which suggested an inner communication peculiar to Ylir and somehow making sport with all outsiders not privy to their private code. Very like Dosadi in this.

His wife of the moment, safely ensconced on Tutalsee, had been quite the opposite: gregarious, sportive, noisy.

Something about that Ylir case had sent McKie back to this wife with a sharpened awareness of her needs. The marriage had gone well for a long time, longer than any of the others. And he saw now why Jedrik reminded him of that one: they both protected themselves with a tough armor of femininity, but were extremely vulnerable behind that facade. When the armor collapsed, it collapsed totally. This realization puzzled McKie because he read his own reaction clearly: he was frightened.

In the eyeblink this evaluation took, Jedrik read him:

"We have not left Dosadi. We've taken it with us."

So that was why she'd made this contact, to be certain he mixed this datum into his evaluations. McKie looked out the open window. It would be dusk soon here on Tandaloor. The Gowachin home planet was a place which had defied change for thousands of standard years. In some respects, it was a backwater.

The ConSentiency will never be the same.

The tiny trickle of Dosadi which Aritch's people had hoped to cut off was now a roaring cataract. The people of Dosadi would insinuate themselves into niche after niche of ConSentient civilization. What could resist even the lowliest Dosadi? Laws would change. Relationships would assume profound and subtle differences. Everything from the most casual friendship to the most complex business relationship would take on some Dosadi character.

McKie recalled Aritch's parting question as Aritch had sent McKie to the jumpdoor which would put him on Dosadi.

"Ask yourself if there might be a price too high to pay for the Dosadi lesson."

That had been McKie's first clue to Aritch's actual motives and the word *lesson* had bothered him, but he'd missed the implications. With some embarrassment, McKie recalled his glib answer to Aritch's question:

"It depends on the lesson."

True, but how blind he'd been to things any Dosadi

would have seen. How ignorant. Now, he indicated to Jedrik that he understood why she'd called such things to his attention.

"Aritch didn't look much beyond the uses of outrage and injustice . . ."

"And how to turn such things to personal advantage."

She was right, of course. McKie stared out at the gathering dusk. Yes, the species tried to make everything its own. If the species failed, then forces beyond it moved in, and so on, *ad infinitum*.

I do what I do.

He recalled those words of the sleeping monster with a shudder, felt Jedrik recoil. But she was proof even against this.

"What powers your ConSentiency had."

Past tense, right. And not *our* ConSentiency because that already was a thing of the past. Besides . . . she was Dosadi.

"And the illusions of power," she said.

He saw at last what she was emphasizing, and her own shared memories in his mind made the lesson doubly impressive. She'd known precisely what McKie's personal ego-focus might overlook. Yet, this was one of the glues which held the ConSentiency together.

"Who can imagine himself immune from any retaliation?" he quoted.

It was right out of the BuSab Manual.

Jedrik made no response.

McKie needed no more emphasis from her now. The lesson of history was clear. Violence bred violence. If this violence got out of hand, it ran a course depressing in its repetitive pattern. More often than not, that course was deadly to the innocent, the so-called "enlistment phase." The ex-innocents ignited more violence and more violence until either reason prevailed or all were destroyed. There were a sufficient number of cinder blocks which once had been planets to make the lesson clear. Dosadi had come within a hair of joining that uninhabited, uninhabitable list.

Before breaking contact, Jedrik had another point to make.

"You recall that in those final days, Broey increased the rations for his Human auxiliaries, his way of saying to them: 'You'll be turned out onto the Rim soon to fend for yourselves.' "

"A *Dosadi* way of saying that."

"Correct. We always held that thought in reserve: that we should breed in such numbers that some would survive no matter what happened. We would thus begin producing species which could survive there without the city of Chu . . . or any other city designed solely to produce nonpoisonous foods."

"But there's always a bigger force waiting in the wings."

"Make sure Aritch understands that."

Choose containable violence when violence cannot be avoided. Better this than epidemic violence.

—Lessons of Choice, The BuSab Manual

The senior attendant of the Courtarena, a squat and dignified Gowachin of the Assumptive Phylum, confronted McKie at the arena door with a confession:

"I have delayed informing you that some of your witnesses have been excluded by Prosecution challenge."

The attendant, whose name was Darak, gave a Gowachin shrug, waited.

McKie glanced beyond the attendant at the truncated oval of the arena entrance which framed a lower section of the audience seats. The seats were filled. He had expected some such challenge for this first morning session of the trial, saw Darak's words as a vital revelation. They were accepting his gambit. Darak had signaled a risky line of attack by those who guided Ceylang's performance. They expected McKie to protest. He glanced back at Aritch, who stood quietly submissive three steps behind his Legum. Aritch gave every appearance of having resigned himself to the arena's conditions.

"The forms must be obeyed."

Beneath that appearance lay the hoary traditions of Gowachin Law—*The guilty are innocent. Governments always do evil. Legalists put their own interests first. Defense and prosecution are brother and sister. Suspect everything.*

Aritch's Legum controlled the initial posture and McKie had chosen defense. It hadn't surprised him to be told that Ceylang would prosecute. McKie had countered by insisting that Broey sit on a judicial panel which would be limited to three members. This had caused a delay during which Bildoon had called McKie, probing for any betrayal. Bildoon's approach had been so obvious that McKie had at first suspected a feint within a feint.

"McKie, the Gowachin fear that you have a Caleban at your command. That's a force which they . . ."

"The more they fear the better."

McKie had stared back at the screen-framed face of Bildoon, observing the signs of strain. Jedrik was right: the non-Dosadi were very easy to read.

"But I'm told you left this Dosadi in spite of a Caleban contract which prohibited . . ."

"Let them worry. Good for them."

McKie watched Bildoon intently without betraying a single emotion. No doubt there were others monitoring this exchange. Let them begin to see what they faced. Puppet Bildoon was not about to uncover what those shadowy forces wanted. They had Bildoon here on Tandaloor, though, and this told McKie an essential fact. The PanSpechi chief of BuSab was being offered as bait. This was precisely the response McKie sought.

Bildoon had ended the call without achieving his purpose. McKie had nibbled only enough to insure that Bildoon would be offered again as bait. And the puppet masters still feared that McKie had a Caleban at his beck and call.

No doubt the puppet masters had tried to question their God Wall Caleban. McKie hid a smile, thinking how that conversation must have gone. The Caleban had only to quote the letter of the contract, and if the questioners became accusatory the Caleban would respond with anger, ending the exchange. And the Caleban's words would be so filled with terms subject to ambiguous translation that the puppet masters would never be certain of what they heard.

As he stared at the patiently waiting Darak, McKie saw that they had a problem, those shadowy figures behind Aritch. Laupuk had removed Mrreg from their councils and his advice would have been valuable now. McKie had deduced that the correct reference was "The Mrreg" and that

Aritch headed the list of possible successors. Aritch might be Dosadi-trained but he was not Dosadi-born. There was a lesson in this that the entire ConSentiency would soon learn.

And Broey as a judge in this case remained an unchangeable fact. Broey was Dosadi-born. The Caleban contract had kept Broey on his poison planet, but it had not limited him to a Gowachin body. Broey knew what it was to be both Human and Gowachin. Broey knew about the Pcharkys and their use by those who'd held Dosadi in bondage. And Broey was now Gowachin. The forces opposing McKie dared not name another Gowachin judge. They must choose from the other species. They had an interesting quandary. And without a Caleban assistant, there were no more Pcharkys to be had on Dosadi. The most valuable *coin* the puppet masters had to offer was lost to them. They'd be desperate. Some of the older ones would be very desperate.

Footsteps sounded around the turn of the corridor behind Aritch. McKie glanced back, saw Ceylang come into view with her attendants. McKie counted no less than twenty leading Legums around her. They were out in force. Not only Gowachin pride and integrity, but their sacred view of Law stood at issue. And the desperate ones stood behind them, goading. McKie could almost see those shadowy figures in the shape of this entourage.

Ceylang, he saw, wore the black robes and white-striped hood of Legum Prosecutor, but she'd thrown back the hood to free her mandibles. McKie detected tension in her movements. She gave no sign of recognition, but McKie saw her through Dosadi eyes.

I frighten her. And she's right.

Turning to address the waiting attendant and speaking loudly to make sure that the approaching group heard, McKie said:

"Every law must be tested. I accept that you have given me formal announcement of a limit on my defense."

Darak, expecting outraged protest and a demand for a list of the excluded witnesses, showed obvious confusion.

"Formal announcement?"

Ceylang and entourage came to a stop behind Aritch.

McKie went on in the same loud voice:

"We stand here within the sphere of the Courtarena. All matters concerning a dispute in the arena are formal in this place."

The attendant glanced at Ceylang, seeking help. This response threatened him. Darak, hoping someday to be a High Magister, should now be recognizing his inadequacies. He would never make it in the politics of the Gowachin Phyla, especially not in the coming Dosadi age.

McKie explained as though to a neophyte:

"Information to be verified by my witnesses is known to me in its entirety. I will present the evidence myself."

Ceylang, having stooped to hear a low-voiced comment from one of her Gowachin advisors, showed surprise at this. She raised one of her ropey tendrils, called, "I protest. The Defense Legum cannot give . . ."

"How can you protest?" McKie interrupted. "We stand here before no judicial panel empowered to rule on any protest."

"I make *formal* protest!" Ceylang insisted, ignoring an advisor on her right who was tugging at her sleeve.

McKie permitted himself a cold smile.

"Very well. Then we must call Darak into the arena as witness, he being the only party present who is outside our dispute."

The edges of Aritch's jaws came down in a Gowachin grimace.

"At the end, I warned them not to go with the Wreave," he said. "They cannot say they came here unwarned."

Too late, Ceylang saw what had happened. McKie would be able to question Darak on the challenges to the witnesses. Some of those challenges were certain to be overturned. At the very least, McKie would know who the Prosecution feared. He would know it in time to act upon it. There would be no delays valuable to Prosecution. Tension, fear, and pride had made Ceylang act precipitately. Aritch had been right to warn them, but they counted on McKie's fear of the interlocked Wreave triads. Let them count. Let them blunt their awareness on that and on a useless concern over the excluded witnesses.

McKie motioned Darak through the doorway into the arena, heard him utter an oath. The reason became apparent as McKie pressed through in the crowded surge of the Prosecutor's party. The instruments of Truth-by-Pain had been arrayed on their ancient rack below the judges. Seldom brought out of their wrappings even for display to visiting dignitaries these days, the instruments had not been employed in the arena within the memory of a living witness. McKie had expected this display. It was obvious that Darak and Ceylang had not. It was interesting to note the members of Ceylang's entourage who were watching for McKie's response.

He gave them a grin of satisfaction.

McKie turned his attention to the judicial panel. They had given him Broey. The ConSentiency, acting through BuSab, held the right of one appointment. Their choice delighted McKie. Bait, indeed! Bildoon occupied the seat on Broey's right. The PanSpechi chief of bureau sat there all bland and reserved in his unfamiliar Gowachin robes of water green. Bildoon's faceted eyes glittered in the harsh arena lighting. The third judge had to be the Gowachin choice and undoubtedly maneuvered (as Bildoon had been) by the puppet masters. It was a Human and McKie, recognizing him, missed a step, recovered his balance with a visible effort.

What were they doing?

The third judge was named Mordes Parando, a noted challenger of BuSab actions. He wanted BuSab eliminated—either outright or by removing some of the bureau's key powers. He came from the planet Lirat, which provided McKie with no surprises. Lirat was a natural cover for the shadowy forces. It was a place of enormous wealth and great private estates guarded by their own security forces. Parando was a man of somewhat superficial manners which might conceal a genuine sophisticate, knowledgeable and erudite, or a completely ruthless autocrat of Broey's stamp. He was certainly Dosadi-trained. And his features bore the look of the Dosadi Rim.

There was one more fact about Parando which no one outside Lirat was supposed to know. McKie had come upon it quite by chance while investigating a Palenki who'd been an estate guard on Lirat. The turtlelike Palenki were notoriously dull, employed chiefly as muscle. This one had been uncommonly observant.

"Parando makes advice on Gowachin Law."

This had been responsive to a question about Parando's relationship with the estate guard being investigated. McKie, not seeing a connection between question and answer, had not pursued the matter, but had tucked this datum away for future investigation. He had been mildly interested at the time because of the rumored existence of a legalist enclave on Lirat and such enclaves had been known to test the limits of legality.

The people behind Aritch would expect McKie to recognize Parando. Would they expect Parando to be recognized as a legalist? They were certain to know the danger of putting Parando on a Gowachin bench. Professional legalists were absolutely prohibited from Gowachin judicial service.

"Let the people judge."

Why would they need a legalist here? Or were they expecting McKie to recognize the Rim origins of Parando's body? Were they warning McKie not to raise *that* issue here? Body exchange and the implications of immortality represented a box of snakes no one wanted to open. And the possibility of one species spying on another . . . There was fragmentation of the ConSentiency latent in this case. More ways than one.

If I challenge Parando, his replacement may be more

dangerous. If I expose him as a legalist after the trial starts . . . Could they expect me to do that? Let us explore it.

Knowing he was watched by countless eyes, McKie swept his gaze around the arena. Above the soft green absorbent oval where he stood were rank on rank of benches, every seat occupied. Muted morning light from the domed translucent ceiling illuminated rows of Humans, Gowachin, Palenki, Sobarips . . . McKie identified a cluster of Ferret Wreaves just above the arena, limber thin with a sinuous flexing in every movement. They would bear watching. But every species and faction in the ConSentiency would be represented here. Those who could not come in person would watch these proceedings via the glittering transmitter eyes which looked down from the ceiling's edges.

Now, McKie looked to the right at the witness pen set into the wall beneath the ranked benches. He identified every witness he'd called, even the challenged ones. The forms were being obeyed. While the ConSentient Covenant required certain modifications here, this arena was still dominated by Gowachin Law. To accent that, the blue metal box from the Running Phylum occupied the honor place on the bench in front of the judicial panel.

Who will taste the knife here?

Protocol demanded that Prosecutor and Defense approach to a point beneath the judges, abase themselves, and call out acceptance of the arena's conditions. The Prosecutor's party, however, was in disarray. Two of Ceylang's advisors were whispering excited advice to her.

The members of the Judicial panel conferred, glancing at the scene below them. They could not act formally until the obeisance.

McKie passed a glance across the panel, absorbed Broey's posture. The Dosadi Gowachin's enlightened greed was like an anchor point. It was like Gowachin Law, changeable only on the surface. And Broey was but the tip of the Dosadi advisory group which Jedrik had approved.

Holding his arms extended to the sides, McKie marched

forward, abased himself face down on the floor, stood and
called out:

"I accept this arena as my friend. The conditions here are
my conditions but Prosecution has defiled the sacred traditions of this place. Does the court give me leave to slay her
outright?"

There was an exclamation behind him, the sound of
running, the sudden flopping of a body onto the arena's matted floor. Ceylang could not address the court before this
obeisance and she knew it. She and the others now also knew
something else just as important—that McKie was ready to
slay her despite the threat of Wreave vendetta.

In a breathless voice, Ceylang called out her acceptance
of the arena's conditions, then:

"I protest this trick by Defense Legum!"

McKie saw the stirring of Gowachin in the audience. A
trick? Didn't Ceylang know yet how the Gowachin dearly
loved legal tricks?

The members of the judicial panel had been thoroughly
briefed on the surface demands of the Gowachin forms,
though it was doubtful that Bildoon understood sufficiently
what went on beneath those forms. The PanSpechi confirmed this now by leaning forward to speak.

"Why does the senior attendant of this court enter ahead
of the Legums?"

McKie detected a fleeting smile on Broey's face, glanced
back to see Darak standing apart from the prosecution
throng, alone and trembling.

McKie took one step forward.

"Will the court direct Darak to the witness pen? He is
here because of a formal demand by the Prosecutor."

"This is the senior attendant of your court," Ceylang argued. "He guards the door to . . ."

"Prosecution made formal protest to a matter which occurred in the presence of this attendant," McKie said. "As
an attendant, Darak stands outside the conflicting interests.
He is the only reliable witness."

Broey stirred, looked at Ceylang, and McKie realized how strange the Wreave must appear to a Dosadi. This did not deter Broey, however.

"Did you protest?"

It was a direct question from the bench. Ceylang was required to answer. She looked to Bildoon for help but he remained silent. Parando also refused to help her. She glanced at Darak. The terrified attendant could not take his attention from the instruments of pain. Perhaps he knew something specific about their presence in the arena.

Ceylang tried to explain.

"When Defense Legum suggested an illegal . . ."

"Did you protest?"

"But the . . ."

"This court decides on all matters of legality. Did you protest?"

"I did."

It was forced out of her. A fit of trembling passed over the slender Wreave form.

Broey waved Darak to the witness pen, had to add a vocal order when the frightened attendant failed to understand. Darak almost ran to the shelter of the pen.

Silence pervaded the arena. The silence of the audience was an explosive thing. They sat poised in the watching ovals, all of those species and factions with their special fears. By now, they'd heard many stories and rumors. Jump-doors had spread the Dosadi emigres all across the Con-Sentiency. Media representatives had been excluded from Dosadi and this court on the Gowachin argument that they were "prey to uninformed subjective reactions," but they would be watching here through the transmitter eyes at the ceiling.

McKie looked around at nothing in particular but taking in every detail. There were more than three judges in this arena and Ceylang certainly must realize that. Gowachin Law turned upon itself, existing "only to be changed." But that watching multitude was quite another matter. Ceylang must be made to understand that she was a sacrifice of the arena. ConSentient opinion stood over her like a heavy sledge ready to smash down.

It was Parando's turn.

"Will opposing Legums make their opening arguments now?"

"We can't proceed while a formal protest is undecided," McKie said.

Parando understood. He glanced at the audience, at the ceiling. His actions were a direct signal: Parando knew which *judges* really decided here. To emphasize it, he ran a hand from the front of his neck down his chest, the unique Rim Raider's salute from Dosadi signifying "Death before surrender." Subtle hints in the movement gave McKie another datum: Parando was a Gowachin in a Human body. They'd dared put two Gowachin on that panel!

With Dosadi insight, McKie saw why they did this. They were prepared to produce the Caleban contract here. They were telling McKie that *they* would expose the body-exchange secret if he forced them to it. All would see that loophole in the Caleban contract which confined the Dosadi-born, but released outsiders in Dosadi flesh.

They think I'm really Jedrik in this flesh!

Parando revealed even more. His people intended to find the Jedrik body and kill it, leaving this *McKie* flesh forever in doubt. He could protest his McKie identity all he wanted. They had but to demand that he prove it. Without the other person . . . What had their God Wall Caleban told them?

"He is McKie, she is McKie. He is Jedrik, she is Jedrik."

His mind in turmoil, McKie wondered if he dared risk an immediate mind contact with Jedrik. Together, they'd already recognized this danger. Jedrik had hidden herself on McKie's hideaway, a floating island on Tutalsee. She was there with a special Taprisiot contract prohibiting unwanted calls which might inadvertently reveal her location.

The judges, led by Parando, were acting, however, moving

for an immediate examination of Darak. McKie forced himself to perform as a Legum.

His career in ruins, the attendant answered like an automaton. In the end, McKie restored most of his witnesses. There were two notable exceptions: Grinik (that flawed thread which might have led to The Mrreg) and Stiggy. McKie was not certain why they wanted to exclude the Dosadi weapons genius who'd transformed a BuSab wallet's contents into instruments of victory. Was it that Stiggy had broken an *unbreakable* code? That made sense only if Prosecution intended to play down the inherent Dosadi superiority.

Still uncertain, McKie prepared to retire and seek a way to avoid Parando's gambit, but Ceylang addressed the bench.

"The issue of witnesses having been introduced by Defense," she said, "Prosecution wishes to explore this issue. We note many witnesses from Dosadi called by Defense. There is a noteworthy omission whose name has not yet been introduced here. I refer to a Human by the name of Jedrik. Prosecution wishes to call Keila Jedrik as . . ."

"One moment!"

McKie searched his mind for the forms of an acceptable escape. He knew that his blurted protest had revealed more than he wanted. But they were moving faster than he'd expected. Prosecution did not really want Jedrik as a witness, not in a Gowachin Courtarena where the roles were never quite what they appeared to non-Gowachin. This was a plain message to McKie.

"We're going to find her and kill her."

With Bildoon and Parando concurring, a jumpdoor was summoned and Ceylang played her trump.

"Defense knows the whereabouts of witness Keila Jedrik."

They were forcing the question, aware of the emotional bond between McKie and Jedrik. He had a choice: argue that a personal relationship with the witness excluded her. But Prosecution and all the judges had to concur. They obviously would not do this—not yet. A harsh lock on his emotions, McKie gave the jumpdoor instructions.

Presently, Jedrik stepped onto the arena floor, faced the judges. She'd been into the wardrobe at his bower cottage and wore a yellow and orange sarong which emphasized her height and grace. Open brown sandals protected her feet. There was a flame red blossom at her left ear. She managed to look exotic and fragile.

Broey spoke for the judges.

"Do you have knowledge of the issues at trial here?"

"What issues are at trial?"

She asked it with a childlike innocence which did not even fool Bildoon. They were forced to explain, however, because of those other *judges* to whom every nuance here was vital. She heard them out in silence.

"An alleged experiment on a sentient population confined to a planet called Dosadi . . . lack of informed consent by subject population charged . . . accusations of conspiracy against certain Gowachin and others not yet named . . ."

Two fingers pressed to his eyes in the guise of intense listening, McKie made contact with Jedrik, suggesting, conferring. They had to find a way out of this trap! When he looked up, he saw the suspicions in Parando's face: *Which body, which ego? McKie? Jedrik?*

In the end, Ceylang hammered home the private message, demanding whether Jedrik had "any personal relationship with Defense Legum?"

Jedrik answered in a decidedly un-Dosadi fashion.

"Why . . . yes. We are lovers."

In itself, this was not enough to exclude her from the arena unless Prosecution and the entire judicial panel agreed. Ceylang proposed the exclusion. Bildoon and Parando were predictable in their agreement. McKie waited for Broey.

"Agreed."

Broey had a private compact with the shadow forces then. Jedrik and McKie had expected this, but had not anticipated the form confirmation would take.

McKie asked for a recess until the following morning.

With the most benign face on it, this was granted. Broey announced the decision, smiling down at Jedrik. It was a measure of McKie's Dosadi conditioning that he could not find it in himself to blame Broey for wanting personal victory over the person who had beaten him on Dosadi.

Back in his quarters, Jedrik put a hand on McKie's chest, spoke with eyes lowered.

"Don't blame yourself, McKie. This was inevitable. Those judges, none of them, would've allowed any protest from you before seeing me in person on that arena floor."

"I know."

She looked up at him, smiling.

"Yes . . . of course. How like one person we are."

For a time after that, they reviewed the assessment of the aides chosen for Broey. Shared memories etched away at minutiae. Could any choice be improved? Not one person was changed—Human or Gowachin. All of those advisors and aides were Dosadi-born. They could be depended upon to be loyal to their origins, to their conditioning, to themselves individually. For the task assigned to them, they were the best available.

McKie brought it to a close.

"I can't leave the immediate area of the arena until the trial's over."

She knew that, but it needed saying.

There was a small cell adjoining his office, a bedog there, communications instruments, Human toilet facilities. They delayed going into the bedroom, turned to a low-key argument over the advisability of a body exchange. It was procrastination on both sides, outcome known in advance. Familiar flesh was familiar flesh, less distracting. It gave each of them an edge which they dared not sacrifice. McKie could play Jedrik and Jedrik could play McKie, but that would be dangerous play now.

When they retired, it was to make love, the most tender experience either had known. There was no submission, only a giving, sharing, an open exchange which tightened

McKie's throat with joy and fear, sent Jedrik into a fit of un-Dosadi sobbing.

When she'd recovered, she turned to him on the bed, touched his right cheek with a finger.

"McKie."

"Yes?"

"I've never had to say this to another person, but . . ." She silenced his attempted interruption by punching his shoulder, leaning up on an elbow to look down at him. It reminded McKie of their first night together, and he saw that she had gone back into her Dosadi shell . . . but there was something else, a difference in the eyes.

"What is it?"

"Just that I love you. It's a very interesting feeling, especially when you can admit it openly. How odd."

"Stay here with me."

"We both know I can't. There's no safe place here for either of us, but the one who . . ."

"Then let's . . ."

"We've already decided against an exchange."

"Where will you go?"

"Best you don't know."

"If . . ."

"No! I wouldn't be safe as a witness; I'm not even safe at your side. We both . . ."

"Don't go back to Dosadi."

"Where is Dosadi? It's the only place where I could ever feel at home, but Dosadi no longer exists."

"I meant . . ."

"I know."

She sat up, hugged her knees, revealing the sinewy muscles of her shoulders and back. McKie studied her, trying to fathom what it was she hid in that Dosadi shell. Despite the intimacy of their shared memories, something about her eluded him. It was as though he didn't want to learn this thing. She would flee and hide, of course, but . . . He listened carefully as she began to speak in a faraway voice.

"It'd be interesting to go back to Dosadi someday. The differences . . ."

She looked over her shoulder at him.

"There are those who fear we'll make over the ConSentiency in Dosadi's image. We'll try, but the result won't be Dosadi. We'll take what we judge to be valuable, but that'll change Dosadi more than it changes you. Your masses are less alert, slower, less resourceful, but you're so numerous. In the end, the ConSentiency will win, but it'll no longer be the ConSentiency. I wonder what it'll be when . . ."

She laughed at her own musings, shook her head.

"And there's Broey. They'll have to deal with Broey and the team we've given him. Broey Plus! Your ConSentiency hasn't the faintest grasp of what we've loosed among them."

"The predator in the flock."

"To Broey, your people are like the Rim—a natural resource."

"But he has no Pcharkys."

"Not yet."

"I doubt if the Calebans ever again will participate in . . ."

"There may be other ways. Look how easy it is for us."

"But we were printed upon each other by . . ."

"Exactly! And they continue to suspect that you're in my body and I'm in yours. Their entire experience precludes the free shift back and forth, one body to another . . ."

"Or this other thing . . ."

He caressed her mind.

"Yes! Broey won't suspect until too late what's in store for him. They'll be a long time learning there's no way to sort you from . . . me!"

This last was an exultant shout as she turned and fell upon him. It was a wild replay of their first night together. McKie abandoned himself to it. There was no other choice, no time for the mind to dwell on depressing thoughts.

In the morning, he had to tap his implanted amplifiers to bring his awareness to the required pitch for the arena. The process took a few minutes while he dressed.

Jedrik moved softly with her own preparations, straightened the bedog and caressed its resilient surface. She summoned a jumpdoor then, held him with a lingering kiss. The jumpdoor opened behind her as she pushed away from him.

McKie smelled familiar flowers, glimpsed the bowers of his Tutalsee island before the door blinked out of existence, hiding Jedrik and the island from him. Tutalsee? The moment of shocked understanding delayed him. She'd counted on that! He recovered, sent his mind leaping after her.

I'll force an exchange! By the Gods . . .

His mind met pain, consuming, blinding pain. It was agony such as he'd not even imagined could exist.

Jedrik!

His mind held an unconscious Jedrik whose awareness had fled from pain. The contact was so delicate, like holding a newborn infant. The slightest relaxation and he knew he would lose her to . . . He felt that terrifying monster of the first exchange hovering in the background, but love and concern armed him against fear.

Frantic, McKie held that tenuous contact while he called a jumpdoor. There was a small delay and when the door opened, he saw through the portal the black, twisted wreckage which had been his bower island. A hot sun beat down on steaming cinders. And in the background, a warped metal object which might have been one of Tutalsee's little four-place flitters rolled over, gurgled, and sank. The visible wreckage said the destructive force had been something like a pentrate, swift and all-consuming. The water around the island still bubbled with it. Even while he watched, the island began breaking up, its cinders drifting apart on the long, low waves. A breeze flattened the steaming smoke. Soon, there'd be nothing to show that beauty had floated here. With a pentrate, there would be nothing to recover . . . not even bodies to . . .

He hesitated, still holding his fragile grasp on Jedrik's unconscious presence. The pain was only a memory now. Was it really Jedrik in his awareness, or only his remembered imprint of her? He tried to awaken the sleeping presence, failed. But small threads of memory emerged, and he saw that the destruction had been Jedrik's doing, response to attack. The attackers had wanted a live hostage. They hadn't anticipated that violent, unmistakable message.

"You won't hold *me* over McKie's head!"

But if there were no bodies . . .

Again, he tried to awaken that unconscious presence. Her memories were there, but she remained dormant. The effort strengthened his grip upon her presence, though. And he told himself it had to be Jedrik, or he wouldn't know what had happened on the bower island.

Once more, he searched the empty water. Nothing.

A pentrate would've torn and battered everything around it. Shards of metal, flesh reduced to scattered cinders . . .

She's dead. She has to be dead. A pentrate . . .

But that familiar presence lay slumbering in his mind.

The door clacker interrupted his reverie. McKie released the jumpdoor, turned to look through the bedside viewer at the scene outside his Legum quarters. The expected deputation had arrived. Confident, the puppet masters were moving even before confirmation of their Tutalsee gambit. They could not possibly know yet what McKie knew. There could be no jumpdoor or any other thread permitted to connect this group to Tutalsee.

McKie studied them carefully, keeping a bridle on his rage. There were eight of them, so contained, so well schooled in Dosadi self-control. So transparent to a Jedrik-amplified McKie. They were four Humans and four Gowachin. Overconfident. Jedrik had seen to that by leaving no survivors.

Again, McKie tried to awaken that unconscious presence. She would not respond.

Have I only built her out of my memories?

There was no time for such speculation. Jedrik had made her choice on Tutalsee. He had other choices to make here and now—for both of them. That ghostly presence locked in his mind would have to wait.

McKie punched the communicator which linked him to Broey, gave the agreed-upon signal.

"It's time."

He composed himself then, went to the door.

They'd sent no underlings. He gave them that. But they addressed him as Jedrik, made the anticipated demands, gloated over the hold they had upon him. It was only then that McKie saw fully how well Jedrik had measured these people; and how she had played upon her McKie in those last hours together like an exquisitely tuned instrument. Now, he understood why she'd made that violent choice.

As anticipated, the members of the delegation were extremely surprised when Broey's people fell upon them without warning.

*For the Gowachin, to stand alone against all adversity is
the most sacred moment of existence.*

—The Gowachin, a BuSab analysis

The eight prisoners were dumped on the arena floor,
bound and shackled. McKie stopped near them,
waiting for Ceylang to arrive. It was not yet dawn. The
ceiling above the arena remained dark. A few of the transmitter eyes around the upper perimeter glittered to reveal
that they were activated. More were coming alive by the
moment. Only a few of the witness seats were occupied,
but people were streaming in as word was passed. The judicial bench remained empty.

The outer areaway was a din of Courtarena security
forces coming and going, people shouting orders, the clank
of weapons, a sense of complete confusion there which
gradually resolved itself as Broey led his fellow judges up
onto their bench. The witness pen was also filling, people
punching sleep from their eyes, great gaping yawns from
the Gowachin.

McKie looked to Broey's people, the ones who'd brought
in the prisoners. He nodded for the captors to leave, giving
them a Dosadi hand signal to remain available. They left.

Ceylang passed them as she entered, still fastening her
robe. She hurried to McKie's side, waited for the judges to
be seated before speaking.

"What is the meaning of this? My attendants . . ."

Broey signaled McKie.

McKie stepped forward to address the bench, pointed to
the eight bound figures who were beginning to stir and push
themselves upright.

"Here you see my client."

Parando started to speak, but Broey silenced him with a

sharp word which McKie did not catch. It sounded like "frenzy."

Bildoon sat in fearful fascination, unable to wrest his attention from the bound figures, all of whom remained silent. Yes, Bildoon would recognize those eight prisoners. In his limited, ConSentient fashion, Bildoon was sharp enough to recognize that he was in personal danger. Parando, of course, knew this immediately and watched Broey with great care.

Again, Broey nodded to McKie.

"A fraud has been perpetrated upon this court," McKie said. "It is a fraud which was perpetrated against those great and gallant people, the Gowachin. Both Prosecution and Defense are its victims. The Law is its ultimate victim."

It had grown much quieter in the arena. The observer seats were jammed, all the transmitter eyes alive. The faintest of dawn glow touched the translucent ceiling. McKie wondered what time it was. He had forgotten to put on any timepiece.

There was a stir behind McKie. He glanced back, saw attendants belatedly bringing Aritch into the arena. Oh, yes—they would have risked any delay to confer with Aritch. Aritch was supposed to be the other McKie expert. Too bad that this Human who looked like McKie was no longer the McKie they thought they knew.

Ceylang could not hold her silence. She raised a tendril for attention.

"This Tribunal . . ."

McKie interrupted.

". . . is composed of three people. Only three."

He allowed them a moment to digest this reminder that Gowachin trial formalities still dominated this arena, and were like no other such formalities in the ConSentiency. It could've been fifty judges up there on that bench. McKie had witnessed Gowachin trials where people were picked at random off the streets to sit in judgment. Such jurists took their duties seriously, but their overt behavior could lead another sentient species to question this. The Gowachin chattered back and forth, arranged parties, exchanged jokes, asked each other rude questions. It was an ancient pattern. The jurists were required to become "a single organism." Gowachin had their own ways of rushing that process.

But this Tribunal was composed of just three judges, only one of them visibly Gowachin. They were separate entities, their actions heavy with mannerisms foreign to the Gowachin. Even Broey, tainted by Dosadi, would be unfamiliar to the Gowachin observers. No "single organism" here holding to the immutable forms beneath Gowachin Law. That had to be deeply disturbing to the Legums who advised Ceylang.

Broey leaned forward, addressed the arena.

"We'll dispense with the usual arguments while this new development is explored."

Again, Parando tried to interrupt. Broey silenced him with a glance.

"I call Aritch of the Running Phylum," McKie said.

He turned.

Ceylang stood in mute indecision. Her advisors remained at the back of the arena conferring among themselves. There seemed to be a difference of opinion among them.

Aritch shuffled to the death-focus of the arena, the place where every witness was required to stand. He glanced at the instruments of pain arrayed beneath the judicial bench, cast a wary look at McKie. The old High Magister appeared harried and undignified. That hurried conference to explore this development must've been a sore trial to the old Gowachin.

McKie crossed to the formal position beside Aritch, addressed the judges.

"Here we have Aritch, High Magister of the Running Phylum. We were told that if guilt were to be found in this arena, Aritch bore that guilt. He, so we were led to believe, was the one who made the decision to imprison Dosadi. But how can that be so? Aritch is old, but he isn't as old as

Dosadi. Then perhaps his alleged guilt is to be found in concealing the imprisonment of Dosadi. But Aritch summoned an agent of BuSab and sent that agent openly to Dosadi."

A disturbance among the eight shackled prisoners interrupted McKie. Several of the prisoners were trying to get to their feet, but the links of the shackles were too short.

On the judicial bench, Parando started to lean forward, but Broey hauled him back.

Yes, Parando and others were recalling the verities of a Gowachin Courtarena, the constant reversals of concepts common throughout the rest of the ConSentiency.

To be guilty is to be innocent. Thus, to be innocent is to be guilty.

At a sharp command from Broey, the prisoners grew quiet.

McKie continued.

"Aritch, conscious of the sacred responsibilities which he carried upon his back as a mother carries her tads, was deliberately named to receive the punishment blow lest that punishment be directed at all Gowachin everywhere. Who chose this innocent High Magister to suffer for all Gowachin?"

McKie pointed to the eight shackled prisoners.

"Who are these people?" Parando demanded.

McKie allowed the question to hang there for a long count. Parando knew who these eight were. Did he think he could divert the present course of events by such a blatant ploy?

Presently, McKie spoke.

"I will enlighten the court in due course. My duty, however, comes first. My client's *innocence* comes first."

"One moment."

Broey held up a webbed hand.

One of Ceylang's advisors hurried past McKie, asked and received permission to confer with Ceylang. A thwarted Parando sat like a condemned man watching this conversation as though he hoped to find reprieve there. Bildoon had hunched forward, head buried in his arms. Broey obviously controlled the Tribunal.

The advisor Legum was known to McKie, one Lagag of a middling reputation, an officer out of breeding. His words to Ceylang were low and intense, demanding.

The conference ended, Lagag hurried back to his companions. They now understood the tenor of McKie's *defense*. Aritch must have known all along that he could be sacrificed here. The ConSentient Covenant no longer permitted the ancient custom where the Gowachin audience had poured into the arena to kill with bare hands and claws the *innocent* defendant. But let Aritch walk from here with the brand of innocence upon him; he would not take ten paces outside the arena's precincts before being torn to pieces.

There'd been worried admiration in the glance Lagag had given McKie in passing. Yes . . . now they understood why McKie had maneuvered for a small and vulnerable judicial panel.

The eight prisoners began a new disturbance which Broey silenced with a shout. He signaled for McKie to continue.

"Aritch's design was that I expose Dosadi, return and defend him against the charge that he had permitted illegal psychological experiments upon an unsuspecting populace. He was prepared to sacrifice himself for others."

McKie sent a wry glance at Aritch. Let the High Magister try to fight in half-truths in that defense!

"Unfortunately, the Dosadi populace was *not* unsuspecting. In fact, forces under the command of Keila Jedrik had moved to take control of Dosadi. Judge Broey will affirm that she had succeeded in this."

Again, McKie pointed to the shackled prisoners.

"But these conspirators, these people who designed and profited from the Dosadi Experiment, ordered the death of Keila Jedrik! She was murdered this morning on Tutalsee to prevent my using her at the proper moment to prove Aritch's *innocence*. Judge Broey is witness to the truth of what I say. Keila Jedrik was brought into this arena yesterday only that she might be traced and killed!"

McKie raised both arms in an eloquent gesture of completion, lowered his arms.

Aritch looked stricken. He saw it. If the eight prisoners denied the charges, they faced Aritch's fate. And they must know by now that Broey wanted them *Gowachin-guilty*. They could bring in the Caleban contract and expose the body-exchange plot, but that risked having McKie defend or prosecute them because he'd already locked them to his actual *client*, Aritch. Broey would affirm this, too. They were at Broey's mercy. If they were *Gowachin-guilty*, they walked free only here on Tandaloor. *Innocent*, they died here.

As though they were one organism, the eight turned their heads and looked at Aritch. Indeed! What would Aritch do? If he agreed to sacrifice himself, the eight might live. Ceylang, too, focused on Aritch.

Around the entire arena there was a sense of collective held breath.

McKie watched Ceylang. How candid had Aritch's people been with their Wreave? Did she know the full Dosadi story?

She broke the silence, exposing her knowledge. She chose to aim her attack at McKie on the well-known dictum that, when all else failed, you tried to discredit the opposing Legum.

"McKie, is this how you defend these eight people whom only *you* name as client?" Ceylang demanded.

Now, it was delicate. Would Broey go along?

McKie countered her probe with a question of his own.

"Are you suggesting that you'd prosecute these people?"

"I didn't charge them! You did."

"To prove Aritch's innocence."

"But you call them client. Will you defend them?"

A collective gasp arose from the cluster of advisors behind her near the arena doorway. They'd seen the trap. If McKie accepted the challenge, the judges had no choice but to bring the eight into the arena under Gowachin forms. Ceylang had trapped herself into the posture of prosecutor against the eight. She'd said, in effect, that she affirmed their guilt. Doing so, she lost her case against Aritch and her life was immediately forfeit. She was caught.

Her eyes glittered with the unspoken question.

What would McKie do?

Not yet, McKie thought. *Not yet, my precious Wreave dupe.*

He turned his attention to Parando. Would they dare introduce the Caleban contract? The eight prisoners were only the exposed tip of the shadowy forces, a vulnerable tip. They could be sacrificed. It was clear that they saw this and didn't like it. No Gowachin Mrregs here with that iron submission to responsibility! They loved life and its power, especially the ones who wore Human flesh. How precious life must be for those who'd lived many lives! *Very* desperate, indeed.

To McKie's Dosadi-conditioned eyes, it was as though he read the prisoners' thoughts. They were safest if they remained silent. Trust Parando. Rely on Broey's enlightened greed. At the worst, they could live out what life was left to them here on Tandaloor, hoping for new bodies before the flesh they now wore ran out of vitality. As long as they still lived they could hope and scheme. Perhaps another Caleban could be hired, more Pcharkys found . . .

Aritch broke, unwilling to lose what had almost been his.

The High Magister's Tandaloor accent was hoarse with protest.

"But I did supervise the tests on Dosadi's population!"

"To what tests do you refer?"

"The Dosadi . . ."

Aritch fell silent, seeing the trap. More than a million Dosadi Gowachin already had left their planet. Would Aritch make targets of them? Anything he said could open the door to proof that the Dosadis were superior to non-Dosadis. Any Gowachin (or Human, for that matter) could well become a target in the next few minutes. One had only to denounce a selected Human or Gowachin as Dosadi. ConSentient fears would do the rest. And any of his arguments could be directed into exposure of Dosadi's real purpose. He obviously saw the peril in that, had seen it from the first.

The High Magister confirmed this analysis by glancing at the Ferret Wreaves in the audience. What consternation it would create among the secretive Wreaves to learn that another species could masquerade successfully as one of their own!

McKie could not leave matters where they stood, though. He threw a question at Aritch.

"Were the original transportees to Dosadi apprised of the nature of the project?"

"Only *they* could testify to that."

"And their memories were erased. We don't even have historical testimony on this matter."

Aritch remained silent. Eight of the original designers of the Dosadi project sat near him on the arena floor. Would he denounce them to save himself? McKie thought not. A person deemed capable of performing as The Mrreg could not possess such a flaw. Could he? Here was the real point of no return.

The High Magister confirmed McKie's judgment by turning his back on the Tribunal, the ages-old Gowachin gesture of submission. What a shock Aritch's performance must have been for those who'd seen him as a possible Mrreg. A poor choice except at the end, and that'd been as much recognition of total failure as anything else.

McKie waited, knowing what had to happen now. Here was Ceylang's moment of truth.

Broey addressed her.

"You have suggested that you would prosecute these eight prisoners. The matter is in the hands of Defense Legum."

Broey shifted his gaze.

"How say you, Legum McKie?"

The moment to test Broey had come. McKie countered with a question.

"Can this Courtarena suggest another disposition for these eight prisoners?"

Ceylang held her breath.

Broey was pleased. He had triumphed in the end over Jedrik. Broey was certain in his mind that Jedrik did not occupy this Legum body on the arena floor. Now, he could show the puppet masters what a Dosadi-born could do. And McKie saw that Broey intended to move fast, much faster than anyone had expected.

Anyone except Jedrik, and she was only a silent (memory?) in McKie's awareness.

Having given the appearance of deliberation, Broey spoke.

"I can order these eight bound over to ConSentient jurisdiction if McKie agrees."

The eight stirred, subsided.

"I agree," McKie said. He glanced at Ceylang. She made no protest, seeing the futility. Her only hope now lay in the possible deterrent presence of the Ferret Wreaves.

"Then I so order it," Broey said. He spared a triumphant glance for Parando. "Let a ConSentient jurisdiction decide if these eight are guilty of murder and other conspiracy."

He was well within the bounds of the Covenant between the ConSentiency and Gowachin, but the Gowachin members of his audience didn't like it. Their Law was best! Angry whistlings could be heard all around the arena.

Broey rose half-out of his seat, pointed at the instruments of pain arrayed beneath him. Gowachin in the audience fell silent. They, better than anyone, knew that no person here, not even a member of the audience, was outside the Tribunal's power. And many understood clearly now why those bloody tools had been displayed here. Thoughtful people had anticipated the problem of keeping order in this arena.

Responding to the silent acceptance of his authority, Broey sank back into his seat.

Parando was staring at Broey as though having just discovered the presence of a monster in this Gowachin form. Many people would be reassessing Broey now.

Aritch held his attitude of complete submission.

Ceylang's thoughts almost hummed in the air around her. Every way she turned, she saw only a tangle of unmanageable tendrils and a blocked passage.

McKie saw that it was time to bring matters to a head. He crossed to the foot of the judicial bench, lifted a short spear from the instruments there. He brandished the barbed, razor-edged weapon.

"Who sits on this Tribunal?"

Once, Aritch had issued such a challenge. McKie, repeating it, pointed with the spear, answered his own question.

"A Gowachin of my choice, one supposedly wronged by the Dosadi project. Were you wronged, Broey?"

"No."

McKie faced Parando.

"And here we have a Human from Lirat. Is that not the case, Parando?"

"I am from Lirat, yes."

McKie nodded.

"I am prepared to bring a parade of witnesses into this arena to testify as to your occupation on Lirat. Would you care to state that occupation?"

"How dare you question this Tribunal?"

Parando glared down at McKie, face flushed.

"Answer his question."

It was Broey.

Parando looked at Bildoon, who still sat with face concealed in his arms, face down on the bench. Something about the PanSpechi repelled Parando, but he knew he had to have Bildoon's vote to overrule Broey. Parando nudged the PanSpechi. Inert flesh rolled away from Parando's hand.

McKie understood.

Facing doom, Bildoon had retreated into the creche. Somewhere, an unprepared PanSpechi body was being rushed into acceptance of that crushed identity. The emergence of a new Bildoon would require considerable time. They did not have that time. When the creche finally brought forth a functioning persona, it would not be heir to Bildoon's old powers in BuSab.

Parando was alone, exposed. He stared at the spear in McKie's hand.

McKie favored the arena with a sweeping glance before speaking once more to Parando.

"I quote that renowned expert on Gowachin Law, High Magister Aritch: 'ConSentient Law always makes aristocrats of its practitioners. Gowachin Law stands beneath that pretension. Gowachin Law asks: Who knows the people? Only such a one is fit to judge in the Courtarena.' That is Gowachin Law according to High Magister Aritch. That is the law in this place."

Again, McKie gave Parando a chance to speak, received only silence.

"Perhaps you are truly fit to judge here," McKie suggested. "Are you an artisan? A philosopher? Perhaps you're a humorist? An artist? Ahhh, maybe you are that lowliest of workmen, he who tends an automatic machine?"

Parando remained silent, gaze locked on the spear.

"None of these?" McKie asked. "Then I shall supply the answer. You are a professional legalist, one who gives legal advice, even to advice on Gowachin Law. You, a Human, not even a Legum, dare to speak of Gowachin Law!"

Without any muscular warning signal, McKie leaped forward, hurled the spear at Parando, saw it strike deeply into the man's chest.

One for Jedrik!

With bubbling gasp, Parando sagged out of sight behind the bench.

Broey, seeing the flash of anger in McKie's effort, touched the blue box in front of him.

Have no fear, Broey. Not yet. I still need you.

But now, more than Broey knew it was really McKie in this flesh. Not Jedrik. Those members of the shadow force watching this scene and able to plot would make the expected deduction because they did not know how freely and completely Jedrik and McKie had shared. To the shadow force, McKie would've known Parando's background. They'd trace out that mistake in short order. So this was McKie in the arena. But he'd left Dosadi. There could be only one conclusion in the plotters' minds.

McKie had Caleban help!

They had Calebans to fear.

And McKie thought: *You have only McKie to fear.*

He grew aware that grunts of Gowachin approval were sounding all around the arena. They accepted him as a Legum, thus they accepted his argument. Such a judge deserved killing.

Aritch set the precedent. McKie improved on it.

Both had found an approved way to kill a flawed judge, but McKie's act had etched a Gowachin precedent into the ConSentient legal framework. The compromise which had brought Gowachin and ConSentient Law into the Covenant of shared responsibility for the case in this arena would be seen by the Gowachin as a first long step toward making their Law supreme over all other law.

Aritch had half-turned, looking toward the bench, a glittering appraisal in his eyes which said the Gowachin had salvaged something here after all.

McKie strode back to confront Ceylang. He faced her as the forms required while he called for judgment.

"Bildoon?"

Silence.

"Parando?"

Silence.

"Broey?"

"Judgment for Defense."

The Dosadi accent rang across the arena. The Gowachin Federation, only member of the ConSentiency which dared permit a victim to judge those accused of victimizing him, had received a wound to its pride. But they'd also received something they would consider of inestimable value—a foothold for their Law in the ConSentiency, plus a memorable court performance which was about to end in the drama they loved best.

McKie stepped to within striking distance of Ceylang, extended his right hand straight out to the side, palm up.

"The knife."

Attendants scurried. There came the sound of the blue box being opened. Presently, the knife handle was slapped firmly into McKie's palm. He closed his fingers around it, thinking as he did so of all those countless others who had faced this moment in a Gowachin Courtarena.

"Ceylang?"

"I submit to the ruling of this court."

McKie saw the Ferret Wreaves rise from their seats as one person. They stood ready to leap down into the arena and avenge Ceylang no matter the consequences. They could do nothing else but carry out the role which the Gowachin had designed for them. Few in the arena had misunderstood their presence here. No matter the measurement of the wound, the Gowachin did not suffer such things gladly.

An odd look of camaraderie passed between Ceylang and McKie then. Here they stood, the only two non-Gowachin in the ConSentient universe who had passed through that peculiar alchemy which transformed a person into a Legum. One of them was supposed to die immediately, and the other would not long survive that death. Yet, they understood each other the way siblings understand each other. Each had shed a particular *skin* to become something else.

Slowly, deliberately, McKie extended the tip of his blade toward Ceylang's left jowl, noting the myriad pocks of her triad exchanges there. She trembled but remained firm. Deftly, with the swiftest of flicking motions, McKie added another pock to those on her left jowl.

The Ferret Wreaves were the first to understand. They sank back into their seats.

Ceylang gasped, touched a tendril to the wound. Many times she had been set free by such a wound, moving on to new alliances which did not completely sunder the old.

For a moment, McKie thought she might not accept, but the increasing sounds of approval all around the arena overcame her doubts. The noise of that approval climbed to a near deafening crescendo before subsiding. Even the Gowachin joined this. How dearly they loved such legal nuances!

Pitching his voice for Ceylang alone, McKie spoke.

"You should apply for a position in BuSab. The new director would look with favor upon your application."

"You?"

"Make a Wreave bet on it."

She favored him with the grimace which passed for a smile among Wreaves, spoke the traditional words of triad farewell.

"We were well and truly wed."

So she, too, had seen the truth in their unique closeness.

McKie betrayed the extent of his esoteric knowledge by producing the correct response.

"By my mark I know you."

She showed no surprise. A good brain there, not up to Dosadi standards, but good.

Well and truly wed.

Keeping a firm lock on his emotions (the Dosadi in him helped), McKie crossed to confront Aritch.

"Client Aritch, you are innocent."

McKie displayed the fleck of Wreave blood on the knife tip.

"The forms have been obeyed and you are completely exonerated. I rejoice with all of those who love justice."

At this point in the old days, the jubilant audience would've fallen on the hapless client, would've fought for bloody scraps with which to parade through the city. No doubt Aritch would've preferred that. He was a traditionalist. He confirmed that now.

"I am glad to quit these times, McKie."

McKie mused aloud.

"Who will be the Mrreg now that you're . . . disqualified? Whoever it is, I doubt he'll be as good as the one he replaces. It will profit that next Mrreg to reflect upon the fragile and fugitive value to be gained from the manipulation of others."

Glowering, Aritch turned and shambled toward the doorway out of the arena.

Some of the Gowachin from the audience already were leaving, no doubt hoping to greet Aritch outside. McKie had no desire to witness that remnant of an ancient ritual. He had other concerns.

Well and truly wed.

Something burned in his eyes. And still he felt that soft and sleeping presence in his awareness.

Jedrik?

No response.

He glanced at Broey who, true to his duty as a judge, would be the last to leave the arena. Broey sat blandly contemplating this place where he'd displayed the first designs of his campaign for supremacy in the ConSentiency. He would accept nothing less short of his own death. Those shadowy puppet masters would be the first to feel his rule.

That fitted the plan McKie and Jedrik had forged between them. In a way, it was still the plan of those who'd bred and conditioned Jedrik for the tasks she'd performed so exquisitely.

It was McKie's thought that those nameless, faceless Dosadis who stood in ghostly ranks behind Jedrik had made a brave choice. Faced with the evidence of body exchange all around, they'd judged that to be a deadly choice—the conservatism of extinction. Instead, they'd trusted sperm and ova, always seeking the new and better, the changed, the adapted. And they'd launched their simultaneous campaign to eliminate the Pcharkys of their world, reserving only that one for their final gamble.

It was well that this explosive secret had been kept here. McKie felt grateful to Ceylang. She'd known, but even when it might've helped her, she'd remained silent. BuSab would now have time to forge ways of dealing with this problem. Ceylang would be valuable there. And perhaps more would be learned about PanSpechi, Calebans, and Taprisiots. If only Jedrik . . .

He felt a fumbling in his memories.

"If only Jedrik what?"

She spoke laughingly in his mind as she'd always spoken there.

McKie suppressed a fit of trembling, almost fell.

"Careful with our body," she said. "It's the only one we have now."

"Whose body?"

She caressed his mind.

"Ours, love."

Was it hallucination? He ached with longing to hold her in his arms, to feel her arms around him, her body pressed to him.

"That's lost to us forever, love, but see what we have in exchange."

When he didn't respond, she said:

"One can always be watching while the other acts . . . or sleeps."

"But where are you?"

"Where I've always been when we exchanged. See?"

He felt her parallel to him in the shared flesh and, as he voluntarily drew back, he came to rest in contact with her mutual memories, still looking from his own eyes but aware that someone else peered out there, too, that someone else turned this body to face Broey.

Fearful that he might be trapped here, McKie almost panicked, but Jedrik gave him back the control of their flesh.

"Do you doubt me, love?"

He felt shame. There was nothing she could hide from him. He knew how she felt, what she'd been willing to sacrifice for him.

"You'd have made their perfect Mrreg."

"Don't even suggest it."

She went pouring through his arena memories then and her joy delighted him.

"Oh, marvelous, McKie. Beautiful! I couldn't have done it better. And Broey still doesn't suspect."

Attendants were taking the eight prisoners out of the arena now, all of them still shackled. The audience benches were almost empty.

A sense of joy began filtering through McKie.

I lost something but I gained something.

"You didn't lose as much as Aritch."

"And I gained more."

McKie permitted himself to stare up at Broey then, studying the Gowachin judge with Dosadi eyes and two sets of awareness. Aritch and the eight accused of murder were things of the past. They and many others like them would be dead or powerless before another ten-day. Broey already had shown the speed with which he intended to act. Supported by his troop of Jedrik-chosen aides, Broey would occupy the seats of power, consolidating lines of control in that shadow government, eliminating every potential source of opposition he could touch. He believed Jedrik dead and, while McKie was clever, McKie and BuSab were not a primary concern. One struck at the real seats of power. Being Dosadi, Broey could not act otherwise. And he'd been almost the best his planet had ever produced. Almost.

Jedrik-within chuckled.

Yes, with juggernaut certainty, Broey would create a single target for BuSab. And Jedrik had refined the simulation pattern by which Broey could be anticipated. Broey would find McKie waiting for him at the proper moment.

Behind McKie would be a new BuSab, an agency directed by a person whose memories and abilities were amplified by the one person superior to Broey that Dosadi had ever produced.

Standing there in the now silent arena, McKie wondered: *When will Broey realize he does our work for us?*

"When we show him that he failed to kill *me!*"

In the purest obedience to Gowachin forms, without any sign of the paired thoughts twining through his mind, McKie bowed toward the surviving jurist, turned, and left. And all the time, Jedrik-within was planning . . . plotting . . . planning . . .

THE EYES OF
HEISENBERG

1

They would schedule a rain for this morning, Dr. Thei Svengaard thought. *Rain always makes the parents uneasy . . . not to mention what it does to the doctors.*

A gust of winter wetness rattled against the window behind his desk. He stood, thought of muting the windows, but the Durants—this morning's parents—might be even more alarmed by the unnatural silence on such a day.

Dr. Svengaard stepped to the window, looked down at the thronging foot traffic—day shifts going to their jobs in the megalopolis, night shifts headed toward their tumbled rest. There was a sense of power and movement in the comings and goings of the people in spite of their troglodyte existence. Most of them, he knew, were childless Sterries . . . sterile, sterile. They came and they went, numbered, but numberless.

He had left the intercom open to his reception room and he could hear his nurse, Mrs. Washington, distracting the Durants with questions and forms.

Routine.

That was the watchword. This must all appear normal, casual routine. The Durants and all the others fortunate enough to be chosen *and* to become parents must never suspect the truth.

Dr. Svengaard steered his mind away from such thoughts,

reminding himself that guilt was not a permissible emotion for a member of the medical profession. Guilt led inevitably to betrayal . . . and betrayal brought messy consequences. The Optimen were exceedingly touchy where the breeding program was concerned.

Such a thought with its hint of criticism filled Svengaard with a momentary disquiet. He swallowed, allowed his mind to dwell on the Folk response to the Optimen, *They are the power that loves us and cares for us.*

With a sigh, he turned away from the window, skirted the desk and went through the door that led via the ready room to the lab. In the ready room, he paused to check his appearance in the mirror: gray hair, dark brown eyes, strong chin, high forehead and rather grim lips beneath an aquiline nose. He'd always been rather proud of the remote dignity in his appearance-cut and had come to terms with the need of adjusting the remoteness. Now, he softened the set of his mouth, practiced a look of compassionate interest.

Yes, that would do for the Durants—granting the accuracy of their emotional profiles.

Nurse Washington was just ushering the Durants into the lab as Dr. Svengaard entered through his private door. The skylights above them drummed and hissed with the rain. Such weather suddenly seemed to fit the room's mood: washed glass, steel, plasmeld and tile . . . all impersonal. It rained on everyone . . . and all humans had to pass through a room such as this . . . even the Optimen.

Dr. Svengaard took an instant dislike to the parents. Harvey Durant was a lithe six-footer with curly blond hair, light blue eyes. The face was wide with an apparent innocence and youth. Lizbeth, his wife, stood almost the same height, equally blonde, equally blue-eyed and young. Her figure suggested Valkyrie robustness. On a silver cord around her neck she wore one of the omnipresent Folk talismans, a brass figure of the female Optiman, Calapine. The breeder cult nonsense and religious overtones of the figure did not escape Dr. Svengaard. He suppressed a sneer.

The Durants were parents, however, and robust—living testimony to the skill of the surgeon who had cut them. Dr. Svengaard allowed himself a moment of pride in his profession. Not many people could enter the tight little group of subcellular engineers who kept human variety within bounds.

Nurse Washington paused in the door behind the Durants, said, "Dr. Svengaard, Harvey and Lizbeth Durant." She left without waiting for acknowledgments. Nurse Washington's timing and discretion always were exquisitely correct.

"The Durants, how nice," Dr. Svengaard said. "I hope my nurse didn't bore you with all those forms and questions. But I guess you knew you were letting yourselves in for all that routine when you asked to watch."

"We understand," Harvey Durant said. And he thought, *Asked to watch, indeed! Does this old fake think he can pull his little tricks on us?*

Dr. Svengaard noted the rich, compelling baritone of the man's voice. It bothered him, added to his dislike.

"We don't want to take any more of your time than absolutely necessary," Lizbeth Durant said. She clasped her husband's hand and through their secret code of finger pressures said: *"Do you read him? He doesn't like us."*

Harvey's fingers responded, *"He's a Sterrie prig, so full of pride in his position that he's half blind."*

The woman's no-nonsense tone annoyed Dr. Svengaard. She already was staring around the lab, quick, searching looks. *I must keep control here*, he thought. He crossed to them, shook hands. Their palms were sweaty.

Nervous. Good, Dr. Svengaard thought.

The sound of a viapump at his left seemed reassuringly loud to him then. You could count on the pump to make parents nervous. That was why the pumps were loud. Dr. Svengaard turned toward the sound, indicated a sealed crystal vat on a force-field stand near the lab's center. The pump sound came from the vat.

"Here we are," Dr. Svengaard said.

Lizbeth stared at the vat's milky translucent surface. She wet her lips with her tongue. "In there?"

"And as safe as can be," Dr. Svengaard said.

He cherished the small hope then that the Durants might yet leave, go home and await the outcome.

Harvey took his wife's hand, patted it. He, too, stared at the vat. "We understand you've called in this specialist," he said.

"Dr. Potter," Svengaard said. "From Central." He glanced at the nervous movements of the Durants' hands, noting the omnipresent tattooed index fingers—gene type and station. They could add the coveted "V" for viable now, he thought, and he suppressed a momentary jealousy.

"Dr. Potter, yes," Harvey said. Through their hands, he signaled Lizbeth, *"Notice how he said Central?"*

"How could I miss it?" she responded.

Central, she thought. The place conjured pictures of the lordly Optimen, but this made her think of the Cyborgs who secretly opposed the Optimen, and the whole thing filled her with profound disquiet. She could afford to think of nothing but her son now.

"We know Potter's the best there is," she said. "and we don't want you to think we're just being emotional and fearful . . ."

". . . but we're going to watch," Harvey said. And he thought, *This stiff-necked surgeon had better realize we know our legal rights.*

"I see," Dr. Svengaard said. *Damn these fools!* he thought. But he held his voice to a soothing monotone and said, "Your concern is a matter of record. I admire it. However, the consequences . . ."

He left the words hanging there, reminding them that he had legal rights, too, could make the cut with or without their permission, and couldn't be held responsible for any upset to the parents. Public Law 10927 was clear and direct. Parents might invoke it for the right to watch, but the cut *would* be made at the surgeon's discretion. The human race had a planned future which excluded genetic monsters and wild deviants.

Harvey nodded, a quick and emphatic motion. He gripped his wife's hand tightly. Bits of Folk horror stories and official myths trickled through his mind. He saw Svengaard partly through this confusion of stories and partly through the clandestine forbidden literature grudgingly provided by the Cyborgs to the Parents Underground—through Stedman and Merck, through Shakespeare and Huxley. His youth had fed on such a limited past that he knew superstition could not help but remain.

Lizbeth's nod came slower. She knew what their chief concern here had to be, but that was still her son in the vat.

"Are you sure," she asked, deliberately baiting Svengaard, "that there's no pain?"

The extent of the Folk nonsense which bred in the *necessary* atmosphere of popular ignorance filled Dr. Svengaard with resentment. He knew he'd have to end this interview quickly. The things he *might* be saying to these people kept intruding on his awareness, interfering with what he *had* to say.

"That fertilized ovum has no nerve trains," he said. "It's physically less than three hours old, its growth retarded by controlled nitrate respiration. Pain? The concept doesn't apply."

The technical terms would have little meaning to them, Dr. Svengaard knew, other than to emphasize the distance between mere parents and a submolecular engineer.

"I guess that was rather foolish of me," Lizbeth said. "The . . . it's so simple, not really like a human yet." And she signaled to Harvey through their hands, *"What a simpleton he is! As easy to read as a child."*

Rain beat a tarantella against the skylight. Dr. Svengaard waited it out, then: "Ah, now, let us make no mistakes." And he thought what an excellent moment it was to give these fools a catechism refresher. "Your embryo may be less than three hours old, but it already contains every basic enzyme

it'll need when fully developed. An enormously complicated organism."

Harvey stared at him in assumed awe at the *greatness*
which could understand such mysteries as the shaping and
moulding of life.

Lizbeth glanced at the vat.

Two days ago, selected gametes from Harvey and herself
had been united there, gripped in stasis, allowed to go
through limited mitosis. The process had produced a viable
embryo—not too common a thing in their world where only
a select few were freed of the contraceptive gas and allowed
to breed, and only a rare number of those produced viables.
She wasn't supposed to understand the intricacies of the process, and the fact that she did understand had to be hidden at
all times. *They*—the genetic Optimen of Central—stamped
savagely on the slightest threat to their supremacy. And *they*
considered knowledge in the wrong hands to be the most
terrible threat.

"How . . . big is . . . he now?" she asked.

"Diameter less than a tenth of a millimeter," Dr. Svengaard said. He relaxed his face into a smile. "It's a morula
and back in the primitive days it wouldn't yet have completed its journey to the uterus. This is the stage when it's
most susceptible to us. We must do our work now before the
formation of the trophoblast."

The Durants nodded in awe.

Dr. Svengaard basked in their respect. He sensed their
minds fumbling over poorly remembered definitions from
the limited schooling they'd been permitted. Their records
said she was a creche librarian and he an instructor of the
young—not much education required for either.

Harvey touched the vat, jerked his hand away. The crystal surface felt warm, filled with subtle vibrations. And there
was that constant *thrap-thrap-thrap* of the pump. He sensed
the deliberateness of that annoying sound, reading the way
he'd been trained in the Underground the subtle betrayals
in Svengaard's manner. He glanced around the laboratory—

glass pipes, square gray cabinets, shiny angles and curves of plasmeld, omnipresent gauges like staring eyes. The place smelled of disinfectants and exotic chemicals. Everything about the lab carried that calculated double purpose— functional yet designed to awe the uninitiated.

Lizbeth focused on the one mundane feature of the place she could really recognize for certain—a tile sink with gleaming faucets. The sink sat squeezed between two mysterious constructions of convoluted glass and dull gray plasmeld.

The sink bothered Lizbeth. It represented a place of disposal. You flushed garbage into a sink for grinding before it was washed into the sewage reclamation system. Anything small could be dumped into a sink and lost.

Forever.

Anything.

"I'm not going to be talked out of watching," she said.

Damn! Dr. Svengaard thought. *There was a catch in her voice.* That little catch, that hesitation was betrayal. It didn't fit with her bold appearance. Overemphasis on maternal drive in her cutting . . . no matter how successful the surgeon had been with the rest of her.

"Our concern is for you as much as for your child," Dr. Svengaard said. "The trauma . . ."

"The law gives us the right," Harvey said. And he signaled to Lizbeth, *"The whole pattern's more or less what we anticipated."*

Trust this clod to know the law, Dr. Svengaard thought. He sighed. Statistical prediction said one in one hundred thousand parents would insist, despite all the subtle and not so subtle pressures against it. Statistics and visible fact, however, were two distinct matters. Svengaard had noted how Harvey glared at him. The man's cutting had been strong on male protectiveness—too strong, obviously. He couldn't stand to see his *mate* thwarted. Doubtless he was an excellent provider, model husband, never participated in Sterrie orgies—a leader.

A clod.

"The law," Dr. Svengaard said, and his voice dripped rebuke, "also requiries that I point out the dangers of psychological trauma to the parents. I was *not* suggesting I'd try to prevent you from watching."

"We're going to watch," Lizbeth said.

Harvey felt a surge of admiration for her then. She played her role so beautifully, even to that catch in her voice.

"I couldn't stand the waiting otherwise," Lizbeth said. "Not knowing . . ."

Dr. Svengaard wondered if he dared press the matter—perhaps an appeal to their obvious awe, a show of Authority. One look at Harvey's squared shoulders and Lizbeth's pleading eyes dissuaded him. They were going to watch.

"Very well," Dr. Svengaard sighed.

"Will we watch from here?" Harvey asked.

Dr. Svengaard was shocked. "Of course not!" What primitives, these clods. But he tempered the thought with realization that such ignorance resulted from the carefully fostered mystery that surrounded gene shaping. In a calmer tone, he said, "You'll have a private room with a closed-circuit connection to this lab. My nurse will escort you."

Nurse Washington proved her competence then by appearing in the doorway. She'd been listening, of course. A good nurse never left such matters to chance.

"Is this all we get to see here?" Lizbeth asked.

Dr. Svengaard heard the pleading tone, noted the way she avoided looking directly at the vat. All his pent-up scorn came out in his voice as he said, "What else is there to see, Mrs. Durant? Surely you didn't expect to see the morula."

Harvey tugged at his wife's arm, said, "Thank you, Doctor."

Once more, Lizbeth's eyes scanned the room, avoiding the vat. "Yes, thank you for showing us . . . this room. It helps to see how . . . prepared you are for . . . every emergency." Her eyes focused on the sink.

"You're quite welcome, I'm sure," Dr. Svengaard said. "Nurse Washington will provide you with the list of permissible names. You might occupy part of your time choosing a name for your son if you've not already done so." He nodded to the nurse. "See the Durants to Lounge Five, please."

Nurse Washington said, "If you'll follow me, please?" She turned with that air of overworked impatience which Svengaard suspected all nurses acquired with their diplomas. The Durants were sucked up in her wake.

Svengaard turned back to the vat.

So much to do—Potter, the specialist from Central, due within the hour . . . and he wouldn't be happy about the Durants. People had so little understanding of what the medical profession endured. The psychological preparation of parents subtracted from time better devoted to more important matters . . . and it certainly complicated the security problem. Svengaard thought of the five "Destroy After Reading" directives he'd received from Max Allgood, Central's boss of T-Security, during the past month. It was disturbing, as though some new danger had set Security scurrying.

But Central insisted on the socializing with parents. The Optimen must have good reason, Svengaard felt. Most things *they* did made wonderful sense. Sometimes, Svengaard knew, he fell into a feeling of orphanage, a creature without past. All it took to shake him from the emotional morass, though, was a moment's contemplation: *"They are the power that loves us and cares for us." They* had the world firmly in their grip, the future planned—a place for every man and every man in his place. Some of the old dreams— space travel, the questing philosophies, farming of the seas—had been shelved temporarily, put aside for more important things. The day would come, though, once *they* solved the unknowns behind submolecular engineering.

Meanwhile, there was work for the willing—maintaining the population of workers, suppressing deviants, husbanding the genetic pool from which even the Optimen sprang.

Svengaard swung the meson microscope over the Durant vat, adjusted for low amplification to minimize Heisenberg interference. One more look wouldn't hurt, just on the chance he might locate the pilot-cell and reduce Potter's problem. Even as he bent to the scope, Svengaard knew he was rationalizing. He couldn't resist another search into this morula which had the potential, might be shaped into an Optiman. The wonderous things were so rare. He flicked the switch, focused.

A sigh escaped him, "Ahhhhh . . ."

So passive the morula at low amplification; no pulsing as it lay within the stasis—yet so beautiful in its semidormancy . . . so little to hint that it was the arena of ancient battles.

Svengaard put a hand to the amplification controls, hesitated. High amplification posed its dangers, but Potter could re-adjust minor marks of meson interference. And the *big* look was very tempting.

He doubled amplification.

Again.

Enlargement always reduced the appearance of stasis. Things moved here, and in the unfocused distances there were flashes like the dartings of fish. Up cut of the swarming arena came the triple spiral of nucleotides that had led him to call Potter. Almost Optiman. Almost that beautiful perfection of form and mind that could accept the indefinite balancing of Life through the delicately adjusted enzyme prescriptions.

A sense of loss pervaded Svengaard. His own prescription, while it kept him alive, was slowly killing him. It was the fate of all men. They might live two hundred years, sometimes even more . . . but in the end the balancing act failed for all except the Optimen. They were perfect, limited only by their physical sterility, but that was the fate of many humans and it subtracted nothing from endless life.

His own childless state gave Svengaard a sense of communion with the Optimen. *They'd* solve that, too . . . someday.

He concentrated on the morula. A sulfur-containing

amino acid dependency showed faint motion at this amplification. With a feeling of shock, Svengaard recognized it—isovalthine, a genetic marker for latent myxedema, a warning of potential thyroid deficiency. It was a disquieting flaw in the otherwise near-perfection. Potter would have to be alerted.

Svengaard backed off amplification to study the mitochondrial structure. He followed out the invaginated unit-membrane to the flattened, sac-like cristae, returned along the external second membrane, focused on the hydrophilic outer compartment. Yes . . . the isovalthine was susceptible to adjustment. Perfection might yet be for this morula.

Flickering movement appeared at the edge of the microscope's field.

Svengaard stiffened, thought, *Dear God, no!*

He stood frozen at the viewer as a thing seen only eight previous times in the history of gene-shaping took place within his field of vision.

A thin line like a distant contrail reached into the cellular structure from the left. It wound through a coiled-coil of alpha helices, found the folded ends of the polypeptide chains in a myosin molecule, twisted and dissolved.

Where the trail had been now lay a new structure about four Angstroms in diameter and a thousand Angstroms long—sperm protamine rich in arginine. All around it the protein factories of the cytoplasm were undergoing change, fighting the stasis, realigning. Svengaard recognized what was happening from the descriptions of the eight previous occurrences. The ADP-ATP exchange system was becoming more complex—"resistant." The surgeon's job had been made infinitely more complex.

Potter will be furious, Svengaard thought.

Svengaard turned off the microscope, straightened. He wiped perspiration from his hands, glanced at the lab clock. Less than two minutes had passed. The Durants weren't even in their lounge yet. But in those two minutes, some force . . . some energy from *outside* had made a seemingly purposeful adjustment within the embryo.

Could this be what's stirred up Security . . . and the Optimen? Svengaard wondered.

He had heard this thing described, read the reports . . . but actually to have seen it himself! To have seen it . . . so sure and purposeful . . .

He shook his head. *No! It was not purposeful! It was merely an accident, chance, nothing more.*

But the vision wouldn't leave him.

Compared to that, he thought, *how clumsy my efforts are. And I'll have to report it to Potter. He'll have to shape that twisted chain . . . if he can now that it's resistant.*

Full of disquiet, not at all satisfied that he had seen an accident, Svengaard began making the final checks of the lab's preparations. He inspected the enzyme racks and their linkage to the computer dosage-control—plenty of cytochrome b_5 and P-450 hemoprotein, a good reserve store of ubiquinone and sulfhydryl, arsenate, azide and oligomycin, sufficient protein-bound phosphohistidine. He moved down the line—acylating agents, a store of (2,4-dinitrophenol) and the isoxazolidon-3 groups with reduction NADH.

He turned to the physical equipment, checked the meson scalpel's micromechanism, read the life-system gauges on the vat and the print-out of the stasis mechanism.

All in order.

It had to be. The Durant embryo, that beautiful thing with its wondrous potential, was now *resistant*—a genetic unknown . . . if Potter could succeed where others had failed.

2

D r. Vyaslav Potter stopped at the Records Desk on his way into the hospital. He was faintly tired after the long tube-shunt from Central to Seatac Megalopolis, still he told an off-color joke about primitive reproduction to the gray-haired duty nurse. She chuckled as she hunted up Svengaard's latest report on the Durant embryo. She put the report on the counter and stared at Potter.

He glanced at the folder's cover and looked up to meet the nurse's eyes.

Is it possible? he wondered. *But . . . no: she's too old—wouldn't even make a good playmate. Anyway, the big-domes wouldn't grant us a breeding permit.* And he reminded himself: I'm a Zeek . . . $J^4 11118^2 K$. The Zeek gene-shaping had gone through a brief popularity in the region of Timbuctu Megalopolis during the early nineties. It produced curly black hair, a skin one shade lighter than milk chocolate, soft brown eyes and a roly-poly face of utmost benignity, all on a tall, strong body. A Zeek. A Vyaslav Potter.

It had yet to produce an Optiman, male or female, and never a viable gamete match.

Potter had long since given up. He was one of those who'd voted to discontinue the Zeek. He thought of the Optimen with whom he dealt and sneered at himself, *There but for the brown eyes* . . . But the sneer no longer gave him a twinge of bitterness.

"You know," he said, smiling at the nurse, "these Durants whose emb I have this morning—I cut them both. Maybe I've been in this business too long."

"Oh, go on with you, Doctor," she said with an arch turn of her head. "You're not even middle-aged. You don't look a day over a hundred."

He glanced at the folder. "But here are these kids bringing me their emb to cut and I . . ." He shrugged.

"Are you going to tell them?" she asked. "I mean that you had them, too."

"I probably won't even see them," he said. "You know how it is. Anyway, sometimes people are happy with their cut . . . sometimes they wish they'd had a little more of this, less of that. They tend to blame the surgeon. They don't understand, *can't* understand the problems we have in the cutting room."

"But the Durants seem like a very successful cut," she said. "Normal, happy . . . perhaps a little over-worried about their son, but . . ."

"Their genotype is one of the most successful," he said. He tapped the record folder with a forefinger. "Here's the proof: they had a viable with potential." He lifted a thumb in the time-honored gesture for Optiman.

"You should be very proud of them," she said. "My family's had only fifteen viables in a hundred and eighty-nine years, and never an . . ." She repeated Potter's thumb gesture.

He pursed his lips into a moue of commiseration, wondering how he let himself get drawn into these conversations with women, especially with nurses. It was that little seed of hope that never died, he suspected. It was cut from the same stuff that produced the wild rumors, the quack "breeder doctors" and the black market in "true breed" nostrums. It was the thing that sold the little figurines of Optiman-Calapine because of the unfounded rumor that she had produced a viable. It was the thing that wore out the big toes of fertility idols from the kisses of the hopeful.

His moue of commiseration became a cynical sneer. *Hopeful! If they only knew.*

"Were you aware the Durants are going to watch?" the nurse asked.

His head jerked up and he glared at her.

"It's all over the hospital," she said. "Security's been alerted. The Durants have been scanned and they're in Lounge Five with closed circuit to the cutting room."

Anger blazed through him. "Damn it to hell! Can't they do anything right in this stupid place?"

"Now, Doctor," she said, stiffening into the prim departmental dictator. "There's no call to lose your temper. The Durants quoted the law. That ties our hands and you know it."

"Stupid damn' law," Potter muttered, but his anger had subsided. *The law!* he thought. *More of the damn' masquerade.* He had to admit, though, that they needed the law. Without Public Law 10927, people might ask the wrong kinds of questions. And no doubt Svengaard had done his bumbling best to try to dissuade the Durants.

Potter assumed a rueful grin, said, "Sorry I snapped like that. I've had a bad week." He sighed. "They just don't understand."

"Is there any other record you wish, Doctor?" she asked.

Rapport was gone, Potter saw. "No, thanks," he said. He took the Durant folder, headed for Svengaard's office. Just his luck: a pair of watchers. It meant plenty of extra work. Naturally!

The Durants couldn't be content with seeing the tape *after* the cut. Oh, no. *They* had to be on the scene. That meant the Durants weren't as innocent as they might appear—no matter what this hospital's Security staff said. The public just did not insist anymore. That was supposed to have been *cut* out of them.

The statistical few who defied their genetic shaping now required special attention.

And Potter reminded himself, *I did the original cut on this pair. There was no mistake.*

He ran into Svengaard outside the latter's office, heard the man's quick resume. Svengaard then began babbling about his Security arrangements.

"I don't give a damn what your Security people say," Potter barked. "We've new instructions. Central Emergency's to be called in every case of this kind."

They went into Svengaard's office. It pretended to wood paneling—a corner room with a view of flowered roof gardens and terraces built of the omnipresent three-phase regenerative plasmeld, the "plasty" of the Folk patios. Nothing must age or degenerate in this best of all Optiman worlds. Nothing except people.

"Central Emergency?" Svengaard asked.

"No exceptions," Potter said. He sat in Svengaard's chair, put his feet on Svengaard's desk, and brought the little ivory-colored phone box to his stomach with its screen only inches from his face. He punched in Security's number and his own code identification.

Svengaard sat on a corner of the desk across from him, appearing both angry and cowed. "They were scanned, I tell you," he said. "They were carrying no unusual devices. There's nothing unusual about them."

"Except they insist on watching," Potter said. He jiggled the phone key. "What's keeping those ignoramuses?"

Svengaard said, "But the law—"

"Damn the law!" Potter said. "You know as well as I do that we could route the view signal from the cutting room through an editing computer and show the parents anything we want. Has it ever occurred to you to wonder why we don't do just that?"

"Why . . . they . . . ahh . . ." Svengaard shook his head. The question had caught him off balance. Why wasn't that done? The statistics showed a certain number of parents would insist on watching and . . .

"It was tried," Potter said. "Somehow, the parents detected the computer's hand in the tape."

"How?"

"We don't know."

"Weren't the parents questioned and . . ."

"They killed themselves."

"Killed them—How?"

"We don't know."

Svengaard tried to swallow in a dry throat. He began to get a picture of intense excitement just under Security's surface. He said, "What about the statistical ratio of—"

"Statistical, my ass!" Potter said.

A heavy masculine voice came from the phone: "Who're you talking to?"

Potter focused on the screen, said, "I was talking to Sven. This viable he called me on—"

"It is a viable?"

"Yes! It's a viable with the full potential, but the parents insist on watching the—"

"I'll have a full crew on the way by tube in ten minutes," said the voice on the phone. "They're at Friscopolis. Shouldn't take 'em more than a few minutes."

Svengaard rubbed wet palms against the sides of his working smock. He couldn't see that face on the phone, but the voice sounded like Max Allgood, T Security's boss.

"We'll delay the cut until your people get here," Potter said. "The records are being faxed to you and should be on your desk in a few minutes. There's another—"

"Is that embryo everything we were told?" asked the man on the phone. "Any flaws?"

"A latent myxedema, a projective faulty heart valve, but the—"

"Okay, I'll call you after I've seen the—"

"Damn it to hell!" Potter erupted. "Will you let me get

ten words out of my mouth without interrupting?" He glared into the screen. "There's something here more important than flaw and the parents." Potter glanced up at Svengaard, back to the screen. "Sven reports he saw an *outside* adjustment of the arginine deficiency."

A low whistle came from the phone, then, "Reliable?"

"Depend on it."

"Did it follow the pattern of the other eight?"

Potter glanced up at Svengaard, who nodded.

"Sven says yes."

"They won't like that."

"I don't like it."

"Did Sven see enough to get any . . . new ideas on it?"

Svengaard shook his head.

"No," Potter said.

"There's a strong possibility it isn't significant," the man on the phone said. "In a system of increasing determinism—"

"Oh, yes," Potter sneered. "In a system of increasing determinism you get more and more indeterminism. You might as well say in a foofram of increasing haggersmaggle—"

"Well, it's what *they* believe."

"So they say. *I* believe Nature doesn't like being meddled with."

Potter stared into the screen. For some reason, he recalled his youth, the beginning of his medical studies and the day he'd learned how *very* close his genotype had been to the Optiman. He found that the old core of hatred had become mildly amused tolerance and cynicism.

"I don't see why they put up with you," the man on the phone said.

"Because I was *very* close," Potter whispered. He wondered then how close the Durant embryo would be. *I'll do my best,* he thought.

The man on the phone cleared his throat, said, "Yes, well I'll depend on you to handle things at your end. The em-

bryo ought to provide some verification of the outside
inter—"

"Don't be a total ass!" Potter snapped. "The emb will
bear out Sven's report to the last enzyme. You tend to your
job; we'll do ours." He slapped the cut-off, pushed the
phone back onto the desk and sat staring at it. "Pompous
damned . . . no—he's what he is because he's what he is.
Comes from living too close to *them*. Comes from the
original cut. Maybe I'd be an ass too if that's what I had
to be."

Svengaard tried to swallow in a dry throat. He'd never
before heard such an argument or such frank talk from the
men who operated out of Central.

"Shocked you, eh, Sven?" Potter asked. He dropped his
feet to the floor.

Svengaard shrugged. He felt ill-at-ease.

Potter studied the man. Svengaard was good within his
limits, but he lacked creative imagination. A brilliant surgeon, but without that special quality he was often a dull
tool.

"You're a good man, Sven," Potter said. "Dependable.
That's what your record says, you know. Dependable. You'll
never be anything else. Weren't meant to be. In your particular niche, though, you're *it.*"

Svengaard heard only the praise, said, "It's good to be ap-
preciated, of course, but—"

"But we have work to do."

"It will be difficult," Svengaard said. "Now."

"Do you think that *outside* adjustment was an accidental
thing?" Potter asked.

"I—I'd like to believe that"—Svengaard wet his lips with
his tongue—"it wasn't *determined,* that no agency . . ."

"You'd like to lay it to uncertainty, to Heisenberg," Potter said. "The principle of uncertainty, some result of our
own meddling—everything an accident in the capricious
universe."

Svengaard felt stung by a quality of harshness in Potter's

voice, said, "Not precisely. I meant only that I hoped no super causal agency had a hand in—"

"God? You don't really mean you're afraid this is the action of a deity?"

Svengaard looked away. "I remember in school," he said. "You were lecturing. You said we always have to be ready to face the fact that the reality we see will be shockingly different from anything our theories led us to suspect."

"Did I say that? Did I really say that?"

"You did."

"Something's out there, eh? Something beyond our instruments. It's never heard of Heisenberg. It isn't uncertain at all. It moves." His voice lowered. "It moves directly. It adjusts things." He cocked his head to one side. "Ah-hah! The ghost of Heisenberg is confounded!"

Svengaard glared at Potter. The man was mocking him. He spoke stiffly, "Heisenberg did point out that we have our limits."

"You're right," Potter said. "There's a caprice in our universe. He taught us that. There's always something we can't interpret or understand . . . or measure. He set us up for this present dilemma, eh?" Potter glanced at his finger watch, back to Svengaard. "We tend to interpret everything around us by screening it through that system which is native to us. Our civilization sees indeterminately through the eyes of Heisenberg. If he taught us truly, how can we tell whether the unknown's an accident or the deliberate intent of God? What's the use of even asking?"

Svengaard spoke defensively, "We appear to manage, somehow."

Potter startled him by laughing, head tipped back, body shaking with enjoyment. The laughter subsided and presently Potter said, "Sven, you are a gem. I mean that. If it weren't for the ones like you, we'd still be back in the muck and mire, running from glaciers and saber-tooth tigers."

Svengaard fought to keep anger from his voice, said, "What do *they* think this arginine adjustment is?"

Potter stared at him, measuring, then, "Damned if I haven't underestimated you, Sven. Apologies, eh?"

Svengaard shrugged. Potter was acting oddly today—astonishing reactions, strange eruptions of emotion. "Do you *know* what they say about this?" he asked.

"You heard Max on the phone," Potter said.

So that was Allgood, Svengaard thought.

"Certainly, I know," Potter growled. "Max has it all wrong. *They* say gene-shaping inflicts itself on nature—on a nature that can never be reduced to mechanical systems and, therefore, to stationary matter. You can't stop the movement, see? It's an extended system phenomenon, energy seeking a level that's—"

"Extended system?" Svengaard asked.

Potter looked up at the man's scowling face. The question focused Potters' attention abruptly on the differences in thought patterns between those who lived close to Central and those who touched the Optiman world only through reports and second-hand associations.

We are so different, Potter thought. *Just as the Optimen are different from us and Sven here is different from the Sterries and breeders. We're cut off from each other . . . and none of us has a past. Only the Optimen have a past. But each has an individual past . . . selfishly personal . . . and ancient.*

"Extended system," Potter said. "From the microcosmos to the macrocosmos, *they* say all is order and systems. The *idea* of matter is insubstantial. All is collisions of energy—some appearing large, swift and spectacular . . . some small, gentle and slow. But this too is relative. The aspects of energy are infinite. Everything depends on the viewpoint of the observer. For each change of viewpoint, the energy rules change. There exist an infinite number of energy rules, each set dependent on the twin aspects of viewpoint and background. In an extended system, this *thing* from outside assumes the aspect of a node appearing on a standing wave. That's what *they* say."

Svengaard slipped off the desk, stood in a rapture of awe. He felt that he'd had a fleeting glimpse, a wisp of understanding that penetrated every question he might ask about the universe.

Could that be what it's like to work out of Central? he wondered.

"That's a great summation, isn't it?" Potter demanded. He stood up. "A truly *great* idea!" A chuckle shook him.

"You know, a guy named Diderot had that idea. It was around 1750 or thereabout. *They* spoon-feed it to us now. Great wisdom!"

"Maybe Diderot was . . . one of *them*," Svengaard ventured.

Potter sighed, thinking, *How ignorant a man can become on a diet of managed history.* He wondered then how his own diet had been adjusted and managed.

"Diderot was one of us," Potter growled.

Svengaard stared at him, shocked to silence by the man's . . . blasphemy.

"It comes down to this," Potter said. "Nature doesn't like being meddled with."

A chime sounded beneath Svengaard's desk.

"Security?" Potter asked.

"That's the all clear," Svengaard said. "They're ready for us now."

"Central's Security hotshots are all in place," Potter said. "You will note that they didn't stoop to report to you or to me. They watch us too, you know."

"I've . . . nothing to hide," Svengaard said.

"Of course you haven't," Potter said. He moved around the desk, threw an arm across Svengaard's shoulders. "Come along. It's time for us to put on the mask of Archeus. We're going to give form and organization to a living body. Veritable gods, we are."

Svengaard felt himself still lost in confusion. "What'll *they* do . . . to the Durants?" he asked.

"Do? Not a damn' thing—unless the Durants force it.

The Durants won't even know they're being watched. But Central's little boys will know everything that goes on in that lounge. The Durants won't be able to belch without the gas being subjected to a full and complete analysis. Come along."

But Svengaard held back. "Doctor Potter," he asked, "what do *you* think introduced that arginine chain into the Durant morula?"

"I'm closer to you than you think," Potter said. "We're fighting . . . instability. We've upset the biological stability of the inheritance patterns with our false isomers and our enzyme adjustments and our meson beams. We've undermined the chemical stability of the molecules in the germ plasm. You're a doctor. Look at the enzyme prescriptions we all have to take—how profound the adjustment we have to make to stay alive. It wasn't always that way. And *whatever* set up that original stability is still in there fighting. *That's* what I think."

3

The cutting room nurses positioned the vat under the enzyme console, readied the tubes and the computer-feed-analysis board. They worked quietly, efficiently as Potter and Svengaard examined the gauges. The computer nurse racked her tapes and there came a brief whirring-clicking as she tested her board.

Potter felt himself filled with the wakeful anxiety that always came over him before surgery. He knew it would give way presently to the charged sureness of action, but he felt snappish at the moment. He glanced at the vat gauges. The Krebs cycle was holding at 86.9, a good sixty points above death level. The vat nurse came over, examined his breather mask. He checked his microphone, "Mary had a little lamb, its fleece was black as hades—the surgeon took the credit for . . . a joke on all the ladies."

He heard a distinct chuckle from the computer nurse, glanced at her, but she had her back to him and her face already hidden by hood and mask.

The vat nurse said, "Microphone working, Doctor."

He couldn't see her lips moving behind her mask, but her cheeks rippled as she spoke.

Svengaard flexed his fingers in their gloves, took a deep breath. It smelled faintly of ammonia. He wondered why

Potter always joked with the nurses. It seemed demeaning, somehow.

Potter moved across to the vat. His sterile suit crinkled with a familiar snapping hiss as he walked. He glanced up at the wall screen, the replay monitor which showed approximately what the surgeon saw and which was the view watched by the parents. The screen presented him with a view of itself as he turned his forehead pickup lens toward it.

Damn' parents, he thought. *They make me feel guilty . . . all of them.*

He returned his attention to the crystal vat now bristling with instruments. The pump's churgling annoyed him.

Svengaard moved to the other side of the vat, waiting. The breather mask hid the lower half of his face, but his eyes appeared calm. He radiated a sense of steadiness, reliability.

How does he really feel? Potter wondered. And he reminded himself that in an emergency there wasn't a better cutting-room assistant than Sven.

"You can begin increasing the pyruvic acid," Potter said.

Svengaard nodded, depressed the feeder key.

The computer nurse started her reels turning.

They watched the gauges as the Krebs cycle began rising—87.0 . . . 87.3 . . . 87.8 . . . 88.5 . . . 89.4 . . . 90.5 . . . 91.9 . . .

Now, Potter told himself, *the irreversible movement of growth has started. Only death can stop it.* "Tell me when the Krebs cycle reaches one hundred and ten," he said.

He swung the scope and micromanipulators into place, leaned into the rests. *Will I see what Sven saw?* he wondered. He knew it wasn't likely. The lightning from *outside* had never struck twice in the same place. It came. It did what no human hand could do. It went away.

Where? Potter wondered.

The inter-ribosomal gaps swam into focus. He scanned

them, boosted amplification and went down into the DNA spirals. Yes—there was the situation Sven had described. The Durant embryo was one of those that could cross over into the more-than-human land of Central . . . if the surgeon succeeded.

The confirmation left Potter oddly shaken. He shifted his attention to the mitochondrial structures, saw the evidence of the arginine intrusion. It squared precisely with Sven's description. Alpha-helices had begun firming up, revealing the telltale striations at the aneurin shifts. This one was going to resist the surgeon. This was going to be a tough one.

Potter straightened.

"Well?" Svengaard asked.

"Pretty much as you described it," Potter said. "A straightforward job." That was for the watching parents.

He wondered then what Security was discovering about the Durants. Would this pair be loaded down with search and probe devices disguised as conventional artifacts? Possibly. But there were rumors of new techniques being introduced by the Parents Underground . . . and of Cyborgs moving out of the dark shadows which had hidden them for centuries—if there were Cyborgs at all. Potter was not convinced.

Svengaard spoke to the computer nurse, "Start backing off the pyruvic."

"Backing off pyruvic," she said.

Potter swung his attention to the priority rack beside him, checked the presentation—in the first row the pyrimidines, nucleic acids and proteins, then aneurin, riboflavin, pyridoxin, pantothenic acid, folic acid, choline, inositol, sulfhydryl . . .

He cleared his throat, lining up his plan for the attack on the morula's defenses. "I will attempt to find a pilot cell by masking the cysteine at a single locus," he said. "Stand by with sulfhydryl and prepare an intermediary tape for protein synthesis."

"Ready for masking," Svengaard said. He nodded to the

computer nurse who racked the intermediary tape into position with a smooth sureness.

"Krebs cycle?" Potter asked.

"One hundred and ten coming up," Svengaard said.

Silence.

"Mark," Svengaard said.

Again, Potter bent to the scope. "Begin the tape," he said. "Two minims of sulfhydryl."

Slowly, Potter increased amplification, chose a cell for the masking. The momentary clouding of intrusion cleared away and he searched the surrounding cells for clues that mitosis would take off on his *directed* tangent. It was slow . . . slow. He'd just begun and his hands already felt sweaty in their gloves.

"Stand by with adenosine triphosphate," he said.

Svengaard presented the feeder tube in the micromanipulators, nodded to the vat nurse. ATP already. This was going to be a tough one.

"Begin one minim ATP," Potter said.

Svengaard depressed the feeder key. The whirring of the computer tapes sounded overly loud.

Potter lifted his head momentarily, shook it. "Wrong cell," he said. "We'll try another one. Same procedure." Again, he leaned into the scope and the rests, moved the micromanipulators, pushing amplification up a notch at a time. Slowly, he traced his way down into the cellular mass. *Gently . . . gently . . .* The scope itself could cause irreversible damage in here.

Ahhh, he thought, recognizing an active cell deep in the morula. Vat-stasis had produced only a relative slowing in here. The cell was the scene of intense chemical activity. He recognized doubled base pairs strung on a convoluted helix of sugar phosphate as they passed his field of vision.

His beginning anxiety had passed and he felt the old sureness with the often repeated sensation that the morula was an ocean in which he swam, that the cellular interior was his natural habitat.

"Two minims of sulfhydryl," Potter said.

"Sulfhydryl, two minims," Svengaard said. "Standing by with ATP."

"ATP," Potter said, then, "I'm going to inhibit the exchange reaction in the mitochondrial systems. Start oligomycin and azide."

Svengaard proved his worth then by complying without hesitation. The only sign that he recognized the dangers in this procedure was a question, "Shall I have an uncoupling agent ready?"

"Stand by with arsenate in number one," Potter said.

"Krebs cycle going down," the computer nurse said. "Eighty-nine point four."

"Intrusion effect," Potter said. "Give me point six minim of azide."

Svengaard depressed the key.

"Point four minim oligomycin," Potter said.

"Oligomycin, point four," Svengaard said.

Potter felt that he lived now only through his eyes on the microscope and his hands on the micromanipulators. His existence had moved into the morula, fused with it.

His eyes told him that peripheral mitosis had stopped . . . as it should under these ministrations. "I *think* we have it," he said. He planted a marker on the scope position, shifted focus and went down into the DNA spirals, seeking the hydroxyl deformity, the flaw that would produce a faulty heart valve. Now he was the artist, the master cutter—the pilot cell determined. Now he moved to reshape the delicate chemical factory of the inner structure.

"Prepare for the cut," he said.

Svengaard armed the meson generator. "Armed," he said.

"Krebs cycle seventy-one," the computer nurse said.

"First cut," Potter said. He let off the single, aimed burst, watched the tumbling chaos that followed. The hydroxyl appendage vanished. Nucleotides reformed.

"Hemoprotein P-450," Potter said. "Stand by to reduce it with NADH." He waited, studying the globular proteins that formed before him, watching for biologically active molecules. *Now!* Instinct and training combined to tell him the precise instant. "Two and a half minims of P-450," he said.

A corner of turmoil engaged a group of polypeptide chains in the heart of the cell.

"Reduce it," Potter said.

Svengaard touched the NADH feeder key. He couldn't see what Potter saw, but the surgeon's forehead lens reproduced a slightly off-parallax view of the scope field. That plus Potter's instructions told of the slow spread of change in the cell.

"Krebs cycle fifty-eight," the computer nurse said.

"Second cut," Potter said.

"Armed," Svengaard said.

Potter searched out the myxedema-latent isovaithine, found it. "Give me a tape on structure," he said. "S- (isopropylcarboxymethyl) cystein."

Computer tape hissed through the reels, stopped, resumed at a slow, steady pace. The isovaltine comparison image appeared in the upper right quadrant of Potter's scope field. He compared the structures, point for point, said, "Tape off." The comparison image vanished.

"Krebs cycle forty-seven," the computer nurse said.

Potter took a deep, trembling breath. Another twenty-seven points and they'd be in the death range. The Durant embryo would succumb.

He swallowed, aimed off the meson burst.

Isovalthine tumbled apart.

"Ready with cycloserine," Svengaard said.

Ahhh, good old Sven, Potter thought. *You don't have to tell him every step of the way what to do.*

"Comparison on D-4-aminoisoxazolidon-3," Potter said.

The computer nurse readied the tape, said, "Comparison ready."

The comparison image appeared in Potter's view field. "Check," he said. The image vanished. "One point eight minims." He watched the interaction of the enzymic functional groups as Svengaard administered the cycloserine. The amino group showed a nice, open field of affinity. Transfer-RNA fitted readily into its niches.

"Krebs cycle thirty-eight point six," the computer nurse said.

We'll have to chance it, Potter thought. *This embryo won't take more adjustment.*

"Reduce vat stasis to half," he said. "Increase ATP. Give me micro-feed on ten minims of pyruvic acid."

"Reducing stasis," Svengaard said. And he thought, *This will be close.* He keyed the ATP and pyruvic acid feeders.

"Give me the Krebs cycle on the half point," Potter said.

"Thirty-five," the nurse said. "Thirty-four point five. Thirty-four. Thirty-three point five." Her voice picked up speed with a shocked breathlessness: "Thirty-three . . . thirty-two . . . thirty-one . . . thirty . . . twenty-nine . . ."

"Release all stasis," Potter said. "Present the full amino spectrum with activated histidine. Start pyridoxin—four point two minims."

Svengaard's hands sped over the keys.

"Back-feed the protein tape," Potter ordered. "Give it the full DNA record on computer automatic."

Tapes hissed through the reels.

"It's slowing," Svengaard said.

"Twenty-two," the computer nurse said. "Twenty-one nine . . . twenty-two . . . twenty-one nine . . . twenty-two one . . . twenty-two two . . . twenty-two one . . . twenty two two . . . twenty-two three . . . twenty-two four . . . twenty-two three . . . twenty-two four . . . twenty-two five . . . twenty-two six . . . twenty-two five . . ."

Potter felt the see-saw battle through every nerve. The morula was down at the edge of the death range. It could live or it could die in the next few minutes. Or it could come out of this crippled. Such things happened. When the flaw was too gross, the vat was turned off, flushed out. But Potter felt an identification with this embryo now. He felt he couldn't afford to lose it.

"Mutagen desensitizer," he said.

Svengaard hesitated. The Krebs cycle was following a slow sine curve that dipped perilously into the death cycle now. He knew why Potter had made this decision, but the carcinogenic peril of it had to be weighed. He wondered if he should argue the step. The embryo hung less than four points from a deadly plunge into dissolution. Chemical mutagens administered at this point could shock it into a spurt of growth or destroy it. Even if the mutagen treatment worked, it could leave the embryo susceptible to cancer.

"Mutagen desensitizer!" Potter repeated.

"Dosage?" Svengaard asked.

"Half minim on fractional-minim feed. I'll control it from here."

Svengaard shifted the feeder keys, his eyes on the Krebs-cycle repeater. He'd never heard of applying such drastic treatment this close to the borderline. Mutagens usually were reserved for the partly-flawed Sterrie embryo, a move that sometimes produced dramatic results. It was like shaking a bucket of sand to level the grains. Sometimes the germ plasm presented with a mutagen sought a better level on its own. They'd even produced an occasional viable this way . . . but never an Optiman.

Potter reduced amplification, studied the flow of movement in the embryo. Gently, he depressed the feeder key, searched for Optiman signs. The cellular action remained unsteady, partly blurred.

"Krebs cycle twenty-two eight," the computer nurse said.

Climbing a bit, Potter thought.

"Very slow," Svengaard said.

Potter maintained his vigil within the morula. It was growing, expanding in fits and starts, fighting with all the enormous power contracted in its tiny domain.

"Krebs cycle thirty point four," Svengaard said.

"I am withdrawing mutagens," Potter said. He backed off the microscope to a peripheral cell, desensitized the nucleo-proteins, searched for the flawed configurations.

The cell was clean.

Potter traced down into the coiled-coil helices of the DNA chains with a dawning wonder.

"Krebs cycle thirty-six eight and climbing," Svengaard said. "Shall I start the choline and aneurin?"

Potter spoke automatically, his attention fixed on the cell's gene structure. "Yes, start them." He completed the scope tracing, shifted to another peripheral cell.

Identical.

Another cell—the same.

The altered gene pattern held true, but it was a pattern, Potter realized, which hadn't been seen in humankind since the second century of gene shaping. He thought of calling for a comparison to be sure. The computer would have it, of course. No record was ever lost or thrown away. But he dared not . . . there was too much at stake in this. He knew he didn't need the comparison, though. This was a classic form, a classroom norm which he had stared at almost daily all through his medical education.

The super-genius pattern that had caused Sven to call in a Central specialist was there, firmed up by the cutting-room adjustments. It was close-coupled, though, with a fully stable fertility pattern. The longevity basics lay locked in the configurations of the gene structure.

If this embryo reached maturity and encountered a fertile mate, it could breed healthy, living children without the interference of the gene surgeon. It needed no enzyme prescription to survive. It would outlive ten standard humans without that prescription . . . and with a few delicate enzymic adjustments might join the ranks of the immortals.

The Durant embryo could father a new race—like the live-forevers of Central, but dramatically unlike them. This embryo's progeny might fit themselves into the rhythms of natural selectivity . . . completely outside Optiman control.

It was the template pattern from which no human could deviate too far and live, yet it was the single thing feared most by Central.

Every gene surgeon had this drummed into him during his education, *"Natural selectivity is a madness that sends its human victims groping blindly through empty lives."*

Optiman reason and Optiman logic must do the selecting.

As though he straddled Time, Potter felt the profound certainty that the Durant embryo, if it matured, *would* encounter a fertile mate. This embryo had received a gift from *outside*—a wealth of sperm-arginine, the key to its fertility pattern. In the flood of mutagen which opened the active centers of the DNA, this embryo's gene patterns had shaken down into a stable form no human dared attempt.

Why did I introduce the mutagens just then? Potter wondered. *I knew it was the needed thing. How did I know? Was I an instrument of some other force?*

"Krebs cycle fifty-eight and climbing steadily," Svengaard said.

Potter longed for the freedom to discuss this problem with Svengaard . . . but there were the damnable parents and the Security people . . . watching. *Was it possible anyone else had seen enough and knew enough of this pattern to realize what had happened here?* he wondered.

Why did I introduce the mutagens?

"Can you see the pattern yet?" Svengaard asked.

"Not yet," Potter lied.

The embryo was growing rapidly now. Potter studied the proliferation of stable cells. It was beautiful.

"Krebs cycle sixty-four seven," Svengaard said.

I've waited too long, Potter thought. *The bigdomes of Central will ask why I waited so long to kill this embryo. I cannot kill it! It's too beautiful.*

Central maintained its power by keeping the world at large in ignorance of the ruling fist, by doling out living time in the form of precious enzyme prescriptions to its half-alive slaves.

The Folk had a saying: *"In this world there are two worlds—one that works not and lives forever; one that lives not and works forever."*

Here in a crystal vat lay a tiny ball of cells, a living creature less than six-tenths of a millimeter in diameter, and it carried the full potential of living out its life beyond Central's control.

This morula had to die.

They'll order it killed, Potter thought. *And I will be suspect . . . finished. And if this thing did get loose in the world, what then? What would happen to gene surgery? Would we go back to correcting minor defects . . . the way it was before we started shaping supermen?*

Supermen!

In his mind, he did what no voice could do: he cursed the Optimen. They were enormous power, instant life or death. Many were geniuses. But they were as dependent on the enzymic fractions as any clod of the Sterries or Breeders. There were men as brilliant among the Sterries and Breeders . . . and among the surgeons.

But none of these could live forever, secure in that ultimate, brutal power.

"Krebs cycle one hundred even," Svengaard said.

"We're over the top now," Potter said. He risked a glance at the computer nurse, but she had her back to him, fussing with her board. Without that computer record, it might be possible to conceal what had happened here. With that record open to examination by Security and by the Optimen, it could not be hidden. Svengaard had not seen enough. The forehead lens only approximated the full field vision. The vat nurses couldn't even guess at it. Only the computer nurse with her tiny monitor screen might know . . . and the full record lay in her machine now—a pattern of magnetic waves on strips of tape.

"That's the lowest I've ever seen it go without killing the embryo," Svengaard said.

"How low?" Potter asked.

"Twenty-one nine," Svengaard said. "Twenty's bottom, of course, but I've never heard of an embryo coming back from below twenty-five before, have you, Doctor?"

"No," Potter said.

"Is it the pattern we want?" Svengaard asked.

"I don't want to interfere too much yet," Potter said.

"Of course," Svengaard said. "Whatever happens, it was inspired surgery."

Inspired surgery! Potter thought. *What would this dolt say if I told him what I have here? A totally viable embryo! A total. Kill it, he'd say. It'll need no enzyme prescription and it can breed true. It hasn't a defect . . . not one. Kill it, he'd say. He's a dutiful slave. The whole sorry history of gene shaping could be justified by this one embryo. But the minute they see this tape at Central, the embryo will be destroyed.*

Eliminate it, they'll say . . . because they don't like to use words too close to kill or death.

Potter bent to the scope. How lovely the embryo was in its own terrifying way.

He risked another glance at the computer nurse. She turned, mask down, met his gaze, smiled. It was a knowing, secretive smile, the smile of a conspirator. Now, she reached up to mop the perspiration from her face. Her sleeve brushed a switch. A rasping, whirring scream came from the computer board. She whirled to it, grated, "Oh, my God!" Her hands sped over the board, but tape continued to hiss through the transponder plates. She turned, tried to wrestle the transparent cover from the recording console. The big reels whirled madly under the cover plate.

"It's running wild!" she shouted.

"It's locked on Erase!" Svengaard yelled. He jumped to her side, tried to get the cover plate off. It jammed in its tracks.

Potter watched like a man in a trance as the last of the tape flashed through the heads, began whipping on the take-up reels.

"Oh, Doctor, we've lost it!" the computer nurse wailed.

Potter focused on the little monitor screen at the computer nurse's station. *Did she watch the operation closely?* he asked himself. *Sometimes they follow the cut move by move . . . and computer nurses are a savvy lot. If she watched, she'll have a good idea what we achieved. At the very least, she'll suspect. Was that tape erasure really an accident? Do I dare?*

She turned, met his gaze. "Oh, Doctor, I'm so sorry," she said.

"It's all right, nurse," Potter said. "There's nothing very special about this embryo now, aside from the fact that it will live."

"We missed it, eh?" Svengaard asked. "Must've been the mutagens."

"Yes," Potter said. "But without them it'd have died."

Potter stared at the nurse. He couldn't be sure, but he thought he saw a profound relief wash over her features.

"I'll cut a verbal tape of the operation," Potter said. "That should be enough on this embryo."

And he thought, *When does a conspiracy begin? Was this such a beginning?*

There was still so much this conspiracy required. No knowledgeable eye could ever again look at this embryo through the microscope without being a part of the conspiracy . . . or a traitor.

"We still have the protein synthesis tape," Svengaard said. "That'll give us the chemical factors by reference— and the timing."

Potter thought about the protein synthesis tape. Was there danger in it? No, it was only a reference for what had been used in the operation . . . not *how* anything had been used.

"So it will," Potter said. "So it will." He gestured to the monitor screen. "Operation's finished. You can cut the direct circuit and escort the parents to the reception room. I'm very sorry we achieved no more than we did, but this'll be a healthy human."

"Sterrie?" Svengaard asked.

"Too soon to guess," Potter said. He looked at the computer nurse. She had managed to get the cover off at last and had stopped the tapes. "Any idea how that happened?"

"Probably solonoid failure," Svengaard said.

"This equipment's quite old," the nurse said. "I've asked for replacement units several times, but we don't seem to be very high on the priority lists."

And there's a natural reluctance at Central to admit anything can wear out, Potter thought.

"Yes," Potter said. "Well, I daresay you'll get your replacements now."

Did anyone else see her trip that switch? Potter wondered. He tried to remember where everyone in the room had been looking, worried that a Security monitor might've been watching her. *If Security saw that, she's dead,* Potter thought. *And so am I.*

"The technician's report on repairs will have to be part of the record on this case," Svengaard said. "I presume you'll—"

"I'll see to it personally, Doctor," she said.

Turning away, Potter had the impression that he and the computer nurse had just carried on a silent conversation. He noted that the big screen was now a gray blank, the Durants no longer watching. *Should I see them myself?* he wondered. *If they're part of the Underground, they could help. Something has to be done about the embryo. Safest to get it out of here entirely . . . but how?*

"I'll take care of the tie-off details," Svengaard said. He began checking the vat seals, life systems repeaters, dismantling the meson generator.

Someone has to see the parents, Potter thought.

"The parents'll be disappointed," Svengaard said. "They generally know why a specialist is called in . . . and probably got their hopes up."

The door from the ready room opened to admit a man Potter recognized as an agent from Central Security. He was a moon-faced blond with features one tended to forget five minutes after leaving him. The man crossed the room to stand in front of Potter.

Is this the end for me? Potter wondered. He forced his voice into a steady casual tone, asked, "What about the parents?"

"They're clean," the agent said. "No tricky devices—conversation normal . . . plenty of small talk, but normal."

"No hint of the other things?" Potter asked. "Any way they could've penetrated Security without instruments?"

"Impossible!" the man snorted.

"Doctor Svengaard believes the father's overly endowed with male protectiveness and the mother has too much maternalism," Potter said.

"The records show you shaped 'em," the agent said.

"It's possible," Potter said. "Sometimes you have to concentrate on gross elements of the cut to save the embryo. Little things slip past."

"Anything slip past on this one today?" the agent asked. "I understand the tape's been erased . . . an accident."

Does he suspect? Potter asked himself. The extent of his own involvement and personal danger threatened to overwhelm Potter. It took the greatest effort to maintain a casual tone.

"Anything's possible of course," Potter said. He shrugged. "But I don't think we have anything unusual here. We lost the Optishape in saving the embryo, but that happens. We can't win them all."

"Should we flag the embryo's record?" the agent asked.

He's still fishing, Potter told himself. He said, "Suit yourself. I'll have a verbal tape on the cut pretty soon—probably just as accurate as the visual one. You might wait and analyze that before you decide."

"I'll do that," the agent said.

Svengaard had the microscope off the vat now. Potter relaxed slightly. No one was going to take a casual, dangerous look at the embryo.

"I guess we brought you on a wild goose chase," Potter said. "Sorry about that, but they did insist on watching."

"Better ten wild goose chases than one set of parents knowing too much," the agent said. "How was the tape erased?"

"Accident," Potter said. "Worn equipment. We'll have the technical report for you shortly."

"Leave the worn equipment thing out of your report," the agent said. "I'll take that verbally. Allgood has to show every report to the Tuyere now."

Potter permitted himself an understanding nod. "Of course." The men who worked out of Central knew about such things. One concealed personally disquieting items from the Optimen.

The agent glanced around the cutting room, said, "Someday we won't have to use all this secrecy. Won't come any too soon for me." He turned away.

Potter watched the retreating back, thinking how neatly the agent fitted into the demands of his profession. A superb cut with just one flaw—too neat a fit, too much cold logic, not enough imaginative curiosity and readiness to explore the avenues of chance.

If he'd pressed me, he'd have had me, Potter thought. *He should've been more curious about the accident. But we tend to copy our masters—even in their blind spots.*

Potter began to have more confidence of success in his impetuous venture. He turned back to help Svengaard with the final details, wondering, *How do I know the agent's satisfied with my explanation.* No feeling of disquiet accompanied the question. *I know he's satisfied, but how do I know it?* Potter asked himself.

He realized then that his mind had been absorbing correlated gene information—the inner workings of the cells and their exterior manifestations—for so many years that this weight of data had fused into a new level of understanding. He was reading the tiny betrayals in gene-type reactions.

I can read people!

It was a staggering realization. He looked around the room at the nurses helping with the tie-off. When his eyes found the computer nurse, he *knew* she had deliberately destroyed the record tape. He knew it.

4

Lizbeth and Harvey Durant walked hand in hand from the hospital after their interview with the Doctors Potter and Svengaard. They smiled and swung their clasped hands like children off on a picnic—which in a sense they were.

The morning's rain had been shut off and the clouds were being packed off to the east, toward the tall peaks that looked down on Seatac Megalopolis. The overhead sky showed a clear cerulean blue with a goblin sun riding high in it.

A mob of people in loose marching order was coming through the park across the way, obviously the exercise period for some factory team or labor group. Their uniformed sameness was broken by flashes of color—an orange scarf on a woman's head, a yellow sash across a man's chest, the scarlet of a fertility fetish dangling on a gold loop from a woman's ear. One man had equipped himself bright green shoes.

The pathetic attempts at individuality in a world of gene-stamped sameness stabbed through Lizbeth's defenses. She turned away lest the scene tear the smile from her lips, asked, "Where'll we go?"

"Hmmm?" Harvey held her back, waiting on the walk for the group to pass.

Among the marchers, faces turned to stare enviously at Harvey and Lizbeth. All knew why the Durants were here. The hospital, a great pile of plasmeld behind them, the fact that they were man and woman together, the casual dress, the smiles—all said the Durants were on breeder-leave from their appointed labors.

Each individual in that mob hoped with a lost desperation for this same escape from the routine that bound them all. Viable gametes, breeder leave—it was the universal dream. Even the known Sterries hoped, and patronized the breeder quacks and the manufacturers of doombah fetishes.

They have no pasts, Lizbeth thought, focusing abruptly on the common observation of the Folk philosophers. *They're all people without pasts and only the hope for a future to cling to. Somewhere our past was lost in an ocean of darkness. The Optimen and their gene surgeons have extinguished our past.*

Even their own breeder-leave lost its special glow in the face of this. The Durants might not be constrained to leap up at the rising bell and hurry apart to their labors, but they were still people without a past . . . and their future might be lost in an instant. The child being formed in the hospital vat . . . in some small way it might still be part of them, but the surgeons had changed it. They had cut it off sharply from its past.

Lizbeth recalled her own parents, the feeling of estrangement from them, of differences which went deeper than blood.

They were only partly my parents, she thought. *They knew it . . . and I knew it.*

She felt the beginnings of estrangement from her own unformed son then, an emotion that colored present necessities. *What's the use?* she wondered. But she knew what the use was—to end forever all this amputation of pasts.

The last envious face passed. The mob became moving backs, bits of color. They turned a corner and were gone, cut off.

Is it a corner we've turned and no coming back? Lizbeth wondered.

"Let's walk to the cross-town shuttle tube," Harvey said.

"Through the park?" she asked.

"Yes," Harvey said. "Just think—ten months."

"And we can take our son home," she said. "We're very lucky."

"It seems like a long time—ten months," Harvey said.

Lizbeth answered as they crossed the street and entered the park. "Yes, but we can come see him every week when they shift him to the big vat—and that's only three months away."

"You're right," Harvey said. "It'll be over before we know it. And thank the powers he's not a specialist or *anything else*. We can raise him at home. Our work time'll be reduced."

"That Doctor Potter's wonderful," she said.

As they talked, their clasped hands moved with the subtle pressures and finger shifts of the secret conversation— the *No-Spoken-Word* hand code that classified them as couriers of the Parents Underground.

"They're still watching us," Harvey signaled.

"I know."

"Svengaard is out—a slave of the power structure."

"Obviously. You know, I had no idea the computer nurse was one of us."

"You saw that, too?"

"Potter was looking at her when she tripped the switch."

"Do you think the Security people saw her?"

"Not a chance. They were all concentrated on us."

"Maybe she's not one of us," Harvey signaled. And he spoke aloud, "Isn't it a beautiful day. Let's take the floral path."

Lizbeth's finger pressures answered, *"You think that nurse is an accidental?"*

"Could be. Perhaps she saw what Potter'd accomplished and knew there was only one way to save the embryo."

"*Someone will have to contact her immediately then.*"

"*Cautiously. She might be unstable, emotional—a breeder neurotic.*"

"*What about Potter?*"

"*We'll have to get people to him right away. We'll need his help getting the embryo out of there.*"

"*That'll give us nine of Central's surgeons,*" she said.

"*If he goes along,*" Harvey signaled.

She looked at him with a smile that completely masked her sudden worry. "*You have doubts?*"

"*It's only that I think he was reading me at the same time I read him.*"

"*Oh, he was,*" she said. "*But he was slow and lame about it compared to us.*"

"*That's how I read him. He was like a first reader, an amateur stumbling along, gaining confidence as he went.*"

"*He's untrained,*" she said. "*That's obvious. I was worried you'd read something in him that escaped me.*"

"*I guess you're right.*"

Across the park, dust had shattered the sunlight into countless pillars that stood up through an arboretum. Lizabeth stared at the scene as she answered, "*No doubt of it, darling. He's a natural, someone who's stumbled onto the talent accidentally. They do occur, you know—have to. Nothing can keep us from communicating.*"

"*But they certainly try.*"

"*Yes,*" she signaled. "*They were very intent on it there today, probing and scanning us in that lounge. But people who think mechanically will never guess—I mean that our weapons are people and not things.*"

"*It's their fatal blind spot,*" he agreed. "*Central's carved out the genetic ruts with logic—and logic keeps digging the ruts deeper and deeper. They're so deep now they can't see over the edges to the outside.*"

"*And that wide, wide universe out there calling to us,*" she signaled.

5

M ax Allgood, Central's chief of Tachy-Security, climbed
Administration's plasmeld steps slightly ahead of his
two surgeon companions as befitted the director of the Optimen's swift and terrible hand of power.

The morning sun behind the trio sent their shadows darting across the white building's angles and planes.

They were admitted to the silver shadows of the entrance
portico where a barrier dropped for the inevitable delay.
Quarantine scanners searched and probed them for inimi-
cal microbes.

Allgood turned with the patience of long experience in
this procedure, studied his companions—Boumour and
Igan. It amused him that they must drop their titles here. No
doctors were admitted to these precincts. Here they must be
pharmacists. The title "doctor" carried overtones which
spread unrest among the Optimen. *They* knew about doctors, but only as ministers to the *mere* humans. A doctor
became a euphemism in here, just as no one said *death* or
kill or implied that a machine or structure would wear out.
Only new Optimen in their acolyte apprenticeship, or *meres*
of young appearance served in Central, although some of
the *meres* had been preserved by their masters for remarkable lengths of time.

Boumour and Igan both passed the test of youthfulness,

although Boumour's face was of that pinched-up elfin type which tended to suggest age before its time. He was a big man with heavy shoulders, powerful. Igan looked lean and fragile beside him, a beaked face with long jaw and tight little mouth. The eyes of both men were Optimen color—blue and penetrating. They were probably near-Opts, both of them. Most Central surgeon-pharmacists were.

The pair moved restlessly under Allgood's gaze, avoiding his eyes. Boumour began talking in a low voice to Igan with one hand on the man's shoulder moving nervously, kneading. The movement of Boumour's hand on Igan's shoulder carried an odd familiarity, a suggestion to Allgood that he had seen something like this somewhere before. He couldn't place where.

The quarantine probing-scanning continued. It seemed to Allgood that it was lasting longer than usual. He turned his attention to the scene across from the building. It was strangely peaceful, at odds with the mood of Central as Allgood knew it.

Allgood realized that his access to secret records and even to old books gave him an uncommon knowledge about Central. The Optiman demesne reached across leagues of what had once been the political entities of Canada and northern United States. It occupied a rough circle some seven hundred kilometers in diameter and with two hundred levels below ground. It was a region of multitudinous controls—weather control, gene control, bacterial control, enzyme control . . . human control . . .

In this little corner, the heart of Administration, the ground had been shaped into an Italian chiaroscuro landscape—blacks and grays with touches of pastels. The Optimen were people who could barber a mountain at a whim: *"A little off the top and leave the sideburns."* Throughout Central, nature had been smoothed over, robbed of her dangerous sharpness. Even when the Optimen staged some natural display, it lacked an element of drama which was a general lack in their lives.

Allgood often wondered at this. He had seen pre-Optiman films and recognized the differences. Central's manicured niceties seemed to him all tied up with the omnipresent red triangles indicating pharmacy outlets where the Optimen might check their enzyme prescriptions.

"Are they taking a long time about it or is it just me?" Boumour asked. His voice carried a rumbling quality.

"Patience," Igan said. A mellow tenor there.

"Yes," Allgood said. "Patience is a man's best ally."

Boumour looked up at the Security chief, studying, wondering. Allgood seldom spoke except for effect. He, not the Optimen, was the Conspiracy's greatest threat. He was body and soul with his masters, a super puppet. *Why did he order us to accompany him today?* Boumour wondered. *Does he know? Will he denounce us?*

There was a special ugliness about Allgood that fascinated Boumour. The Security chief was a stocky little Folk *mere* with moon face and darting almond eyes, a dark bush of hair low on his forehead—a Shang-cut by the look of his overt gene markers.

Allgood turned toward the quarantine barrier and with a sudden feeling of awakening, Boumour realized the man's ugliness came from within. It was the ugliness of fear, of created fear and personal fear. The realization gave Boumour an abrupt sensation of relief which he signaled to Igan through finger pressures on the man's shoulder.

Igan pulled away suddenly to stare out across from the building where they stood. *Of course Max Allgood fears,* he thought. *He lives in a mire of fears, named and nameless . . . just as the Optimen do . . . poor creatures.*

The scene across from Central began to impress itself on Igan's senses. Here, at this moment, it was a day of absolute Spring, planned that way in the lordly heart of Weather Control. Administration's steps looked down on a lake, round and perfect like an enameled blue plate. On a low hill beyond the lake, plasmeld plinths stood out like white stones: elevator caps reaching down into the locked fastness of the Optimen quarters below—two hundred levels.

Far beyond the hill, the sky began to turn dark blue and oily. It was streaked suddenly with red, green and purple fires in a rather flat pattern. Presently, there came a low clap of contained thunder. Across the reaches of Central, some Upper Optiman was staging a tame storm for entertainment.

It struck Igan as a pointless display, lacking danger or drama . . . which he decided were two words for the same thing.

The storm was the first thing Allgood had seen this day to fit his interpretation of Central's inner rhythms. Things of an ominous nature set the pattern for his view of Central. People vanished into here never to be seen again and only he, Allgood, the chief of Tachy-Security, or a few trusted agents knew their fate. Allgood felt the thunderclap keyed to his mood, a sound that portended absolute power. Under the storm sky now turning acid yellow and dispersing the air of Spring, the plinths on the hill above the lake became pagan cenotaphs set out against a ground as purple-green as camomile.

"It's time," Boumour said.

Allgood turned to find the quarantine barrier lifted. He led the way into the Hall of Counsel with its shimmering adamantine walls above ranks of empty plasmeld benches. The trio moved through tongues of perfumed vapor that swayed aside as they breasted them.

Optiman acolytes wearing green capes fastened at the shoulders with diamond lanulas came from side shadows to pace them. Worked into the green of their robes were shepherd's pipes of platinum and they swung golden thuribles that wafted clouds of antiseptic pink smoke into the air.

Allgood kept his attention on the end of the hall. A giant globe as red as a mandrake stem hung in walking beams there. It was some forty meters in diameter with a section folded back like a segment cut from an orange to reveal the interior. This was the Tuyere's control center, the tool of strange powers and senses with which *they* watched and ruled their minions. Lights flashed in there, phosphor greens and the blue cracklings of arcs. Great round gauges spelled out messages and red lights winked response. Numbers flowed on beams through the air and esoteric symbols danced on ribbons of light.

Up through the middle, like the core of the fruit, stretched a white column supporting a triangular platform at the globe's center. At the points of the triangle, each on a golden plasmeld throne, sat the Optimen trio known as the Tuyere— friends, companions, elected rulers for this century and with seventy-eight years yet to serve. It was a wink of time in their lives, an annoyance, often disquieting because they must face realities which all other Optimen could treat as euphemisms.

The acolytes stopped some twenty paces from the red globe, but continued swinging their thuribles. Allgood moved one pace ahead, motioned Boumour and Igan to halt behind him. The Security chief felt he knew just how far he could go here, that he must go to the limits. *They need me,* he told himself. But he held no illusions about the dangers in this interview.

Allgood looked up into the globe. A dancing lacery of power placed a deceptive transparency over the interior. Through that curtain could be seen shapes, outlines—now clear, now enfolded.

"I came," Allgood said.

Boumour and Igan echoed the greeting, reminding themselves of all the protocol and forms which must be observed here: *"Always use the name of the Optiman you address. If you do not know the name, ask it humbly."*

Allgood waited for the Tuyere to answer. Sometimes he felt they had no sense of time, at least of seconds and minutes and perhaps not even of days. It might be true. People of infinite lives might notice the passing seasons as clock ticks.

The throne support turned, presenting the Tuyere one by

one. They sat in clinging translucent robes, almost nude, flaunting their similarity to the *meres*. Facing the open segment now was Nourse, a Greek god figure with blocky face, heavy brows, a chest ridged by muscles that rippled as he breathed. How evenly he breathed, with what controlled slowness.

The base turned, presented Schruille, the bone slender, unpredictable one with great round eyes, high cheeks and a flat nose above a mouth which seemed always pulled to a thin line of disapproval. Here was a dangerous one. Some said he spoke of things which other Optimen could not. In Allgood's presence, Schruille had once said "death," although referring to a butterfly.

Again, the base turned—and here was Calapine, her robe girdled with crystal plastrons. She was a thin, high-breasted woman with golden brown hair and chill, insolent eyes, full lips and a long nose above a pointed chin. Allgood had caught her watching him strangely on occasion. At such times he tried not to think about the Optimen who took *mere* playmates.

Nourse spoke to Calapine, looking at her through the prismatic reflector which each throne raised at a shoulder. She answered, but the voices did not carry to the floor of the hall.

Allgood watched the interplay for a clue to their mood. It was known among the Folk that Nourse and Calapine had been bedmates for periods that spanned hundreds of *mere* lifetimes. Nourse had a reputation of strength and predictability, but Calapine was known as a wild one. Mention her name and likely someone would look up and ask, "What's she done now?" It was always said with a touch of admiration and fear. Allgood knew that fear. He had worked for other ruling trios, but none who had his measure as did these three . . . especially Calapine.

The throne base stopped with Nourse facing the open segment. "You came," he rumbled. "Of course you came. The ox knows its owner and the ass its master's crib."

So it's going to be one of those days, Allgood thought. *Ridicule!* It could only mean they knew how he had stumbled . . . but didn't they always?

Calapine swiveled her throne to look down at the *meres.* The Hall of Counsel had been patterned on the Roman Senate with false columns around the edges, banks of benches beneath glittering scanner eyes. Everything focused down onto the figures standing apart from the acolytes.

Looking up, Igan reminded himself he had feared and hated these creatures all his life—even while he pitied them. How lucky he'd been to miss the Optiman cut. It'd been close, but he'd been saved. He could remember the hate of his childhood, before it had become tempered by pity. It'd been a clean thing then, sharp and real, blazing against the Givers of Time.

"We came as requested to report on the Durants," Allgood said. He took two deep breaths to calm his nerves. These sessions were always dangerous, but doubly so since he'd decided on a double game. There was no turning back, though, and no wish to since he'd discovered the dopplegangers of himself they were growing. There could be only one reason they'd duplicate him. Well, they'd learn.

Calapine studied Allgood, wondering if it might be time to seek diversion with the ugly Folk male. Perhaps here was an answer to boredom. Both Schruille and Nourse indulged. She seemed to recall having done that before with another Max, but couldn't remember if it had helped her boredom.

"Say what it is we give you, little Max," she said.

Her woman's voice, soft and with laughter behind it, terrified him. Allgood swallowed. "You give life, Calapine."

"Say how many lovely years you have," she ordered.

Allgood found his throat contained no moisture. "Almost four hundred, Calapine," he rasped.

Nourse chuckled. "Ahead of you stretch many more lovely years if you serve us well," he said.

It was the closest to a direct threat Allgood had ever heard from an Optiman. They worked their wills by indirection, by euphemistic subtlety. They worked through *meres* who could face such concepts as death and killing.

Who have they shaped to destroy me? Allgood wondered.

"Many little tick-tock years," Calapine said.

"Enough!" Schruille growled. He detested these interviews with the underclasses, the way Calapine baited the Folk. He swiveled his throne and now all the Tuyere faced the open segment. Schruille looked at his fingers, the ever youthful skin, and wondered why he had snapped that way. An enzymic imbalance? The thought touched him with disquiet. He generally held his silence during these sessions—as a defense because he tended to get sentimental about the pitiful *meres* and despise himself for it afterward.

Boumour moved up beside Allgood, said, "Does the Tuyere wish now the report on the Durants?"

Allgood stifled a feeling of rage at the interruption. Didn't the fool know that the Optimen must always appear to lead the interview?

"The words and images of your report have been seen, analyzed and put away," Nourse rumbled. "Now, it is the non-report that we wish."

Non-report? Allgood asked himself. *Does he think we've hidden something?*

"Little Max," Calapine said. "Have you bowed to our necessity and questioned the computer nurse under narcosis?"

Here it comes, Allgood thought. He took a deep breath, said, "She has been questioned, Calapine."

Igan took his place beside Boumour, said, "There's something I wish to say about that if I—"

"Hold your tongue, pharmacist," Nourse said. "We talk to Max."

Igan bowed his head, thought, *How dangerous this is! And all because of that fool nurse. She wasn't even one of us. No Cyborg-of-the-register knows her. A member of no cell or platoon. An accidental, a Sterrie, and she puts us in this terrible peril!*

Allgood saw that Igan's hands trembled, wondered, *What's driving these surgeons? They can't be such fools.*

"Was it not a deliberate thing that nurse did?" Calapine asked.

"Yes, Calapine," Allgood said.

"Your agents did not see it, yet we knew it had to be," Calapine said. She turned to scan the instruments of the control center, returned her attention to Allgood. "Say now why this was."

Allgood sighed. "I have no excuses, Calapine. The men have been censured."

"Say now why the nurse acted thus," Calapine ordered.

Allgood wet his lips with his tongue, glanced at Boumour and Igan. They looked at the floor. He looked back to Calapine, at her face shimmering within the globe. "We were unable to discover her motives, Calapine."

"Unable?" Nourse demanded.

"She . . . ahh . . . ceased to exist during the interrogation, Nourse," Allgood said. As the Tuyere stiffened, sitting bolt upright in their thrones, he added, "A flaw in her genetic cutting, so the pharmacists tell me."

"A profound pity," Nourse said, settling back.

Igan looked up, blurted, "It could've been a deliberate self-erasure, Nourse."

That damn' fool! Allgood thought.

But Nourse stared now at Igan. "You were present, Igan?"

"Boumour and I administered the narcotics."

And she died, Igan thought. *But we did not kill her. She died and we'll be blamed for it. Where could she have learned the trick of stopping her own heart? Only Cyborgs are supposed to know and teach it.*

"Deliberate . . . self-erasure?" Nourse asked. Even when considered indirectly, the idea held terrifying implications.

"Max!" Calapine said. "Say now if you used excessive . . . cruelty." She leaned forward, wondering why she wanted him to admit barbarity.

"She suffered nothing, Calapine," Allgood said.

Calapine sat back disappointed. *Could he be lying?* She read her instruments: Calmness. He wasn't lying.

"Pharmacist," Nourse said, "explain your opinion."

"We examined her carefully," Igan said. "It couldn't have been the narcotics. There's no way . . ."

"Some of us think it was a genetic flaw," Boumour said.

"There's disagreement," Igan said. He glanced at Allgood, feeling the man's disapproval. It had to be done, though. The Optimen must be made to know disquiet. When they could be tricked into acting emotionally, they made mistakes. The plan called for them to make mistakes now. They must be put off balance—subtly, delicately.

"Your opinion, Max?" Nourse asked. He watched carefully. They'd been getting poorer models lately, doppleganger degeneration.

"We've already taken cellular matter, Nourse," Allgood said, "and are growing a duplicate. If we get a true copy, we'll check the question of genetic flaw."

"It is a pity the doppleganger won't have the original's memories," Nourse said.

"Pity of pities," Calapine said. She looked at Schruille "Is this not true, Schruille?"

Schruille looked up at her without answering. Did she think she could bait him the way she did the *meres*?

"This woman had a mate?" Nourse asked.

"Yes, Nourse," Allgood said.

"Fertile union?"

"No, Nourse," Allgood said. "A Sterrie."

"Compensate the mate," Nourse said. "Another woman, a bit of leisure. Let him think she was loyal to us."

Allgood nodded, said, "We are giving him a woman, Nourse, who will keep him under constant surveillance."

A trill of laughter escaped Calapine. "Why has no one mentioned this Potter, the genetic engineer?" she asked.

"I was coming to him, Calapine," Allgood said.

"Has anyone examined the embryo?" Schruille asked, looking up suddenly.

"No, Schruille," Allgood said.

"Why not?"

"If this is a concerted action to escape genetic controls, Schruille, we don't want members of the organization to know we suspect them. Not yet. First, we must learn all about these people—the Durants, their friends, Potter . . . everyone."

"But the embryo's the key to the entire thing," Schruille said. "What was done to it? What is it?"

"It is bait, Schruille," Allgood said.

"Bait?"

"Yes, Schruille, to catch whoever else may be involved."

"But what was done to it?"

"How can that matter, Schruille, as long as we can . . . as long as we have complete control over it."

"The embryo is being guarded most adroitly, I hope," Nourse said.

"Most adroitly, Nourse."

"Send the pharmacist Svengaard to us," Calapine ordered.

"Svengaard . . . Calapine?" Allgood asked.

"You need not know why," she said. "Merely send him."

"Yes, Calapine."

She stood up to signify the end of the interview. The acolytes turned around, still swinging their thuribles, prepared now to escort the *meres* from the hall. But Calapine was not finished. She stared at Allgood, said, "Look at me, Max."

He looked, recognizing that strange, studying set to her eyes.

"Am I not beautiful?" she asked.

Allgood stared at her, the slender figure with its outlines softened by the robe and curtains of power within the globe. She was beautiful as were many Optimen females. But the beauty repelled him with its threatening perfection. She would live indefinitely, already had lived forty or fifty thousand years. But one day his lesser flesh would reject the medical replacements and the enzyme prescriptions. He would die while she went on and on and on.

His lesser flesh rejected her.

"You are beautiful, Calapine," he said.

"Your eyes never admit it," she said.

"What do you want, Cal?" Nourse asked. "Do you want this . . . do you want Max?"

"I want his eyes," she said. "Just his eyes."

Nourse looked at Allgood, said, "Women." His voice held a note of false camaraderie.

Allgood stood astonished. He had never heard that tone from an Optiman before.

"I make a point," Calapine said. "Don't interrupt my words with male jokes. In your heart of hearts, Max, how do you feel about me?"

"Ahhhh," Nourse said. He nodded.

"I shall say it for you," she said as Allgood remained mute. "You worship me. Never forget that, Max. You worship me." She looked at Boumour and Igan, dismissed them with a wave of her hand.

Allgood lowered his eyes, feeling the truth in her words. He turned, and with the acolytes flanking them, led Igan and Boumour out of the hall.

As they emerged onto the steps, the acolytes held back and the barrier dropped. Igan and Boumour turned left, noting a new building at the end of the long esplanade which fronted Administration. They saw its machicolated walls, the openings fitted with colored filters which sent bursts of red, blue and green light upon the surrounding air, and they recognized that it blocked the way they had intended to take out of Central. A building suddenly erected, another Optiman toy. They saw it and planned their steps accordingly with the automatic acceptance that marked them as regulars in the Optiman demesne. The *meres* and inhabitants of Central seemed to know their way through the arabesques of its roads and streets by an instinct. The place defied cartographers because the Optimen were too subject to change and whim.

"Igan!"

It was Allgood calling from behind them.

They turned, waited for him to catch up.

Allgood planted himself in front of them, hands on hips, said, "Do you worship her, too?"

"Don't speak foolishness," Boumour said.

"No," Allgood said. His eyes appeared to be sunk in pockets above the high cheekbones. "I belong to no Folk cult, no breeder congregation. How can I worship her?"

"But you do," Igan said.

"Yes!"

"They are the real religion of our world," Igan said. "You do not have to belong to a cult or carry a talisman to know this. Calapine merely told you that, if there is a conspiracy, those belonging to it are heretics."

"Is that what she meant?"

"Of course."

"And she must know what is done to heretics," Allgood said.

"Without a doubt," Boumour said.

6

Svengaard had seen this building in the tri-casts and entertainment vids. He'd heard descriptions of the Hall of Counsel—but actually to be standing here at the quarantine wall with the copper sheen of sunset over the hills across from it . . . he'd never dreamed this could occur.

Elevator caps stood out like plasmeld warts on the hillock in front of him. There were other low hills beyond with piled buildings on them that could've been mistaken for rock outcroppings.

A lone woman passed him on the esplanade pulling a ground-effect cart filled with oddly shaped bundles. Svengaard found himself worried about what the bundles might contain, but he knew he dared not ask or show undue curiosity.

The red triangle of a pharmacy outlet glowed on a pillar beside him. He passed it, glanced back at his escort.

He had come halfway across the continent in the tube with an entire car to himself except for the escort, an agent from T-Security. Deep into Central they'd come, the gray-suited T-Security agent always beside him.

Svengaard began climbing the steps.

Already, Central was beginning to weigh on him. There was a sense of something disastrous about the place. Even though he suspected the source of the feeling, he couldn't shake it off. It was all the Folk nonsense you could never quite evade, he'd decided. The Folk were a people for the most part without legends or ancient myths except where such matters touched the Optimen. In the Folk memories, Central and the Optimen were fixed with sinister omens compounded of awesome fear and adulation.

Why did they summon me? Svengaard asked himself. The escort refused to say.

They were stopped by the wall and waited now, silent, nervous.

Even the agent was nervous, Svengaard saw.

Why did they summon me?

The agent cleared his throat, said, "You have all the protocol straight?"

"I think so," Svengaard said.

"Once you get into the hall, keep pace with the acolytes who'll escort you from there. You'll be interviewed by the Tuyere—Nourse, Schruille and Calapine. Remember to use their names when you address them individually. Use no such words as death or kill or die. Avoid the very concepts if you can. Let them lead the interview. Best not to volunteer anything."

Svengaard took a trembling breath.

Have they brought me here to advance me? he wondered. *That must be it. I've served my apprenticeship under such men as Potter and Igan. I'm being promoted to Central.*

"And don't say 'doctor,'" the escort said. "Doctors are pharmacists or genetic engineers in here."

"I understand," Svengaard said.

"Allgood wants a complete report on the interview afterward," the agent said.

"Yes, of course," Svengaard said.

The quarantine barrier lifted.

"In you go," the agent said.

"You're not coming with me?" Svengaard asked.

"Not invited," the agent said. He turned, went down the steps.

Svengaard swallowed, entered the silver gloom of the portico, stepped through to find himself in the long hall with an escort of six acolytes, three to a side, swinging thuribles from which pink smoke wafted. He smelled the antiseptics in the smoke.

The big red globe at the end of the hall dominated the place. Its open segment showing flashing and winking lights; the moving shapes inside fascinated Svengaard.

The acolytes stopped him twenty paces from the opening and he looked up at the Tuyere, recognizing them through the power curtains—Nourse in the center flanked by Calapine and Schruille.

"I came," Svengaard said, mouthing the greeting the agent had told him to use. He rubbed sweaty palms against his best tunic.

Nourse spoke with a rumbling voice, "You are the genetic engineer, Svengaard."

"Thei Svengaard, yes . . . Nourse." He took a deep breath, wondering if they'd caught the hesitation while he remembered to use the Optiman's name.

Nourse smiled.

"You assisted recently in the genetic alteration of an embryo from a couple named Durant," Nourse said. "The chief engineer at the cutting was Potter."

"Yes, I was the assistant, Nourse."

"There was an accident during this operation," Calapine said.

There was a strange musical quality in her voice, and Svengaard recognized she hadn't asked a question, but had reminded him of a detail to which she wanted him to give his attention. He felt the beginnings of a profound disquiet.

"An accident, yes . . . Calapine," he said.

"You followed the operation closely?" Nourse asked.

"Yes, Nourse." And Svengaard found his attention swinging to Schruille, who sat there brooding and silent.

"Now then," Calapine said, "you will be able to tell us what it is Potter has concealed about this genetic alteration."

Svengaard found that he had lost his voice. He could only shake his head.

"He concealed nothing?" Nourse asked. "Is that what you say?"

Svengaard nodded.

"We mean you no harm, Thei Svengaard," Calapine said. "You may speak."

Svengaard swallowed, cleared his throat. "I . . ." he said. ". . . the question . . . I saw nothing . . . concealed." He fell silent, then remembered he was supposed to use her name and said, "Calapine," just as Nourse started to speak.

Nourse broke off, scowled.

Calapine giggled.

Nourse said, "Yet you tell us you followed the genetic alteration."

"I . . . wasn't on the microscope with him every second," Svengaard said. "Nourse. I . . . uh . . . the duties of the assistant—instructions to the computer nurse, keying the feeder tapes and so on."

"Say now if the computer nurse was a special friend of yours," Calapine ordered.

"I . . . she'd . . ." Svengaard wet his lips with his tongue. *What do they want?* "We'd worked together for a number of years, Calapine. I can't say she was a friend. We worked together."

"Did you examine the embryo after the operation?" Nourse asked.

Schruille sat up, stared at Svengaard.

"No, Nourse," Svengaard said. "My duties were to secure the vat, check life support systems." He took a deep breath. Perhaps they were only testing him after all . . . but such odd questions!

"Say now if Potter is a special friend," Calapine ordered.

"He was one of my teachers, Calapine, someone I've worked with on delicate gentic problems."

"But not in your particular circle," Nourse said.

Svengaard shook his head. Again, he sensed menace. He

didn't know what to expect—perhaps that the great globe would roll over, crush him, reduce his body to scattered atoms. But no, the Optimen couldn't do that. He studied the three faces as they became clear through the power curtains, seeking a sign. Clean, sterile faces. He could see the genetic markers in their features—they might be any Sterries of the Folk except for the Optiman aura of mystery. Folk rumor said they were sterile by choice, that they saw breeding as the beginning of death, but the genetic clues of their features spoke otherwise to Svengaard.

"Why did you call Potter on this particular problem?" Nourse asked.

Svengaard took a tight, quavering breath, said, "He . . . the embryo's genetic configuration . . . near-Opt. Potter is familiar with our hospital. He . . . I have confidence in him; brilliant sur—genetic engineer."

"Say now if you are friendly with any other of our pharmacists," Calapine said.

"They . . . I work with them when they come to our facility," Svengaard said.

"Calapine," Nourse supplied.

A trill of laughter shook her.

A dark flush spread up from Svengaard's collar. He began to feel angry. What kind of test was this? Couldn't they do anything but sit there, mocking, questioning?

Anger gave Svengaard command of his voice and he said, "I'm only head of genetic engineering at one facility, Nourse—a lowly district engineer. I handle routine cuttings. When something requires a specialist, I follow orders, call a specialist. Potter was the indicated specialist for this case."

"*One* of the specialists," Nourse said.

"One I know and respect," Svengaard said. He didn't bother adding the Optiman's name.

"Say now if you are angry," Calapine ordered, and there was that musical quality in her voice.

"I'm angry."

"Say why."

"Why am I here?" Svengaard asked. "What kind of interrogation is this? Have I done something wrong? Am I to be censured?"

Nourse bent forward, hands on knees. "You dare question us?"

Svengaard stared at the Optiman. In spite of the tone of the question, the square, heavy-boned face appeared reassuring, calming. "I'll do anything I can to help you," Svengaard said. "Anything. But how can I help or answer you when I don't know what you want?"

Calapine started to speak, but stopped as Nourse raised a hand.

"Our most profound wish is that we could tell you," Nourse said. "But surely you know we can have no true discourse. How could you understand what we understand? Can a wooden bowl contain sulphuric acid? Trust us. We seek what is best for you."

A sense of warmth and gratitude permeated Svengaard. Of course he trusted them. They were the genetic apex of humankind. And he reminded himself: "*They are the power that loves us and cares for us.*"

Svengaard sighed. "What do you wish of me?"

"You have answered all our questions," Nourse said. "Even our non-questions are answered."

"Now, you will forget everything that has happened here between us," Calapine said. "You will repeat our conversation to no person."

Svengaard cleared his throat. "To no one . . . Calapine?"

"No one."

"Max Allgood has asked that I report to him on—"

"Max must be denied," she said. "Fear not, Thei Svengaard. We will protect you."

"As you command," Svengaard said. "Calapine."

"It is not our wish that you think us ungrateful of your loyalty and services," Nourse said. "We are mindful of your good opinion and would not appear cold nor callous in your eyes. Know that our concern is for the larger good of humankind."

"Yes, Nourse," Svengaard said.

It was a gratuitous speech, its tone disturbing to Svengaard, but it helped clear his reason. He began to see the direction of their curiosity, to sense their suspicions. Those were his suspicions now. Potter had betrayed his trust, had he? The business with the accidentally destroyed tape had not been an accident. Very well—the criminals would pay.

"You may go now," Nourse said.

"With our blessing," Calapine said.

Svengaard bowed. And he marked that Schruille had not spoken or moved during the entire interview. Svengaard wondered why this fact, of itself, should be a suddenly terrifying thing. His knees trembled as he turned, the acolytes flanking him with their smoking thuribles, and left the hall.

The Tuyere watched until the barrier dropped behind Svengaard.

"Another one who doesn't know what Potter achieved," Calapine said.

"Are you sure Max doesn't know?" Schruille asked.

"I'm sure," she said.

"Then we should've told him."

"And told him how we knew?" she asked.

"I know the argument," Schruille said. "Blunt the instrument, spoil the work."

"That Svengaard, he's one of the reliable ones," Nourse said.

"It is said we walk the sharp edge of a knife," Schruille said. "When you walk the knife, you must be careful *how* you place your feet."

"What a disgusting idea," Calapine said. She turned to Nourse. "Are you still hobbying da Vinci, dearest?"

"His brush stroke," Nourse said. "A most exacting discipline. I should have it in forty or fifty years. Soon at any rate."

"Provided you've placed each step correctly," Schruille said.

Presently, Nourse said, "Sometimes, Schruille, you allow cynicism to carry you beyond the bounds of propriety." He turned, studied the instrument gauges, sensors, peek-eyes and read-outs across from Calapine on the inner wall of the globe. "It's reasonably quiet today. Shall we leave the control with Schruille, Cal, and go down for a swim and a pharmacy session."

"Body tone, body tone," Schruille complained. "Have you ever considered doing twenty-five laps of the pool instead of twenty?"

"You say the most astonishing things of late," Calapine said. "Would you have Nourse upset his enzyme balance? I fail completely in my attempts to understand you."

"Fail to try," Schruille said.

"Is there anything we can do for you?" she asked.

"My cycle has plunged me into dreadful monotony," Schruille said. "Is there something you can do about that?"

Nourse looked at Schruille in the prismatic reflector. The man's voice with its suggestion of a whine had grown increasingly annoying of late. Nourse was beginning to regret that community of tastes and bodily requirements had thrown them together. Perhaps when the Tuyere's service was done . . .

"Monotony," Calapine said. She shrugged.

"There's a certain triumph in well-considered monotony," Nourse said. "That's Voltaire, I believe."

"It sounded like the purest Nourse," Schruille said.

"I sometimes find it helpful," Calapine said, "to invoke a benign concern for the Folk."

"Even among ourselves?" Schruille asked.

"Consider the fate of the poor computer nurse," she said. "In the abstract, naturally. Can you not feel sorrow and pity?"

"Pity's a wasteful emotion," Schruille said. "Sorrow is akin to cynicism." He smiled. "This will pass. Go to your swim. When the vigor's on you, think of me . . . here."

Nourse and Calapine stood, ordered the carrier beams into position.

"Efficiency," Nourse said. "We must seek more efficiency in our minions. Things must be made to run more smoothly."

Schruille looked up at them waiting for the beams. He wanted only to be free of the wanton rambling of their voices. They missed the point, insisted on missing it.

"Efficiency?" Calapine asked. "Perhaps you're right."

Schruille no longer could contain the emotions at war within him. "Efficiency's the opposite of craftsmanship," he said. "Think on that!"

The beams came. Nourse and Calapine slid down and away without answering, leaving Schruille to close the segment. He sat alone at last within the green-blue-red winking of the control center—alone except for the glittering eyes of scanners activated along the upper circle of the globe. He counted eighty-one of them alive and staring at him and at the responses of the globe. Eighty-one of his fellows . . . or groups of his fellows were out there observing him and his work as he observed the Folk and their work.

The scanners imparted a vague uneasiness to Schruille. Before the Tuyere's service, he could never remember watching the control center or its activities. Too much that was painful and unthinkable occurred here. Were the former masters of the control center curious about how the new trio dispatched its duties? Who were the watchers?

Schruille dropped his attention to the instruments. In moments like this he often felt like Chen Tzu-ang's "Master of Dark Truth" who saw the whole world in a jade bottle. Here was the jade bottle—this globe. A flick of the power ring on the arm of his throne and he could watch a couple making love in Warsopolis, study the contents of an embryo vat in Greater London or loose hypnotic gas with taming suggestions into a warren of New Peking. The touch of a key and he could analyze the shifting motives of an entire work force in the megalopolis of Roma.

Searching within himself, Schruille could not find the impulse to move a single control.

He thought back, trying to remember how many scanners

had watched the first years of the Tuyere's service. He was sure it had never exceeded ten or twelve. But now—eighty-one.

I should've warned them about Svengaard, he thought. *I could've said that we shouldn't rely on the assumption there's a special Providence for fools. Svengaard is a fool who disturbs me.*

But Nourse and Calapine would have defended Svengaard. He knew it. They'd have insisted the man was reliable, honorable, loyal. They'd wager anything on it.

Anything? Schruille wondered. *Is there something they might not wager on Svengaard's loyalty?*

Schruille could almost hear Nourse pontificating, *"Our judgment of Svengaard is the correct one."*

And that, Schruille thought, *is what disturbs me. Svengaard worships us . . . as does Max. But worship is nine-tenths fear.*

In time, everything becomes fear.

Schruille looked up at the watching scanners, spoke aloud: "Time-time-time . . ."

Let that chew at their vitals, he thought.

7

The place was a pumping station for the sewage reclamation system of Seatac Megalopolis. It lay at the eleven hundred foot level on the spur line that sent by-product irrigation water into Grand Coulee system. A four-story box of sampling pipes, computer consoles and access cat-walks aglow with force-buoyed lights, it throbbed to the pulse of the giant turbines it controlled.

The Durants had come down through the personnel tubes during the evening rush hour, moving in easy random stages that insured they weren't followed and that they carried no tracer devices. Five inspection tubes had passed them as clean.

Still, they were careful to read the faces and actions of the people who jostled past. Most of the people were dull pages, hurried, intent on their own business. Occasionally, they exchanged a mutual reading-glance with another courier, or identified sub-officials with the fear goading them on Optiman errands.

No one noticed a couple in workman brown, their hands clasped, who emerged onto Catwalk Nine of the pumping station.

The Durants paused there to survey their surroundings. They were tired, elated and more than a little awed at having been summoned into the control core of the Parents

Underground. The smell of hydrocarbons filled the air around them. Lizbeth sniffed.

Her silent conversation through their clasped hands carried overtones of tension. Harvey worked to reassure her.

"It's probably our Glisson we're to see," he said.

"There could be other Cyborgs with the same name," she said.

"Not likely."

He urged her out onto the catwalk, past a hover light. They took a left branching past two workmen reading Pitot gauges, their faces in odd shadows created by the lights from below.

Lizbeth felt the lonely exposure of their position, signaled, *"How can we be sure* they *aren't watching us here?"*

"This must be one of our places," he said. *"You know."*

"How can it be?"

"Route the scanners through editing computers," he said. *"The Opts see only what we want them to see then."*

"It's dangerous to feel sure of such things," she said. Then, *"Why have they summoned us?"*

"We'll know in a few minutes," he said.

The walk led through a dust-excluding lock port into a tool bunker, gray walls punctured by outlets for transmission tubes, the inevitable computer controls blinking, ticking, chuckling, whirring. The place smelled of a sweet oil.

As the port clanged shut behind the Durants, a figure came from their left and sat on a padded bench across from them.

The Durants stared silently, recognizing and repelled by the recognition. The figure's outline suggested neither man nor woman. It looked planted there in the seat, and as they watched, it pulled thin cables from pockets in its gray coveralls, plugged the cables into the computer wall.

Harvey brought his attention up to the square, deeply seamed face and the light gray eyes with their stare of blank directness, that coldly measured observation which was a trademark of the Cyborg.

"Glisson," Harvey said, "you summoned us?"

"I summoned you," the Cyborg said. "It has been many years, Durant. Do you still fear us? I see that you do. You are late."

"We're unfamiliar with this area," Harvey said.

"We came carefully," Lizbeth said.

"Then I taught you well," Glisson said. "You were reasonably good pupils."

Through their clasped hands, Lizbeth signaled *"They're so hard to read, but something's wrong."* She averted her eyes from the Cyborg, chilled by the weighted stare. No matter how she tried to think of them as flesh and blood, her mind could never evade the knowledge that such bodies contained miniaturized computers linked directly to the brain, that the arms were not arms but prosthetic tools and weapons. And the voice—always such a clipped-off unemotional quality.

"You should not fear us, madam," Glisson said. "Unless you are not Lizbeth Durant."

Harvey failed to repress the snap of anger, said, "Don't talk to her that way! You don't own us."

"What is the first lesson I taught you after you were recruited?" Glisson asked.

Harvey brought himself under control, forced a rueful smile onto his mouth. "To hold our tempers," he said. Lizbeth's hand continued to tremble in his.

"That lesson you did not learn well," Glisson said. "I overlook your fallibility."

Through their hands, Lizbeth signaled, *"It was prepared for violence against us."*

Harvey acknowledged.

"First," Glisson said, "you will report on the genetic operation." There was a pause while the Cyborg changed its jacked connections to the computer wall. "Do not be distracted by my work. I distribute tools—thus"—it indicated the bunker—"this space which appears on *their* screens as a space filled with tools, will never be investigated."

A bench slid from the wall to the Durants' right. "If you are fatigued, sit," Glisson said. The Cyborg indicated its cable linkage to the wall computer. "I sit only that I may carry on the work of this space while we speak." The Cyborg smiled, a stiff rictus to signify that the Durants must realize such as Glisson did not feel fatigue.

Harvey urged Lizbeth to the bench. She sat as he signaled, *"Caution. Glisson's maneuvering us. Something's being hidden."*

Glisson turned slightly to face them, said, "A verbal, factual, complete report. Leave out nothing, no matter how trivial it may seem to you. I have limitless capacity for data."

They began recounting what they had observed of the genetic operation, taking up from each other on cue without a break as good couriers were taught to do. Harvey experienced the odd feeling during the recital that he and Lizbeth became part of the Cyborg's mechanism. Questions came so mechanically from Glisson's lips. Their answers felt so clinical. He had to keep reminding himself, *This is our son we discuss.*

Presently, Glisson said, "There seems no doubt we've another viable immune to the gas. Your evidence virtually completes the picture. We have other data, you know."

"I didn't know the surgeon was one of us," Lizbeth said.

There was a pause while Glisson's eyes went even blanker than usual. The Durants felt they could almost see the esoteric formulae flitting through Glisson's thinking-banks. It was said the Cyborgs composed most of their thoughts only in higher math, translating to common language as it suited them.

"The surgeon was not one of us," Glisson said. "But he soon will be."

What strategic formula produced those words, Harvey wondered. "What about the computer tape on the operation?" he asked.

"It's destroyed," Glisson said. "Even now, your embryo

is being removed to a safe place. You will join him soon." A mechanical chuckle escaped the Cyborg's lips.

Lizbeth shivered. Harvey felt the tension of her through their hands. He said, "Is our son safe?"

"Safe," Glisson said. "Our plans insure that safety."

"How?" Lizbeth asked.

"You will understand soon," Glisson said. "An ancient and reliable way of safe concealment. Be assured: viables are valuable weapons. We do not risk our valuable weapons."

Lizbeth signaled, *The cut—ask now.*"

Harvey wet his lips with his tongue, said, "There are . . . when a Central surgeon's called in, usually it means the embryo could be cut to Optiman. Did they . . . is our son . . ."

Glisson's nostrils flared. The face took on a look of hauteur that said such ignorance insulted a Cyborg. The clipped voice said, "We would require a complete tape record, including the enzymic data even to guess. The tape is gone. Only the surgeon knows the result of the operation for certain. We have yet to question him."

Lizbeth said: "Svengaard or the computer nurse might've said something that—"

"Svengaard is a dolt," Glisson said. "The computer nurse is dead."

"They killed her?" Lizbeth whispered.

"How she died isn't important," Glisson said. "She served her purpose."

With his hand, Harvey signaled, *The Cyborgs had something to do with her death!*"

"I saw," she answered.

Harvey said, "Are you . . . will we be allowed to talk to Potter?"

"Potter will be offered full Cyborg status," Glisson said. "Talking will be his decision . . . afterward."

"We want to know about our son!" Lizbeth flared.

Harvey signaled frantically, *Apologize!*"

"Madam," Glisson said, "let me remind you the so-called

Optiman cut is not a state to which we aspire. Remember your vows."

She squeezed Harvey's hand to silence his signals, said, "I'm sorry. It was such a shock to learn . . . the possibility . . ."

"Your emotional excesses are taken into account as a mitigating circumstance," Glisson said. "It is well, therefore, that I warn you of a thing to happen. You will hear things about your son which you must *not* let excite you."

"What things?" Lizbeth whispered.

"An outside force of unknown origin sometimes interferes with the anticipated course of a genetic operation," Glisson said. "There is reason to believe this happened with your son."

"What do you mean?" Harvey asked.

"Mean!" Glisson sneered. "You ask questions to which there are no answers."

"What does this . . . *thing* do?" Lizbeth supplied.

Glisson looked at her. "It behaves somewhat in the fashion of a charged particle, penetrates the genetic core and alters the structure. If this has happened to your son, you may consider it beneficial because it apparently prevents the Optiman cut."

The Durants digested this.

Presently, Harvey said, "Do you require more of us? May we go now?"

"You will remain here," Glisson said.

They stared.

"You will wait for further orders," Glisson said.

"But we'll be missed," Lizbeth said. "Our apartment, they'll—"

"We've raised dopplegangers to play your roles long enough for you to escape Seatac," Glisson said. "You can never go back. You should've known this."

Harvey's lips moved, then, "Escape? What's . . . why are . . ."

"There is violence," Glisson said. "Even now. The

death-wish cults will have their day." The Cyborg raised its gaze toward the ceiling. "War . . . blood . . . killing. It will be as it was before when the skies flamed and the earth ran molten."

Harvey cleared his throat. *Wars . . . before.* Glisson gave the impression that wars had been recent, perhaps only yesterday. And for this Cyborg that might be true. It was said that Glisson's grandsire had fought in the Optiman-Cyborg war. No one of the Underground Folk knew how many identities Glisson had lived.

"Where'll we go?" Harvey asked. He signaled Lizbeth not to interrupt.

"A place has been prepared," Glisson said.

The Cyborg arose, unplugged its linkage with the computer panel, said, "You will wait here. Do not attempt to leave. Your needs will be provided for."

Glisson left by the lock port and it sealed with a heavy thump.

"They're as bad as the Optimen," Lizbeth signaled.

"The day will come when we're free of both them and the Opts," Harvey said.

"It'll never happen," she said.

"Don't say that!" he ordered.

"If only we knew a friendly surgeon," she said. *"We could take our son and run."*

"That's foolishness! *How could we service the vat without machinery for—"*

"I've that machinery right inside me," she said. *"I was . . . born with it."*

Harvey stared at her, shocked speechless.

"I don't want the Cyborgs or the Opts controlling our son's life," she said, *"regulating his mind with hypnotic gas, making duplicates of him for their own purposes, pushing him and leading him and—"*

"Don't work yourself into a state," he said.

"You heard him," she said. *"Dopplegangers! They can regulate anything—our very being! They can condition us*

to . . . to . . . do anything! For all we know, we've been conditioned to be here right now!"

"Liz, you're being unreasonable."

"Unreasonable? Look at me! They can take a piece of my skin and grow an identical copy. Me! Identical! How do you know I'm me? How do you know I'm the original me? How do I know?"

He gripped her free arm and for a moment had no words. Presently, he forced himself to relax, shook his head. "You're you, Liz. *You're not flesh grown from a cell. You're . . . all the things we've shared . . . and been . . . and done together. They couldn't duplicate memories . . . not that with a doppleganger."*

She pressed her cheek against the rough fabric of his jacket, wanting the comfort of it, the tactile sensation that told her body he was here and he was real.

"They'll make dopplegangers of our son," she said. *"That's what they're planning. You know it."*

"Then we'll have many sons."

"For what reason?" She looked up at him, her lashes damp with unshed tears. *"You heard what Glisson said. Something from outside adjusted our embryo. What was it?"*

"How can I know?"

"Somebody must know."

"I know you," he said. *"You want to think it's God."*

"What else could it be?"

"Anything—chance, accident, some higher order manipulator. Maybe someone's discovered something they're not sharing."

"One of us? They wouldn't!"

"Nature, then," he said. "Nature asserting itself in the interest of Man."

"Sometimes you sound like a cultist!"

"It isn't the Cyborgs," he said. "We know that."

"Glisson said it was beneficient."

"But it's genetic shaping. That's blasphemy to them. Physical alteration of the bioframe, that's their way."

"*Like Glisson*," she said. "*That robot with flesh.*" Again, she pressed her cheek against him. "*That's what I fear—they'll do that to our son . . . our sons.*"

"*The courier service outnumbers the Cyborgs a hundred to one,*" he said. "*As long as we stick together, we'll win.*"

"*But we're just flesh,*" she said, "*and so weak.*"

"*And we can do something all those Sterries together can't do,*" he reminded her. "*We can perpetuate our own kind.*"

"*What does it matter?*" she asked. "*Optimen never die.*"

8

S vengaard waited for night and checked the area
through the observation screens in his office before
going down to the vat room. In spite of the fact that this
was *his* hospital and he had a perfect right here, he was
conscious of doing a forbidden thing. The significance of
the interview at Central hadn't escaped him. The Optimen
wouldn't like this, but he had to look in that vat.

He paused in the darkness of the vat room, stood there
near the door, realizing with a sense of detachment that he
had never before been in here without the full blaze of lights.
There were only the glow bulbs behind gauges and telltales
now—faint dots and circles of luminescence by which to
orient himself.

The *thrap-thrap-thrap* of viapumps created an odd con-
trapuntal rhythm which filled the gloom with a sense of urgency. Svengaard imagined all the embryos in there
(twenty-one at the morning count) their cells reaching out,
doubling and redoubling and re-redoubling in the strange
ecstasy of growth—becoming unique, distinct, discrete individuals.

Not for them the contraceptive gas that permeated Folk
breathing spaces. Not yet. Now, they could grow almost as
their ancestors had grown before the genetic engineers.

Svengaard sniffed.

His nostrils, instinctively alerted by the darkness, sensed the amniotic saltiness of the air. From its odor, this room could almost have been a primal seashore with life burgeoning in its ooze.

Svengaard shuddered and reminded himself, *I'm a submolecular engineer, a gene surgeon. There's nothing strange here.*

But the thought failed to convince him.

He pushed himself away from the door, headed down the line looking for the vat with the Durant embryo. In his mind lay the clear memory of what he had seen in that embryo— the intrusion that had flooded the cells with arginine. Intrusion. Where had it originated? Was Potter correct? Was it an unknown creator of stability? Stability . . . order . . . systems. Extended systems . . . infinite aspects of energy that left all matter insubstantial.

These suddenly were frightening thoughts here in the whispering gloom.

He stumbled against a low instrument stand, cursed softly. His stomach felt tight with the urgency of the viapumps and the real urgency in the fact that he had to finish here before the duty nurse made her hourly rounds.

An insect shape, shadow against shadows, stood out against the wall in front of him. He froze and it took a moment for him to recognize the familiar outlines of the meson microscope.

Svengaard turned to the luminous numbers on the vats— twelve, thirteen, fourteen . . . fifteen. Here it was. He checked the name on the tag, reading it in the glow of a gauge bulb: "Durant."

Something about this embryo had the Optimen upset and Security in an uproar. His regular computer nurse was gone—where, nobody could say. The replacement walked like a man.

Svengaard wheeled out the microscope, moving gently in the darkness, positioned the instrument over the vat, made the connections by feel. The vat throbbed against his fingers. He rigged for scanning, bent to the viewer.

Up out of the swarming cellular mass came a hydrophilic gene segment. He centered on it, the darkness forgotten as he pushed his awareness into the scope-lighted field of the viewer. Meson probes slid down . . . down into the mitochondrial structure. He found the alphahelices and began checking out polypeptide chains.

A puzzled frown creased his brow. He switched to another cell. Another.

The cells were low in arginine—he could see that. Thoughts brushed their way through his mind as he peered and hunted, *How could the Durant embryo, of all embryos, be low on arginine? Any normal male would have more sperm protamine than this. How could the ADP-ATP exchange system carry no hint of Optiman? The cut wouldn't make this much difference.*

Abruptly, Svengaard sent his probes down into the sex identifiers, scanned the overlapping helices.

Female!

He straightened, checked number and tag. "Fifteen. Durant."

Svengaard bent to the inspection chart, read it in the gauge glow. It showed the duty nurse's notations for the eighty-first hour. He glanced at his watch: still twenty minutes before she made the eighty-second hour check.

The Durant embryo could not possibly be female, he thought. *Not from Potter's operation.*

Someone had switched embryos, he realized. One embryo would activate the vat's life-system responses much like another. Without microscopic examination, the change couldn't be detected.

Who?

In Svengaard's mind, the most likely candidates were the Optimen. They'd removed the Durant embryo to a safe place and left a substitute.

Why?

Bait, he thought. *Bait.*

Who are they trying to catch?

He straightened, mouth dry, heart pumping rapidly. A sound at the wall to his left brought him whirling around. The vat room's emergency computer panel had come to life, tapes beginning to turn, lights winking. A read-out board clattered.

But there was no operator!

Svengaard whirled to run from the room, collided with a blocky, unmoving shape. Arms and hands gripped him with unmerciful pressure and he saw beyond his captor a section of the vat room wall open with dim light there and movement.

Then darkness exploded in his skull.

9

Seatac Hospital's new computer nurse got Max Allgood on the phone after only a short delay while Security traced him. Allgood's eyes appeared sunken. His mouth was pulled into a thin line.

"Yes?" he said. "Oh, it's you."

"Something important's come up," she said. "Svengaard's in the vat room examining the Durant embryo under microscope."

Allgood rolled his eyes. "Oh, for the love . . . Is that why you got me out of . . . is that why you called me?"

"But there was a noise and you said—"

"Forget it."

"I tell you there was a commotion of some kind in that room and now Doctor Svengaard's gone. I didn't see him go."

"He probably left by another door."

"There is no other door."

"Look, sweetie, I have half a hundred agents there covering that room like a blanket. A fly couldn't move in that room without our scanners picking it up."

"Then check with them to see where Svengaard's gone."

"Oh, for—"

"Check!"

"All right!" Allgood turned to his hot line, got the duty

agent. The computer nurse could hear him through her open line. "Where's Svengaard?"

A muffled voice responded, "Just went in and examined the Durant embryo under microscope, then left."

"Went out the door?"

"Just walked out."

Allgood's face came back onto the computer nurse's screen. "You hear that?"

"I heard, but I've been down at the end of the hall ever since he went in. He didn't come out."

"You probably turned your back for five seconds."

"Well . . ."

"You did, didn't you?"

"I may've looked away just for a second, but—"

"So you missed him."

"But I heard a commotion in there!"

"If there was anything wrong, my men would've reported it. Now, forget this. Svengaard's no problem. *They* said he'd probably do this and we could ignore it. They're never wrong about such things."

"If you're sure."

"I'm sure."

"Say, why are we so interested in that embryo?"

"You don't need to know, sweetie. Get back to work and let me get some sleep."

She broke the connection, still wondering about the noise she had heard. It had sounded like something being hit.

Allgood sat staring at the blank screen after the nurse signed off. *Noise? Commotion?* He formed a circle with his mouth, exhaled slowly. *Crazy damn' female!*

Abruptly, he stood up, turned back to his bed. The doxie playmate he'd brought in for the night lay there in the rosy light of a gloom dispeller, half awake, looking at him. Her eyes under long lashes filled him with sudden rage.

"Get the hell out of here!" he roared.

She sat upright in the bed, wide awake, staring.

"Out!" he said, pointing to the door.

She tumbled out of bed, grabbed her clothing and ran out the door, a flash of pink flesh.

Only when she'd gone did Allgood realize who she'd reminded him of—Calapine, a dull Calapine. He wondered at himself then. The Cyborg had said the adjustments they made, the instruments they'd implanted, would help him control his emotions, permit him to lie with impunity even to Optimen. This outburst now—it frightened him. He stared down at one of his slippers abandoned on the gray rug, its mate vanished somewhere. He kicked the slipper, began pacing back and forth.

Something was wrong. He could feel it. He'd lived almost four hundred *lovely* years, most of them in Optiman service. He had a well-trained instinct for rightness and wrongness. It was survival.

Something was wrong.

Had the Cyborg lied to him? Was he being used for some trick of their own?

He stumbled over the slipper, ignored it.

Noise. Commotion.

With a low curse, he returned to the hot line, got his duty agent. The man's face on the screen looked like an infant's —puffy lips and big, eager eyes.

"Go down to that vat room and inspect it," Allgood said. "The fine tooth. Look for signs of a commotion."

"But if anybody sees us—"

"Damn it to hell! Do as I say!"

"Yes, sir!"

The agent clicked off.

Allgood threw off his robe, all thought of sleep forgotten, ran through a quick shower and began dressing.

Something was wrong. He could feel it. Before leaving his quarters he put out a call to have Svengaard picked up and brought in for questioning.

10

By eight A.M., the streets and speedwalks of Seatac's industrial district-north swarmed with machine and foot traffic—the jostling impersonals of people following the little strung-out channels of their private concerns. Weather control had said the day would be held to a comfortable seventy-eight Fahrenheit with no clouds. An hour from now as the day settled into its working tempo, traffic would become more sparse. Dr. Potter had seen the city at that pace many times, but he had never before been immersed in the shift-break swarm.

He was aware that the Parents Underground had chosen this time for its natural concealment. He and his guide were just two more impersonals here. Who would notice them? This didn't subtract, though, from his fascinated interest in a scene that was new to him.

A big female Sterrie in the green-white striped uniform of a machine-press operator in the heavy industry complex pushed past him. She looked to Potter like a B2022419^{k}G8 cut with cream skin and heavy features. In a gold loop in her right ear she wore a dancing doll breeder fetish.

Almost in lock step behind her trotted a short man with hunched-up shoulders carrying a short brass rod. He flashed an impish grin at Potter as they passed, as much as to say: "Here's the only way to get through a crowd like this."

Potter's guide turned Potter aside onto the step-down walk and then into a side street. The guide was an enigma to Potter, who couldn't place the cut. The man wore a plain brown service suit, coveralls. He appeared reasonably normal except for a pale, almost sickly skin. His deeply set eyes glittered almost like lenses. A skull cap concealed his hair except for a few dark brown strands that looked almost artificial. His hands when they touched Potter to guide him felt cold and faintly repellent.

The crowd thinned here as the step-down walk rounded a corner into a byway canyon between two towering windowless buildings. There was dust in this cavernous street rising up and almost concealing a distant tracery of bridges. Potter wondered at the dust. It was as though the director of local weather allowed dust here in an unconscious passion for naturalness.

A bulky man hurried past them and Potter was caught by the look of his hands—thick wrists, bulging knuckles, horned callouses. He had no idea what work could cause such deformity.

The guide steered them now onto a succession of drop walks and into the cave of an alley. The swarm was left behind. A feeling of detachment seized Potter. He felt he was re-living an old and familiar experience.

Why did I come with this person? he wondered.

The guide wore the wheeled blazon of a transport driver on his shoulder, but he'd said right out he was from the Parents Underground.

"I know what you did for us," he'd said. "Now, we will do something for you." A turn of the head. "Come."

They'd talked only briefly after that, but Potter had known from the first the guide had correctly identified himself. This was no trick.

Then why did I accept the invitation? Potter asked himself. Certainly it wasn't for the veiled promises of extended life and instant knowledge. There were Cyborgs behind this, of course, and he suspected this guide might be one of them.

Most of the Optimen and Servant Uppers tended to discount the Folk rumors that Cyborgs did exist, but Potter had never joined the cynics and scoffers. He could no more explain why than he could explain his presence here in this alley cave walking between dark plasmeld walls illuminated by the ghost flicker of overhead glowtubes.

Potter suspected he had at last rebelled against one of the three curses of their age—moderation, drugs and alcohol. Narco-pleasures and alcohol had tempted him in their time . . . and finally moderation. He knew it wasn't normal for the times. Better to take up with one of the wild sex cults. But pointless sex without even the faint hope of issue had palled on him, although he knew this for a sign of final dissolution.

The alley opened into one of the lost squares of the megalopolis—a triangular paving and fountain that looked to be real stone, green with the slime of ages.

The Optimen don't know about this place, Potter thought. They despised stone which eroded and wore away—in their time. Regenerative plasmeld was the thing. It stood unmoved and unmoving for all time.

The guide slowed as they reached the open air. Potter noted a faint smell of chemicals about the man, oily sweetness, and a tiny scar running diagonally down the back of his neck into his collar.

Why didn't he try to blackmail me into coming? Potter wondered. *Could he be that sure? Could anyone know me that well?*

"We have a job for you," the guide had said. "An operation you must perform."

Curiosity is my weakness, Potter thought. *That's why I'm here.*

The guide put a hand on Potter's arm, said, "Stop. Wait without moving."

The tone was conversational, calm, but Potter felt hidden tensions. He looked up and around. The buildings were windowless, faceless. A wide door stood out in the angle of another alleyway ahead. They had come almost around the fountain without encountering another person. Nothing stirred or moved around them. There was only the faint rumbling of distant machinery.

"What is it?" Potter whispered. "Why're we waiting?"

"Nothing," the guide said. "Wait."

Potter shrugged.

His mind veered back to the first encounter with this creature. *How could they know what I achieved with that embryo? It must be the computer nurse. She's one of them.*

The guide had refused to say.

I came because I hoped they could help me solve the mystery of the Durant embryo, he thought. *They were the source of the arginine intrusion—that's what I suspect.*

He thought of Svengaard's description—a contrail-like intrusion. It had deposited arginine-rich sperm protamine through the coiled alpha-helices of the embryo's cells. Then had come the operation—the cysteine masked, neutralized with sulfhydryl and the ATP phase . . . oligomycin and azide . . . the exchange reaction inhibited.

Potter stared up at the patch of blue sky framed by the buildings around the square. His mind, concentrated on the Durant cutting, had encountered a new idea. He no longer saw the sky. His awareness was back within the swarming cell structure, following the mitochondrial systems like an undersea hunter.

"It could be repeated," Potter whispered.

"Silence," the guide hissed.

Potter nodded. *On any embryo at all,* he thought. *The key's the arginine flooding. I could duplicate that myself on the basis of Sven's description. Gods! We could make billions of Durant embryos! And every one of them self-viable!*

He took a deep breath, dismayed by the realization that—with the record tape erased—his memory might be the only container of that entire operation and its implications. Svengaard and the computer nurse could have only part of it. They hadn't been *in* there, immersed in the heart of the cell.

A brilliant surgeon might deduce what had happened and be able to reproduce the operation from the partial records, but only if he were set the problem. Who would ever take up this problem? Not the Optimen. Not that dolt Svengaard.

The guide tugged at Potter's arm.

Potter looked down into that flat, chill-eyed face with its lack of genetic identification.

"We are observed," the guide said in an oddly depersonalized tone. "Listen to me very carefully. Your life depends on it."

Potter shook his head, blinked. He felt removed from his own person, become only a set of senses to record this man's words and actions.

"You will go through that door ahead of us," the guide said.

Potter turned, looked at the door. Two men carrying paper-wrapped parcels emerged from the alley in front of it, hurried around the square opposite them. The guide ignored them. Potter heard a babble of young voices growing louder in the alley. The guide ignored these, too.

"Inside that building, you will take the first door on your left," he said. "You will see a woman there operating a voicebox. You will say to her: 'My shoe pinches.' She will say: 'Everyone has troubles.' She will take care of you from there."

Potter found his voice: "What if . . . she's not there?"

"Then go through the door behind her desk and out through the adjoining office into a rear hall. Turn left and go to the rear of the building. You will find there a man in a loader supervisor's uniform, striped gray and black. You will repeat the procedure with him."

"What about you?" Potter asked.

"That is not your concern. Quickly, now!" The guide gave him a push.

Potter stumbled toward the door just as a woman in a

teacher's uniform emerged from the alley leading a file of children between him and the bolt hole.

Potter's shocked senses took in the scene—children, all dressed in tight shorts that revealed their long flamingo legs. They were all around him suddenly and he was bulling his way through toward the door.

Behind him, someone screamed.

Potter lurched against the door, found the handle, looked back.

His guide had gone around to the opposite side of the fountain which concealed him now from the waist down, but what remained visible was enough to make Potter gasp and freeze. The man's chest was bare revealing a single milky white dome from which blazed a searing light.

Potter turned left, saw a line of men emerging from another alley to be crisped and burned down by that searing light. The children were shouting, crying, falling back into the alley from which they had emerged, but Potter ignored them, fascinated by this slaughter-machine which he'd thought was a human being.

One of the guide's arms lifted, pointed overhead. From the extended fingers, lancets of searing blue stabbed upward. Where the light terminated, aircars tumbled from the sky. The air all around had become an ozone-crackling inferno punctuated by explosions, screams, hoarse shouts.

Potter stood there watching, unable to move, forgetful of his instructions or the door or his hand upon the door's handle.

Return fire was coming now at the guide. His clothing shriveled, vanished in smoke to reveal an armored body with muscles that had to be plasmeld fibers. The ravening beams continued to blaze from his hands and chest.

Potter found he no longer could bear to watch. He wrenched the door open, stumbled through into the relative gloom of a yellow-walled foyer. He slammed the door behind him as an explosion rocked the building. The door rattled behind him.

On his left, a door was flung open. A tiny blue-eyed blonde woman stood there staring at him. Potter found himself oddly recognizing the markers of her genetic cut, reassured by the touch of humanity in these tiny betrayals. He could see the cabinet of a voicebox in the room behind her.

"My shoe pinches," Potter said.

She gulped. "Everyone has troubles."

"I am Dr. Potter," he said. "I think my escort has just been killed."

She stepped aside, said, "In here."

Potter lurched past her into an office with lines of empty desks. His mind was a turmoil. He felt shaken to his roots by the implications of the violence he had just witnessed.

The woman took his arm, herded him toward another door. "Through here," she said. "We'll have to go into the service tubes. That's the only way. They'll have this place surrounded in minutes."

Potter stopped, figuratively dug in his heels. He hadn't counted on violence. He didn't know what he had expected, but not that.

"Where're we going?" he demanded. "Why do you want me?"

"Don't you know?" she asked.

"He . . . never said."

"Everything'll be explained," she said. "Hurry."

"I don't move a millimeter until you tell me," he said.

A raw street oath escaped her lips. She said, "If I must I must. You're to implant the Durant embryo in its mother. It's the only way we can get it out of here."

"*In* the mother?"

"In the ancient way," she said. "I know it's disgusting, but it's the only way. Now, hurry!"

Potter allowed himself to be herded through the door.

11

In the control center, their red Survey Globe, the Tuyere occupied the thrones on the pivoting triangle, reviewing data and reviewing data—correlating, deducing, commanding. The 120-degree scan of curved wall available to each of them flashed with data in numerous modes—pictorially in the spying screens, as probability function in mathematical read-outs, as depth-module decision analogues, as superior /inferior unit apportionments pictured in free-flowing pyramids, as visual reports reduced to cubed grids of binaries according to relative values, as motivational curves weighted for action/reaction and presented in flowing green lines . . .

In the upper quadrants, scanner eyes glittered to show how many of the Optimen were sitting in on the globe's activity—over a thousand this morning.

Calapine worried the prescription ring on her left thumb, felt the abortive hum of power in it as she twisted and slid it along her skin. She was restless, full of demands for which she could find no names. The duties of the globe were becoming repellent, her companions hateful. In here, time settled into more of a continuous blur without days or nights. Every companion she had ever known grew to be the same companion, merged, endlessly merged.

"Once more have I studied the protein synthesis tape on

the Durant embryo," Nourse said. He glanced at Calapine in the reflector beside his head, drummed the arm of his throne with fingers that moved back and forth, back and forth on the carved plasmeld.

"Something we've missed, something we've missed," Calapine mocked. She looked at Schruille, caught him rubbing his hands along his robe at his thighs, a motion that seemed filled with stark betrayal of nervousness.

"Now it happens I've discovered the thing we missed," Nourse said.

A movement of Schruille's head caught Nourse's attention. He turned. For a moment, they stared at each other in the prisms. Nourse found it interesting that Schruille betrayed a tiny skin blemish beside his nose.

Odd, Nourse thought. *How could one of us have a blemish such as that? Surely there could be no enzymic imbalance.*

"Well, what is it?" Schruille demanded.

"You've a blemish beside your nose," Nourse said.

Schruille stared at him.

"You deduce this from the embryo's tape?" Calapine asked.

"Eh? Oh . . . no, of course not."

"Then what is it you've discovered?"

"Yes. Well . . . it seems rather obvious now that the operation Potter performed may be repeatable—given that general type of embryo and proper administration of sperm protamine."

Schruille shuddered.

"Have you deduced the course of the operation?" Calapine asked.

"Not precisely, but in outline, yes."

"Potter could repeat it?" she asked.

"Perhaps even Svengaard."

"Guard and preserve us," Calapine muttered. It was a ritual formula whose words seldom caught an Optiman's conscious attention, but she heard herself this time and the word "preserve" stood out as though outlined in fire.

She whirled away.

"Where is Max?" Schruille asked.

The whine in Schruille's voice brought a sneer to Nourse's lips.

"Max is working," Nourse said. "He is busy."

Schrille looked up at the watching scanners, thinking of all their fellows behind those lensed eyes—the Actionists seeing events as a new demand upon their talents, not realizing what violence might be unleashed here; the Emotionals, fearful and complaining, rendered almost ineffective by guilt feelings; the Cynics, interested by the new *game* (most of the watchers, Schruille felt, were Cynics); the Hedonists, angered by the current sense of urgent emergency, worried because such matters interfered with their enjoyments; and the Effetes, looking in all this for something new at which to sneer.

Will we now develop a new party? Schruille asked himself. *Will we now have the Brutals, all sensitivity immured by the needs of self-preservation? Nourse and Calapine haven't faced this as yet.*

Again, he shuddered.

"Max calls," Calapine said. "I have him in my transient screen."

Schruille and Nourse flicked their channel duplicators, looked down at Allgood's swarthy, solid, muscular figure in the transient screen.

"I report," Allgood said.

Calapine watched the Security chief's face. He appeared oddly distracted, fearful.

"What of Potter?" Nourse asked.

Allgood blinked.

"Why does he delay his answer?" Schruille asked.

"It's because he worships us," Calapine said.

"Worship is a product of fear," Schruille said. "Perhaps there's something he wishes to show us, a projection or an evidential sub-datum. Is that it, Max?"

Allgood stared out of the screen, looking from one to the

other. They'd gotten tied up in that lost-time sense again, the endless word play and disregard for time in the quest for data, data, data—that side effect of endless life, the supra-involvement in trivia. This time, he hoped it would go on without end.

"Where is Potter?" Nourse demanded.

Allgood swallowed. "Potter has . . . temporarily eluded us." He knew better than to lie or evade now.

"Eluded?" Schruille asked.

"How?" Nourse asked.

"There was . . . violence," Allgood said.

"Show us this violence," Schruille said.

"No," Calapine said. "I will take Max's word for it."

"Do you doubt Max?" Nourse asked.

"No doubts," Schruille said. "But I will see this violence."

"How can you?" Calapine asked.

"Leave if you wish," Schruille said. He measured out his words: "I . . . will . . . see . . . this . . . violence." He looked at Allgood. "Max?"

Allgood swallowed. This was a development he had not anticipated.

"It happened," Nourse said. "We know that, Schruille."

"Of course it happened," Schruille said. "I saw the mark where it was edited out of our channels. Violence. Now, I wish to bypass the safety valve which protects our sensitivities." He snorted. "Sensitivities!"

Nourse stared at him, noting that all traces of a whine had gone from Schruille's voice.

Schruille looked up at the scanners, saw that many were winking off. He was disgusting even the Cynics, no doubt. A few remained, though.

Will they stay through to the end? he wondered.

"Show the violence, Max," Schruille ordered.

Allgood shrugged.

Nourse swiveled his throne around, putting his back to the screen. Calapine put her hands over her eyes.

"As you command," Allgood said. His face vanished

from the screen, was replaced by a high view looking down into a tiny square between windowless buildings. Two tiny figures walked around a fountain in the square. They stopped and a close-up showed the faces—Potter and an unknown, a strange-looking man with frighteningly cold eyes.

Again, the long view—two other men emerging from an alley carrying paper-wrapped packages. Behind them trooped a file of children with adult monitor in teacher's uniform.

Abruptly, Potter was lurching, pushing through the children. His companion was running the other way around the fountain.

Schruille risked a glance at Calapine, caught her peeking between her fingers.

A shrill, piercing cry from the screen, brought his attention jerking back.

Potter's companion had become a thing of horror, clothing fallen away, a milky bulb arising from his chest to flare with brilliant light.

The screen went blank, came alive again to a view from a slightly different angle.

A quick glance showed that Calapine had dropped all pretense of hiding her eyes, was staring at the screen. Nourse, too, watched through his shoulder prism.

Another blaze of light leaped from the figure in the screen. Again the scene went blank.

"It's a Cyborg," Schruille said. "Know that as you watch."

Again, the scene came alive from a different angle and this time from very high. The action in the plasmeld canyon was reduced to a movement of midges, but there was no difficulty in finding the center of violence. Lancets of blazing light leaped upward from a lurching figure in the square. Aircars exploded and fell from the sky in pieces.

One Security vehicle plummeted in behind the Cyborg. A pulsing beam of coherent light emerged from it to cut a smoking furrow down the side of a building. The Cyborg whirled, lifted a hand from which a blinding blue finger seemed to extend into infinity. The finger met the diving car, split it in half. One half hit a building, ricocheted and smashed into the Cyborg.

A ball of yellow brilliance took shape in the square. In a second, a reverberating explosion shook the scene.

Schruille looked up to find the circle of watching scanners complete, every lensed eye blazing red.

Calapine cleared her throat. "Potter went into that building on the right."

"Is that all you can say?" Schruille asked.

Nourse swiveled his throne, glared at Schruille.

"Was it not interesting?" Schruille asked.

"Interesting?" Nourse demanded.

"It is called warfare," Schruille said.

Allgood's face reappeared on the screen, looking up at them with a veiled intensity.

He's naturally curious at our reaction, Schruille thought.

"Do you know of *our* weapons, Max?" Schruille asked.

"This talk of weapons and violence disgusts me," Nourse said. "What is the good of this?"

"Why do we have weapons if they were not intended for use?" Schruille asked. "Do you know the answer, Max?"

"I know of your weapons," Allgood said. "They are the ultimate safeguard for your persons."

"Of course we have weapons!" Nourse shouted. "But why must we—"

"Nourse, you demean yourself," Calapine said.

Nourse pushed himself back in his throne, hands gripping the arms. *"Demean myself!"*

"Let us review this new development," Schruille said. "Cyborgs we knew existed. They have eluded us consistently. Thus, they control computer editing channels and have sympathy among the Folk. Thus, we see, they have an Action Arm which can sacrifice . . . I say *sacrifice* a member for the good of the whole."

Nourse stared at him, wide-eyed, drinking the words.

"And we," Schruille said, "we had forgotten how to be thoroughly brutal."

"Faaah!" Nourse barked.

"If you injure a man with a weapon," Schruille said, "which is the responsible party—the weapon or the one who wields it?"

"Explain yourself," Calapine whispered.

Schruille pointed to Allgood in the screen. "There is our weapon. We've wielded it times without number until it learned to wield itself. We've not forgotten how to be brutal, we've merely forgotten that we *are* brutal."

"What rot!" Nourse said.

"Look," Schruille said. He pointed up to the watching scanners, every one of them alive. "There's my evidence," Schruille said. "When have so many watched in the globe?"

A few of the lights began to wink out, but came back as the channels were taken over by other watchers.

Allgood watching from the screen felt the thrill of complete fascination. A tight sensation in his chest prevented deep breaths, but he ignored it. The Optimen facing violence! After a lifetime playing with euphemisms, Allgood found the thought of this almost unacceptable. It had been so swift. But then these were the live-forevers, the people who could not fail. He wondered then at the thoughts which raced through their minds.

Schruille, the usually silent and watchful, looked down at Allgood and said, "Who else has eluded us, Max?"

Allgood found himself unable to speak.

"The Durants are missing," Schruille said. "Svengaard has not been found. Who else?"

"No one, Schruille. No one."

"We want them captured," Schruille said.

"Of course, Schruille."

"Alive," Calapine said.

"Alive, Calapine?" Allgood asked.

"If it's possible," Schruille said.

Allgood nodded. "I obey, Schruille."

"You may get back to your work now," Schruille said.

The screen went blank.

Schruille busied himself with the controls in the arm of his throne.

"What're you doing?" Nourse demanded and he heard the petulance in his own voice, despising it.

"I remove the censors which excluded violence from our eyes except as a remote datum," Schruille said. "It is time we observed the reality of our land."

Nourse sighed. "If you feel it's necessary."

"I know it's necessary."

"Most interesting," Calapine said.

Nourse looked at her. "What do you find interesting in this obscenity?"

"This exhilaration I feel," she said. "It's most interesting."

Nourse whirled away from her, glared at Schruille. He could see now that there definitely was a skin blemish on Schruille's face—beside his nose.

12

To Svengaard, raised in the ordered world of the Optimen, the idea that they were fallible came as heresy. He tried to put it out of his mind and his ears. To be fallible was to be subject to death. Only the lower orders suffered thus. Not the Optimen. How could they be fallible?

He knew the surgeon sitting across from him in the pale dawn light that filtered through narrow slots in a domed ceiling. The man was Toure Igan, one of Central's surgical elite, a person to whom only the most delicate geneticomedical problems were posed.

The room they occupied was a tight little space stolen between the walls of an air-system cap servicing the subterranean warrens of the Cascade Complex. Svengaard sat in a comfortable chair, but his arms and legs were bound. Other people were using the space, crowding past the little table where Igan sat. The people carried oddly shaped packages. For the most part they ignored Igan and his companion.

Svengaard studied the dark, intense features of the Central surgeon. Crease lines in the man's face betrayed the beginning of enzymic failure. He was starting to age. But the eyes were the blue of a summer sky and still young.

"You must choose sides," Igan had said.

Svengaard allowed his attention to wander. A man passed carrying a golden metallic ball. From one of his pockets protruded a short silver chain on which dangled a breeder fetish in the shape of a lingam.

"You must answer," Igan said.

Svengaard looked at the wall beside him—plasmeld, the inevitable plasmeld. The space stank of disinfectants and the ersatz-garden effect of air purifier perfumes.

People continued to pass through the narrow room. The sameness of their garments began to weigh on Svengaard. Who were these people? That they were members of the Underground, that was obvious. But *who* were they?

A woman touched him, crowding past. Svengaard looked up into a white smile in a black face, recognized a Zeek female, a face like Potter's but the skin darker . . . a surgical mistake. She wore a bracelet of human hair on her right wrist. It was blonde hair. Svengaard stared at the bracelet until the woman rounded the curve of the room out of his sight.

"It's open battle now," Igan said. "You must believe me. Your own life depends on it."

My own life? Svengaard wondered. He tried to think about his own life, identify it. He had a tertiary wife, little more than a playmate, a woman like himself whose every request for a breeder permit had been denied. For a moment, he couldn't picture her face, lost the shape of it in memories of previous wives and playmates.

She isn't my life, he thought. *Who is my life?*

He was conscious of a fatigue that went to the bone, and a hangover from the narcotics his captors had administered during the night. He remembered the hands seizing him, that gasping look into a wall that could not be a door but was, the lighted space beyond. And he remembered awakening here with Igan across from him.

"I've held nothing back," Igan said. "I've told you everything. Potter barely escaped with his life. The order's already out to get you. Your computer nurse is dead. Many people have died. More will die. They have to be sure, don't you understand? They can leave nothing to chance."

What is my life? Svengaard asked himself. And he thought now about his comfortable apartment, the artifacts and entertainment reels, the reference works, his friends, the safely ordinary routine of his position.

"But where would I go?" Svengaard asked.

"A place has been prepared."

"No place is safe from *them,*" Svengaard said. In saying this, he sensed for the first time the depth of his own resentment against the Optimen.

"Many places are safe," Igan said. "*They* merely pretend to supersensual perception. Their real powers lie in machines and instruments, the secret surveillance. But machines and instruments can be twisted to other purposes. And the Optimen depend on Folk to do their violence."

Svengaard shook his head. "This is all nonsense."

"Except for one thing," Igan said, "*they* are as we—variously human. We know this from experience."

"But why would they do these things you accuse them of?" Svengaard protested. "It's not sensible. They're *good* to us."

"Their sole interest is in maintaining themselves," Igan said. "They walk a tightrope. As long as there's no significant change in their environment, they'll continue living . . . indefinitely. Let significant change creep into their lives and they are like us—subject to the whims of nature. For them, you see, there can be no nature—no nature they don't control."

"I don't believe it," Svengaard said. "They're the ones who love us and care for us. Look at all they've done for us."

"I have looked." Igan shook his head. Svengaard was being more pig-headed than they'd expected. He screened out contrary evidence and stuck to the old formulas.

"You want them to succumb," Svengaard accused. "Why do you want this?"

"Because they've deprived us of evolution," Igan said.

Svengaard stared at him. "What?"

"They've made themselves the only free individuals in our world," Igan said. "But individuals don't evolve. Populations evolve, not individuals. We have no population."

"But the Folk—"

"Yes, the Folk! Who among us are allowed to mate?" Igan shook his head. "You're a gene surgeon, man! Haven't you identified the pattern yet?"

"Pattern? What pattern? What do you mean?" Svengaard pushed himself up in the chair, cursed his bindings. His arms and legs felt numb.

"The Optimen hold to one cardinal rule of mating," Igan said. "Return to the standard average. They allow a random interchange with the standard average organism to suppress development of unique individuals. Such few unique individuals as occur are not allowed to breed."

Svengaard shook his head. "I don't believe you," he said. But he could feel the beginnings of doubt. His own case—no matter which mate he chose, the breeding permit was denied. He'd examined the genetic matchings himself, had seen configurations he would've sworn were viable—but the Optimen said no.

"You do believe me," Igan said.

"But look at the long lives they give us," Svengaard said. "I can expect almost two hundred years."

"Medicine does that, not the Optimen," Igan said. "Delicate, careful refinement of the enzymic prescription's the key. That plus a proscribed life in which emotional upset is held to a minimum. Selected exercises and a diet chosen for your specific needs. It could be done for almost anyone."

"Indefinite life?" Svengaard whispered.

"No! But long life, much longer than we get now. I'm going on four hundred years, myself—as are several of my contemporaries. Almost four hundred *lovely* years," he said, remembering Calapine's vicious phrase . . . and Nourse's chuckle.

"Four hundred—you?" Svengaard asked.

"I agree it's nothing compared to *their* many thousands,"

Igan said. "But almost anyone could have these years, except *they* don't permit it."

"Why?" Svengaard asked.

"This way they can offer the bonus years to the selected few," Igan said, "a reward for service. Without this rule they have no *coin* to buy us. You knew this! You've been trying to sell yourself to them for this coin all your life."

Svengaard looked down at his bound hands. *Is that my life?* he wondered. *Fettered hands? Who will buy my fettered hands?*

"And you should hear Nourse chuckle at my pitiful four hundred years," Igan said.

"Nourse?"

"Yes! Nourse of the Tuyere, Nourse the Cynic, Nourse of the more than forty thousand years! Why do you think Nourse is a Cynic?" Igan demanded. "There're older Optimen, much older. Most of *those* aren't Cynics."

"I don't understand," Svengaard said. He stared at Igan, feeling weak, battered, unable to counter the force of these words and arguments.

"I forget you're not of Central," Igan said. "They classify themselves by the tiny bit of emotion they're permitted. They're Actionists, Emotionals, Cynics, Hedonists and Effetes. They pass through cynicism on their way to hedonism. The Tuyere already's well occupied in pursuit of personal pleasure. There's a pattern here, too, and none of it's good."

Igan studied Svengaard, weighing the effect of his words. Here was a creature barely above the Folk. He was medieval man. To him, Central and the Optimen were the "primum mobile" in control of all celestial systems. Beyond Central lay only the empyrean home of the Creator . . . and for the Svengaards of the world there was little distinction between Optiman and Creator. Both were higher than the moon and totally without fault.

"Where can we run?" Svengaard asked. "There's no place to hide. *They* control the enzymic prescriptions. The minute one of us walks into a pharmacy for renewal, that's the end."

"We have our sources," Igan said.

"But why would you want me?" Svengaard asked. He kept his eyes on his bindings.

"Because you're a unique individual," Igan said. "Because Potter wants you. Because you know of the Durant embryo."

The Durant embryo, Svengaard thought. *What's the significance of the Durant embryo? It all comes back to that embryo.*

He looked up, met Igan's eyes.

"You find it difficult to see the Optimen in my description of them," Igan said.

"Yes."

"They're a plague on the face of the earth," Igan said. "They're the earth's disease!"

Svengaard recoiled from the bitterness of Igan's voice.

"Saul has erased his thousands and David his ten thousands," Igan said. "But the Optimen erase the future."

A blocky hulk of a man squeezed past the narrow space beside the table, planted himself with his back to Svengaard.

"Well?" he asked. The voice carried a disturbing tone of urgency, just in that one word. Svengaard tried to see the face, but couldn't move far enough to the side. There was just that wide belted back in a gray jacket.

"I don't know," Igan said.

"We can spare no more time," the newcomer said. "Potter has completed his work."

"The result?" Igan asked.

"He says successful. He used enzymic injection for quick recovery. The mother will be ready to move soon." A thick hand moved over the shoulder to point a thumb at Svengaard. "What do we do with him?"

"Bring him," Igan said. "What's Central doing?"

"Ordered arrest and confinement of every surgeon."

"So soon? Did they get Dr. Hand?"

"Yes, but he took the black door."

"Stopped his heart," Igan said. "The only thing. We can't let them question one of us. How many does that leave us?"

"Seven."

"Including Svengaard?"

"Eight then."

"We'll keep Svengaard restrained for the time being," Igan said.

"They're beginning to pull their special people out of Seatac," the big man said.

Svengaard could see only half of Igan's face past the newcomer, but that half showed a deep frown of concentration. The one visible eye looked at Svengaard, disregarded him.

"It's obvious," Igan said.

"Yes—they're going to destroy the megalopolis."

"Not destroy, sterilize."

"You've heard Allgood speak of the Folk?"

"Many times. *Vermin in their warrens.* He'll step on the entire region without a qualm. Is everything ready to move?"

"Ready enough."

"The driver?"

"Programed for the desired response."

"Give Svengaard a shot to keep him quiet, then. We won't have time for him once we're on the road."

Svengaard stiffened.

The bulky back turned. Svengaard looked up into a pair of glistening eyes, gray, measuring, devoid of emotion. One of the thick hands lifted, carrying a springshot ampule. The hand touched his neck and there was a jolt.

Svengaard stared up at that faceless face while the fuzzy clouds closed around his mind. His throat felt thick, tongue useless. He willed himself to protest, but no sound came. Awareness became a tightening globe centered on a tiny patch of ceiling with slotted openings. The scene condensed, smaller and smaller—a frantic circle like an eye with slotted pupils.

He sank into a cushioned well of darkness.

13

Lizbeth lay on a bench with Harvey seated beside her, steadying her. There were five people here in a cubed space no bigger than a large packing box. The box had been fitted into the center of a normal load on an overland transporter van. A single glowtube in the corner above her head illuminated the interior with a sickly yellow light. She could see Doctors Igan and Boumour on a rough bench opposite her, their feet stretched across the bound, gagged, and unconscious figure of Svengaard on the floor.

It was already night outside, Harvey had said. That must mean they'd come a goodly distance, she thought. She felt vaguely nauseated and her abdomen ached around the stitches. The thought of carrying her son within her carried a strange reassurance. There was a sense of fulfillment in it. Potter had said she could likely do without her regular enzymes while she carried the embryo. He'd obviously been thinking the embryo would be removed into a vat when they reached a safe place. But she knew she'd resist that. She wanted to carry her son full term. No woman had done that for thousands of years, but she wanted it.

"We're picking up speed," Igan said. "We must be out of the tubes onto the skyway."

"Will there be checkpoints?" Boumour asked.

"Bound to be."

Harvey sensed the accuracy of Igan's assessment. Speed? Yes—their bodies were compensating for heavier pressure on the turns. Air was coming in a bit faster through the scoop ventilator under Lizbeth's bench. There was a new hardness to the ground-effect suspension, less bounce. The turbines echoed loudly in the narrow box and he could smell unburned hydrocarbons.

Checkpoints? Security would use every means to see that no one escaped Seatac. He wondered then what was about to happen to the megalopolis. The surgeons had spoken of poison gas in the ventilators, sonics. Central had many weapons, they said. Harvey put out an arm to hold Lizbeth as they rounded a sharp corner.

He didn't know how he felt about Lizbeth carrying their son within her. It was odd. Not obscene or disgusting . . . just odd. An instinctive response had come to focus within him and he looked around for dangers from which he could protect her. But there was only this box filled with the smell of stale sweat and oil.

"What's the cargo around us?" Boumour asked.

"Odds and ends," Igan said. "Machinery parts, some old art works, inconsequential things. We took anything we could pirate to make a seemingly normal load."

Inconsequentials, Harvey thought. He found himself fascinated by this revelation. Inconsequentials. They carried parts to things that might never be built.

Lizbeth's hand groped out, found his. "Harvey?"

He bent over her. "Yes, dear?"

"I feel . . . so . . . funny."

Harvey cast a despairing look at the doctors.

"She'll be all right," Igan said.

"Harvey, I'm afraid," she said. "We're not going to get through."

"That's no way to talk," Igan said.

She looked up, found the gene surgeon studying her across the narrow space of the box. His eyes were a pair of glittering instruments in a slim, supercilious face. *Is he a*

Cyborg, too? she wondered. The cold way the eyes stared at her broke through her control.

"I don't care about myself!" she hissed. "But what about my son?"

"Best calm yourself, madame," Igan said.

"I can't," she said. "We're not going to make it!"

"That's no way to act," Igan said. "Our driver is the finest Cyborg available."

"He'll never get us past *them,*" she moaned.

"You'd best be quiet," Igan said.

Harvey at last had an object from which to protect his wife. "Don't talk to her that way!" he barked.

Igan spoke in a long-suffering tone, "Not you, too, Durant. Keep your voice down. You know as well as I do they'll have listening stations along the skyway. We shouldn't be speaking now unless it's absolutely necessary."

"Nothing can get past *them* tonight," Lizbeth whispered.

"Our driver is little more than a shell of flesh around a reflex computer," Igan said. "He's programed for just this task. He'll get us through if anyone can."

"If anyone can," she whispered. She began to sob—wracking, convulsive movements that shook her whole body.

"See what you've done!" Harvey said.

Igan sighed, brought up a hand containing a capsule, extended the capsule to Harvey. "Give her this."

"What's that?" Harvey demanded.

"Just a sedative."

"I don't want a sedative," she sobbed.

"It's for your own good, my dear," Igan said. "Really, this could dislodge the embryo. You should remain calm and quiet this soon after the operation."

"She doesn't want it," Harvey said. His eyes glared with anger.

"She has to take it," Igan said.

"Not if she doesn't want it."

Igan forced his voice into a reasonable tone. "Durant, *I'm* only trying to save our lives. You're angry now and you—"

"You're damn' right I'm angry! I'm tired of being ordered around!"

"If I've offended you, I'm sorry, Durant," Igan said. "But I must caution you that your present reaction is conditioned by your gene shaping. You've excess male protectiveness. Your wife will be all right. This sedative is harmless. She's hysterical because she has too much *maternal* drive. These are flaws in your gene shaping, but you'll both be all right if you remain calm."

"Who says we're flawed?" Harvey demanded. "I'll bet you're a Sterrie who's never—"

"That's quite enough, Durant," the other doctor said. It was a rumbling, powerful voice.

Harvey looked at Boumour, noted the pinched-up elfin face on the big body. The surgeon appeared powerful and dangerous, the face strangely inhuman.

"We cannot fight among ourselves," Boumour rumbled. "We may be getting near the checkpoint. They're sure to have listening devices."

"We aren't flawed," Harvey growled.

"Perhaps you're right," Igan said. "But you're both reducing our chances of escape. If one of you breaks up at that checkpoint, that's the end of us." He shifted his hand, extended the capsule to Lizbeth. "Please take this, madam. It contains a tranquilizer. Quite harmless, I assure you."

Hesitantly, Lizbeth took the capsule. It felt cold and gelatinous against her fingers—repulsive. She wanted to hurl the thing at Igan, but Harvey touched her cheek.

"Maybe you'd better take it," he said. "For the baby."

She brought up her hand, popped the capsule against the back of her tongue, gulped it. It must be all right if Harvey agreed. But she didn't like the hurt, baffled look in his eyes.

"Now relax," Igan said. "It's fast acting—three or four minutes and you'll feel quite calm." He sat back, glanced down at Svengaard. The trussed figure still appeared to be unconscious, chest rising and falling in an even rhythm.

For what felt like a long time now, Svengaard had been

increasingly aware of hunger and a swooping, turning motion that rolled his body against a hard surface. There was a sensation of swiftness about the motion. He smelled human perspiration, heard the roar of turbines. The sound was beginning to press on his consciousness. There was light, dim and fuzzy through uncooperative eyelids. He felt a gag biting his lips, bindings on hands and feet.

Svengaard opened his eyes.

For a moment, he failed to focus, then he found himself staring up at a low ceiling, a tiny glowtube in the corner with a speaker grill beneath it bulging beside a dull ruby call light. The ceiling seemed too close to him and there was a blurred shadow shape to his right—a leg stretched across him. The single light emitted a yellow glow that almost failed to dispel the darkness.

The ruby light began winking, red fire flashing on and off, on and off.

"Checkpoint!" Igan hissed. "Silence everyone!"

They sensed the van begin to slow. Its air suspension became softer and softer. The turbines whined downscale. They rocked to a stop and the turbines whispered into standby.

Svengaard's gaze darted around the enclosure. A rough bench above him to his right . . . two figures seated on it. A sharp edge of metal protruded from the bench support beside his cheek. Softly, gently, Svengaard moved his head toward the metal projection, felt it touch flesh through the gag. He gave a gentle push of his head upward and the gag pulled down slightly. The projection scratched his cheek, but he ignored it. Another gentle tug and the gag lowered another fraction of a millimeter. He turned his eyes, checking his surroundings, saw Lizbeth's face above him to the left, her eyes closed, hands in front of her mouth. There was a sense of suspended terror about her.

Again, Svengaard moved his head.

There were voices somewhere in a remote distance—sharp sounds of questions, murmurous answers.

Lizbeth's hands lowered to reveal her mouth. The lips moved soundlessly.

The sound of talking had stopped.

Slowly, the van began to move.

Svengaard twisted his head. The binding of his gag broke free. He coughed it from his mouth, shouted, "Help! Help! I'm a prisoner! Help!"

Igan and Boumour leaped with shock. Lizbeth screamed, "No! Oh, no!"

Harvey surged forward, crashed a fist into Svengaard's jaw, fell on him with one hand over the man's mouth. They held their positions in an agony of listening as the van continued to gather speed.

Igan took a trembling breath, looked across into the wide staring eyes of Lizbeth.

The voice of their driver came through the speaker grill: "What is the trouble? Can't you observe the simplest precautions?"

The dispassionate, accusing quality of the voice chilled Harvey. He wondered about the driver then, why the creature took this tone rather than telling them if they'd been exposed. Svengaard felt limp and unconscious beneath him, Harvey realized. He experienced a wild desire to throttle the surgeon here and now, could almost feel his hands around the man's throat.

"Did they hear us?" Igan whispered.

"Apparently not," the driver rasped. "No sign of pursuit. I presume you'll not permit another such lapse. Please report on what happened."

"Svengaard wakened from the narcotic sooner than we expected."

"But he was gagged."

"He . . . managed to get the gag off, somehow."

"Perhaps you should kill him. Obviously, he will not take reconditioning."

Harvey pushed himself off Svengaard. Now that the Cyborg had made the suggestion, he no longer felt like killing

Svengaard. Who was it up there in the van's cab? Harvey wondered. Cyborgs tended to sound alike, that computer personality with its altitude of logic so far above the human. This one, though, came through even more remote than usual.

"We'll . . . consider what to do," Igan said.

"Svengaard is again secure?"

"He's been taken care of."

"No thanks to you," Harvey said, staring at Igan. "You were right over him."

Igan's faced paled. He remembered his frozen immobility after that leap of fear. Anger surged through him. What right had this clod to question a surgeon? He spoke stiffly, "I regret that I'm not a man of violence."

"Something you'd better learn," Harvey said. He felt Lizbeth's hand on his shoulder, allowed her to guide him back onto their bench. "If you have more of that knock-out stuff, maybe you'd better use another dose of it on him before he wakes up again."

Igan suppressed a sharp reply.

"In the bag under our bench," Boumour said. "A reasonable suggestion."

Woodenly, Igan groped for a slapshot and administered it to Svengaard.

Again, the driver's voice barked through the speaker: "Attention! We must not presume from the lack of immediate and obvious pursuit that they failed to hear the outcry. I am executing Plan Gamma."

"Who is that driver?" Harvey whispered.

"I didn't see which one they programed," Boumour said. He studied Harvey. That had been an appropriate question. The driver did sound odd, much more so than the usual Cyborg abnormality. They'd said the driver would be a programed reflex computer, a machine designed to give the surest response to achieve their escape. Who did they choose for that program?

"What's Plan Gamma?" Lizbeth whispered.

"We're abandoning the prepared escape route," Boumour said. He stared at the forward wall of their box. Abandoning the prepared route . . . which meant they'd be completely dependent now upon the abilities of the Cyborg driver . . . and whichever scattered cells of the Underground remained and were available. Any one of those cells could've been compromised, of course. Boumour's usually stolid nature began to entertain odd wisps of fear.

"Driver!" Harvey called.

"Silence," the driver snapped.

"Stick to the original plan," Harvey said. "They have the medical facilities there if my wife—"

"Your wife's safety is not the overriding factor," the driver said. "Elements along the prepared route must not be discovered. Do not distract me with your objections. Plan Gamma is being executed."

"Easy does it," Boumour said as Harvey surged forward, supporting himself with a hand on the bench. "What can you do, Durant?"

Harvey sagged back onto the bench, groped for and found Lizbeth's hand. She squeezed it, signaled, *"Wait. Don't you read the doctors? They're frightened too . . . and worried."*

"I'm worried about you," Harvey signaled.

So her safety—and presumably ours—aren't the overriding concern, Boumour thought. *What then is the overriding concern? What program controls our computer-in-flesh?*

14

Only Nourse of the Tuyere occupied a throne in the Survey Globe, his attention on the rays, the winking lights and gauges, the cascading luminescences that reported affairs of the Folk. A telltale told him it was night outside in this hemisphere—darkness that spread across the land from Seatac to the megalopolis of N'Scotia. He saw the physical darkness as a sign of frightening events to come and wished Schruille and Calapine would return.

The visual-report screen came alight. Nourse turned to face it as Allgood's features appeared there. The Security boss bowed to Nourse.

"What is it?" Nourse asked.

"Seatac Checkpoint East reports a van with an odd load of containers has just gone through, Nourse. Its turbines carried masking mutes which we deciphered. The mutes concealed sounds of breathing—five persons hidden in the load. Voices cried out from within as the van pulled away. Acting on your instructions, we put a drop marker onto the van and now have it under observation. What are your orders?"

It begins, Nourse thought. *While I'm alone here it begins.*

Nourse looked to the instruments covering the checkpoints. Seatac East. The van was a moving green pinpoint on a screen. He read the banked binaries describing the incident, compared them with a total-plan motivational analysis. The probability analogues he derived filled him with a sense of doom.

"The voices have been identified, Nourse," Allgood said. "The voice prints were—"

"Svengaard and Lizbeth Durant," Nourse said.

"Where she is, her husband cannot be far away," Allgood said.

Allgood's logical little announcements began to annoy Nourse. He contained the emotion while noting the man had overlooked the use of the Optiman's name-in-address. It was a small sign, but significant, especially when Allgood appeared not to notice his own lapse.

"Which leaves us two unidentified," Nourse said.

"We can make an educated guess . . . Nourse."

Nourse glanced at his probability analogues, said, "Two of our wayward pharmacists."

"One may be Potter, Nourse."

Nourse shook his head. "Potter remains in Seatac."

"They may have a portable vat, Nourse, and that embryo with them," Allgood said, "but we failed to detect appropriate machinery."

"You would not hear the machinery being used," Nourse said. "Or, hearing it, you would not identify it."

Nourse looked up to the banks of scanners—every one of them alive—showing the Optimen observing their Survey Globe. Night or day, the watching channels were jammed. *They know what I mean,* he thought. *Are they disgusted, or is this just another interesting aspect of violence?*

As could have been predicted, Allgood said, "I fail to understand Nourse's meaning."

"No need," Nourse said. He looked at the face in the screen. So young it appeared, but Nourse had begun to notice a thing: There was much youngness in Central, but no youth. Even the Sterrie servants betrayed this fact to the unveiled eye. He felt himself to be like the Sterrie Folk suddenly, watching each other for evidence of aging, hoping by comparison that their own appearance prospered.

"What are Nourse's instructions?" Allgood asked.

"Svengaard's outcry indicates he's a prisoner," Nourse said. "But we must not overlook the possibility this is an elaborate ruse." He spoke in a resigned, tired voice.

"Shall we destroy the van, Nourse?"

"Destroy . . ." Nourse shuddered. "No, not yet. Keep it under surveillance. Put out a general alert. We must discover where they're headed. Every contact they make must be noted and marked down for attention."

"If they elude us, Nourse, it could—"

"You've flagtapped the appropriate enzyme prescriptions?"

"Yes, Nourse."

"Then they cannot run far . . . or long."

"As you say, Nourse."

"You may go," Nourse said.

He watched the screen long after it had turned blank. Destroy the van? That would be an ending. He felt then that he did not want this *game* to end—ever. A curious feeling of elation crept through him.

The globe's entrance segment swung open below him. Calapine entered followed by Schruille. They rode the climbing beam to their seats on the triangular dais. Neither spoke. They appeared withdrawn, oddly calm. Nourse, thought of a controlled storm as he looked at them—the lightning and the thunder contained, that it might not harm their fellows.

"Is it not time?" Calapine asked.

A sigh escaped Nourse.

Schruille activated the sensor contact with the scanners in the mountains. There was moonlight suddenly in the receiving screens, the sounds of nightbirds, a rustling of dry leaves. Far off across moon-frosted hills lay lines and patches of lights tracing the coast and harbors of the megalopolis and the multi-level skyway networks.

Calapine stared at the scene, thinking of jewels and casual baubles, the playthings of idleness. She'd not had the inclination in several centuries to indulge in such toys. *Why should I think of them now?* she wondered. *These are not toys, these lights.*

Nourse examined the binary pyramids, the action analogues showing the course of Folk activity within the megalopolis.

"All is normal . . . and in readiness," he said.

"Normal!" Schruille said.

"Which of us?" Calapine whispered.

"I have seen the necessity longest," Schruille said. "I will do it." He rolled a looping ring in the arm of his throne and as he moved it was appalled by the simplicity of the action. This ring and the powers it controlled had been at hand for eons, an insensitive linkage of machinery. All it took was a simple turning motion, a hand and the will behind the hand.

Calapine watched the scene in her screens—moonlight on hills, the megalopolis beyond, an animated toy subject to her whims. The last cadre of special personnel had departed, she knew. Irreplaceable objects that might be damaged had been removed. All was ready and doomed.

Winking flares began to appear through the necklaces of light—golden yellow flares. The Tuyere's screens blurred as sonics vibrated the distant scanners. Lights began going out. Across the entire region, the lights went out—in groups and one by one. A low green fog rolled across the scene, filling in the valleys, overrunning the hills.

Presently, no lights were visible. Only the green fog remained. It continued to creep out beneath the impersonal moon, moving out and across and through until it remained and nothing more.

Schruille watched the stacked numerical analogues, the unemotional reporters which merely counted, submitted deductions of sortings, remainders . . . zeroes. Nothing showed Folk dying in the tubes and warrens, in the streets . . . at their labors . . . at their play.

Nourse sat weeping.

They are dead, all dead, he thought. *Dead.* The word felt peculiar in his mind, devoid of personal meaning. It was a term that could be applied to bacteria perhaps . . . or to weeds. One sterilized an area before bringing in lovely flowers. *Why do I weep?* He tried to remember if he'd ever wept before. *Perhaps there was a time when I wept,* he thought. *But it was so long ago. Ago . . . ago . . . ago . . . time . . . time . . . wept . . . wept.* They were words suddenly without meaning. *That's the trouble with endless life,* he thought. *With too much repetition, everything loses meaning.*

Schruille studied the green fog in his screens. *A few repairs, and we'll be able to send in new Folk,* he thought. *We'll repopulate with Folk of a safer cut.* He wondered then where they'd find the safer Folk. The globe's analysis boards revealed that the Seatac problem was only one of many such pockets. Symptoms were everywhere the same.

He could see the flaw. It centered on the isolation of one generation from another. Lack of traditions and continuity became an obsession with the Folk . . . because they seemed to communicate no matter what repressions were tried. Folk sayings would crop up to reveal the deep current beneath.

Schruille quoted to himself: *"When God first created a dissatisfied man, He put that man outside Central."*

But we created these Folk, Schruille thought. *How did we create dissatisfied men?*

He turned then and saw that Calapine and Nourse were weeping.

"Why do you weep?" Schruille demanded.

But they remained silent.

15

Where the last skyway ended, the van took the turn away from the undermountain tube, and held to the wide surface track on the Lester by-way. It led upward through old tunnels to the wilderness reserve and breeder-leave resorts along an almost deserted air-blasted road-bed. There were no slavelights up here, only the moon and the stabbing cyclops beam of the van's headlight.

An occasional omnibus passed them on the down-track, the passenger seats occupied by silent, moody couples, their breeder-leave ended, heading back to the megalopolis. If any of them focused on the van, it was dismissed as a supply carrier for the resorts.

On a banked curve below the Homish Resort Complex, the Cyborg driver made a series of adjustments to his lift controls. Venturis narrowed. Softness went out of the ride. Turbines whined upward to a near destructive keening. The van turned off the roadbed.

Within the narrow box that concealed them, Harvey Durant clutched the bench with one hand and Lizbeth with the other as the van lurched and bounced across the eroded mounds of an ancient railroad right of way, crashed through a screen of alders and turned onto a game track that followed the right of way upward through buck brush and rhododendrons.

"What's happening?" Lizbeth wailed.

The driver's voice rasped through the speaker, "We have left the road. There is nothing to fear."

Nothing to fear, Harvey thought. The idea appeared so ludicrous he had to suppress a chuckle which he realized might be near hysteria.

The driver had turned off all exterior lights and was relying now on the moon and his infra-red vision.

The Cyborg-boosted vision revealed the trail as a snail track through the brush. The van gulped this track for two kilometers, leaving a dusty, leaf-whirling wake to a point where the game trail intersected a forest patrol road—a cleared track matted with dead sallow and bracken from the passage of the patrol vehicles. Here, it turned right like a great hissing prehistoric monster, labored up a hill, roared down the other side and to the top of another hill where it stopped.

Turbines whined down to silence and the van settled onto its skids. The driver emerged, a blocky stub-legged figure with glittering prosthetic arms attached for its present needs. A side panel was ripped off and the Cyborg began unloading cargo, tossing it indiscriminately down through a stand of hemlock into a deep gully.

Within their compartment, Igan lurched to his feet, put his mouth near the speaker-phone, hissed, "Where are we?"

Silence.

"That was stupid," Harvey said. "How do you know why he's stopped?"

Igan ignored the insult. It came after all from a semi-educated dolt. "You can hear him shifting cargo," Igan said. He leaned across Harvey, pounded a palm against the compartment's side. "What's going on out there?"

"Oh, sit down," Harvey said. He put a hand on Igan's chest, pushed. The surgeon stumbled backward onto the opposite bench.

Igan started to bounce back, his face dark, eyes glaring. Boumour restrained him, rumbled, "Serenity, friend Igan."

Igan settled back. Slowly, a look of patience came over his features. "It's odd," he said, "how one's emotions have a way of asserting themselves in spite of—"

"That will pass," Boumour said.

Harvey found Lizbeth's hand, clutched it, signaled, *"Igan's chest—it's convex and hard as plasmeld. I felt it under his jacket."*

"You think he's Cyborg?"

"He breathes normally."

"And he has emotions. I read fear on him."

"Yes . . . but . . ."

"We will be careful."

Boumour said, "You should place more trust in us, Durant. Doctor Igan had deduced that our driver would not be moving cargo unless certain sounds were safe."

"How do we know who's moving cargo?" Harvey asked.

A look of caution fled across Boumour's massive calm. Harvey read it, smiled.

"Harvey!" Lizbeth said. *"You don't think the—"*

"It's our driver out there," Harvey reassured her. *"I can smell the wilderness in the air. There's been no sound of a struggle. One doesn't take a Cyborg without a struggle."*

"But where are we?" she asked.

"In the mountains, the wilderness," Harvey said. *"From the feel of the ride, we're well off the main by-ways."*

Abruptly, their compartment lurched, slid sideways. The single light was extinguished. In the sudden darkness, the wall behind Harvey dropped away. He clutched Lizbeth, whirled, found himself looking out into darkness . . . moonlight . . . their driver a blocky shadow against a distant panorama of the megalopolis with its shimmering networks of light. The moon silvered the tops of trees below them and there was a sharp smell of forest duff, resinous, dank, churned up by the van and not yet settled. The wilderness lay silent as though waiting, analyzing the intrusion.

"Out," the driver said.

The Cyborg turned. Harvey saw the features suddenly illuminated by moonlight, said, "Glisson!"

"Greetings, Durant," Glisson said.

"Why you?" Harvey asked.

"Why not?" Glisson asked. "Get out of there now."

Harvey said: "But my wife isn't—"

"I know about your wife, Durant. She's had plenty of time since the treatment. She can walk if she doesn't exert herself."

Igan spoke at Harvey's ear, "She'll be quite all right. Sit her up gently and help her down."

"I . . . feel all right," Lizbeth said. "Here." She put an arm over Harvey's shoulder. Together, they slid down to the ground.

Igan followed, asked, "Where are we?"

"We are someplace headed for someplace else," Glisson said. "What is the condition of our prisoner?"

Boumour spoke from within the compartment, "He's coming around. Help me lift him out."

"Why've we stopped?" Harvey asked.

"There is steep climbing ahead," Glisson said. "We're dropping the load. A van isn't built for this work."

Boumour and Igan shouldered past them carrying Svengaard, propped him against a stump beside the track.

"Wait here while I disengage the trailer," Glisson said. "You might be considering whether we should abandon Svengaard."

Hearing his name, Svengaard opened his eyes, found himself staring out and down at the distant lights of the megalopolis. His jaw ached where Harvey had struck him and there was a throbbing in his head. He felt hungry, thirsty. His hands were numb beyond the bindings. A dry smell of evergreen needles filled his nostrils. He sneezed.

"Perhaps we *should* get rid of Svengaard," Igan said.

"I think not," Boumour said. "He's a trained man, a possible ally. We're going to need trained men."

Svengaard looked toward the voices. They stood beside the van which was a long silvery shape behind a stubby double cab. A wrenching of metal sounded there. The trailer slid backward on its skids almost two meters before stopping against a mound of dirt.

Glisson returned, squatted beside Svengaard. "What is our decision?" asked the Cyborg. "Kill him or keep him?"

Harvey gulped, felt Lizbeth clutch his arm.

"Keep him yet awhile," Boumour said.

"If he causes no more trouble," Igan said.

"We could always use his parts," Glisson said. "Or try to grow a new Svengaard and retrain it." The Cyborg stood. "An immediate decision isn't necessary. It is a thing to consider."

Svengaard remained silent, frozen by the emotionless clarity of the man's speech. *A hard, brutal man,* he thought. *A tough man, prepared for any violence. A killer.*

"Into the cab with him then," Glisson said. "Everyone into the cab. We must get . . ." The Cyborg broke off, stared out toward the megalopolis.

Svengaard turned toward the strings of blue-white light glittering far away and cold. A winking golden flare had appeared amidst the lights on his left. Another blazed up beyond it—a giant's bonfire set against the background of distant, moon-frosted mountains. More yellow flares appeared to the right. A bone-chilling rattle of sonics shook him, jarred a sympathetic metal dissonance from the van.

"What's happening?" Lizbeth hissed.

"Quiet!" Glisson said. "Be quiet and observe."

"Gods of life," Lizbeth whispered, "what is it?"

"It is the death of a megalopolis," Boumour said.

Again, sonics rattled the van.

"That hurts," Lizbeth whimpered.

Harvey pulled her close, muttered, "Damn them!"

"Up here it hurts," Igan said, his voice chillingly formal. "Down there it kills."

Green fog began emerging from the wilderness some ten

kilometers below them. It rolled out and down like a furious downy sea beneath the moon, engulfing everything—hills, the gem-like lights, the yellow flares.

"Did you think they would use the death fog?" Boumour asked.

"We knew they would use it," Glisson said.

"I suppose so," Boumour said. "Sterilize the area."

"What is it?" Harvey demanded.

"It comes from the vents where they administered the contraceptive gas," Boumour said. "One particle on your skin—the end of you."

Igan moved around, stared down at Svengaard. "They are the ones who love us and care for us," he mocked.

"What's happening?" Svengaard asked.

"Can you not hear?" Igan asked. "Can you not see? Your friends the Optimen are sterilizing Seatac. Did you have friends there?"

"Friends?" There was a broken quality to Svengaard's voice. He turned back to stare at the green fog. The distant lights had all been extinguished.

Again, sonics chattered through them, shook the ground, rattled the van.

"What do you think of *them* now?" Igan asked.

Svengaard shook his head, unable to speak. He wondered why he had no sensory fuse system to shut off this scene. He felt chained to awareness through sense organs gone abnormal beyond any previous experience . . . a permissive aberration. His senses were deceiving him, that was it. This was a special case of self-deception.

"Why don't you answer me?" Igan asked.

"Leave him alone," Harvey said. "We've griefs of our own. Haven't you any feelings?"

"He sees it and does not believe," Igan said.

"How could they?" Lizbeth whispered.

"Self-preservation," Boumour rumbled. "A trait our friend Svengaard doesn't seem to have. Perhaps it was cut out of him."

Svengaard stared at the rolling green cloud. So silent and stealthy it was. The great reach of darkness where once there had been light and life filled him with a raw awareness of his own mortality. He thought of friends down there—the hospital staff—embryos, his playmate-wife.

All destroyed.

Svengaard felt emptied, incapable of any emotion—even grief. He could only question, *What was their purpose?*

"Into the cab with him," Glisson said. "On the floor in the rear."

Ungentle hands lifted Svengaard—he identified Boumour and Glisson. The driver's unemotional quality confused Svengaard. He had never before encountered quite that abstract detachment in a human being.

They pushed him onto the floor of the van's cab. The sharp edge of a seat brace dug into his side. Feet came in around him. Someone put a foot on his stomach, recoiled. The turbines came alive. A door was slammed. They glided into motion.

Svengaard sank into a kind of stupor.

Lizbeth seated above him heaved a deep sigh. Hearing it, Svengaard was roused to a feeling of compassion for her, his first emotion since the shock of seeing the megalopolis die.

Why did they do it? he asked himself. *Why?*

In the darkness, Lizbeth gripped Harvey's hand. She could see in an occasional patch of moonglow the outline of Glisson directly ahead of her. The Cyborg's minimal movement, the sense of power in every action, filled her with growing disquiet. The scar of her operation itched. She wanted to scratch, but feared calling attention to herself. The Courier Service had been a long time building its own organization, deceiving both the Cyborgs and the Optimen. They'd done it partly through self-effacement. Now, in her fear, she sank back into that treatment.

Through their hands, Harvey signaled, *"Boumour and Igan, I read them now. They're new Cyborgs. Probably just a first linkage with implanted computers. They're just learn-*

ing the price, shedding their normal human emotional reactions, learning to counterfeit emotion."

She absorbed this, seeing them through Harvey's deduction. He often read people better than she did. She reread what she had seen of the two surgeons.

"Do you read it?" he signaled.

"You're right. Yes."

"It means a total break with Central. They can never go back."

"That explains Seatac," she signaled. She began to tremble.

"And we can't trust them," Harvey said. He pressed her close, soothing her.

The van labored up through the foothills skirting open meadows, following ancient tracks, an occasional streambed. Shortly before dawn, it swerved left down a fire-break and into a stand of pines and cedars, squeezed its way through a narrow lane there with its blowers kicking up a heavy cloud of forest duff behind. Glisson pulled to a stop behind an old building, moss on its sides, small curtained windows. Pseudo-ducks with a weedy patina and grass-grown signs that they hadn't been animated in years, made a short file near the building—pale moon-figures—in the light of a single bulb high up under the building's eaves.

Turbines whined to silence. They could hear then the hum of machinery and looking toward the sound saw the dull silver outline of a ventilator tower among the trees.

A door at the corner of the building opened. A heavy-headed man with a big jaw, stoop-shouldered, emerged blowing his nose into a red handkerchief. He looked old, his face a mask of subservience.

Glisson said, "It's the sign. All is safe here . . . for the moment." He slipped out, approached the old man, coughed.

"A lot of sickness around these days," the old man said. His voice was as ancient as his face, wheezing, slurring the consonants.

"You're not the only one with troubles," Glisson said.

The old man straightened, shed the stooped look and subservient manner. "S'pose you're wanting a hidey hole," he said. "Don't know if it's safe here. Don't even know if I oughta hide you."

"I will give the orders here," Glisson said. "You will obey."

The old man studied Glisson a moment, then a look of anger washed over his face. "You damn' Cyborgs!" he said.

"Hold your tongue," Glisson said, his voice flat. "We need food, a safe place to spend the day. I shall require your help in hiding this van. You must know the surrounding terrain. And you will arrange other transportation for us."

"Best cut it up and bury it," the old man said, his voice surly. "Been a hornet's nest stirred up. Guess you know that."

"We know," Glisson said. He turned, beckoned to the van. "Come along. Bring Svengaard."

Presently, the others joined him. Boumour and Igan supported Svengaard between them. The bindings on Svengaard's feet had been released, but he appeared barely able to stand. Lizbeth walked with the bent-over care that said she wasn't sure her incision had healed despite the enzymic speed-up medication.

"We will lodge here during daylight," Glisson said. "This man will direct you to quarters."

"What word from Seatac?" Igan asked.

Glisson looked at the old man, said, "Answer."

The oldster shrugged. "Courier through here couple of hours ago. Said no survivors."

"Any report on a Dr. Potter?" Svengaard croaked.

Glisson whirled, stared at Svengaard.

"Dunno," the old man said. "What route he take?"

Igan cleared his throat, glanced at Glisson, then at the old man. "Potter? I believe he was in the group coming out by the power tubes."

The old man flicked a glance at the ventilator tower growing more distinct among the trees by the second as daylight crept across the mountains. "Nobody come through the tubes," he said. "They shut off the ventilators and flooded the tubes with that gas first thing." He looked at Igan. "Ventilators been going again for about three hours."

Glisson studied Svengaard, asked, "Why are you interested in Potter?"

Svengaard remained silent.

"Answer me!" Glisson ordered.

Svengaard tried to swallow. His throat ached. He felt driven into a corner. Glisson's words enraged him. Without warning, Svengaard lurched forward dragging Igan and Boumour, lashed out at Glisson with a foot.

The Cyborg dodged with a blurring movement, caught the foot, jerked Svengaard from the two surgeons, whirled, swung Svengaard wide and released him. Svengaard landed on his back, skidded across the ground, stopped. Before he could move, Glisson was standing over him. Svengaard lay there sobbing.

"Why are you interested in Potter?" Glisson demanded.

"Go away, go away, go away!" Svengaard sobbed.

Glisson straightened, looked around at Igan and Boumour. "You understand this?"

Igan shrugged. "It's emotion."

"Perhaps a shock reaction," Boumour said.

Through their hands, Harvey signaled Lizbeth, *"He's been in shock, but this mean's he's coming out of it. These are medical people! Can't they read anything?"*

"Glisson reads it," she answered. *"He was testing them."*

Glisson turned around, looked squarely at Harvey. The bold understanding in the Cyborg's eyes shot a pang of fear through Harvey.

"Careful," Lizbeth signaled. *"He's suspicious of us."*

"Take Svengaard inside," Glisson said.

Svengaard looked up at their driver. Glisson, the Durants called him. But the old man from the building had labeled Glisson a Cyborg. Was it possible? Were the half-men being revived to challenge the Optimen once more? Was that the reason for Seatac's death?

Boumour and Igan lifted him, checked the fetters on his hands. "Let's have no more foolishness," Boumour said.

Are they like Glisson? Svengaard asked himself. *Are they, too, part man, part machine? And what about the Durants?*

Svengaard could feel the tear dampness in his eyes. *Hysteria,* he thought. *Coming out of shock.* He began to wonder at himself then with an odd feeling of guilt. Why does Potter's death strike me more deeply than the death of an entire megalopolis, the extinction of my wife and friends? What did Potter symbolize to me?

Boumour and Igan half carried, half walked him into the building, down a narrow hall and into a poorly lighted, gloomy big room with a ceiling that went up to bare beams two stories above. They dropped him onto a dusty couch—bare plastic and hydraulic contour-shapers that adjusted reluctantly. The light came from two glowglobes high up under the beams. It exposed oddments of furniture scattered around the room and mounds of strange shapes covered by slick, glistening fabric. A table to his left, he realized, was made of planks. Wood! A contour cot lay beyond it, and an ancient roll-top desk with a missing drawer, and mismatched chairs. A stained, soot-blackened fireplace, with an iron crane reaching across its mouth like a gibbet, occupied half the wall across from him. The entire room smelled of dampness and rot. The floor creaked as people moved. Wood flooring!

Svengaard looked up at tiny windows admitting a sparse gray daylight that grew brighter by the second. Even at its brightest he knew it wouldn't dispel the gloom of this place. Here was sadness that made him think of people without number—dead, forgotten. Tears rolled down his cheeks.

What's wrong with me? he wondered.

There came a sound from the yard of the van's turbines being ignited. He heard it lift, leave . . . fade away. Harvey and Lizbeth entered the room.

Lizbeth looked at Svengaard, then at Boumour and Igan who had taken up vigil on the cot. With her crouched, protective walk, she crossed to Svengaard, touched his shoul-

THE EYES OF HEISENBERG • 451

der. She saw his tears, evidence of humanity, and she wished then that he were her doctor. Perhaps there was a way. She decided to ask Harvey.

"Please trust us," she said. "We won't harm you. *They* are the ones who killed your wife and friends, not us."

Svengaard pulled away.

How dare she have pity on me? he thought. But she had reached some chord in him. He could feel himself shattering.

Oppressive silence settled over the room.

Harvey came up, guided his wife to a chair at the table.

"It's wood," she said, touching the surface, wonder in her voice. Then, "Harvey, I'm very hungry."

"They'll bring food as soon as they've disposed of the van," he said.

She clutched his hand and Svengaard watched, fascinated by the nervous movement of her fingers.

Glisson and the old man returned presently, slamming the door behind them. The building creaked with their movement.

"We'll have a forest patrol vehicle for the next stage," Glisson said. "Much safer. There's a thing you all should know now." The Cyborg moved a cold, weighted stare from face to face. "There was a marker on top of the van's load section which we abandoned last night."

"Marker?" Lizbeth said.

"A device for tracing us, following us," Glisson said.

"Ohhh!" Lizbeth put a hand over her mouth.

"I do not know how closely they were following," Glisson said. "I was altered for this task and certain of my devices were left behind. They may know where we are right now."

Harvey shook his head. "But why . . . ?"

"Why haven't they moved against us?" Glisson asked. "It's obvious. They hope we'll lead them to the vitals of our organization." Something like rage came into the Cyborg's features. "It may be we can surprise them."

16

In the Survey Room, the great globe's instrumented inner walls lay relatively quiescent. Calapine and Schruille of the Tuyere occupied the triple thrones. The dais turned slowly, allowing them to scan the entire surface. Kaleidoscopic colors from the instruments played a somnolent visible melody across Calapine's features—a wash of greens, reds, purples.

She felt tired with a definite emotion of self-pity. There was something wrong with the enzymic analyzers. She felt sure of it, wondering if the Underground had somehow compromised the function of the pharmacy computers.

Schruille was no help. He'd laughed at the suggestion.

Allgood's features appeared on a call screen before Calapine. She stopped the turning dais as he bowed, said, "I call to report, Calapine." She noted the dark circles under his eyes, the drugged awareness in the way he held his head stiffly erect.

"You have found them?" Calapine asked.

"They're somewhere in the wilderness area, Calapine," Allgood said. "They have to be in there."

"Have to be!" she sneered. "You're a foolish optimist, Max."

"We know some of the hiding places they could've chosen, Calapine."

"For every one you know, they've nine you don't know," she said.

"I have the entire area ringed, Calapine. We're moving in slowly, checking everywhere as we go. They're there and we'll find them."

"He babbles," she said, glancing at Schruille.

Schruille returned a mirthless smile, looked at Allgood through the prismatic reflector. "Max, have you found the source of the substitute embryo?"

"Not yet, Schruille."

He stared up at them, his face betraying his obvious confusion at the militancy and violence of *his* Optimen.

"Do you seek in Seatac?" Calapine demanded.

Allgood wet his lips with his tongue.

"Out with it!" she snapped. *Ahhh, the fear in his eyes.*

"We're searching there, Calapine, but the—"

"You think we were too precipitate?" she asked.

He shook his head.

"You're acting strangely," Schruille said. "Are you afraid of us?"

He hesitated, then, "Yes, Schruille."

"Yes, Schruille!" Calapine mimicked.

Allgood looked at her, the fear in his eyes tempered by anger. "I'm taking every action I know, Calapine."

She marked a sudden precision in his manner behind the anger. Her eyes went wide with wonder. Was it possible? She looked at Schruille, wondering if he had seen it.

"Max, why did you call us?" Schruille asked.

"I . . . to report, Schruille."

"You've reported nothing."

Hesitantly, Calapine brought up her instruments for a special probe of Allgood, stared at the result. Horror mingled with rage in her. Cyborg! They had defiled Max! Her Max!

"There's only need for you to obey us," Schruille said.

Allgood nodded, remained silent.

"You!" Calapine hissed. She leaned toward the screen. "You dared! Why? Why, Max?"

Schruille said, "What . . . ?"

But in the shocked instant of her questions, Allgood had seen that he was discovered. He knew it was his end, could see it in her eyes. "I saw . . . I found the dopplegangers," he stammered.

An angry twist of her hand rolled one of the rings on her throne arm. Sonics sent a shock wave chattering across Allgood, blurred his image. His lips moved soundlessly, eyes staring. He collapsed.

"Why did you do that?" Schruille asked.

"He was Cyborg!" she grated, and pointed to the evidence of the instruments.

"Max? Our Max?" He looked at the instruments, nodded.

"*My* Max," she said.

"But he worshipped you, loved you."

"He does nothing now," she whispered. She blanked the screen, continued to stare at it. Already, the incident was receding from her mind.

"Do you enjoy direct action?" Schruille asked.

She met his gaze in the reflector. *Enjoy direct action? There was indeed a kind of elation in . . . violence.*

"We have no Max now," Schruille said.

"We'll waken another doppleganger," she said. "Security can function without him for now."

"Who'll waken the doppleganger?" Schruille asked. "Igan and Boumour are no longer with us. The pharmacist, Hand, is gone."

"What's keeping Nourse?" she asked.

"Enzymic trouble," Schruille said, a note of glee in his voice. "He said something about a necessary realignment of his prescription. Bonellia hormone derivatives, I believe."

"Nourse can awaken the doppleganger," she said. She wondered momentarily then why they needed the doppleganger. Oh, yes. Max was gone.

"There's more to it than merely awakening Max's duplicate," Schruille said. "They're not as good as they once were, you know. The new Max must be educated for his role, fitted into it gently. It could be weeks . . . months."

"Then one of us can run Security," she said.

"You think we're ready for it?" Schruille asked.

"There's a *thrill* in this sort of decision-making," she said. "I don't mind saying I've been deeply bored during the past several hundred years. But now—now, I feel alive, vital, alert, fascinated." She looked up at the glowing banks of scanner eyes, a full band of them, showing their fellow Optimen watching activities in the Survey Room. "And I'm not alone in this."

Schruille glanced up at the glittering arctic circle of the globe's inner wall. "Aliveness," he murmured. "But Max . . . he is dead."

She remembered then, said, "Any Max can be replaced." She looked at Schruille, turning her head to stare past the prism. "You're very blunt today, Schruille. You've spoken of death twice that I recall."

"Blunt? I?" He shook his head. "But I didn't *erase* Max."

She laughed aloud. "My own reactions thrill me, Schruille!"

"And do you find changes in your enzymic demands?"

"A few. What is that? Times change. It's part of being. Adjustments must be made."

"Indeed," he said.

"Where'd they find a substitute for the Durant embryo?" she asked, her mind shooting off at a tangent.

"Perhaps the new Max can discover," Schruille said.

"He must."

"Or you will grow another Max?" Schruille said.

"Don't mock me, Schruille."

"I wouldn't dare."

Again, she looked directly at him.

"What if they produced their own embryo for the substitution?" Schruille asked.

She turned away. "In the name of all that's proper, how?"

"Air can be filtered clean of contraceptive gas," Schruille said.

"You're disgusting!"

"Am I? But haven't you wondered what Potter concealed?"

"Potter? We know what he concealed."

"A person devoted to the preservation of life . . . such as that is," Schruille said. "What did he hide in his mind?"

"Potter is no more."

"But what did he conceal?"

"You think he knew the source of the . . . outside interference?"

"Perhaps. And *he* would know where to find an embryo."

"Then the record will show the source, as you said yourself."

"I've been reconsidering."

She stared at him in the prism. "It's not possible."

"That I could reconsider?"

"You know what I mean—what you're thinking."

"But it *is possible*."

"It isn't!"

"You're being stubborn, Cal. A female should be the last person to deny such a possibility."

"Now, you're being truly disgusting!"

"We know Potter found a self-viable," Schruille pressed. "They could have many self-viables—male and female. We know historically the capabilities of such raw union. It's part of our *natural* ancestry."

"You're unspeakable," she breathed.

"You can face the concept of death but not this," Schruille said. "Most interesting."

"Disgusting!" she barked.

"But possible," Schruille said.

"The substitute embryo wasn't self-viable!" she pounced.

"All the more reason they might've been willing to sacrifice it for one that was, eh?"

"Where would they find the vat facilities, the chemicals, the enzymes, the—"

"Where they've always been."

"What?"

"They've put the Durant embryo back into its mother," Schruille said. "We can be certain of this. Would it not be equally logical to leave the embryo there to begin with—never remove it, never isolate the gametes in a vat at all?"

Calapine found herself speechless. She sensed a sour taste in her mouth, realized with a feeling of shock that she wanted to vomit. *Something's wrong with my enzyme balance,* she thought.

She spoke slowly, precisely, "I am reporting to pharmacy at once, Schruille. I do not feel well."

"By all means," Schruille said. He glanced up and around at the watching scanners—a full circle of them.

Delicately, Calapine eased herself out of her throne, slid down the beam to the lock segment. Before letting herself out, she cast a look up at the dais, faintly remembering. *Which Max was . . . erased?* she asked herself. *We've had many of him . . . a successful model for our Security.* She thought of the others, Max after Max after Max, each shunted aside when his appearance began to annoy his masters. They stretched into infinity, images in an endless system of mirrors.

What is erasure to such as Max? she wondered. *I am an unbroken continuity of existence. But a doppleganger doesn't remember. A doppleganger breaks the continuity.*

Unless the cells remember.

Memory . . . cells . . . embryos . . .

She thought of the embryo within Lizbeth Durant. Disgusting, but simple. So beautifully simple. Her gorge began to rise. Whirling, Calapine dropped down to the Hall of Counsel, ran for the nearest pharmacy outlet. As she ran, she clenched the hand that had slain Max and helped destroy a megalopolis.

17

S he's sick, I tell you!"
Harvey bent over Igan shaking him out of sleep.
They were in a narrow earth-walled room, ceiling of plasmeld
beams, a dim yellow glowglobe in one corner. Sleeping
pads were spread against the walls, Boumour and Igan on
two of them foot to foot, the bound form of Svengaard on
another, two of the pads empty.

"Come quickly!" Harvey pleaded. "She's sick."

Igan groaned, sat up. He glanced at his watch—almost
sunset on the surface. They'd crawled in here just before
daylight and after a night of laboring on foot up seemingly
endless woods trails behind a Forest Patrol guide. Igan still
ached from the unaccustomed exercise.

Lizbeth sick?

She'd had three days since the embryo had been placed
within her. The others had healed this rapidly, but they
hadn't been subject to a night of stumbling along rough forest trails.

"Please hurry," Harvey pleaded.

"I'm coming," Igan said. And he thought, *Listen to his
tone change now that he needs me.*

Boumour sat up opposite him, asked, "Shall I join you?"

"Wait here for Glisson," Igan said.

"Did Glisson say where he was going?"

"To arrange for another guide. It'll be dark soon."

"Doesn't he ever sleep?" Boumour asked.

"Please!" Harvey begged.

"Yes!" Igan snapped. "What're her symptoms?"

"Vomiting . . . incoherent."

"Let me get my bag." Igan retrieved a thick black case from the floor near his head, glanced across at Svengaard. The man's breathing still showed the even rhythm of the narcotic they'd administered before collapsing into sleep themselves. Something had to be done about Svengaard. He slowed them down.

Harvey pulled at Igan's sleeve.

"I'm coming! I'm coming!" Igan said. He freed his arm, followed Harvey through a low hole at the end of the room and into a room similar to the one they'd just vacated. Lizbeth lay on a pad beneath a single glowglobe across from them. She groaned.

Harvey knelt beside her. "I'm right here."

"Harvey," she whispered. "Oh, Harvey."

Igan joined them, lifted a pulmonometer-sphagnomometer from his bag. He pressed it against her neck, read the dial. "Where do you hurt?" he asked.

"Ohhhh," she moaned.

"Please," Harvey said, looking at Igan. "Please do something."

"Stand out of the way," Igan said.

Harvey stood up, backed off two steps. "What is it?" he whispered.

Igan ignored him, taped an enzymic vampire gauge to Lizbeth's left wrist, read the dials.

"What's wrong with her?" Harvey demanded.

Igan unclipped his instruments, restored them to his bag. "Nothing's wrong with her."

"But she's—"

"She's perfectly normal. Most of the others reacted the same way. It's realignment of her enzymic demand system."

"Isn't there some—"

"Calm down!" Igan stood up, faced Harvey. "She barely needs any prescription material. Pretty soon, she can do without altogether. She's in better health than you are. And she could walk into a pharmacy right now. The prescription flag wouldn't even identify her."

"Then why's she . . . ?"

"It's the embryo. It compensates for her needs to protect itself. Does it automatically."

"But she's sick!"

"A bit of glandular maladjustment, nothing else." Igan picked up his bag. "It's all part of the ancient process. The embryo says produce this, produce that. She produces. Puts a certain strain on her system."

"Can't you do anything for her?"

"Of course I can. She'll be extremely hungry in a little while. We'll give her something to settle her stomach and then feed her. Provided they can produce some food in this hole."

Lizbeth groaned, "Harvey?"

He knelt beside her, clasped her hands. "Yes, dear?"

"I feel terrible."

"They'll give you something in a few minutes."

"Ohhhhh."

Harvey turned a fierce scowl up at Igan.

"As soon as we can," Igan said. "Don't worry. This is normal." He turned, ducked out into the other room.

"What's wrong?" Lizbeth whispered.

"It's the embryo," Harvey said. "Didn't you hear?"

"Yes. My head aches."

Igan returned with a capsule and a cup of water, bent over Lizbeth. "Take this. It'll settle your stomach."

Harvey helped her sit up, held her while she swallowed the capsule.

She took a quavering breath, returned the cup. "I'm sorry to be such a—"

"Quite all right," Igan said. He looked at Harvey. "Best

bring her in the other room. Glisson will return in a few minutes. He should have food and a guide."

Harvey helped his wife to her feet, supported her as they followed Igan into the other room. They found Svengaard sitting up staring at his bound hands.

"Have you been listening?" Igan asked.

Svengaard looked at Lizbeth. "Yes."

"Have you thought about Seatac?"

"I've thought."

"You're not thinking of releasing him," Harvey said.

"He slows us too much," Igan said. "And we *cannot* release him."

"Then perhaps I should do something about him," Harvey said.

"What do you suggest, Durant?" Boumour asked.

"He's a danger to us," Harvey said.

"Ahh," Boumour said. "Then we leave him to you."

"Harvey!" Lizbeth said. She wondered if he'd suddenly gone mad. Was this his reaction to her request that they seek Svengaard as her doctor?

But Harvey was remembering Lizbeth's moans. "If it's him or my son," he said, "the choice is easy."

Lizbeth took his hand, signaled, *"What're you doing? You can't mean this!"*

"What is he, anyway?" Harvey asked, staring at Igan. And he signaled Lizbeth, *"Wait. Watch."*

She read her husband then, pulled away.

"He's a gene surgeon," Harvey said. His voice dripped scorn. "He's existed for *them*. Can he justify his existence? He's a nonviable, nonliving nonentity. He has no future."

"Is that your choice?" Boumour asked.

Svengaard looked up at Harvey. "Do you talk of murdering me?" he asked. The lack of emotion in his voice surprised Harvey.

"You don't protest?" he asked.

Svengaard tried to swallow. His throat felt full of dry

cotton. He looked at Harvey, measuring the bulk of the man, the corded muscles. He remembered the excessive male protectiveness in Harvey's nature, the gene-error that made him a slave to Lizbeth's slightest need.

"Why should I argue," Svengaard asked, "when much of what he says is true and when he's already made up his mind?"

"How will you do it, Durant?" Boumour asked.

"How would you like me to do it?" Harvey asked.

"Strangulation might be interesting," Boumour said, and Harvey wondered if Svengaard, too, could hear the Cyborg clinical detachment in the man's voice.

"A simple snap of the neck is quicker," Igan said. "Or an injection. I could supply several from my kit."

Harvey felt Lizbeth trembling against him. He patted her arm, disengaged himself.

"Harvey!" she said.

He shook his head, advanced on Svengaard.

Igan retreated to Boumour's side, stood watching.

Harvey knelt behind Svengaard, closed his fingers around the surgeon's throat, bent close to the ear opposite his audience. In a whisper audible only to Svengaard, Harvey said, "They would as soon see you dead. They don't care one way or another. How do you feel about it?"

Svengaard felt the hands on his throat. He knew he could reach up with his bound hands and try to remove those clutching fingers, but he knew he'd fail. There was no doubting Harvey's strength.

"Your own choice?" Harvey whispered.

"Do it, man!" Boumour called.

Only seconds ago, Svengaard realized, he'd been resigned to death, wanted death. Suddenly, that wish was the farthest thing from his desires.

"I want to live," he husked.

"Is that your choice?" Harvey whispered.

"Yes!"

"Are you talking to him?" Boumour asked.

"Why do you want to live?" Harvey asked in a normal voice. He relaxed his fingers lightly, a subtle communication to Svengaard. Even an untrained person could *read* this.

"Because I've never *been* alive," Svengaard said. "I want to try it."

"But how can you justify your existence?" Harvey asked, and he allowed his fingers to tighten ever so slightly.

Svengaard looked at Lizbeth, sensing at last the direction of Harvey's thoughts. He glanced at Boumour and Igan.

"You haven't answered my question," Boumour said. "What are you discussing with our prisoner?"

"Are they both Cyborgs?" Svengaard asked.

"Irretrievably," Harvey said. "Without human feelings—or near enough to it that it makes no difference."

"Then how can you trust them with your wife's care?" Harvey's fingers relaxed.

"That is a way I could justify my existence," Svengaard said.

Harvey removed his hands from Svengaard's throat, squeezed the man's shoulders. It was instant communication, more than words, something that went from flesh to flesh. Svengaard knew he had an ally.

Boumour crossed to stand over them, demanded, "Are you going to kill him or aren't you?"

"No one here's going to kill him," Harvey said.

"Then what've you been doing?"

"Solving a problem," Harvey said. He kept a hand on Svengaard's arm. Svengaard found he could understand Harvey's intent just by the pressure of that hand. It said, *"Wait. Be still. Let me handle this."*

"And what is your intention now toward our prisoner?" Boumour demanded.

"I intend to free him and put my wife in his care," Harvey said.

Boumour glared at him. "And if that incurs our displeasure?"

"What idiocy!" Igan blared. "How can you trust *him* when we're available?"

"This is a fellow human," Harvey said. "What he does for my wife will be out of humanity and not like a mechanic treating her as a machine for transporting an embryo."

"This is nonsense!" Igan snapped. But he realized then that Harvey had recognized their Cyborg nature.

Boumour raised a hand to silence him as Igan started to continue talking. "You have not indicated how you will do this if we oppose it," he said.

"You're not full Cyborgs," Harvey said. "I see in you fears and uncertainties. It's new to you and you're changing. I suspect you're very vulnerable yet."

Boumour backed off three steps, his eyes measuring Harvey. "And Glisson?" Boumour asked.

"Glisson wants only trustworthy allies," Harvey said. "I'm giving him a trustworthy ally."

"How do you know you can trust Svengaard?" Igan demanded.

"Because you have to ask, you betray your ineffectiveness," Harvey said. He turned, began unfastening Svengaard's fetters.

"It's on your head," Boumour said.

Harvey freed Svengaard's hands, knelt and removed the bindings from his feet.

"I'm going for Glisson," Igan said. He left the room.

Harvey stood up, faced Svengaard. "Do you know about my wife's condition?" he asked.

"I heard Igan," Svengaard said. "Every surgeon studies history and genetic origins. I have an academic knowledge of her condition."

Boumour sniffed.

"There's Igan's medical kit," Harvey said, pointing to the black case on the floor. "Tell me why my wife was sick."

"You're not satisfied with Igan's explanation?" Boumour asked. He appeared outraged by the thought.

"He said it was natural," Harvey said. "How can sickness be natural?"

"She has received medication," Svengaard said. "Do you know what it was?"

"It had the same markings as the pill he gave her in the van," Harvey said. "A tranquilizer he called it then."

Svengaard approached Lizbeth, looked at her eyes, her skin. "Bring the kit," he said, nodding to Harvey. He guided Lizbeth to an empty pad, finding himself fascinated by the idea of this examination. Once he had thought of this as disgusting; now, the idea that Lizbeth carried an embryo in her in the ancient way held only mystery for him, a profound curiosity.

Lizbeth sent a questioning look at Harvey as Svengaard eased her back onto the pad. Harvey nodded reassuringly. She tried to smile, but a strange fear had come over her. The fear didn't originate with Svengaard. His hands were full of gentle assurance. But the prospect of being examined frightened her. She could feel terror warring with the drug Igan had given her.

Svengaard opened the kit, remembering the diagrams and explanations from the study tapes of his school years. They had been the subject of ribald jokes then, but even the jokes helped him now because they tended to fix vital facts in his mind.

> Cling to the wall, for if you fall,
> You then must learn to do the crawl!

In his memory, he could hear the chant and the uproarious burst of laughter.

Svengaard bent to his examination, excluding all else but the patient and himself. Blood pressure . . . enzymes . . . hormone production . . . bodily secretions . . .

Presently, he sat back, frowned.

"Is something wrong?" Harvey asked.

Boumour stood, arms folded, behind Harvey. "Yes, do tell us," he said.

"Menstrual hormone complex is much too high," Svengaard said. And he thought, *"Cling to the wall . . ."*

"The embryo controls these changes," Boumour sneered.

"Yes," Svengaard said. "But why this shift in hormone production?"

"From your superior knowledge, you'll now tell us," Boumour said.

Svengaard ignored the mocking tone, looked up at Boumour. "You've done this before. Have you had any spontaneous abortions in your patients?"

Boumour frowned.

"Well?" Svengaard said.

"A few." He supplied the information grudgingly.

"I suspect the embryo isn't firmly attached to the endometrium," Svengaard said. "To the wall of the uterus," he said, recognizing Harvey's need for explanation. "The embryo must cling to the uterus wall. The way of this is prepared by hormones present during the menstrual cycle."

Boumour shrugged. "Well, we expect to lose a certain percentage."

"My wife is not a *certain percentage*," Harvey growled. He turned, focused a glare on Boumour that sent the man retreating three steps.

"But these things happen," Boumour said. He looked at Svengaard, who was preparing a slapshot ampule from Igan's kit. "What're you doing?"

"Giving her a little enzymic stimulation to produce the hormones she needs," Svengaard said. He glanced at Harvey, seeing the man's fears and need for reassurance. "It's the best thing we can do now, Durant. It should work if her system hasn't been too upset by all this." He waved a hand indicating their flight, the emotional stress, the exertion.

"Do whatever you think you should," Harvey said. "I know it's your best."

Svengaard administered the shot, patted Lizbeth's arm.

"Try to rest. Relax. Don't move around unless it's necessary."

Lizbeth nodded. She had been reading Svengaard, seeing his genuine concern for her. His attempt to reassure Harvey had touched her, but there were fears she couldn't suppress.

"Glisson," she whispered.

Svengaard saw the direction of her thoughts, and said, "I won't permit him to move you until I'm sure you're all right. He and his guide will just have to wait."

"*You* won't permit!" Boumour sneered.

As though to punctuate his words, the ground around them rumbled and shook. Dust puffed through the low entrance and, like a magician's trick, Glisson materialized there as the concealing dust settled.

At the first sign of disturbance, Harvey had dropped to the floor beside Lizbeth. He held her shoulders, shielded her with his body.

Svengaard still knelt beside the medical kit.

Boumour had whirled to stare at Glisson. "Sonics?" Boumour hissed.

"Not sonics," Glisson said. The Cyborg's usually flat voice carried a sing-song twang.

"He has no arms," Harvey said.

They all noticed it then. From the shoulders down where Glisson's arms had been now dangled only the empty linkages for Cyborg prosthetic attachments.

"*They* have sealed us in here," Glisson said. Again, that sing-song twang as though something about him had been broken. "As you can see, I am disarmed. Do you not think that amusing? Do you see now why we could never fight *them* openly? When they wish it, they can destroy anything . . . anyone."

"Igan?" Boumour whispered.

"Igans are easy to destroy," Glisson said. "I have seen it. Accept the fact."

"But what'll we do?" Harvey demanded.

"Do?" Glisson looked down at him. "We will wait."

"One of you could stand off an entire Security force to get Potter away," Boumour said. "But all you can do now is wait?"

"Violence is not my function," Glisson said. "You will see."

"What'll they do?" Lizbeth hissed.

"Whatever they wish to do," Glisson said.

18

"There, it is done," Calapine said.

She looked at Schruille and Nourse in the reflectors.

Schruille indicated the kinesthetic analogue relays of the Survey Globe's inner wall. "Did you observe Svengaard's emotion?"

"He was properly horrified," Calapine said.

Schruille pursed his lips, studied her reflection. A session with the pharmacy had restored her composure, but she occupied her throne in a subdued mood. The kaleidoscopic play of lights from the wall gave an unhealthy cast to her skin. There was a definite flush to her features.

Nourse glanced up at the observer lights—the span of arctic wall glowed with a dull red intensity, every position occupied. With hardly an exception, the Optiman community watched developments.

"We have a decision to make," Nourse said.

"You look pale, Nourse," Calapine said. "Did you have pharmacy trouble?"

"No more than you." He spoke defensively. "A simple enzymic heterodyning. It's pretty well damped out."

"I say bring them here now," Schruille said.

"To what purpose?" Nourse asked. "We have the pattern of their flight very well fixed. Why let them escape again?"

"I don't like the thought of unregistered self-viables—who knows how many—running loose out there," Schruille said.

"Are you sure we could take them alive?" Calapine asked.

"The Cyborg admits ineffectiveness against us," Schruille said.

"Unless that's a trick," Nourse said.

"I don't think so," Calapine said. "And once we have them here we can extract the information we need from their raw brains with the utmost precision."

Nouse turned, stared at her. He couldn't understand what had happened to Calapine. She spoke with the callous brutality of a Folk woman. She was like an awakened ghoul, as though violence were her rising bell.

What is her setting bell? he wondered. And he was shocked at his own thought.

"If they have means of destroying themselves?" Nourse asked. "I remind you of the computer nurse and a sad number of our own surgeons who appear to be in league with these criminals. We were powerless to prevent their self-destruction."

"How callous you are, Nourse," Calapine said.

"Callous? I?" He shook his head. "I merely wish to prevent further pain. Let us destroy them ourselves and go on from here."

"Glisson's a full Cyborg," Schruille said. "Can you imagine what his memory banks would reveal?"

"I remember the one who escorted Potter," Nourse said. "Let us take no risk. His quietude could be a trick."

"A contact narcotic in their present cell," Schruille said. "That's my suggestion."

"How do you know it'll work on the Cyborgs?" Nourse asked.

"Then they could escape once more," Schruille said. He shrugged. "What does it matter?"

"Into another megalopolis," Nourse said. "Is that it?"

"We know the infection's widespread," Schruille said.

"Certainly, there were cells right here in Central. We've cleaned out those, but the—"

"I say stop them now!" Nourse snapped.

"I agree with Schruille," Calapine said. "What's the risk?"

"The sooner we stop them the sooner we can return to our own pursuits," Nourse said.

"This *is* our pursuit," Schruille said.

"You like the idea of sterilizing another megalopolis, don't you, Schruille?" Nourse sneered. "Which one this time? How about Loovil?"

"Once was enough," Schruille said. "But likes and dislikes really have nothing to do with it."

"Let us put it to a vote then," Calapine said.

"Because you're two to one against me, eh?" Nourse said.

"She means a *full* vote," Schruille said. He looked up at the observation lights. "We've obviously a full quorum."

Nouse stared at the indicators knowing he'd been neatly trapped. He dared not protest a full vote—any vote. And his two companions appeared so sure of themselves. *"This is our pursuit."*

"We've allowed the Cyborgs to interfere," Nourse said, "because they increased the proportion of viables in the genetic reserve. Did we do this merely to destroy the genetic reserve?"

Schruille indicated a bank of binary pyramids on the Globe's wall. "If they endanger us, certainly. But the issue is unregistered *self*-viables, their possible immunity to the contraceptive gas. Where else could they have produced the substitute embryo?"

"If it comes down to it, we don't need any of them," Calapine said.

"Destroy them all?" Nourse asked. "All the Folk?"

"And raise a new crop of dopplegangers," she said. "Why not?"

"Duplicates don't always come true," Nourse said.

"Nothing limits us," Schruille said.

"Our sun isn't infinite," Nourse said.

"We'll solve that when the need arises," Calapine said. "What problem can defy us? We're not limited by time."

"Yet we're sterile," Nourse said. "Our gametes refuse to unite."

"And well they do," Schruille said. "I'd not have it otherwise."

"All we wish now is a simple vote," Calapine said. "A simple vote on whether to capture and bring in one tiny band of criminals. Why should that arouse major debate?"

Nourse started to speak, thought better of it. He shook his head, looked from Calapine to Schruille.

"Well?" Schruille asked.

"I think this little band is the real issue," Nourse said. "One Sterrie surgeon, two Cyborgs and two viables."

"And Durant was ready to kill the Sterrie," Schruille said.

"No." It was Calapine. "He wasn't ready to erase anyone." She found herself suddenly interested in the train of Nourse's reasoning. It was his logic and reason, after all, which had always attracted her.

Schruille, seeing her waver, said, "Calapine!"

"We all saw Durant's emotions," Nourse said. He waved at the instrument wall in front of him. "He would've killed no one. He was . . . *educating* Svengaard, talking to Svengaard with his hands."

"As they do between themselves, he and his wife," Calapine said. "Certainly!"

"You say we should raise a new crop of dopplegangers." Nourse said. "Which seed shall we use? The occupants of Seatac, perhaps?"

"We could take the seed cells first," Schruille said, and he wondered how he had been put so suddenly on the defensive. "I say let's vote on it. Bring them here for full interrogation or destroy them."

"No need," Nourse said. "I've changed my mind. Bring them here . . . if you can."

"Then it's settled," Schruille said. He rapped the signal into his throne arm. "You see, it's really very simple."

"Indeed?" Nourse said. "Then why do Calapine and I find ourselves suddenly reluctant to use violence? Why do we long for the old ways when Max shielded us from ourselves?"

19

The Hall of Counsel had not seen such a gathering since the debate over legalizing limited Cyborg experiments on their own kind some thirty thousand years before. The Optimen occupied a rainbow splashing of multicolored cushions on the banks of plasmeld benches. Some appeared nude, but most out of awareness of such a gathering's traditional nature came clothed in garments of their immediate historical whims. There were togas, kilts, gowns and ruffs, three-cornered hats and derbies, G-strings and muu-muus, fabrics and styles reaching back into prehistory.

Those who could not jam into the hall watched through half-a-million scanner eyes that glittered around the upper line of the walls.

It was barely daylight over Central, but not an Optiman slept.

The Survey Globe had been moved aside and the Tuyere occupied a position on the front bench center at the end of the hall. The prisoners had been brought in on a pneumoflot tumbril by acolytes. They sat on the tumbril's flat surface immobilized within dull blue plasmeld plastrons that permitted only the shallowest of breaths.

As she looked down on them from her bench, seeing the five figures so rigidly repressed, Calapine permitted herself a faint pity for them. The woman—such terror in her eyes. The rage in Harvey Durant's face. The resigned waiting in Glisson and Boumour. And Svengaard—a look of wary awakening.

Yet Calapine felt something was missing here. She couldn't name the missing thing, felt it only as a negative blankness within herself.

Nourse is right, she thought. *These five are important.*

Some Optiman up near the front of the hall had brought a tinkle-player and its little bell music could be heard above the murmurous whispering of the throng in the hall. The sound appeared to grow louder as the Optimen quieted in anticipation. The tinkle-player was stilled in mid-melody.

It grew quieter and quieter in the hall.

Despite her fear, Lizbeth stared around her in the growing silence. She had never before seen an Optiman in the flesh—only on the screens of the public announcement system. (In her lifetime it'd been mostly the members of the Tuyere, although older Folk mentioned the Kagiss trio preceding them.) They looked so varied and colorful—and so distant. She had the demoralizing feeling that nothing of this moment had happened by chance, that there was a terrifying symmetry in being here, now with this company.

"They are completely immobilized," Schruille said. "There's nothing to fear."

"Yet they are terrified," Nourse said. And he recalled suddenly a moment out of his youth. He'd been taken to an antiquary's home, one of the Hedonists proudly displaying his plasmeld copies of lost statues. There'd been a giant fish, one headless figure on a horse (very daring, that), a hooded monk and a man and woman clasped in a mutual embrace of terror. The man and woman, he realized now, had been recalled by the faces of Lizbeth and Harvey Durant.

They are, in a way, our parents, Nourse thought. *We spring from the Folk.*

Calapine realized abruptly what it was she missed here. There was no Max. He was gone, she knew, and she wondered momentarily what had happened to him. Outgrew his usefulness, she decided. The new Max must not be ready yet.

Odd that Max should go just like that, she thought. *But the lives of the Folk were like gossamer. One day you saw them; the next day you saw through the place where they had been. I must ask what happened to Max.* But she knew she wouldn't ever get around to that. The answer might require a disgusting word, a concept where even euphemisms would be repellent.

"Pay particular attention to the Cyborg Glisson," Schruille said. "Isn't it strange that our instruments reflect no emotions from him?"

"Perhaps he has no emotions," Calapine said.

"Hah!" Schruille barked. "Very good."

"I don't trust him," Nourse said. "My grandsire spoke of Cyborg tricks."

"He's virtually a robot," Schruille said. "Programed to respond with the closest precise answer to preserve his being. His present docility is interesting."

"Isn't it our purpose to interrogate them?" Nourse asked.

"In a moment," Schruille said. "We will peel them down to the raw brain and open their memories to our examination. First, it is well to study them."

"You're so callous, Schruille," Calapine said.

A murmurous agreement spread upward through the hall.

Schruille glanced at her. Calapine's voice had sounded so strange then. He found himself filled with a sudden disquiet.

Glisson's Cyborg eyes moved, heavy-lidded, coldly probing, glistening with their lensed alterations that expanded his spectrum of visibility.

"Do you see it, Durant?" he asked, his voice chopped into bits by the necessity of short breaths.

Harvey found his voice. "I . . . can't . . . believe . . . it."

"They are talking," Calapine said, her voice bright. She

looked at the Durant male, surprised a look of loathing and pity in his eyes.

Pity? she wondered.

A glance at the tiny repeater bracelet on her wrist, confirmed the assessment of the Survey Globe. *Pity. Pity! How dare he pity me!*

"Har . . . vey," Lizbeth whispered.

Frustrated rage contorted Harvey's face. He moved his eyes, could not quite swing them far enough to see her. "Liz," he muttered. "Liz, I love you."

"This is a time for hate, not love," Glisson said, his detached tone giving the words an air of unreality. "Hate and revenge," Glisson said.

"What are you saying?" Svengaard asked. He'd listened with mounting amazement to their words. For a time, he'd thought of pleading with the Optimen that he'd been a prisoner, held against his will, but a sixth sense told him the attempt would be useless. He was nothing to these lordly creatures. He was foam in the backwash of a wave at a cliff base. They were the cliff.

"Look at them as a doctor," Glisson said. "They are dying."

"It's true," Harvey said.

Lizbeth had pressed her eyes closed against tears. Now, her eyes sprang open and she stared up at the people around her, seeing them through Harvey's eyes and Glisson's.

"They *are* dying," she breathed.

It was there for the trained eyes of an Underground courier to read. Mortality on the faces of the immortals! Glisson had seen it, of course, through his Cyborg abilities to see and respond, read-and-reflect.

"The Folk are *so* disgusting at times," Calapine said.

"They can't be," Svengaard said. There was an unreadable tone in his voice and Lizbeth wondered at it. The voice lacked the despair she could have expected.

"I say they *are* disgusting!" Calapine intoned. "No mere pharmacist should contradict me."

Boumore stirred out of a profound lethargy. The as yet alien computer logic within him had recorded the conversation, replayed it, derived corollary meanings. He looked up now as a new and partial Cyborg, read the subtle betrayals in Optiman flesh. The thing was there! Something had gone wrong with the live-forevers. The shock of it left Boumour with a half-formed feeling of emptiness, as though he ought to respond with some emotion for which he no longer had the capacity.

"Their words," Nourse said. "I find their conversation mostly meaningless. What is it they're saying, Schruille?"

"Let us ask them now about the self-viables," Calapine said. "And the substitute embryo. Don't forget the substitute embryo."

"Look up there in the top row," Glisson said. "The tall one. See the wrinkles on his face?"

"He looks so old," Lizbeth whispered. She felt a curiously empty feeling. As long as the Optimen were there—unchangeable, eternal—her world contained a foundation that could never tremble. Even as she'd opposed them, she'd felt this. Cyborgs died . . . eventually. The Folk died. But Optimen went on and on and on . . .

"What is it?" Svengaard asked. "What's happening to them?"

"Second row on the left," Glisson said. "The woman with red hair. See the sunken eyes, the stare?"

Boumour moved his eyes to see the woman. Flaws in Optiman flesh leaped out as his gaze traversed the short arc permitted him.

"What're they saying?" Calapine demanded. "What is this?" Her voice sounded querulous even to her own ears. She felt fretful, annoyed by vague aches.

A muttering sound of discontent moved upward through the benches. There were little pockets of giggling and bursts of peevish anger, laughter.

We're supposed to interrogate these criminals, Calapine thought. *When will it start? Must I begin it?*

She looked at Schruille. He had scrunched down in his seat, glaring at Harvey Durant. She turned to Nourse, encountered a supercilious half-smile on his face, a remote look in his eyes. There was a throbbing at Nourse's neck she had never noticed before. A mottled patch of red veins stood out on his cheek.

They leave everything to me, she thought.

With a fretful movement of her shoulders, she touched her bracelet controls. Lambent purple light washed over the giant globe at the side of the hall. A beam of the light spilled out from the globe's top as though decanted onto the floor. It reached out toward the prisoners.

Schruille watched the play of light. Soon the prisoners would be raw, shrieking creatures, he knew, spilling out all their knowledge for the Tuyere's instruments to analyze. Nothing would remain of them except nerve fibers along which the burning light would spread, drinking memories, experiences, knowledge.

"Wait!" Nourse said.

He studied the light. It had stopped its reaching movement toward the prisoners at his command. He felt they were making some gross error known only to himself and he looked around the abruptly silent hall wondering if any of the others could identify the error or speak it. Here was all the secret machinery of their government, everything planned, ordained. Somehow, the inelegant unexpectedness of naked Life had entered here. It was an error.

"Why do we wait?" Calapine asked.

Nourse tried to remember. He knew he had opposed this action. Why?

Pain!

"We must not cause pain," he said. "We must give them the chance to speak without duress."

"They've gone mad," Lizbeth whispered.

"And we've won," Glisson said. "Through my eyes, all my fellows can see—we've won."

"They're going to destroy us," Boumour said.

"But we've won," Glisson said.

"How?" Svengaard asked. And louder: "How?"

"We offered them Potter as bait and gave them a taste of violence," Glisson said. "We knew they'd look. They had to look."

"Why?" Svengaard whispered.

"Because we've changed the environment," Glisson said. "Little things, a pressure here, a shocking Cyborg there. And we gave them a taste for war."

"How?" Svengaard asked. "How?"

"Instinct," Glisson said. The word carried a computed finality, a sense of inhuman logic from which there was no escape. "War's an instinct with humans. Battle. Violence. But their systems have been maintained in delicate balance for so many thousands of years. Ah, the price they paid—tranquillity, detachment, boredom. Comes now violence with its demands and their ability to change has atrophied. They're heterodyning, swaying farther and farther from that line of perpetual life. Soon they'll die."

"War?" Svengaard had heard the stories of the violence from which the Optimen preserved the Folk. "It can't be," he said. "There's some new disease or—"

"I have stated the fact as computed to its ultimate decimal of logic," Glisson said.

Calapine screamed, "What're they saying?"

She could hear the prisoners' words distinctly, but their meaning eluded her. They were speaking obscenities. She heard a word, registered it, but the next word replaced it in her awareness without linkage. There was no intelligent sequence. Only obscenities. She rapped Schruille's arm. "What are they saying?"

"In a moment we will question them and discover," Schruille said.

"Yes," Calapine said. "The very thing."

"How is it possible?" Svengaard breathed. He could see two couples dancing on the benches high up at the back of the hall. There were couples embracing, making love. Two Optimen began shouting at each other on his right—nose to nose. Svengaard felt that he was watching buildings fall, the earth open and spew forth flames.

"Watch them!" Glisson said.

"Why can't they just compensate for this . . . change?" Svengaard demanded.

"Their ability to compensate is atrophied," Glisson said. "And you must understand that compensation itself is a new environment. It creates even greater demands. Look at them! They're oscillating out of control right now."

"Make them shut up!" Calapine shouted. She leaped to her feet, advanced on the prisoners.

Harvey watched, fascinated, terrified. There was a disjointed quality in her movement, in every response—except her anger. Rage burned at him from her eyes. A violent trembling swept through his body.

"You!" Calapine said, pointing at Harvey. "Why do you stare at me and mumble? Answer!"

Harvey found himself frozen in silence, not by his fear of her anger, but by a sudden overwhelming awareness of Calapine's age. How old was she? Thirty thousand years? Forty thousand? Was she one of the originals—eighty thousand or more years old?

"Speak up and say what you will," Calapine commanded. "I, Calapine, order it. Show honor now and perhaps we will be lenient."

Harvey stared, mute. She seemed unaware of the growing uproar all around.

"Durant," Glisson said, "you must remember there are subterranean things called instincts which direct destiny with the inexorable flow of a river. This is change. See it around us. Change is the only constant."

"But she's dying," Harvey said.

Calapine couldn't make sense of his words, but she found herself touched by the tone of concern for her in his voice.

She consulted her bracelet linkage with the globe. *Concern!* He was worried about her, about Calapine, not about himself or his futile mate!

She turned into an oddly enfolding darkness, collapsed full length on the floor with her arms outstretched toward the benches.

A mirthless chuckle escaped Glisson's lips.

"We have to do something for them," Harvey said. "They have to understand what they're doing to themselves!"

Schruille stirred suddenly, looked up at the opposite wall, saw dark patches where scanners had been deactivated, abandoned by the Optimen who couldn't jam into the hall. He felt an abrupt alarm at the eddies of movement in the crowd all around. Some of the people were leaving—swaying, drifting, running, laughing, giggling. . . .

But we came to question the prisoners, Schruille thought.

The hysteria in the hall slowly impressed itself on Schruille's senses. He looked at Nourse.

Nourse sat with eyes closed, mumbling to himself. "Boiling oil," Nourse said. "But that's too sudden. We need something more subtle, more enduring."

Schruille leaned forward. "I have a question for the man Harvey Durant."

"What is it?" Nourse asked. He opened his eyes, pushed forward, subsided.

"What did he hope to gain by his actions?" Schruille asked.

"Very good," Nourse said. "Answer the question, Harvey Durant."

Nourse touched his own bracelet. The purple beam of light inched closer to the prisoners.

"I didn't want you to die," Harvey said. "Not this."

"Answer the question!" Schruille blared.

Harvey swallowed. "I wanted to—"

"We wanted to have a family," Lizbeth said. She spoke clearly, reasonably. "That's all. We wanted to be a family." Tears started in her eyes and she wondered then what her child would have been like. Certainly, none of them were going to survive this madness.

"What is this?" Schruille asked. "What is this family nonsense?"

"Where did you get the substitute embryo?" Nourse asked. "Answer and we may be lenient." Again the burning light moved toward the prisoners.

"We have self-viables immune to the contraceptive gas," Glisson said. "Many of them."

"You see?" Schruille said. "I told you so."

"Where are these self-viables?" Nourse asked. He felt his right hand trembling, looked at it wonderingly.

"Right under your noses," Glisson said. "Scattered through the population. And don't ask me to identify them. I don't know them all. No one does."

"None will escape us," Schruille said.

"None!" Nourse echoed.

"If we must," Schruille said, "we'll sterilize all but Central and start over."

"With what will you start over?" Glisson asked.

"What?" Schruille screamed the word at the Cyborg.

"Where will you find the genetic pool from which to start over?" Glisson asked. "You are sterile—and terminating."

"We need but one cell to duplicate the original," Schruille said, his voice sneering.

"They why haven't you duplicated yourselves?" Glisson asked.

"You dare question us?" Nourse demanded.

"I will answer for you then," Glisson said. "You've not chosen duplication because the doppleganger is unstable. The trend of the duplicates is downward—extinction."

Calapine heard scattered words—"Sterile . . . terminating . . . unstable . . . extinction . . ." They were hideous words that crept down into the depths where she lay watching a string of fat sausages parade in glowing order before her awareness. They were like seeds with a lambent radiance moving against a background of oiled black velvet.

Sausages. Seeds. She saw them then not precisely as seeds, but as encapsulated life—walled in, shielded, bridging a period unfavorable to life. It made the idea of seeds less repellent to her. They were life . . . always life.

"We don't need the genetic pool," Schruille said.

Calapine heard his voice clearly, felt she could read his thoughts. Words out of one of the glowing sausages forced themselves upon her: *We have our millions in Central. We are enough by ourselves. Feeble, short-lived Folk are a disgusting reminder of our past. They are pets and we no longer need pets.*

"I've decided what we can do to these criminals," Nourse said. He spoke loudly to force his voice over the growing hubbub in the hall. "We will apply nerve excitation a micron at a time. The pain will be exquisite and can be drawn out for centuries."

"But you said you didn't want to cause pain," Schruille shouted.

"Didn't I?" Nourse's voice sounded worried.

I don't feel well, Calapine thought. *I need a long session in the pharmacy. Pharmacy.* The word was a switch that turned on her consciousness. She felt her body stretched out on the floor, pain and wetness at her nose where it had struck the floor in her fall.

"Your suggestion contains some merit, however," Schuiller said. "We could restore the nerves behind our ministrations and carry on the punishment indefinitely. Exquisite pain forever!"

"A hell," Nourse said. "Appropriate."

"They're insane enough to do it," Svengaard rasped.

"How can we stop them?"

"Glisson!" Lizbeth said. "Do something!"

But the Cyborg remained silent.

"This is something you didn't anticipate, isn't it, Glisson?" Svengaard said.

Still, the Cyborg held to silence.

"Answer me!" Svengaard grated.

"They were just supposed to die," Glisson said, voice dispassionate.

"But now they could sterilize all the earth except Central and go on in their madness by themselves," Svengaard said. "And *we* could be tortured forever!"

"Not forever," Glisson said. "They're dying."

A cheer went up from the Optimen at the rear of the hall. None of the prisoners could turn to see what had aroused the sound, but it added a new dimension to the sense of urgency around them.

Calapine lifted herself from the floor. Her nose and mouth throbbed with pain. She turned toward the tumbril, saw a commotion among the Optimen beyond it. They were leaping on benches to watch some excited activity hidden in their midst. A naked body lifted suddenly above the throng, turned over and went down again with a sodden thump. Again, a cheer shook the hall.

What're they doing? Calapine wondered. *They're hurting each other—themselves.*

She wiped a hand across her nose and mouth, looked at the hand. Blood. She could smell it now, a tantalizing smell. Her own blood. It fascinated her. She crossed to the prisoners, showed the hand to Harvey Durant.

"Blood," she said. She touched her nose. Pain! "It hurts," she said. "Why does it hurt, Harvey Durant?" She stared into his eyes. Such sympathy in his eyes. He was human. He cared.

Harvey looked at her, their eyes almost level because of the tumbril's position above the floor. He felt a profound compassion for her suddenly. She was Lizbeth; she was Calapine; she was all women. He saw the concentrated intensity of her attention, the here-now awareness which excluded everything except her need for his words.

"It hurts me, too, Calapine," he said, "but your death would hurt me more."

For an instant, Calapine thought the hall had grown still around her. She realized then that noises of the throng continued unabated. She could hear Nourse chanting, "Good! Good!" and Schruille saying, "Excellent! Excellent!" She realized then that she had been the only one to hear Durant's hideous words. It was blasphemy. She'd lived thousands of years suppressing the very concept of personal death. It could not be said or conceived in the mind. But she had *heard* the words. She wanted to turn away, to believe those words had never happened. But something of the attention she had focused on Harvey Durant held her chained to his meaning. Only minutes ago, she had been where the seed of life spanned the eons. She had felt the wild presence of forces that could move within the mitochrondrial structures of the cells.

"Please," Lizbeth whispered. "Free us. You're a woman. You must have some compassion. What have we done to harm you? Is it wrong to want love and life? We didn't want to harm you."

Calapine gave no sign that she heard. There were only Harvey's words playing over and over in her mind, *"Your death . . . your death . . . your death . . . your death . . ."*

Odd flickerings of heat and chill surged through her body. She heard another cheer from the crowd in the far benches. She felt her own sickness and growing awareness of the cul-de-sac in which she had been trapped. Anger suffused her. She bent to the tumbril's controls, punched a button beneath Glisson.

The carapaces of the shell which held the Cyborg began closing. Glisson's eyes opened wide. A rasping moan escaped him. Calapine giggled, punched another button on the controls. The shells snapped to their former position. Glisson gasped.

She turned to the controls beneath Harvey, poised a finger over the buttons. "Explain your disgusting breach of manners!"

Harvey remained frozen in silence. She was going to crush him!

Svengaard began to laugh. He knew his own position, the

first-class second-rater. Why had he been chosen for this moment—to see Glisson and Boumour without words, Nourse and Schruille babbling on their bench, the Optimen in little knots and eddies of mad violence, Calapine ready to kill her prisoners and doubtless forget it ten seconds later. His laughter went out of control.

"Stop that laughing!" Calapine screamed.

Svengaard trembled with hysteria. He gasped for breath. The shock of her voice helped him gain a measure of control, but it still was immensely ludicrous.

"Fool!" Calapine said. "Explain yourself."

Svengaard stared at her. He could feel only pity now. He remembered the sea from the medical resort at Lapush and he thought he saw now why the Optimen had chosen this place so far from any ocean. Instinct. The sea produced waves, surf—a constant reminder that they had set themselves against eternity's waves. They could not face that.

"Answer me," Calapine said. Her hand hovered above his shell's controls.

Svengaard could only stare at her and at the Optimen in their madness beyond her. They stood exposed before him as though their bodies had been opened to spill twisting entrails on the floor.

They have souls with only one scar, Svengaard thought.

It was carved on them day by day, century by century, eon by eon—the increment of panic that their blessed foreverness might be illusion, that it might after all have an ending. He had never before suspected the price the Optimen paid for infinity. The more of it they possessed, the greater its value. The greater the value, the greater the fear of losing it. The pressure went up and up . . . forever.

But there had to be a breaking point. The Cyborgs had seen this, and in their emotionless manner had missed the real consequences.

The Optimen had themselves hemmed in with euphemisms. They had pharmacists, not doctors, because doctors meant sickness and injury, and that equaled the unthinkable. They had only their pharmacy and its count-less outlets never more than a few steps from any Optiman. They never left Central and its elaborate safeguards. They existed as perpetual adolescents in their nursery prison.

"So you won't speak," Calapine said.

"Wait," Svengaard said as her hand moved toward the buttons beneath him. "When you've killed all the viables and only you remain, when you see yourselves dying one by one, what then?"

"How dare you?" she said. "You think to question an Op-timan whose experience of life makes yours no more than that!" She snapped her fingers.

He looked at her bruised nose, the blood.

"Optiman," Svengaard said. "A Sterrie whose constitu-tion will accept the enzyme adjustment for infinite life . . . until destruction comes from within. I think you want to die."

Calapine drew herself up, glared at him. As she did, she became aware of a sudden odd silence in the hall. She swept a glance around her, saw intent watchfulness in every eye focused upon her. Realization came slowly. *They see the blood on my face.*

"You had infinite life," Svengaard said. "Does that make you necessarily more brilliant, more intelligent? No. You merely lived longer, had more time for experience and edu-cation. Very likely, most of you are educated beyond your intelligence, else you'd have seen long ago that this moment was inevitable—the delicate balance destroyed, all of you dying."

Calapine took a step backward. His words were like pain-ful knives burning into her nerves.

"Look at you!" Svengaard said. "All of you sick. What does your precious pharmacy do? I know without being told: It prescribes wider and wider variant prescriptions, more frequent dosages. It's trying to check the oscillations be-cause that's how it's programmed. It'll go on trying as long as you permit it, but it won't save you."

Someone screamed behind her, "Silence him!"

The cry was taken up around the hall, a deafening chant, foot stamping, hands pounding, "Si-lence him! Si-lence him! Si-lence him!"

Calapine pressed her hands to her ears. She could still feel the chant through her skin. And now she saw Optimen start down off the benches toward the prisoners. She knew bloody violence was only a heartbeat away.

They stopped.

She couldn't understand why, and dropped her hands away from her ears. Screams rained down on her. The names of half-forgotten dieties were invoked. Eyes stared at something on the floor at the head of the hall.

Calapine whirled, saw Nourse writhing there, foamy spittle around his mouth. His skin was a mottled reddish purple and yellow. Clawed hands reached out, scraped the floor.

"Do something!" Svengaard shouted. "He's dying!" Even as he shouted, he felt the strangeness of his words. *Do something!?* His medical training surfaced and spoke no matter what happened.

Calapine backed away, put out her hands in a warding gesture as old as witchcraft. Schruille leaped up, stood on the bench where he'd been sitting. His mouth moved soundlessly.

"Calapine," Svengaard said, "if you won't help him, release me so I can do it."

She leaped to obey, filled with gratitude that she could give this hideous responsibility to another.

The restraining shells fell away at her touch. Svengaard leaped down, almost fell. His legs and arms tingled from the long confinement. He limped toward Nourse, his eyes and mind working as he moved. *Mottled yellow in the skin—most probably an immune reaction to pantothenic acid and a failure of adrenalin suppression.*

The red triangle of a pharmacy outlet glowed on the wall at his left above the benches. Svengaard stooped, picked up Nourse's writhing form, began climbing toward the symbol.

The man was a sudden dead weight in his arms, no movement except a shallow lifting of the breast.

Optimen fell back from him as though he carried plague. Abruptly, someone above him shouted, "Let me out!"

The mob turned away. Feet pounded on the plasmeld. They jammed up at the exits, clawed and climbed over one another. There were screams, curses, hoarse shouts. It was like a cattle pen with a predator loose in the midst of the animals.

Part of Svengaard's awareness registered on a woman at his right. He passed her. She lay stretched across two banks of seats, her back at an odd angle, mouth gaping, eyes staring, blood on her arms and neck. There was no sign of breath. He climbed past a man who dragged himself up the tiered benches, one leg useless, his eyes intent on an exit sign and a doorway which appeared to be filled with writhing shapes.

Svengaard's arms ached from his load. He stumbled, almost fell up the last two steps as he eased Nourse to the floor beside the pharmacy outlet.

There were voices down behind him now—Durant and Boumour shouting to be released.

Later, Svengaard thought. He put his hand to the door control on the pharmacy outlet. The doors refused to open. *Of course*, he thought. *I'm not an Optiman.* He lifted Nourse, put one of the Optiman's hands to the control. The doors slid aside. Behind them lay what appeared to be the standard presentation of a priority rack—pyrimidines, aneurin . . .

Aneurin and inositol, he thought. *Got to counteract the immune reaction.*

A familiar flow-analysis board occupied the right side with a gap for insertion of an arm and the usual vampire needles protruding from their gauges. Svengaard tripped the keys on the master flow gauge, opened the panel. He traced back the aneurin and inositol feeders, immobilized the others, thrust Nourse's arm beneath the needles. They found veins, dipped into flesh. Gauges kicked over.

Svengaard pinched off the return line to stop feedback. Again, the gauges kicked over.

Gently, Svengaard disengaged Nourse's arm from the needles, stretched him on the floor. His face was now a uniform pale white, but his breathing had deepened. His eyelids flickered. His flesh felt cold, clammy.

Shock, Svengaard thought. He removed his own jacket, put it around Svengaard, began massaging the arms to restore circulation.

Calapine came into view on his right, sat down at Nourse's head. Her hands were clasped tightly together, knuckles white. There was an odd clarity in her face, the eyes with a look of staring into distances. She felt she had come a much farther distance than up from the floor of the hall, drawn by memories that would not be denied. She knew she had gone through madness into an oddly detached sanity.

The red ball of the Survey Globe caught her eye, the egg of enormous power that did her bidding even now. She thought about Nourse, her many-times playmate. Playmate and toys.

"Will he die?" she asked. She turned to watch Svengaard.

"Not immediately," Svengaard said. "But that final burst of hysteria . . . he's done irreparable damage to his system."

He grew aware that there were only muted moans and a very few controlled commands in the hall now. Some of the acolytes had rallied to help.

"I released Boumour and the Durants and sent a plea for more . . . medical help," Calapine said. "There are a number of . . . dead . . . many injured."

Dead, she thought. *What an odd word to apply to an Optiman. Dead . . . dead . . . dead . . .*

She felt then how necessity had forced her into a new kind of living awareness, a new rhythm. It had happened down there in a burst of memories that trailed through forty thousand years. None of it escaped her—not a moment of kindness nor of brutality. She remembered all the Max Allgoods, Seatac . . . every lover, every toy . . . Nourse.

Svengaard glanced around at a shuffling sound, saw Boumour approaching with a woman limp in his arms. There was a blue bruise across her cheek and jaw. Her arms hung like sticks.

"Is this pharmacy outlet available?" Boumour asked. His voice held that chilled Cyborg quality, but there was shock in his eyes and a touch of horror.

"You'll have to operate the board manually," Svengaard said. "I keyed out the demand system, jammed the feedback."

Boumour stepped heavily around him with the woman. How fragile she looked. A vein pulsed thickly at her neck.

"I must concoct a muscle relaxant until we can get her to a hospital," Boumour said. "She broke her own arms— contramuscular strain."

Calapine recognized the face, remembered they had disputed mildly about a man once—about a playmate.

Svengaard moved to Nourse's right arm, continued massaging. The move brought the floor of the hall into view and the tumbril. Glisson sat impassively armless in his restraining shell. Lizbeth lay at one side with Harvey kneeling beside her.

"Mrs. Durant!" Svengaard said, remembering his obligation.

"She's all right," Boumour said. "Immobilization for the past few hours was the best thing that could've happened to her."

Best thing! Svengaard thought. *Durant was right: These Cyborgs are as insensitive as machines.*

"Si-lence him," Nourse whispered.

Svengaard looked down at the pale face, saw the broken veins in the cheeks, the sagging, unresponsive flesh. Nourse's eyelids flickered open.

"Leave him to me," Calapine said.

Nourse moved his head, tried to look at her. He blinked, having obvious trouble focusing. His eyes began to water.

Calapine lifted his head, slid under him until he rested on her lap. She began stroking his brow.

"He used to like this," she said. "Go help the others, Doctor."

"Cal," Nourse said. "Oh, Cal . . . I . . . hurt."

Calapine lifted the block that gestating child in front
of her face. She peered into the face now.

He tried to rise, but she said, "You best lie where I've
—

"Call Nearly back," she said. "He's . . . he's hurt

20

"Why do you help them?" Glisson asked. "I don't understand you, Boumour. Your actions aren't logical. What use is it to help them?"

He looked up through the open segment of the Survey Globe at Calapine sitting alone on the dais of the Tuyere. The lights of the interior played a slow rhythm across her face. A glowing pyramid of projected binaries danced on the air in front of her.

Glisson had been released from his shell of restraint, but he still sat on the tumbril, his arm connections dangling empty. A medicouch had been brought in for Lizbeth Durant. She lay on it with Harvey seated beside her. Boumour stood with his back to Glisson, looking up into the globe. His fingers moved nervously, clenching, opening. There was a streak of dried blood down his right sleeve. The elfin face held a look of puzzlement.

Svengaard came in from behind the globe, a slowly moving figure in the red shadows. Abruptly, the hall glared with light. The main globes had gone on automatically as darkness fell outside. Svengaard stopped to check Lizbeth, patted Harvey's shoulder. "She will be all right. She's strong."

Lizbeth's eyes followed him as he moved around to look into the Survey Globe. Svengaard's shoulders sagged with fatigue, but there was a look of elation in his face. He was a man who'd found himself.

"Calapine," Svengaard said, "that was the last of them going out to hospitals."

"I see it," she said. She looked up at the scanners, every one lighted. Somewhat more than half of the Optimen were under restraint—mad. Thousands had died. More thousands lay sorely injured. Those who remained watched their globe. She sighed, wondering at their thoughts, wondering how they faced the fact that all had fallen from the tight wire of immortality. Her own emotions confused her. There was an odd feeling of relief in her breast.

"What of Schruille?" she asked.

"Crushed at a door," Svengaard said. "He's . . . dead." She sighed. "And Nourse?"

"Responding to treatment."

"Don't you understand what's happened to you?" Glisson demanded. His eyes glittered as he stared up at Calapine.

Calapine looked down at him, spoke clearly, "We've undergone an emotional stress that has altered the delicate balance of our metabolism," she said. "You tricked us into it. The evidence is quite clear—there's no turning back."

"Then you understand," Glisson said. "Any attempt to force your systems back into the old forms will result in boredom and a gradual descent into apathy."

Calapine smiled. "Yes, Glisson. We'd not want that. We've been addicted to a new kind of . . . aliveness that we didn't know existed."

"Then you do understand," Glisson said, and there was a grudging quality to his voice.

"We broke the rhythm of life," Calapine said. "All life is immersed in rhythm, but we got out of step. I suppose that was the *outside* interference in those embryos—rhythm asserting itself."

"Well then," Glisson said, "the sooner you can turn things over to us, the sooner things will settle down into—"

"To you?" Calapine asked scornfully. She looked out into

the quick contrasts of the hall's glaring light. How black and white it all was. "I'd sooner condemn us all," she said.

"But you're dying!"

"So are you," Calapine said.

Svengaard swallowed. He could see that the old animosities would not be suppressed easily. And he wondered at himself, a second-rater surgeon who had suddenly found himself as a doctor, ministering to people who needed him. Durant had seen *that*—the need to be needed.

"I may have a plan we could accept, Calapine," Svengaard said.

"To you we will listen," Calapine said, and there was affection in her voice. She studied Svengaard as he searched for words, remembering that this man had saved the lives of Nourse and many others.

We made no plans for the unthinkable, she thought, *Is it possible that this nobody who was once a target for kindly sneers can save us?* She dared not let herself hope.

"The Cyborgs have techniques for bringing the emotions into a more or less manageable stasis," Svengaard said. "Once that's done, I believe I know a way to dampen the enzymic oscillations in most of you."

Calapine swallowed. The scanner-eye lights above her began to flash as the watchers signaled for her to let them into the communications channels. They had questions, of course. She had questions of her own, but she didn't know that she could speak them. She caught a reflection of her own face in one of the prisms, was reminded of the look in Lizbeth's eyes as the woman had pleaded from the tumbril.

"I can't promise infinite life," Svengaard said, "but I believe many of you can have many more thousands of years."

"Why should we agree to help them?" Glisson demanded. There was a measuring quality in his voice, a hint of the querulous.

"You're failures, too!" Svengaard said. "Can't you see that?" He realized he had shouted with the full power of his disillusionment.

"Don't shout at me!" Glisson snapped.

So they do have emotions, Svengaard thought. *Pride . . . anger . . .*

"Are you still suffering under the delusion that you're in control of this situation?" Svengaard asked. He pointed to Calapine. "That one woman up there could still exterminate every non-Optiman on earth."

"Listen to him, you Cyborg fool," Calapine said.

"Let's not be too free with that word 'fool'," Svengaard said. He stared up at Calapine.

"Watch your tongue, Svengaard," Calapine said. "Our patience is not infinite."

"Nor is your gratitude, eh?" Svengaard said.

A bitter smile touched her mouth. "We were talking about survival," she said.

Svengaard sighed. He wondered then if the patterns of thought conditioned by the illusion of infinite life could ever be truly broken. She had spoken there like the old Tuyere. But her resiliency had surprised him before.

The outburst had touched Harvey's fears for Lizbeth. He glared at Svengaard and Glisson, tried to control his terror and rage. This hall awed him with its immensity and its remembered bedlam. The globe towered over him, a monstrous force that could crush them.

"Survival, then," Svengaard said.

"Let us understand each other," Calapine said. "There are those among us who will say that your help was merely our due. You are still our captives. There are those who'll demand you submit and reveal your entire Underground to us."

"Yes, let us understand each other," Svengaard said. "Who are your prisoners? Myself, a person who was not a member of the Underground and knows little about it. You have Glisson, who knows more, but assuredly not all. You have Boumour, one of your escaped *pharmacists*, who knows even less than Glisson. You have the Durants, whose knowledge probably goes little beyond their own cell group. What will you gain even if you milk us dry?"

"Your plan to save us," Calapine said.

"My plan requires cooperation, not coercion," Svengaard said.

"And it will only give us a continuation, not restore us to our original condition, is that it?" Calapine asked.

"You should welcome that," Svengaard said. "It would give you a chance to mature, become useful." He waved a hand to indicate their surroundings. "You've frozen yourselves in immaturity here! You've played with toys! I'm offering you a chance to live!"

Is that it? Calapine wondered. *Is this new aliveness a by-product of the knowledge that we must die?*

"I'm not at all sure we'll cooperate," Glisson said.

Harvey had had enough. He leaped to his feet, glared at Glisson. "You want the human race to die, you robot! You! You're another dead end!"

"Prattle!" Glisson said.

"Listen," Calapine said. She began sampling the communications channels. Bits of sentences poured out into the hall:

"We can restore enzymic balance with our own resources!" . . . "Eliminate these creatures!" . . . "What's his plan? What's his plan?" . . . "Begin the sterilization!" . . . ". . . his plan?" . . . "How long do we have if . . ." . . . "There's no doubt we can . . ."

Calapine silenced the voices with a flick of a switch. "It will be put to a vote," she said. "I remind you of that."

"You will die, and soon, if we don't cooperate," Glisson said. "I want that fully understood."

"You know Svengaard's plan?" Calapine asked.

"His thought patterns are transparent," Glisson said.

"I think not," Calapine said. "I saw him work on Nourse. He manipulated a dispensary to produce a dangerous overdose of aneurin and inostol. Remembering that, I ask myself how many of us will die in the attempt to arrest this process we can all feel within ourselves? Would I have risked such an overdose upon myself? How does this relate to the excitement we feel? Will any of us, having tasted excitement, wish to sink back into a non-emotional . . . boredom?" She looked at Svengaard. "These are some of my questions."

"I know his plan," Glisson sneered. "Quell your emotions and implant an enzymic dispensary within each of you. Make Cyborgs of you." A tight grin etched a line of teeth in Glisson's face. "It's your only hope. Accepting it, you will have lost to us at last."

Calapine glared down at him, shocked.

Harvey was caught by the carping meanness in Glisson's voice. His own schism from the Underground had always known the Cyborgs were too calculating and narrow-minded to be trusted with purely human decisions, but he had never before seen the fact so clearly demonstrated.

"Is that your plan, Svengaard?" Calapine demanded.

Harvey jumped up. "No! That's not his plan!"

Svengaard nodded to himself. *Of course! A fellow human, and a father would know.*

"You pretend to know what I, a Cyborg, do not know?" Glisson asked.

Svengaard looked at Harvey with raised eyebrows.

"Embryos," Harvey said.

Svengaard nodded, looked up at Calapine. "I propose to keep you continually implanted with living embryos," he said. "Living monitors that will make you adjust to your own needs. You will regain your emotions, your . . . zest for life, this excitement you prize."

"You propose to make of us living *vats for embryos?*" Calapine asked, wonder in her voice.

"The gestation process can be delayed for hundreds of years," Svengaard said. "With proper hormone adjustment, this can be applied even to men. Caesarian delivery, of course, but it need not be painful . . . or frequent."

Calapine weighed his words, wondering why she felt no disgust at the suggestion. Once she had felt disgust at the realization that Lizbeth Durant carried an embryo within her, but Calapine realized now her disgust had been compounded of jealousy. Not all the Optimen would accept this, she knew. Some would hope for a return to the old ways. She looked up at the globe's telltales. No one had escaped the poisoning excitement, though. They would have to understand that everyone was going to die . . . sooner or later. Choice of time was all they had.

We didn't have immortality after all, she thought, *only the illusion. We had that, though . . . for eons.*

"Calapine!" Glisson said. "You're not going to accept this—this foolish proposal?"

The mechanical man is outraged at a living solution, she thought. She said, "Boumour, what do you say?"

"Yes," Glisson said, "speak up, Boumour. Point out the illogicality of this . . . *proposal.*"

Boumour turned, studied Glisson, glanced at Svengaard, at the Durants, stared up at Calapine. There was a look of secret wisdom in Boumour's pinched face. "I can still remember . . . how it was," he said. "I . . . think it was better . . . before I . . . was changed."

"Boumour!" Glisson said.

Hit him in his pride, Svengaard thought.

Glisson glared up at Calapine with mechanical intensity. "It's not yet determined that we'll help you!"

"Who needs you?" Svengaard asked. "You've no monopoly on your techniques. You'd save a little time and trouble, that's all. We can find embryos."

Glisson stared from one to the other. "But this isn't the way it was computed! You're not supposed to help them!"

The Cyborg fell silent, eyes glassy.

"*Doctor* Svengaard," Calapine said, "could you give us elite, viable embryos such as the Durants'? You saw the arginine intrusion. Nourse believes this possible."

"It's possible," Svengaard said. He considered. "Yes, it's . . . probable."

Calapine looked up at the scanners. "If we accept this offer," she said, "we go on living. You feel it? We're alive now, but we can remember a recent time when we weren't alive."

"We'll help if we must," Glisson said, and there was that carping tone in his voice.

Only Lizbeth, realizing her own bucolic docility in pregnancy, recognizing the flattening tenor of her emotions, suspected the *logical* fact which had swayed the Cyborg. Docile people could be controlled. That's what Glisson was thinking. She could read it in him, understanding him fully for the first time now that she knew he had pride and anger.

Calapine, reading on the Survey Globe's wall the mounting pressure of a single question from her Optiman audience, set up the analogues for an answer. It came swiftly for the scanners to see, "This process could provide eight to twelve thousand years of additional life even for the Folk."

"Even for the Folk," Calapine whispered. They'd discover this, she knew. There could be no more Security now. Even the Survey Globe had been shown to have flaws and limits. Glisson knew it. She could tell this, reading his silent withdrawal down there. Svengaard certainly would realize it. Possibly even the Durants.

She looked at Svengaard, knowing what she had to do. It would be easy to lose the Folk in this moment, lose them completely.

"If it is done," Calapine said, "it will be done for anyone who wishes it—Folk or Optiman."

This is politics, she thought. *This is the way the Tuyere would do it . . . even Schruille. Especially Schruille. Clever Schruille. Dead Schruille.* She could almost hear him chuckling.

"Can it be done for the Folk?" Harvey asked.

"For anyone," she said, and she smiled at Glisson, letting him see how she'd won. "I think we can put it to a vote now."

Once more, she looked up at the scanners, wondering if she'd gauged her people correctly. Most of them would see what she'd done, of course. But there'd be some clinging to the hope they could restore complete enzymic balance. She knew better. Her body knew. But some might choose to try that dangerous course back to boredom and apathy.

"Green for acceptance of *Doctor* Svengaard's proposal," she said. "Gold against."

Slowly, then with cumulating speed, the circle of scanner lights changed color—green . . . green . . . great washes of it with only here and there a dot or pocket of gold. It was a more overwhelming acceptance than she'd expected and this made her edgy, suspicious. She trusted her voting instincts. Overwhelming acceptance. She consulted the Globe's instruments, read the presentation of the answer: "The Cyborg can be maneuvered through its belief in the omnipotence of logic."

Calapine nodded to herself, thinking of her madness. *And Life cannot be totally maneuvered against the interests of living,* she thought.

"The proposal is accepted," she said.

And she found she did not like the sudden pouncing look on Glisson's face. *We've overlooked something,* she thought. *But we'll find it . . . once we're newly adjusted.*

Svengaard turned to look at Harvey Durant, allowed himself a broad grin. This was like the operating room, he thought. One shaped minutiae and the broad pattern followed. It could be done with precision even as it was done down in the cell.

Harvey weighed Svengaard's grin, read the emotional betrayals on the man's face. All the faces around him carried their own exposure in this instant, all open to be read by a courier trained in the Underground. It was a stand-off between the powerful. The Folk might yet have a chance— thousands of years of chance, if Calapine were to be believed—and she believed it herself. The genetic environment had been shaped into a new pattern and he could see it. This was an indefinite pattern, full of indeterminacy. Heisenberg would've liked this pattern. The movers themselves had been moved—and changed—by moving.

"When can Lizbeth and I leave here?" Harvey asked.